FOUNDATION

This Large Print Book carries the
Seal of Approval of N.A.V.H.

THE COLLEGIUM CHRONICLES, BOOK 1

FOUNDATION

MERCEDES LACKEY

THORNDIKE PRESS
A part of Gale, Cengage Learning

GALE
CENGAGE Learning™

Detroit • New York • San Francisco • New Haven, Conn • Waterville, Maine • London

Fic / Lackey / [Large Type] / [Fantasy]

GALE
CENGAGE Learning™

Copyright © 2008 by Mercedes R. Lackey.
Thorndike Press, a part of Gale, Cengage Learning.

Thorndike Press® Large Print Basic.
The text of this Large Print edition is unabridged.
Other aspects of the book may vary from the original edition.
Set in 16 pt. Plantin.
Printed on permanent paper.

LIBRARY OF CONGRESS CATALOGING-IN-PUBLICATION DATA

Lackey, Mercedes.
  Foundation / by Mercedes Lackey.
    p. cm. — (The collegium chronicles ; 1) (Thorndike Press large print basic)
    ISBN-13: 978-1-4104-1428-1 (alk. paper)
    ISBN-10: 1-4104-1428-0 (alk. paper)
    1. Large type books. I. Title.   -
  PS3562.A246F678 2009
  813'.54—dc22   2009000571

Published in 2009 by arrangement with DAW Books.

$32.95

4/09

Gale

Dedicated to the memory of
Alex the Grey
and the continuing research
of Dr. Irene Pepperberg.

www.alexfoundation.org

HERALDS OF VALDEMAR SERIES

by Mercedes Lackey

1000 BF   0   750 AF   798 AF   850 AF

Founding
of Valdemar

Foundation
of the Herald's
Collegium

THE COLLEGIUM
CHRONICLES
Foundation

Prehistory:
Era of the
Black Gryphon

THE MAGE WARS
The Black Gryphon
The White Gryphon
The Silver Gryphon

Reign
of Elspeth the
Peacemaker

THE LAST HERALD–
MAGE TRILOGY
Magic's Pawn

Reign
of Randale

THE LAST HERALD–
MAGE TRILOGY
Magic's Promise
Magic's Price

OFFICIAL TIMELINE
Sequence of events by Valdemar reckoning

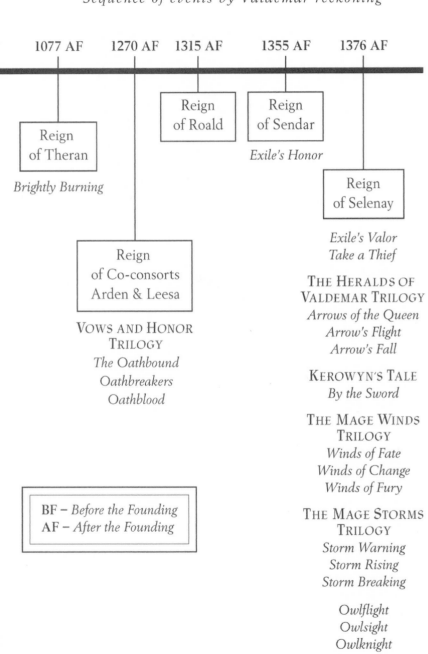

1077 AF   1270 AF   1315 AF   1355 AF   1376 AF

Reign
of Roald

Reign
of Sendar

Reign
of Theran

Exile's Honor

Brightly Burning

Reign
of Selenay

Reign
of Co-consorts
Arden & Leesa

Exile's Valor
Take a Thief

THE HERALDS OF
VALDEMAR TRILOGY
Arrows of the Queen
Arrow's Flight
Arrow's Fall

VOWS AND HONOR
TRILOGY
The Oathbound
Oathbreakers
Oathblood

KEROWYN'S TALE
By the Sword

THE MAGE WINDS
TRILOGY
Winds of Fate
Winds of Change
Winds of Fury

BF – *Before the Founding*
AF – *After the Founding*

THE MAGE STORMS
TRILOGY
Storm Warning
Storm Rising
Storm Breaking

Owlflight
Owlsight
Owlknight

1

Mags did not shiver in the cold; his body was used to it by now. Besides, it was warmer down here in the mine than it was up there, up at the sluices, and almost warmer than it was in the doss room, at least until everyone got packed in and the heat of their bodies combined enough that they could sleep.

He knelt in the shaft in the approved manner, rock just a few finger lengths from his nose, his knees fitted into smooth hollows that he himself had painstakingly cut out. His lamp, strapped to his forehead, cast a dim light on the rock face in front of him. That was the only part of him that was warm — his forehead behind the reflector of the oil lamp.

Around him, behind him in the darkness, came the sounds of tapping and echoes of tapping. He had just begun his half day down here, but of course, he was hungry already. The porridge of barley and oats that they all got for their breakfast didn't last for very long. But he was used to that; in fact, the times when he wasn't hungry were branded in his memory. There had been the day that the cook had fallen ill and the bread had burned and been thrown out by the helpers rather than saved to feed to the children over a period of days — he'd just come off the sluices in time to see the bread in buckets waiting to go into the pig trough. He'd rounded up the rest, and they had all snatched themselves burned loaves before they could be fed to the pigs. They'd gone to sleep quickly that night, stomachs tightly packed with the bread. There was the day he'd stumbled across a cache of apples — probably stolen by one of the house servants — and had eaten his fill. And of course, the day, once a year, when the village priest visited to inspect, a day when they all were washed, given decent clothing, and fed an enormous meal of bread and soup.

His mouth watered just thinking about the soup, and his stomach growled. This afternoon, maybe he could slip off to the piggery again and get at one of the buckets of scraps before they went into the trough. Demmon had found half a meat pasty in one once, the foul bugger, and gloated about it. He was always snitching things and not sharing. And he was always scanting on the work, too, never putting props in his seam, leaving it for the next shift. Served him right he'd got caught in that cave-in. Share around, that was the rule. That way if the grub you snitched was bad, nobody got too sick to work, and if it was good, you all got a taste. Share the warmth, share the rags you snitched so that everybody had some cover, 'cause if someone got cold-sick, it meant you all had to make up for him.

The only thing you couldn't share was the work in the seam. There was only room for one in the little tunnels that riddled the rock like wormholes.

Mags carefully positioned his chisel and tapped at a likely spot in the seam with his hammer. It was a good broad seam, this one, as wide as the tunnel was tall, which meant there was no problem with spending most of his time hammering out waste rock and getting shouted at for not bringing up any sparklies today. In fact, he had three good ones so far, the yellow ones. They were all in the pouch around his neck that he'd bring out at the end of his shift. Master Cole liked the yellow ones. He liked the green ones even better, but his sons usually worked seams that had the green ones in them. He didn't trust the orphans on those seams, though what he thought the orphans would do with a big green sparkly, Mags couldn't imagine. Where would they go with it? Who'd buy a gemstone from a scrawny, raggedy brat? And that assumed they could somehow get off the property in the first place.

This mine produced a lot of different sparklies. Yellow, a pale green that wasn't as good as the dark green ones, dark red, purple ones of all sorts of shades, a paler yellow than the ones Mags had in this seam, a pale blue, and a clear with silver threads running through it. More of that last than anything else, and it was what the youngest mined. When you had more experience, you moved up to the pale yellow and dark red. Then the pale green and the purple. Then the dark yellow and the pale blue. Those took a good eye and a good hand.

Mags' tapping released a chunk of rock. There was nothing in it that he could see, but it wasn't waste — it would go up to the hammer-mill and the sluices. He shoved it behind him for the collector, the youngest kid of all, who would pull out all the rocks from the tunnels and throw them in the donkey cart.

He set his chisel into a good spot and

began tapping again. One more sparkly and he'd get a second slice of barley bread with his broth. Oh, that would be good.

There were two sounds in the mine where he was, the tapping and the steady drip of water. Closer to the mouth, you could hear the bellows that drove fresh air down here, and the creaking of the pumps that pulled water out. Not that they'd drown if the pumps failed, but Master Cole had learned that working in water rusted the tools and meant sparklies were lost. So no working in water.

The rock fractured suddenly and dropped off the face, and there, catching the light was another yellow sparkly as big as Mags' thumb. Extra bread for sure!

But first he had to get it out without breaking it.

He pulled off the rag he kept wrapped around his throat, folded it a few times, and set it on the floor of the tunnel just under the stone. If it already had fractures in it, falling on that wouldn't shatter it. If the gem cutters shattered it later, it was hardly his problem.

Setting his chisel as delicately as he could, he began flaking bits of rock from the face around the sparkly. A tap, a pause to check his progress, another tap, another pause. It

13

was serious, intense work. One slip of the chisel, and so much for the extra bread, and there would be a beating to boot. The others, the sons, could tell from the changed rhythm that he had found something good.

"Mags! That'd better not be a green one!" shouted Jarrik Pieters down the tunnel.

"Ain't!" he grunted. "Yaller."

"Don't break it!" Jarrik shouted back unnecessarily. He could just see Jarrik yelling from his own seam, round face red with exertion and almost-anger, bushy brows furrowing, brown hair (already going thin on top) stringy with sweat, and little, deep-set eyes sparkling greedily at the thought of another sparkly in the pouch. And big mouth gaped wide to yell at Mags not to break it. As if he would! What did Jarrik think he was, an idiot?

Yah, that's exactly what he thinks you are. Or worse. Much worse. An idiot *and* Bad Blood.

Mags heard that a lot. And the other kiddies heard it said of him a lot. Not that any of them knew what it meant.

Most of the new kiddies were picked up to come live and work here once a year when Cole went out and about with his wagon, looking for orphans, kiddies abandoned, lost parents, and generally unwanted. He liked to get them around eleven years old, though he'd take them as young as nine if they were strong and looked like they could do the work. A few had come from as much as two weeks' walk away, sent to meet Cole's wagon by people who wanted 'em off their hands, and right quick.

Ah, but Mags was a different case altogether. Mags was local. And he'd been working for Cole for as long as he could remember.

And for as long as he could remember, every time a member of the Pieters felt like verbally abusing someone, Mags got The Lecture.

Yer Bad Blood, boy. Yer Bad Blood, and it's damn lucky for you that yer here, an' we can put ye to work an' keep those idle hands busy, or ye'd be dancin' at rope's end already.

Bad Blood, because his parents were bandits and had been killed in a raid by the Royal Guard. Bad Blood, because he'd been found in a cradle in the bandit camp after. Bad Blood, so bad that no one had wanted to take him in and he'd been left at the local Temple of the Trine with priests who were probably not at all happy about being saddled with the care of an infant. But then along had come Cole Pieters.

Out of the kindness, the pure kindness of

my heart, I took ye. No one else wanted ye, not even the godly priests. They all knew what ye were. They all figgered one day ye'd turn on 'em. I'm a bloody saint, I am, fer takin' a chance with you.

And so the infant had begun life in the Pieters household with the imaginative name of "the Brat." And from the moment his tiny hands could actually do anything, he'd been put to work, an unpaid, poorly fed, scantily clad, dirty little drudge. He was told, and he believed it, that he'd worked before he could walk, dragging a wad of rag-strips as he crawled, all unknowingly cleaning the floor with it. He'd been Brat for years, going from job to job in the household, from floor duster to spit turner, from pot washer to garden weeder, until he was big enough to see over the side of the sluices. And that was when he'd gone to work at the mine.

And that was when he'd gotten the name of Mags.

Tap, pause. Tap, pause. He put his nose as close to the stone as he could and still see, examining the rock minutely.

He remembered that day. His only instruction had been to watch the older kiddies, do what they did, and look for things that sparkled and had color. He got the stuff that

16

had already been picked over, no one really expected him to find anything. But as he had washed the gravel over and over again in his basin, watching not only the gravel in the pan but making sure he checked the stuff in the sluice as well, he had spotted something. It was no bigger than a grain of wheat, but it was bright, brilliant green. And then he found a yellow one, and a purple, and another green, a third green, and by the time the day was over, he turned over to his astonished overseer a little pile of tiny gem shards, a pile big enough to cover the palm of his hand.

"By the gods, Brat, ye've got th' eyes of a Magpie!" Endal Pieters had exclaimed. And it was the same the next day, and the next, until they started calling him "little Magpie," then Mags, and then — that was his name.

Carefully, Mags put thumb and forefinger to either side of the sparkly, and wiggled it, or tried to. Was it loose? Could he pull it out, like a baby tooth? That was always better than chipping it out.

He felt the thing give a little, heard the tiniest sound of grinding and — it popped out of its socket — in two pieces, not one, but they were both pretty big. He just wouldn't say anything. Two sparklies meant a slice of bread,

"I ain't hearing hammering!" Jarrik shouted. "I ain't hearing hammering, Mags!"

"Pulled two!" he grunted back, took the time to get a drink from his bottle, and tucked the sparklies into the bag around his neck.

"That don't mean no skylarkin'!" Jarrik shouted back. That was his favorite word for shirking lately.

"Gotta pee!" Mags retorted — which he didn't, but his calves and thighs were beginning to cramp something fierce, and he could hear the donkey cart coming. He'd have to clear the tunnel, or at least stop working and cram himself in the end while the kiddie cleaned out the rock, so Jarrik shouted back his grudging permission and Mags backed himself down the tunnel he was working and into the larger shaft. The kiddie — named Felan, skinny, dirt-covered, lank-haired, and wearing patched up burlap breeks and shirt — didn't even look at him, just plunged into the workings with his burlap bag. But Mags didn't expect him to talk; he remembered when he'd been the donkey-boy and had been backhanded for talking to the miners.

Ye ain't here t' talk! Yer here t' work!

Mags stretched his legs as he walked to the played-out seam they were using as the latrine. True waste rock went in here, burying the leavings before they started to smell too bad. The donkey-boy was in charge of that, too.

Mags didn't know the kiddie all that well. So far as he was aware, the boy hadn't spoken a word since he'd arrived. Well, that should make him popular with Jarrik, whose every other sentence was "Too much skylarkin'!" or "Too much jibber-jabber!" accompanied with the back of the hand.

Truth to tell, he didn't really want to know the kiddie's story. There were no good stories here. Every kiddie here was unwanted, burdens on their villages, bastards left on doorsteps, kiddies left orphaned — they arrived, more often than not, with tear-streaked faces, and most of the time, their faces remained tear-streaked. There was little enough to be happy about here, after all.

The food was just enough to keep you alive and no more unless you somehow found or snatched some. They all slept together in a single cellar room without a fireplace, a room dug under the barn and filled with hay and straw too old for the farm animals to eat. At least it wasn't drafty, and being underground it kept from going below freezing and wasn't too hot in the summer. They each got one threadbare blanket, so the best way to sleep was all bundled together in a ball like a wad of puppies, sharing body heat and coverings. Of course, that meant there were a lot of gropings among the older kiddies, but they all knew better than to futter. Everyone knew the story of Missa, who'd futtered and got a big belly. She got beaten and dosed until she lost the baby, and she was never right in the head after. And all the boys old enough to have been the daddy got a beating apiece. So nobody futtered.

Mags couldn't figure out where Missa'd got the energy or the interest to do it anyway. He was always so bone-tired at the end of the day that he fell asleep as soon as he got warm, and there was nothing about *anybody's* skinny body that made him want to put off sleep for even an instant. Maybe it was different for girls, they just had to lay there. Or maybe it would be different when he got older, in the spring and summer, when you didn't ball up all together shivering. But right now his jakko was as tired as the rest of him, and wasn't interested in a thing. Maybe when he was fourteen. He was only thirteen now, or at least, that was what

Master Cole told the priest last time he came.

He kind of hoped it would stay that way. The idea of a few moments of sleep less to appease a part of him that had suddenly got ideas of its own had no appeal.

By the time he made it to the end of the played-out seam, he needed to be there anyway. So it was just as well he'd lied. It wasn't bad; the donkey-boy had recently dumped rock here. He managed to shake the last of the cramps out on the way back, and crawled back into his tunnel, taking a shoring timber with him.

He always put in so many timbers that Master Cole sometimes shouted at him, but he never had a cave-in, and Master Cole couldn't argue with that. He'd noticed on his way out that by his standards, the roof was overdue for a prop, so he brought one in and hammered it in place before going back to work.

Once again, he arranged himself at the face, and began working a little lower. Off in the distance, he heard two of the other kiddies start a timid conversation, quickly hushed when Jarrik roared "No jibber-jabber!"

He was starting to cramp again. All right, time to pull a fake. He had enough stones, he wasn't going to get into trouble unless someone caught him at it — and to do that, they'd have to crawl down this tunnel and he would hear them coming. He stretched himself out, right leg first, then left, all the while tap-tap-pausing on the rock at the side of the tunnel with the chisel alone. Then he flipped over on his back and lay at full length, staring up at the ceiling only a little way above his face, still tapping.

He could only do this when the donkey-boy had cleared out the mined rock. His skin was tough, but not that tough. But the donkey-boy was thorough, he scraped out everything down to the dust, leaving Mags with nice, smooth rock to lie on. Cold, but smooth.

As he lay there, staring at the rock, he heard faint sniffling coming from off in the distance. Jarrik couldn't hear it, likely, or he'd be shouting about that, too. And then there would be a lecture over noon meal about how lucky they all were, how good Master Cole was to give them all shelter and food and clothing, because no one wanted them, not any of them. And how Master Cole was losing money over them, they were such worthless workers, not even earning their keep.

Now, Mags had no idea what the sparklies

were all really called, much less what they were worth, but he had a pretty good idea that all that about not earning their keep was a big, fat lie. Because Master Cole's house didn't get any shabbier, he didn't get any thinner, his wife didn't get raggedy, and his daughters were finding husbands just fine. And all those things took money. So if they weren't earning their keep, then where was all the money coming from?

Of course, the priest tut-tutted and agreed with him when he said these things.

Master Cole would have them all down here, all day and well into the night, if he thought it was possible. But while Mags was still in the house, before he'd gotten big enough to join the sluicing crew, Master Cole had figured out that when he rotated his crews on half a day at the sluice and half a day in the mine, they didn't get sick as often, and weren't crippled from the unnatural positions they had to take down here. Now the only people he had working for him that were bent over and knotted were the ones that dated from before that period, and the ones that had been unfortunate enough to survive a shaft collapse.

They truly did not have anywhere else to go, and it was quite true that no one else would have them. They knew nothing whatsoever except how to sluice rock and mine sparklies. So they survived on the pittance left to them after Cole subtracted "room and board" from their wages.

Cole was supposed to either let the kiddies go at sixteen, or hire them on at full wages. But where could they go? Like the cripples, they only knew mining and sluicing, so who would hire them, and for what?

Of course few of them survived to sixteen.

As usual, Mags felt resolve harden in him. *He* was going to survive. That was why he was so very careful. There would be no rock-falls in his seams. He didn't know what he was going to do when he reached sixteen, but he was going to make it that far. Life might be miserable, but it was preferable to the alternative, because Mags didn't believe in gods or Havens or anything else of that sort. If there were gods, then why did they let people like Master Cole dress in fine clothing and eat meat and white bread, while kiddies who had never done anyone any harm got killed under rock-falls in his mine? Maybe he, Mags, was Bad Blood and deserved to live like this, but there were cursed few of the others who did. . . .

Well, he had best get back to work. He couldn't keep the ruse up for too long. The donkey-boy would notice the lack of rock and report it.

He levered himself back into position and resumed the hunt.

By noon, he had another two sparklies, which virtually assured him of that extra slice of bread, so he joined the line of the rest trudging up to the surface in a better mood than when he had gone down.

When they emerged, blinking, into the thin sunlight, the first thing he saw was Liem Pieters holding out his fat hand for the little bag around his neck. Mags handed it over, and suppressed a grin at Liem's lifted eyebrow. But all the man did was grunt "Extra ration, noon meal and supper," and wave him on.

A couple of the others cast envious glances at him as he headed for the Big House and the back-kitchen door.

By some mysterious alchemy, the kitchen had already heard of his good fortune, for he was presented with a bowl of cabbage soup and two slices of barley bread. He carried both to a long shed with a single big table in it that was called the "schoolroom."

He took the nearest empty seat on one of the long benches and picked up the piece of charcoal waiting there for him. Because that was what you did. You ate, and you learned how to read and write at the same time.

Why? He had no idea. It didn't exactly make sense, and he knew Master Cole fumed over the "wasted time," but for some reason it was something he had to allow.

One of Cole's daughters was there; it was their job to teach the kiddies. She had a big piece of slate mounted onto the wall and chunks of soft, white chalk. This one wore a clean blue dress and had hair that was almost yellow braided in a tail down her back, but otherwise she looked like every other Pieters girl; round white face with very pink cheeks, eyes like a couple of round blue berries shoved into the white dough of her face, and no expression whatsoever. She wrote on the slate, the kiddies wrote what she did on the tabletop in charcoal, they sounded it all out, and then they got to take a bite of food before erasing what they had written and going on.

This was the one part of the day that Mags loved, unreservedly. He was far, far beyond this sort of thing himself, actually. He could read and write entire sentences, and often did so around the word that the others were sounding out. It seemed a kind of magic to him, that he could put these things down and someone else could make the same sense of them that he did. Somewhere, he had heard, there were things called "books" that were full of sentences that told you entire stories and facts about things, and — well, all manner of things it was good to know, or things that answered questions. Master Cole had no books in his house. But other people did.

As if in an echo of his thoughts, the Pieters daughter wrote *book* on the slate. Obediently, but struggling, the others wrote it down. *"B — oo — k. Book,"* they sounded out, while he was writing, *I open my book to read.*

As he erased it, he noticed that Burd, the littlest of the kiddies working the mines, had no bread at all, and kept his attention strictly on his soup, though his face looked as if he was about to cry. No bread — that could only mean he'd come out of the mine empty-handed. And that wasn't fair. Just because the seam had played out, it was hardly fair to punish the kiddy who was unlucky enough to be stuck there. But that was Cole all over . . .

With an internal curse, Mags got Burd's attention by elbowing him while erasing his sentence, and handed him the remaining half slice of bread. Burd stared at him in, first astonishment, then near-worship. He took the half slice and stuffed it quickly in his mouth, as if he was afraid Mags would change his mind.

Mags just finished his soup.

The lesson ended with Endal Pieters coming in and saying it was done with. The daughter — they were all interchangeable to Mags, all identical, all forgettable, all inconsequential because they had no power to punish him — cleaned the slate and scuttled away. The kiddies, Mags included, erased the last words, bolted down whatever food they had left, and got to their feet as Endal watched impatiently.

Then, forming a line because Endal liked precision, they marched out into the cold to take their turn at the sluices.

2

In summer, working the sluices was the best job. There was sun, and fresh air, and if you got hot, you just splashed some water over you. It was hard work, right enough, swirling the heavy pans of gravel around and around in the running water, and by day's end your arms and back ached something terrible, but it was no worse than mining the seam. And if you had to work long hours, either because you were on the morning shift and got up with the sun, or because you were on the afternoon shift and didn't stop till the sun went down, well, that wasn't so bad. You didn't really want to go to bed early in the summer, when you could sluice in the sun and let the heat soak into you, especially after a turn in the mine in the cold. And if you had morning shift and it was hot, the mine felt good by contrast, and it took a while for the heat to leech out of you. Besides, longer hours in the summer got made up for by shorter ones in winter.

The one advantage that the kiddies had over the three night shift miners, the ones all twisted and not right in the head, was that daytime was their shift. Night belonged to the ones Cole cared even less about, if that was possible, and they worked their whole shift in the mine itself, leaving their rock to be sorted through in the day by the kiddies come to the sluice in the morning. They were already twisted up, so the damage was done, and it didn't matter anymore if they got further crippled. As long as they could hobble to the shaft, that suited Cole. If *they* got sick, small loss. Master Cole would find some other cripple to replace whoever sickened and died. Assuming one of the kiddies hadn't had an accident by then and had already gone to night shift.

Some of the kiddies were scared of them, weird buggers that they were. When the kiddies all trudged to the sleeping hole, the night shift would be waking up, blinking at the light, looking like a bunch of cave crickets, pasty-pale under all that dirt, with limbs stuck out at odd angles. They never talked, just mumbled, and what you could understand rarely made any sense.

In summer, despite the night workers getting much shorter shifts than the day workers, Mags felt just a little sorry for them, as much as he could feel sorry for anyone other than himself. They never got clean, they never seemed to care that they didn't. They never saw the sun unless it was coming up or going down. They went from one hole in the ground to another. And he wondered if they looked back on their stints at the sluices with pleasure, or at least, with regret. Or did they just not think about things anymore?

But in fall as it got colder, and in winter, when the water was freezing and there were icicles on the sluice itself, it was bitter work, and he envied the night shift. At least it was relatively warm down in the shaft, compared to the work at the sluice. Maybe being crazy wasn't so bad. It might be worth being crazy to avoid the sluices in winter.

It was fall now; the leaves were starting to drop from the trees, and the water was hand-numbing cold. Mags eyed the water being dumped into the sluice by the bucket-chain with disfavor as he approached. The wheels squeaked and complained, the buckets splashed over the leather belt that took them up and down again into the well, the water splashed down into the sluices. The donkey hitched to the wheel running the whole thing plodded on, head down.

Each of them took a spot on one of the three sluices, wooden troughs that the water from the mine was pumped into, and augmented by water from the well brought up by the bucket-chain. Piles of rock pounded into gravel at the hammer-mill were brought here after sorting. Master Cole's daughters and youngest sons did that; there were a lot of sparklies pounded out by those hammers, fracturing the rock around them but not the crystals themselves. The kiddies got the gravel when the Pieters siblings were done with it. The sorting house was a pleasanter place by far than the sluices. You were allowed to sit down. The doors and windows stood open to the breeze in summer. There was a fire in there, come winter. The only time the kiddies ever saw a fire was when there were leaves and trash being burned, or they took a turn as a kitchen drudge because a drudge had took sick. The sorting house was clean and bright and the work was just tedious, not backbreaking. But then, that was to be expected, since the Pieters kids served there . . . and it was rare indeed that anyone else got a turn in the place. Usually old man Cole or his wife or one of the older boys would bend their heads to work there before they let a kiddie in the door. It had happened once to Mags' knowledge, the year that an ague and a flux went through the whole place, carrying off two Pieters kids and several servants, but leaving the mine workers oddly alone. Maybe even a fever realized what a misery their lives were and figured they had enough punishment.

Mags took his place at the head of the third sluice, with his back to the afternoon sun, so that, weakening as it was, the warmth of it could soak through his raggedy shirt and into his skin. He got the pan that had been left by the kiddie on the last shift under the sluice, scooped up enough to cover the bottom from the gravel pile next to him and began swirling the gravel in the running water, watching for the glint of something colored and shiny.

Again, his thoughts flitted back to the Pieters kids, and that there seemed to be a never-ending supply of mean boys and girls like lumps of dough, as if someone in the kitchen was making them, all alike, and then only baking them halfway. There were the four oldest boys, two girls married off, a couple more that did the teaching, and it seemed like a dozen small 'uns. Surely Cole's wife didn't litter them like kittens! Yet there they were, a horde of them, from the eldest that worked at cutting the sparklies to the youngest that bossed each other in endless and pointless games until the boys were put to work in the sorting house and the girls began learning household duties under the housekeeper's watchful eye.

"Wonder why there's so many Pieters," he muttered, not realizing he had said it aloud until the kiddy next to him — Davey, almost sixteen, and still not crippled, not addle-pated, and making no secret that he was leaving when the priest next came — laughed out loud. Davey was a good head taller than Mags, and like all the kiddies, he was so coated in dirt that it was hard to tell what his skin tone actually was. But his eyes were hard and cold and brown, like pebbles. His hair, matted, with bits of straw still in it, was hacked off short, as Mags' was and, like Mags', was dark, somewhere between brown and black.

" 'Cuz ol' man Cole can't keep his hands off'n the housemaids," the older boy guffawed. "An' don' it make the right-wise born ones hoppin' mad! The boys, anyhow. Ever' time one of them maids squirts out a kid, you kin tell, 'cause they look like thunder."

Mags blinked, spotted a sparkle in the water, and fished out a bit of pale blue like a fingernail paring. "Huh? Why?"

" 'Cuz ol' man Cole likes t' tell 'em, when he don' like what they're doin', that he'll leave the mine an' all t' the bastards if they don' do what they're told." Davey snickered this time. "He got Jarrik t' say he'd marry some ugly stick come spring thataway, instead of some pretty piece that don't come with money. He wasn't half hot about it, an' I hear the girl had some things t' say!"

"How'dye know all that?" Mags glanced at him sideways. Where was Davey getting all this? He talked like he was in and out of the Big House all the time, and Mags knew that wasn't possible. Granted, Davey generally came to bed last, and even in winter he was known for some sort of prowling. Mags figured he just had some angle going, maybe with the stableboy. Or maybe with a kitchen drudge. Neither the stableboy nor the drudges got paid even the pittance that the other servants got, and they took what they could get when they could get it. The stableboy secretly cooked up messes of the oats to eat, and kitchen drudges could snitch bits of this and that as they cleaned pots and pans. Mags had never been hungry as a kitchen drudge.

" 'Cuz I got ears. 'Cuz I don' need as much sleep as you kiddies, so I go sneakin' round the Big House and listenin' under winders." Davey glanced over at Mags and gave him a wink. " 'Cuz when you learn stuff, sometimes y' learn stuff what's worth sumpin'. I learn stuff, makes the cook gimme stuff. I learn stuff, gets me better stuff to wear. Why you think I'm gettin' outa here? I know stuff. I know stuff Jarrik don' want his pa t' know. I know stuff ol' man Cole don' want his wife t' know. Like about them housemaids. He tells her 'twas the boys, but it's him, when the by-blows come." He leaned over conspiratorially and whispered, "I'll tell it all t' you afore I go, if ye get a couple of those yaller sparklies, hide 'em, an' keep 'em for me, then give 'em t' me afore I flit."

Mags felt his heart do a double-beat and bent over the pan to hide his expression. No one had ever made such an offer to him before.

He was tempted — oh, yes — he was tempted. Seriously tempted. This could mean the difference between being stuck here his whole life and getting out, like Davey. If the offer was real. The knowledge might be good for more than just getting out; it might be good for more food, a better blanket, an easier time of it from Jarrik. He, too, might get some of those advantages

36

from the cook, and maybe other things, too.

But it might not be a real offer, and it might be a trap. Maybe Davey never meant to tell him anything once he had the sparklies, or maybe he'd make stuff up to tell, stuff that wasn't true, that would only get Mags in trouble if he tried to use it. And then there was the danger of doing the theft in the first place, Mags had never seen what happened to kiddies who snitched sparklies, because in his time no kiddie had had a reason to try, but it had to be a lot worse than ones caught snitching food or blankets. And Master Cole was just mean enough to have said to Davey, "I'll let you leave here with money in yer pocket and a good suit 'o clothes if you find out who'd snitch sparklies, given a chance." Mags was convinced that there was nothing Master Cole wouldn't try just for the meanness of it.

"That don't sound safe," he muttered, fishing a bright flash of red out of the pan. "I take all the risk, an' fer what? If I git caught, yer off free, an' if you git caught, ye kin say I give it ye and niver say ye ast for it." Davey had never done anyone a kindness so far as Mags knew. He had never been cruel, but he had never done anyone a kindness either. That didn't make him exceptional; just about everybody was that

way. But it also didn't make him trustworthy.

And hadn't he just said he'd been getting
favors from the cook that he hadn't been
sharing with the rest, like he was supposed
to. That made him even less trustworthy.
Like Demmon, he'd been greedy. But unlike Demmon, he'd been sly and had never
told anybody.

For that matter, now that Mags came to
think about it, no one here was really trustworthy on that scale. Even the littlest of the
kiddies would give you up for more food.
That was why everything good got shared
and split, so everyone was equally guilty if
there was guilt to go around.

But Davey hadn't shared. Which meant —
what? Probably nothing good. That he was
sneaky, for sure. And greedy, for sure. And
that anything he did would always be all
about what he got out of it.

Mags was good at watching things out of
the corner of his eye, and for a moment,
Davey's expression turned savage, and more
than angry enough to make the hair on
Mags' neck stand up. Then he laughed.
"Suit yerself. You ain't the only one diggin'
out sparklies. If you won't, summun else
will." And then the older boy turned away,
fixing his attention on his own pan.

Which was the truth; what was also the truth was that Davey himself was deep into a good vein of greens. So Davey could snitch his own sparklies, if he chose. It just might have been a trap.

Well, if Davey thought that turning away would make Mags beg for the chance to get what he was offering, he could think again. He'd played that game years ago, to get the donkeys into harness, showing a wisp of grass and then turning away with it. The donkeys would go for it, every time, and Mags was pretty sure he was smarter than a donkey.

He thought about turning the tables on Davey, going to one of Cole's boys and saying "That there Davey offered stuff if I'd snitch him a sparkly an' give it him afore he flits."

But Davey had never harmed him before this. There were a lot of unspoken rules among the kiddies, and one of them was, you didn't be the one to do the bad first.

If the offer was genuine, and not a trap, then Davey wasn't being the one doing the bad first. And maybe because he was about to flit, the Pieters boys were watching Davey too closely for him to snitch any of his greenies, so he was coming to Mags, who wasn't being watched so closely.

And anyway, that was tellin', and the one thing a kiddie didn't do was tellin' on another. Davey'd have to do him a mort of bad before he'd go so low as tellin'. Tellin' something like this could lead to terrible things, things there were only rumors of in the dark before sleep took them all. Things like tales of kiddies gettin' "caught" in the hammer-mill and crushed to death, or knocked down the well by the bucket-chain and drownded, or goin' to take a pee and the shaft roof come down so hard there was no getting 'em out, 'cause there weren't nothing *to* get out. Things that was supposed to be accidents, but everyone knew they weren't.

So he kept his nose on his business, sending the gravel down the sluice when it was panned out, concentrating on the weak warmth on his back as a counter to the cold numbing of his hands and arms, and watching in that peculiarly unfocused state that let him spot the tiny sparks of color and light that others missed. The little wooden dish at his side filled steadily — though he was careful, all things considered, to keep it on the side away from Davey. Just in case. 'Cause if Davey was angry he hadn't agreed to the snitch, then Davey could be malicious and knock his dish into the water, and he'd have little to show for his shift at the sluice.

But it did occur to him, that Davey's tale just might have a grain of use in it, that it might be worth *his* while to listen under windows now and again. It just might be he could learn something useful there, useful enough to lose some sleep to get it.

The air began to take on a chill as the light from the sun got more gold and less white, and then more amber and less gold, and then went to red as the sun touched the horizon. And because at that point any further panning was pretty much useless, since there would be no way to spot the tiny bits of sparklies in the dark sluice water, Jarrik turned up and ordered them to put pans down and turn over their findings. As usual, Mags turned over a bowl nearly half full with tiny bits. As usual, all he got for his efforts was a grunt.

Then it was off to supper, more cabbage soup and bread with extra bread for Mags, while another of the dough-faced Pieters girls read falteringly out of some holy book or other. Mags had no idea what the book was, or the god. The girl read so badly it was hard to make sense of what she was saying, for most of the words were too big for her, and she sounded them out badly.

41

This was the priest's idea, and Cole obviously wanted to be on the good side of the priest. They got read at by the girls at night-meal, preached at by one of the boys that was supposed to go for a priest at morning. Neither the girl nor the boy put any feeling into it. They both made it look and sound as if they were only doing it 'cause they'd get a beating if they didn't.

Mags ignored it. It was all the same rubbish anyway. Suffer on earth and be rewarded in a heaven he didn't believe in, by gods who didn't see fit to do something about misery right now.

Sometimes, when he had a moment to think, and something turned his mind toward these gods the priests were so big about, he wanted to hit the priests, hit the gods if they existed. But that took energy, and mostly he didn't have the energy to waste. He'd rather have had silence over his meal, or someone to read a book that told you something useful, like how to stay warmer in the winter, or what plants were good to eat. It would have made him mad tonight, to have this girl prattling on about nonsense, except that for a change there was enough food in his belly that he was immediately getting sleepy once he'd stuffed the last of his extra bread in his mouth. He looked up, to see that the three cripples on night shift were just now tottering in. And if he beat the others to the sleep-hole, the straw would still be warm from the cripples' bodies, he'd get the choice of blankets, and he'd be in the middle of the pile of bodies tonight, which was always the warmest place.

The logic was immaculate, and not even the thought of trying out Davey's idea tempted him away from it. He hurried across to the barn, crawled into the pit, wrapped himself up in the least torn of the coverings, and was asleep so quickly and so thoroughly that when the others joined him, he wasn't even aware they were there.

When Jarrik roused them all in the morning, there was a distinct bite to the air, and when they pulled themselves out of the sleep-hole in the thin light of dawn, there was thick frost all over everything. Mags sighed unhappily. Winter would be on them before long. And he didn't envy the kiddies at the sluices this morning at all. There would be ice at the edges of the troughs. By the time his crew took their places there, the water would at least be a little warmer. It was time to think about finding a moment here and there to plait some rush and straw bags, or find the end of a sack some-where. That was what they all used in winter instead of shoes, stuffing the bags full of straw to try and keep off the frostbite. The lucky ones found rags to wrap around their feet, and the really lucky ones, now and then found bits of wool too soiled or ruined in the shearing to spin, that they could stuff in those bags. Maybe something would hap-pen that would give them a few hours off the sluices, like the bucket-chain breaking down. If that happened, Mags could go gather a mort of things that would help. Nuts to hide away, seed-fluff that was almost as good and soft as wool to stuff in the foot bags, cattail roots to eat now.

There were fifteen kiddies here at the mine now, and the three crippled adults. Ten of the oldest got mining duty, him and Davey and Burd and Tansy and Ket in the morning, five others in the afternoon. Of the five left over, one was the donkey-boy, and the other four were on the sluices all day. Those four looked particularly miser-able this morning; they knew what to expect. They'd be getting chilblains before long, painful red-and-purple bumps on their hands caused by the cold water that could crack and even ulcerate. Of course, if they could get their hands warm, the chilblains would go away, but even taking their hands out of the water for a few moments to warm them in their armpits would mean they weren't panning the gravel, and if they weren't panning for sparklies and got caught, they'd get beaten.

Mags had never gotten chilblains, but he considered it luck more than anything. And even without chilblains, when he was working the sluice in winter, his hands hurt with the cold more than enough. The only time they didn't have to work the sluices was when it was *so* cold the troughs froze right up, or when there was a blizzard so thick you couldn't get to the sluices. And when that happened, it was so cold that there was no good place at all to be but the mine. That had only happened twice, and they had all bundled down there, and not even Master Cole had complained about it. Then again, Mags reckoned he didn't much care for his workers freezing to death either.

The mine was definitely the better place to be, come winter. He felt the temperature difference as soon as he was ten feet down the main shaft and the lower he got, following the old cave that the mine had started as, the better he felt. By the time he reached his seam he was almost comfortable. He found the toolbag where it was supposed to be, at the end of the tunnel, which meant someone had been working his seam last night. Which meant that it might need a support . . .

He fetched a timber, but that left him able to only carry his chisel and hammer. He crawled in, found as he had expected that the roof needed shoring, and hammered his timber in place. Then he went to work.

The seam he was following continued to yield good sparklies today. Smaller ones, but more of them. Once he had uncovered them, he went back to his bag for a tool made out of a big nail in a handle, something he used to pry small sparklies with good color out of rock rather than chipping at them.

That was when he overheard Jarrik and one of his brothers talking about something in low, urgent voices.

Thinking immediately that they might be talking about Davey and his "offer," he ghosted over to the side of their shaft and strained his ears as hard as he could to hear what they were saying.

"I ain't never seen anythin' like it," said Melak, a little Jarrik's junior. "I mean, I heerd the stories, but seein' one — it ain't right. It was hot-mad and tryin' and tryin' t' get in, and every way it got stopped, it just tried a new one. Smart. Things like that got no right to be as smart as a man."

"Ain't just that it's smart, neither," Jarrik grumbled. "It's got the luck of a devil. Tyndale shot at it, an' did nothin' but miss."

"It scares me. What's it want?" There was real fear in Melak's voice, something Mags was not accustomed to hearing. "Why won't it go away?"

"It wants somethin' here, I guess," Jarrik replied. "Somethin', or someone. Either way, Pa ain't letting it on the property. He swears he's keepin' it off."

"But how?" Melak *almost* wailed the words. "Ye can't shoot it, ye can't fence it out, and ye can't stop it! We don' know what it wants! What if it wants to get in here and kill one of us?"

"Why would it —" Jarrik stopped.

"You know why," Melak said flatly. "You *know* why. It's more 'n half a spirit, too! It could even be —"

"Don't say it!" Jarrik retorted harshly. "Don't even *think* it. Let Pa handle it. Let Pa handle it, and leave well enough alone!"

Standing there in the dark, listening to them talk about something they feared so much they wouldn't even put a name to it, Mags shivered. When had this — monster, or whatever it was — turned up and started besieging the mine? Days ago?

Now a horde of little things began to make sense. The sluices had been left without a Pieters supervising them, and half the older boys were not at the mine for the past couple of days. The girls had scarcely been seen out-of-doors, and had quickly scuttled back to the Big House when they did come out. The cooks had been less attentive at the giving out of the food, and a fair amount of cabbage and scraps had been joining the broth in the bowls rather than being husbanded in the pot.

At least half of the workmen hadn't been visible over the last three days either.

Maybe that was what had emboldened Davey in the matter of snitching sparklies.

He slipped back to his seam before the brothers noticed that there wasn't any tapping coming from his. And as he carefully pried stones out of the wall, he shivered and wondered.

Most of the time the kiddies were too tired to do anything but sleep when they piled into the sleep-hole. But that didn't keep them from knowing stories about all kinds of horrible things. The Pieters boys had their own store of tales that they told out, pretending to tell them to each other, but really doing it to scare the kiddies working

48

the seams. Most of the stories were about awful things down here in the mines. There were the ghosts of anyone that had died down here, and Mags knew of some few. These ghosts went about looking for someone who was the exact age they had been when they died — and when they found him, they would tear him apart trying to figure out a way into his body.

There were the Knockers, twisted-up little dwarfs no taller than your knee, but monstrous strong. They would wait until everyone was preoccupied and then just snatch a kiddie, grabbing him in his seam before he could utter a sound, bashing his head in with his own hammer, then dragging off the body to eat.

There were the Whisps, ghost-lights that would lead you into dangerous parts of the mine, then drop a rockfall on you. They'd do it by putting you to sleep, then getting you to walk in your sleep to where they were going to kill you.

There were the Horrors, that got into your head and made you crazy, like the night-shift cripples. When the Horrors got you, all you saw was black things coming at you, all claws and red eyes, and you'd drive your head against the wall of the shaft to try and get them out, or you'd make a cave-in yourself to try and stop them, or if they managed to bring you above the ground, you'd throw yourself down the well to be rid of them.

But every one of those was a monster *in* the mine. What about out of it? What was roaming about out there that was so scary the Pieters boys wouldn't name it, wouldn't describe it, and didn't have any bragging ideas on how to get rid of it?

Suddenly, he didn't want to leave at the end of the shift.

And it wasn't just because the sluice water would be so cursed cold.

No, he was afraid that whatever *it* was, it would be up there. Some sort of devil. Mags didn't believe in gods, but he believed, most fervently, in devils.

And if a devil had come here, there was likely only one person it had come for. Well, two, maybe, except the boys were saying that Cole Pieters was driving the thing off himself, so it hadn't come for Master Cole.

All right, then. It had to be coming for Mags. Because Mags was Bad Blood. It would grab him and drink his blood to make itself stronger. And then it would carry him away to torment him forever.

No, he did not want to leave the mine now.

But of course, he had no choice.

3

They heard the commotion before they emerged from the mine, but it didn't sound like monsters were invading Master Cole's property. It sounded more like the day some fool from the local highborn had come nosing about, or at least trying to. He'd brought an armsman with him, but it didn't do him any good. There was two of them, and a half dozen of Cole Pieters' sons, and if they didn't know how to use swords, they didn't need to, as anyone around would know they were damned good with their crossbows. Master Cole had run the man off then, and no mistaking it. He hadn't come back either.

Cole had been hollering about his rights then, and he was doing so now. His voice echoed harshly down the mine shaft. "I know my rights! Ye can't just swan in here and make off with whoever ye choose! These are *my* workers, homeless criminals every one, signed for and turned over to me to use as I need until their time runs out!"

Criminals? Now Mags knew that was a lie, and a big fat one, too. None of them were criminals, not even he. No one had been signed over by gaolers. Everyone here was here through no fault of their own . . .

"Evidently," drawled a new voice, sounding lazy, but with a hard edge of anger beneath the words that Mags doubted Master Cole was hearing. "Evidently you don't know your rights as well as you think you do, Cole Pieters. I *do* have the right to 'swan in here' and take whomever I please. You are the one violating the law, denying a Companion access to his Chosen, and preventing a Herald from exercising his duty."

Mags relaxed. He didn't really know what a Herald or a Companion were, though the latter sounded dirty, and he really didn't care. As long as it wasn't monsters come to tear him to pieces, or devils to torment him, he didn't care.

He emerged, blinking as usual, into the bright light of noon. And there was something of a standoff going on in the yard between the mine and the house and its outbuildings.

There was a man all in white, with two white horses, standing right at a barricade hastily thrown up across the lane leading to the yard. Behind the barricade were Cole Pieters and all of his sons, just like the time when that other fellow had come snooping. Only this time the crossbows weren't trained on the stranger, much to Cole Pieters' obvious fury, as he kept looking back at his sons.

"Pa," said Endal Pieters, his voice flooded with uncertainty, crossbow pointed at the ground and not even cocked. "Pa, that's a Herald. That's a *Herald,* Pa!"

"I can see that!" Pieters snapped. "And the man's daft, and so's his horse! There's nothing here for them to take! I ain't letting go of any of you, no more your sisters, and there's nothin' in *that* trash —" he waved at the emerging mine crew, "— that any of them should come calling for! This is just an excuse to come snooping where they ain't wanted, and they can turn around and —"

"Pa, it's a *Herald* —"

"I don' care if it's the King hisself! I know my rights!" Pieters' face was getting very red indeed. Mags wondered if he was finally going to have that apoplectic fit he'd been threatening to have for years now.

Well, Pieters might or might not know his rights, but the kiddies knew when to stay out of the way. The mining crew going in scuttled across the yard and down the shaft as quick as could be, while the outgoing crew scuttled toward the eating shed as fast as they could. It didn't do to fall under Master Cole's eye when he was like this because if he saw you, then you would be the next thing he took out his anger on when things settled down. It was especially true if he saw you looking at him.

So they all kept their heads down and got across the yard as quick as they could, heading for the colorless daughter waiting in the shed for them, and the equally colorless cook nervously ladling out bowls of soup. And it was a sign of how bad things were that there was no one to take the little sacks from them, the sacks that held their sparklies.

Mags caught Davey looking sly then, and he knew that Davey was thinking up some deviltry to be sure. And right enough, Davey was just about to snatch Burd's little sack from him, when up came Jarrik and took it from him, then took Davey's with a dirty look. Mags was quick to hand his over before Jarrik could even put his hand out for it. He couldn't be rid of it soon enough. Then he headed off across the yard as Jarrik headed for his brothers and the standoff at the gate.

But at that moment, everything changed again.

"That's the one!" the man shouted imperiously, every trace of lazy drawl gone. "Him! You there! Boy!"

Startled, Mags looked to see who the man was shouting at, and to his bewilderment, saw the finger pointing straight at *him.* And one of the horses began rearing and prancing and carrying on like it had a burr under its saddle, tossing its mane and flagging its tail.

Bewilderment turned to panic as all the rest turned to stare at him. Mags looked from side to side for a place to hide, but there wasn't anything. He was caught like a mouse in the middle of a kitchen floor, with hungry cats on every side of him.

"I didn' do nothin'!" he squeaked. "I bin workin'! I bin workin', I tell ya! It ain't me!"

Truly, he had never seen this man or anyone like him in all his life, so how could the fellow be so sure it was *him* he wanted?

"I will be *damned* if ye take my best worker!" Pieters roared. "Ye kin take yer damned horses and be off with ye, or so help me —"

But the man had an even louder voice than Pieters, and the boys were all looking very alarmed now. "You *will* turn over that boy to me, or I'll bring the Guard here and turn over every stone in the place and find every last lie and every last penny you've cheated the Crown out of and every last mistreatment of your servants you've done since you were in swaddling clothes!" he shouted, as Endal plucked at his father's sleeve and begged, "The Guard, Pa! He's gonna call the Guard on us! We cain't hold off the Guard! Be reasonable!"

And that was when things got very strange indeed.

Jarrik pulled Endal away from their father, and shoved him toward Mags. "Get him! Bring him here!" Jarrik growled, and then motioned to two of his brothers, who surrounded their father and bodily shoved him off to the side, arguing with him in harsh whispers.

Meanwhile Endal had crossed the yard, seized Mags by the ear, and was dragging him toward the man, with Mags hissing in pain the entire way.

Endal only let go of his ear when they were within touching distance of the man and the horses, if the barricade hadn't been in the way. Mags had never been this close to a horse before. Not a real horse. The mining carts and machinery were all pulled by donkeys, and he had never been allowed near the stables, nor the Pieters boys when they were mounted.

These horses were big. Very big. They smelled sweetly of cut grass and clover, with overtones of leather. Truth to tell, now that he was this close to them, they scared him. Something that big could mash his foot flat with a silver hoof and never notice, knock him down and trample him and move along without even noticing.

He stared down at the ground, unable to move, while the men shouted over his head. What could this fellow, this Herald, want anyway? He hadn't done anything! He never left the mine!

This . . . couldn't be about his parents, could it? But what did he have to do with what they'd done? He'd only been a baby. . . .

"This boy is coming with me." The man was not shouting now, but he didn't have to, the anger in his voice was like a bludgeon. "You try and stop me, and so help me, I will do exactly what I said I would. The Guard will be here. They will tear this place apart. If you have done one thing wrong, we will find it. And then you will be for it, *Master* Cole."

There was some urgent whispering as Mags stared and stared at his own two feet, until he had memorized every dirt-encrusted line, could have measured out his clawlike toenails in his sleep, knew he would be seeing them perfectly even if he closed his eyes. He couldn't make out what the whispering was about, but it sounded as if the boys were getting their way with the old man. Finally Cole growled, "Then you'll be paying me for him."

The man barked a not-laugh. "Pay you for him? Slavery is illegal in Valdemar, Cole Pieters. You can be thrown in gaol for owning slaves, or selling them."

"I've spent a fortune feeding and clothing this boy!" Cole sputtered. "Eating his head off, taking my charity, giving back naught —"

"A fortune, is it?" The angry drawl was back. "What kind of a fool do you take me for? I'm neither blind nor ignorant. I can see from here what kind of slop you feed these children. A good farmer wouldn't give it to a pig. And if there is a rag on their backs that isn't threadbare and decades old, I will eat it. As for shelter, where are you having them sleep? I don't see a house big enough for them. Are you keeping them in the barn? In a cellar?" His tone got very dangerous, and Mags shivered to hear it. "Exactly what *have* you been spending all

58

the money given to you for the keep of orphans on?"

What money? Mags thought dazedly. But Cole was right on top of that one.

"What money?" he sneered. "Nobbut one person wanted these brats. No fambly wanted 'em, no priest wanted 'em. And their villages couldn 'ford another mouth to feed. Charity! It was my own charity that took 'em in, useless, feckless things that they be! My charity that feeds 'em, and me own kids going short —"

"Oh that's a bit much even for you, Cole Pieters." There was a growl under the drawl. "If you are going to claim all that, then I think perhaps a visit from the Guard *and* Lord Astley's Clerk of Office would be a very, very good thing."

There was a great deal more of that sort of thing, most of it so far over Mags' head that it might as well have been in a foreign tongue. But the man was winning.

Mags only wished if he could tell if that was a good thing or a bad one. Usually he would immediately have said that anything Cole Pieters was against was going to be good for *him,* but now, he wasn't so sure.

Finally, Pieters literally picked Mags up by the scruff of the neck, hauled him off the ground like a scrawny puppy, and shoved him over the barrier at the man, shouting "Take him then! Take him, and be damned to you!"

Without a word, the man mounted one of the two horses, reached down to grab Mags' arm and picked him up like so much dirty laundry, then dumped him on top of the other horse.

Mags froze stiff with fear, his hands going instinctively around the knobby part of the thing he was sitting on, his legs clamping as hard as they could to the horse's sides. But — but — but —

"I dunno howta ride . . ." he tried to gasp out, but it didn't come out any louder than a whisper, and anyway it was already too late. The man was off, the other horse right behind him, and Mags squeezed his eyes and hands shut, and his legs tight, clenching his teeth to stop them from chattering.

I'm gonna fall off. I'm gonna fall off and die.

He'd never been on anything that moved before. He'd never even got a ride in the donkey cart. He opened one eye for just a second, then clamped it tight shut again, feeling dizzy and sick at how fast the ground was going by. Within moments, they were right outside the boundaries of any land *he* knew. He'd never been much past the mine and the Big House.

And suddenly he also realized that he had never had a close-up encounter with anyone that wasn't either a priest, one of the kiddies, one of the servants or miners, or a member of the Pieters family.

And now this stranger was taking him away — somewhere. Where? Why?

Well, he hadn't bound Mags to the horse like a criminal so he couldn't escape, though right now, Mags wouldn't have minded a few ropes tying him on. . . .

This was mad. He'd have been certain that he was *going* mad, except that there was no way he could have been making all this up in his own head.

His stomach was a tight, cold, little knot of fear, there was another icy knot of fear in his throat, every muscle ached from holding on so tightly, and yet he was too terrified to let go even a little bit. All he could do was hang on and endure and hope it ended soon, and that it didn't end with him falling off and breaking his neck.

And then, as suddenly as the ride had begun — it ended. He felt the horse start to slow, then stop, and his eyes flew open.

But he hadn't even begun to take in his surroundings when the man grabbed him as Pieters had, by the scruff of the neck, and hauled him off the horse. At least, though, the man caught him before he fell, and lowered him easily enough to the ground, even if it was at arm's length. But he was wearing white . . . and Mags suddenly realized with an odd sense of shame that *he* was dirty enough to soil the fellow just by what he shed.

The man pushed Mags ahead of him into a building three or four times larger than the Big House, and terrifyingly grand looking, all clean and bright and polished, so much so that suddenly Mags realized just how shabby and neglected the Big House was by sheer contrast. It was two stories tall, made of timber-framed stone all rounded and smooth-polished, and not sharp-edged like the stuff chipped out of a mine, showing all the hundreds of colors that existed in the simple word *tan*. There was glass in all the windows, and Mags knew how ruinously expensive that was, because of the howl that had been sent up when one of the Pieters' boys had shied a rock at something and hit a window instead.

Mags was certain they were just going to go around to the stable or some other outbuilding, where the man would hand him over to someone else, and . . .

But no. The man marched him right in the big front door, all polished wood with shiny brass fittings to it.

And then they were surrounded by people. Well, maybe not *surrounded,* but there were five or six of them at least, and they were all big, all muscled, and all . . .

. . . all in Guard blue.

Now Mags had never actually seen anyone in a Guard uniform before, but they'd been described to him often enough, and with great relish, as one or another Pieters would tell him exactly how the Guard would come to take him one day, how they would tie him up and throw him in a cart and carry him off to be locked up in a dark dungeon until the black beetles ate him because he was Bad Blood and he was going to prove it, inevitably. Or maybe they would just take him and lock him up on a preemptive basis. Because one day he *might* do something awful.

His knees went to water, and his insides, and it was a good thing he hadn't eaten yet because he would have vomited it all up on their shiny, shiny boots. He couldn't move, couldn't speak, couldn't even really hear for the hammering of his heartbeat in his ears, and he didn't resist at all as they half-carried him out of that little room at the front and off away to some other room — he couldn't tell where, they passed so many rooms, with so many people in uniforms in them, only it was a long way from the front. All he grasped was that the floor was all polished wood and the walls were all whitewashed and the place smelled like leather and soap and the oil you used on metal things to keep them from rusting.

A door opened to a wave of steam and more odors of the sort that he had only vaguely whiffed on laundry day in the spring when everything was washed, and it was very hot and very light in there. He could scarcely see for the steam. And the next thing he knew, they had stripped all his rags off him (which wasn't hard, since they went to pieces at a tug), picked him up, and dumped him in a huge thing like the horse trough full of water. He opened his mouth to yell at the cold, only it wasn't cold, it was hot, and the yell didn't come out anyway.

Then two more men, big burly fellows with their sleeves rolled up, took some yellowish soap and a couple of brushes like those he used to use scrubbing the kitchen floor. And then they went to work scrubbing *him* like the kitchen floor. They tsked over his hair and whacked it all off with a big shears before scrubbing his head.

He was so stunned by this turn of events he didn't even squeak. Not even when they stood him up and took cloths and scrubbed at his jakko. Not that there was anything *like* poke-and-tickle, it was like they were scrubbing a sheep or something. It was a good thing he had a tough hide, because they scrubbed at him like they were not going to be happy until they got at least half his skin off. They pulled him out of the water, dumped out the first batch, and left him there shivering for a bit while they filled the big pan again and started all over again.

It took them one more round of water before they were satisfied. By then he was feeling very peculiar, more naked than being without clothes, and tingly all over from the brushes. His skin was a color he'd never seen it before, like one of the Pieters girls, only pinker. His hair, what they'd left of it after shearing most of it off, felt very strange and light. They trimmed off all his nails short, or rather, the fellow that did the hair cutting did. They let him towel himself dry with a piece of cloth big enough to use as a blanket by his standards, and then they shoved clothing at him to put on.

New clothing, near as he could tell. It wasn't white, nor blue, but seemed a bit of odds and ends, most of it too big, but he rolled up sleeves and trews and shoved his feet first into thick warm stockings so soft he almost cried, and then into soft boots that tied up around the foot and leg like the plaited bags he made for winter, only better fitting and a lot stronger.

And then they marched him out again, out to the man in white, who stood by the back door with one of the white horses beside him. He looked up speechlessly at the man, who did not appear angry now, only somewhat resigned and weary and with a good deal of some emotion Mags couldn't identify.

"Well," he said, finally. "Here's your Companion, boy. You haven't raised your eyes to look at him yet, so do so now. And I hope for his sake you aren't as feebleminded as you seem to be."

And with that, he took Mags' chin in his thumb and forefinger, shoved his head up and over to the side, and Mags looked into the face of the horse, and into eyes bluer than the bluest sky, the bluest water, the bluest sparkly that Mags had ever seen . . .

He fell into those eyes. No, he dove into them. Here was something he'd been starving for, and never knew it. Here was love, warmth, and welcome. Here was everything he had ever wanted.

Here was his Companion. *His.* For now, and forever.

:Hello, Mags.: The simple words in his mind gave no indication of the sheer force of *welcome* behind them. *:Oh, my poor Chosen, you are so bewildered!:*

And then came a flood of information that poured easily from Dallen's mind into his, like water into an empty vessel. Or into a dried-up pond after a rain. What a Companion was, and what a Herald was. What they did. Their place in the world, and what the world itself, this *Valdemar* was all about. What he would be doing for the next several years. He understood, most immediately now, what his "Gift" was — Mindspeech — and that it meant he could speak without words to whoever also had that same Gift, and to some who did not — that he could read the thoughts of others, if he exerted himself, as easily as he read his letters. He knew now that he'd had this thing, this Gift, for the last two years, and it hadn't been whispering he'd been overhearing from others; it had been that when he tried to hear what they were saying, he heard it straight from their minds. In the mine, when he'd stolen to the mouths of tunnels, in the sleeping hole when someone had muttered in their sleep. Dallen showed him in that moment the rudiments of how to use that Gift, and how to control it, and promised there would be others who would teach him mastery of it. All of this was filling up his empty head until he was quite sure it was going to overflow, and then . . . it stopped.

He blinked, coming back to himself, and feeling a strange . . . *calm* . . . overlying everything. He had never felt quite like this before. Underneath it was still the terror, but right now it was the calm that was in control. That calm came straight from Dallen, who was a stick to lean on, a shoulder, a support until he could deal with all of this by himself.

He didn't understand more than a fraction of what had been poured into him; it was all so foreign to what he knew life was supposed to be like that he might have been standing among moon-creatures. But he also knew that, eventually, he would understand. That, too, was part of the *calm.*

:Time to pay attention to the rest of the world, Chosen,: Dallen said with an overtone of amusement. *:Otherwise they are going to think that I have stolen your mind away.:*

He blinked, and *fell out* of the entrancement as easily as he had fallen in, staggering a little at the abrupt transition, and looked around to find that he and Dallen were surrounded by a ring of people, all watching them closely.

Everything seemed sharper, clearer; he was aware of the things around him in a way that he had not been until now. The chill against his skin, the soft hide of Dallen under his hand, the way Dallen's breath, hay-scented, huffed against his shoulder.

He looked up into the skeptical eyes of the Herald. *Jakyr,* said memory. *Herald Jakyr.* "His name's Dallen, Herald Jakyr," Mags muttered, still trying to sort through the most immediate of the things dumped into his mind. "I'm . . . Mags. Don't got no other name." He caught a flicker of something from the Herald and scowled, feeling insulted. This man had no call to think of him as some sort of idiot! "And I mebbe scrawny, but I ain't lackwitted," he added with irritation. Then, belatedly, he realized that he had just been impudent to a master; he paled and appended, "Sir."

And involuntarily cringed, waiting for a blow that was, in his mind, inevitable. He had been insolent. He would pay for that.

He couldn't help himself. When you answered smart, you got smacked, if you were lucky, and beaten if you weren't. But Herald Jakyr only chuckled. "Aye, I'll take your word for it, Mags." He placed a hand on Mags' shoulder and his eyes went sad as Mags winced without thinking. "I can see

69

you've had a hard time of it. Well, from now on, things will be better. You have *my* word on it."

Jakyr's words startled Mags, despite all that knowledge that was in him now. So many things he hadn't expected, well, this was one of many. That someone he didn't even know would be *kind* to him. He felt the stirring inside of nameless emotions, things he had not felt, and had not dared to feel, in . . . in as long as he could remember, really. He wanted to laugh. He wanted to cry. His mouth went dry and his eyes wet. It had been so long since someone was *kind* . . .

A long-ago dim memory half came to the surface and then subsided. Rough hands, but a soft voice, comfort and protection. Not complete protection, though, for that voice in memory sometimes sobbed, and sometimes wheedled, and after that had sometimes come pain. Being hidden in a corner by a fire . . . he knew that fire, he knew that place. It was the kitchen of the Big House at the mine. Someone there had been *kind* to him, had cared for him. He remembered a wordless crooning, and warmth.

But the memory slipped away, over-whelmed by the immediacy of the present.

He dared to glance sideways at the Herald. The man's eyes looked weary, but not impatient, and his hand was still firm and warm on Mags' shoulder. "All right, Mags, let's get some food into you, since I took you away from that pig slop they were calling a noon meal. Judging by the look of you —" Jakyr sighed. "My heart tells me to stuff you with things you've likely never tasted before, but my head knows very well what will happen if I do. You'll be sick and miserable, and there will be all my good intentions gone wrong. So. You eat bread, yes?" Mags nodded. "And something like porridge?"

"Not often, sir," Mags replied truthfully. "Most times what you saw. Soup. Barley bread. What we could find."

The men surrounding them murmured to one another, grimacing, and Jakyr winced. "All right, then. Let's start you out with bread and some soup and see how that goes."

Still leaving his hand on Mags' shoulder, Jakyr steered him through the crowd of curious Guardsmen, most of whom were no older than the Pieters boys, and back into the building. Seeing these Guardsmen so young did not give him any measure of comfort; there was no telling what they

71

might or might not do. Dallen seemed to think they were all wonderful people, but . . .

Then that calm came over him again. But as the Herald tried to urge him along, Mags turned — again, involuntarily, not wanting to leave Dallen. It was more than a "want," it was a *need,* the farther he got from Dallen. He felt as if he had to be with Dallen, every moment, every instant. He felt anxiety rising in him, almost to the point of panic, about leaving Dallen alone. What if something happened? What if they tried to persuade Dallen to go? What if they treated the Companion like a mere horse?

:I'm fine, Chosen, they cosset me here like a bride on her wedding day,: the Companion reassured Mags with amusement. *:And I am never more than a thought away from you. You go on, eat, then sleep.:*

Again, that cushion of calm came down over him. So Mags let himself be steered down that long corridor for the second time, until they came to an enormous white-walled, black-beamed room, the biggest he had ever seen, with nothing in it but Guardsmen eating and talking, with row after row of tables and benches. The smell of food was so intense it came near to making him faint. He couldn't identify any of the smells, only that they all made his stomach knot with hunger, and his mouth ache to taste what made all those smells. Rich smells, savory and sweet, and spicy, all blending somehow. Jakyr guided him to the nearest empty seat, and one of the young men that had been with them went away and came back without prompting with an enormous bowl and four thick slices of bread, and a spoon. He put it all down in front of Mags. And when Mags looked into the bowl, he could hardly believe his eyes. It was full of the kind of soup he only saw once a year, when the strangers came to look them all over. Vegetables floated so thickly in the broth that they were pushing each other up to the surface, carrots and peas, three kinds of beans, lentils, bits of chopped root, and soft cooked barley, all in a broth so rich it looked like gravy, not like the watery stuff in the cabbage soup.

But even if new memories hadn't told him that Jakyr was right about getting sick if he ate too much, too fast, his own experience did. *Don't gobble, or you'll be sorry.* So he took the spoon in one hand, a slice of the bread — wheaten bread — in the other. The only time he had seen wheaten bread was when it was burned and thrown in the pig slop. He and the other kiddies got barley or rye bread, coarse stuff that somehow failed to satisfy. He dipped a corner of the bread and sopped up broth. Ate the bite. Took a spoonful of soup that made his mouth sing with flavor and filled his whole head with the intoxicating aroma. Ate that. Dipped the bread again. He repeated this pattern, slowly, carefully. Even though his empty stomach screamed at him to fill it, faster, *now,* he went slowly. He hadn't gotten as far as he had without being able to master his gut. Besides, you didn't gobble food that tasted like this . . . you gobbled food that tasted horrible so you could get it into your stomach before your mouth could protest.

Jakyr watched him, eyes narrowed at first, then relaxing. An approving smile touched his lips. Somewhere under the calm, Mags wondered — why did he care if Mags got sick or not? But the calm said, *Of course he cares. He's a Herald. He just does.* "There's a good lad," he murmured. "Don't worry, there's more where that came from, as much as you want, and when you're used to being better fed, butter for your bread and meat, and —" He grinned then. Mags paused between bites and found himself stretching his mouth in a return smile. It was a peculiar feeling. He couldn't remember the last time he'd smiled. It made him feel strange, but good, to do so. But he didn't have a lot of attention to spare for feelings, not when there was good food to be eaten.

When Mags reached the bottom of the bowl, sopping up the last little bits of broth with the last bite of bread, he sighed, and pushed the bowl and spoon away.

"Had enough for now?" Jakyr asked. Mags nodded. One of the young Guardsmen came over with something, hesitantly. He set down the plate in front of Mags. On it was a sliced apple, whole and sound, not a wormhole or rotten spot to be seen, and a piece of creamy cheese, without a touch of mold to it. "Me gran would say he should have this, too, Herald Jakyr," the young man said, and Mags got it, unbidden from the young man's mind, that he had a little brother about Mags' age, and that Mags himself was wearing this fellow's outgrown shirt, as he was wearing discarded trews, boots, stockings, smallclothes, from four other young Guardsmen. Oddly enough . . . that felt . . . warming. Like they had given him a bit of themselves with the clothing.

"I expect your gran is right," Jakyr agreed, and nodded to Mags to start in on the good things. "Have that, lad, if you can find a corner to tuck it in."

Again, he ate slowly, the cheese first,

savoring the richness of it, soft, creamy, a bit of a bite, and the unexpected crunch of tiny salt crystals, marveling that this was how cheese was supposed to taste. The only cheese he had ever gotten was cheese so covered with mold it was green, and as dried out and hard as a board to boot. Then the apple, so sweet it tasted like the nectar the kiddies used to suck out of the bases of flowers when they got a chance. But by that point, a full belly and being *warm* and the drone of voices as Jakyr talked to the Guardsmen was making him drowsy . . . then sleepy . . . and he felt himself nodding off with a slice of apple still in his hand. He woke up a bit when Jakyr shook him, and obediently let himself be led off by one of the Guardsmen, the same one that had brought him the cheese, to a room, where there was a bed, the first bed *he* had ever slept in. The Guardsman helped him off with his boots, and that was the last thing he remembered before falling into a dream of riding Dallen through apple-flavored clouds to the biggest Big House he had ever seen.

4

Mags' dreams were soothing, for the first time in his memory, and full of something else, too; Dallen explaining things to him. Never in all his life had he encountered anyone with Dallen's patience. He felt like such a dolt, but all those things in his head, they all were so strange, so completely divorced from anything he knew. He kept asking questions and often only got more confused. Finally Dallen stopped where he was in the imaginary landscape; the clouds billowed up about them and whited everything out, so that there was only himself and Dallen,

Over and over, Dallen explained what it was that *he* was, what it was that Dallen was, and why it was important. "I may be a dolt," Mags said once, hanging his head. "But it don't seem real nor possible. How can *I* do all them grand things? How can *you* be talking like a human person?"

And Dallen would begin all over again, explaining it a different way. Always, he was wrapped in that calm, which was a good thing, because it let him listen and try to understand without panicking.

Slowly he began, if not to understand, at least to accept, though none of it made any sense by his lights. Nobody was getting anything out of this so far as he could see. Everything was about what a body got out of something. But the Companions got nothing out of this, and the Heralds, well, all right, they got to live better than Master Cole, but they had to work three times as hard for it. And all the sorting out of things that Heralds did, well, who got anything out of that? It was bewildering. And that was just looking at things the simple way. . . .

When you went at it in a more complicated way, when you started wondering what Companions were, and how they could be as smart as a person, and where they came from and why they were doing all of this, well, it was just plain crazy. And if he had not been enveloped in that calm, he would have been sure he had actually gone mad, and none of this was happening.

Finally Dallen went silent for a long time. :Chosen, when you gave Burd that piece of bread, why did you do it? You got nothing out

78

of it except his gratitude.:

That brought all Mags' questions to a tumbling halt, because even he didn't know why he'd done it. It wasn't like the snitched food that might be bad, with everyone sharing it so nobody got too sick. That half slice of bread wasn't going to make Burd strong enough to do his work and Mags'. And the lack of it wasn't going to keep him from doing his own work. All right, maybe some time in the future, Burd might recall and do him a turn, but he might not. So why had he done it? It wasn't the first time he'd shared with one of the others either . . . generally the littlest or weakest. Then, of course, he'd had to go all hard on them so that they wouldn't think they could depend on him — but he'd felt bad when he did that, too.

" 'Cause . . ." he began, struggling with his own thoughts. "Because . . . it weren't fair. They put him in a played-out seam, how'd they expect him t' find sparklies there? Then they take away his bread 'cause he don't. They knowed he weren't shirking. They knowed he weren't hiding sparklies. It weren't fair. They was takin' away what he shoulda had outa pure meanness. An' there weren't nothin' he could do about it neither."

:That is why we do all of it, Chosen,: Dallen said with immense pride. *:We try to make things fair.:*

Such a strange thought. Such a very strange thought. But it made a kind of equally strange sense.

Slowly he pieced together what Dallen was trying to tell him. That he had been picked out by Dallen to do this thing, because there was something in him that made him right for a task that was going to last a lifetime. That the something was partly what made him give Burd that bread — and many other kindnesses he had done for the other kiddies. That was the complex matter on which all the rest of it rested. It seemed that what he was trying to do — if he understood correctly — was to make things fair.

Which made no sense.

"But life ain't fair —" he protested, having heard *that* over and over again, with varying degrees of smugness on the part of the Pieters' boys.

:Why not?: Dallen asked, stopping him in his tracks.

"Because — because it ain't!" was all he could come up with. It was true. Everyone knew it. Why try and go against what was true?

:And the more people that say that, the more

people there are who use that as their excuse to be cruel, mean, and ugly,: Dallen said implacably. *:'Life isn't fair' is nothing but an excuse people make to justify bad things they do. But why* shouldn't *life be fair? What's keeping it from being fair? Those same cruel, mean, and evil people. I think you understand that, Mags — maybe not in your head, but in your heart, which is more important. And the more people there are who try to make life fair, the more likely it is that it will become fair. Don't you want that?:*

He had to admit that he did. And he had to admit that the idea of *making life fair* had a kind of thrill to it. Even if all he did was share a piece of bread . . .

But all that was really too much to think about for very long. Even in his dreams, his attention came back to the basics, the simple things. And Dallen was perfectly willing, in his dream, to talk about those, too.

Dallen chuckled with sympathy — but promised that he was never, ever going to be hungry again, or cold, or ill-clothed, or dirty. Mags could not quite understand how Dallen could be so very sure of this, but the memories that the Companion shared with him seemed to have no room in them for anything but belief. The idea that he could eat whenever he wanted, as much as he wanted . . . it was like one of those paradises that priest kept mouthing about, but which, of course, *he* did not believe in. But this, this was real. The soup, the bread had been real. The other food on the table had been real. The clothing they had given him, the bed he was sleeping in now, were real.

And in the dream he came to realize something profound; with Dallen beside him, he would never be alone either. He had not realized how much of an aching hunger that filled until it *was* filled — it had been like a wound he'd had for so long that the pain no longer registered with him. It was like the time he had been so hungry that finally hunger ceased to have any meaning — and when he finally *got* food again, it came as a shock to understand how much he'd been starved. And here he had been starved all this time for something else as well. He couldn't put a name to it, but he had been starved for it.

As he groped his way to comprehending all this, Dallen promised he would make sure that Mags understood every little thing that puzzled him, no matter how long it took to explain it.

And Mags began to accept that there was yet another underlying truth to everything that completely went against the way he had thought that the world was — that it was not *he* who was bad and wrong, it was those who had treated him and the other kiddies as they had. Master Cole and his family had had no justification for doing what they had done; in fact, there could *be* no justification, ever, for the way they had abused their workers and servants. This was a complete reversal of the world as he knew it. It went against absolutely everything he had taken for granted.

"But I'm Bad Blood —" he protested over and over, still finding it hard to accept that he had not, somehow, deserved his treatment at the mine. And every time he did, Dallen replied with profound scorn that there was no such thing as Bad Blood. Finally, he began to believe it, at least a little. And what he lacked in belief, Dallen made up for with the calm assurance that lay under everything. Finally, Mags just accepted the assurance without believing, and let Dallen soothe him.

And that was when he woke up, to a room full of empty beds, the sun shining in through the real glass windows. In a bed, under warm blankets. Not cold. Not aching. With a kind of alert lassitude suffusing him, as if his body was saying, *At last, now I can let go, stop being alert, stop being afraid. Now I can rest.*

A sound at the door made him turn his head in time to see a brown-haired, stooped man in green tunic and trews come into the room and head straight for him. "So, the sleeper awakes, and hungry I hope?" the man said.

Who was this? And what did he want? Mags did his best not to try to hide under the covers. Dallen quickly moved to reassure him, and Mags pushed himself up reluctantly, and nodded. He was so used to awakening hungry he hadn't even thought about it. Of course he was hungry. He was *always* hungry.

:This is a Healer. He wants to discover how healthy you are. That is his job.: Mags had never seen a Healer before. When any of the kiddies got hurt or sick, they either got well on their own, or died. When any of the Pieters family got hurt or sick, Cole Pieters sent for one of his fat priest friends.

Mags had gone to sleep fully clothed, and all anyone had done was to cover him up and take his boots off. And for a fraction of a moment, as he pushed the covers back and saw his feet were clad only in socks, he had been afraid the boots had been stolen, until Dallen again washed him with reassurance. While he sat on the edge of the bed and fished for them, the man in green gave him a penetrating look. He was a cheerful sort of fellow, and truth be told, like just about everyone here, he was not the sort of person Mags was used to being around. He must have been about Cole Pieters' age and, like Pieters, he was balding, but there the resemblance ended. He must have been very fit when he was younger; now there was a bit of fat around his middle, but nothing like Pieters' enormous belly. His oblong face with its bushy eyebrows looked as if he smiled much more often than he frowned, and his frank brown eyes had a direct gaze to them that wasn't hard to meet unless you were used to ducking your head and hiding your eyes as Mags was.

"I had the cooks save you some porridge," the man said, watching him shoving his feet into his boots. "I hope your Companion has explained to you that you are expected to be very cleanly —"

Mags ducked his head. "Yessir," he said, and left it at that.

"Well, we'll leave your bath until after you've eaten. Best time for you is in the morning for now, that way you won't conflict with the Guardsmen. Ready?" The man stood up. "I'm Healer Betwick, by the way. I serve the Guard here."

Whatever a Healer was . . . presumably they healed people . . . though how they did that was an utter mystery to Mags. Then again, practically everything going on now was an utter mystery to Mags. "Yessir, Healer Betwick," Mags replied, as Dallen and the memories poured into him showed him what a Healer was.

And yes, they did heal people, in a bewildering variety of ways. This particular shade of green was accepted as *their* color, and if you saw someone wearing it, you knew he was a Healer. Just as, if you saw someone in White, you knew he was a Herald, in Scarlet and he was a Bard. Whatever a Bard was —

Before another flood of memories could start, triggered by that word and half-query, Mags followed the man out of the room into a hallway he only vaguely recalled, and from there, not to the big room with all the tables —

— *Guards' mess,* memory prompted.

But to a spacious and fragrant kitchen full of very busy people. Or, actually, there were only four of them, but they were so extremely busy it seemed as if there were at least eight of them, and Healer Betwick evidently deemed it prudent to stay out of their way.

He motioned to Mags to go and sit on a stool at a little table off to the side and well away from all the activity, then went over to the hearth and fetched a bowl waiting there, keeping warm.

When he brought it back to Mags, the boy saw it was full of porridge with little dark things scattered over the top of it. "What's those?" he asked, a bit apprehensively.

"Currants. Dried ones. They're sweet, you'll like them, and they are good for you."

Reassured that they weren't rabbit drop-pings or something else that didn't belong in food, Mags dug in. The Healer was right, he did like the currants, he liked them a very great deal. Half the time the porridge he'd been fed by Master Cole hadn't even been made with salt; this had been sweet-ened with honey as well as the berries.

While he ate, the Healer talked in an undertone to the cook, who was a large, balding man with enormous biceps. In fact, so far, Mags hadn't seen any women here at all. Which was interesting, because Master Cole had very firm ideas about what was "man's work" and what was not, which meant there would have to be an awful lot of men doing "women's work" here if there were no women about.

:Cole Pieters is wrong about most things.: Dallen sounded amused. :And the few he is right about, he is right entirely by accident.:

Mags nearly choked on his porridge, which caused one of the kitchen staff to make a detour, fetch a mug and pour it full of something, and plunk it down next to Mags, all without missing a beat in his other task. Mags looked at it. It wasn't water . . . it was hot.

:Herb tea. You will like it. Be careful not to burn your mouth.:

The novel sensation of drinking something hot — and flavored — was startling, and a pleasure he had never expected. For that matter, being able to drink water that was fresh and clean, not out of the sluice and full of silt, or stale from sitting in a mildewed bucket all day, or metallic-tasting mine water, had been an unanticipated pleasure. The only time he had ever been able to drink clean water was when he had escaped for a bit to hunt wild food and got a drink from the stream where he went to hunt cress.

The food was doing more than just fill his stomach, it was filling his senses. His nose was so full of the aroma of the tea, all sweet and green, that he felt as if he was floating in it. The porridge had left the flavor of honey and currants in his mouth. And this all seemed to be waking up his thoughts, too. He found himself with a newly-aroused smoldering anger at Cole Pieters. How hard would it have been to give the kiddies clean water to drink? How hard would it have been to give them *hot* water to drink in the winter? It didn't even need any flavoring in it, and the fires were going for the cooking already. That simple device would have cost nothing, yet would have made such a difference. . . .

:Cole Pieters is a vile, cruel man,: Dallen said, his thoughts gone cold and hard. *:And no one was aware just how vile and cruel he is until now. He will be dealt with.:*

Dallen gave him nothing more, shutting off the thought, leaving Mags wondering just what "dealt with" meant.

Mags was carefully scraping the last little bit of the porridge out of the bowl and sucking the last of the sweetness off the spoon when Herald Jakyr came ambling into the kitchen. He was immediately greeted not only by the Healer, but by the cook as well, and his presence evoked smiles from the rest of the staff. He seemed to be a great favorite — the helper in charge of the bread pressed a roll hot from the oven on him, the one in charge of soup begged him to taste it, and the cook himself carved a bit off a haunch of bacon and fried it then and there, to add to the roll. Mags was ignored, which was exactly the way he liked it. He sat and sipped his tea while the adults discussed him as if he was not there.

"The boy's not fit to travel, Jakyr," the Healer said firmly, as Jakyr munched on his snack and the kitchen staff went back to work. "Maybe if it was summer — but he's malnourished and overworked, and travel with winter coming on, even Companion-back . . . I wouldn't advise it. You'll be courting sickness with him, and what if you're caught in weather? What if he got sick and you were stuck in some Waystation somewhere?"

I'm keeping the Herald from going some-where — The thought suffused him with guilt and apprehension, both of which were blown away like mist in the wind by Jakyr's next words before Dallen could say anything other than start that wordless reassurance again.

"I've a bit to do here yet, and I'm not averse to a rest. There's nothing that urgent waiting for me at Haven that we can't afford to let the lad rest and at least start to get some meat on him." Jakyr even seemed a bit relieved. "I've friends enough here to make a pleasure out of necessity."

"And if something urgent should come up?" the Healer persisted, his brows furrowed.

"Then I'll go back alone, and one of the Guard can give the boy an escort to Haven." Jakyr smiled as the Healer nodded with satisfaction. "And if, because of that, they go at a horse's pace and not a Companion's, well, that will do no harm."

"I want that boy eatin' meat afore you take him out of here," the cook tossed over his shoulder, with a scowl. "Gods' a-mercy, if the rest of them mine kids look's bad as him, I'm tempted, sore tempted, to ride over there meself and thrash the bastard till he bleeds."

"It's being dealt with, Scully, never fear," was all that Herald Jakyr said, the same words that Dallen had used. But Mags had no chance to think much about that, since the Healer whisked him away for that threatened bath.

Only this time he didn't have anyone scrubbing at him with floor brushes; in fact, he was left quite alone, and to be honest, he would have been at a bit of a loss if Dallen hadn't told him what to do and how to do it. Soap, that was new. Hot water enough to drown in. More outgrown clothing was

91

waiting for him, dropped off by some young fellow of the Guard, when he got himself well dried off. It, like the last batch, was a bit oversized but soft and warm, and without tears or holes of any sort.

Then he was at a complete loss. Never in all of his life, had he ever had a moment when he was not doing something, except when he was asleep. It was a strange feeling, unsettling, and once again he felt as if the world had suddenly turned upside down. And although he still found himself wrapped in that calm lassitude, he wasn't sleepy as such. He finished cleaning up the room where the baths were so that it was in the same pristine state it had been before, and then stood there in the damp heat, wondering what to do with himself. His hands twitched a little. His body knew what it expected to be doing — it expected him to be down in the mine. What was he supposed to do with himself?

:Would you like to read a real book?:

Of all the things that Dallen could have said, that was one that took him utterly by surprise. His mute assent led Dallen to direct him down a hall and up two flights of stairs to a small room that was comfortably warm and lit with two of those large glazed windows. There were heavily cushioned benches beneath both of them, and the walls were lined with cases crammed with something he had never seen before, but which the memories he had gotten poured into his mind told him were those mysterious objects — *books.* Row upon row of them, thick ones, thin ones, bound in all manner and colors of cloth and leather. The room had a smell like nothing he had ever known; leather, but also an odd, faint, sharpish smell, and a hint of dust. The scent Dallen identified for him as peculiar to books. He stared at them avidly. There must be so many things in those books, and he wanted to read them all.

But which one to start with? There was no way of telling what was inside any of them.

:Let me look through your eyes,: Dallen suggested, and when Mags gave him a puzzled assent, he got a most peculiar sensation, as his own eyes flickered over the backs of the books without his own volition.

:That one,: Dallen suggested, and his eyes rested on the back of one in dull blue leather. Carefully, Mags pulled it out and carried it over to one of the benches.

He was almost afraid to touch the pages with his rough hands, they seemed so fragile to him. When he opened the book, he wasn't sure what he was going to see. But his speculations were not what met his eyes; what he saw was long strings of words in sentences, written small, like rows and rows of ants on the page. It took him a breathless moment to realize that these were words he knew, that he recognized, that he had written. Most of them, anyway.

:I will help you with the others,: Dallen promised. *:Now don't be afraid of the pages. They will withstand being turned, they are tougher than they look. Go ahead.:*

He took a seat on one of the benches, with the weak, but warm sunlight pouring over his back and licked his lips, then plunged in.

Slowly, sentence by sentence, sometimes word by word, Mags began to read his first book.

It was harder work than he thought, but it was also engrossing, once he realized that this book was telling a story. Of course, he didn't understand a lot of it, because it talked about things that were so foreign to his life, but Dallen helped by giving him mental images of what was going on. It was . . . magical. That was the only possible word for it. Here he was, puzzling out a story that someone else had told, someone who probably lived a very long way away from here, and every person that picked up this book would get to learn the same story.

He got so involved in it that when a bell sounded through the building, he jumped. He didn't yelp. Yelping got you hit. But he was genuinely startled, and he sat there for a moment with his heart racing, wondering if he had somehow done something wrong and triggered an alarm.

:That is the bell for noon meal,: Dallen informed him merrily, taking no notice of his panic. And his stomach rumbled. He was so used to being hungry that it hadn't registered with him. But his stomach had gotten two good, big meals so far, and it wanted another.

He could find his way around a mine, so it was not hard now to remember his way back to the mess hall. But even if he had not known how to get there, the stream of Guards all going in one direction would have given him the clue. This time the room was full of men, and he wondered what it was he should do and where he should go.

But one of the young men spotted him, no doubt because in his ordinary, if over-large clothing, he stood out among the blue uniforms like a rock on a snowdrift. The fellow steered him over to a table, and consulted with someone who was bringing platters of food around.

And *that* man returned with another big bowl of soup and a half a loaf of bread. "Healer's orders, Trainee," the man said, putting both in front of him. "Soup fer you, he sez, till ye be used ta eaten regular. Mebbe some cheese an' fruit. An' no beer for ye. I'll bring the tea, foreby."

Mags hardly cared. This time the soup had chunks of chicken meat in it as well as the thick rafts of vegetables, and round white things he couldn't identify, but which tasted glorious. There was more wonderful cheese, and another apple. More herb tea, this time sweetened with honey that somehow blended with the flavors of the herbs and made them stand out more. Part of him still wanted to be wary, afraid that someone would decide to take all this away from him, but Dallen kept up a steady flow of certainty, and eventually he just gave himself over to the food.

He ate until he couldn't eat any more, and he *intended* to go back to his book again. But somehow he found himself in that room full of beds again, and thought he would lie down for just a little bit.

And that decision was the last thing he remembered before sleep claimed him.

It seemed only a moment later that he woke to Dallen's prodding and the sound of a bell again. Outside the windows, the sun was setting. Inside, the sounds from down the hall made him realize that the Guardsmen were heading in the direction of the mess hall. And once again, his stomach growled, telling him in no uncertain terms that it was empty, it had gotten used to being full, and it wanted to be that way again, now.

He spent the next several days in the same way; getting fed, sleeping a very great deal, slowly becoming more and more facile at reading books, absorbing what was in the books that Dallen selected for him.

If he didn't speak much, it was because he spent most of his time watching everything. From time to time, with a vaguely worried look on his face, Herald Jakyr would seek him out in the book room or at meals and ask him some pointed question or other. Mags' answers must have satisfied him, for the Herald would get a relieved look on his face and go off about his business.

That business took him away from the Guard Post more often than not. Mags didn't mind; while he was gone, the Guardsmen generally let him poke around as much as he cared to as long as he was not underfoot.

By watching, he learned how to groom a horse — and by extension, Dallen. He learned how to saddle and bridle one, too, and what to feed it. He learned all manner of useful things, in fact, although the one thing he didn't learn, because he never could bring himself to pick up a weapon, was how to *use* a weapon. He watched the Guardsmen at their practice, and every time he even thought about picking up a knife or a bow, he wanted to crawl away and hide. It made his skin crawl and his stomach tie up in knots in a way that nothing Dallen could do would soothe. He kept thinking about the time when he was still in the kitchen and someone had raised a mining hammer as a weapon to Master Cole.

Master Cole had gathered everyone outside to watch.

"I be judge and jury here," the Master had said harshly. "Ye dared t' raise yer filthy hand t' me, dared t' try an' strike me dead, and me boys as witness to it."

He had glanced around at all of his sons, who had nodded and mumbled "ayes."

"Then I gives ye the sentence ye'd hev served me, if ye could." And he had then taken the massive, stone-headed mallet at his side, and brutally beaten the poor wretch to death, and beyond, into a pulp, while every other person on the property was forced to watch.

Then the mine kiddies had been ordered to take up what was left and leave it in a played-out seam. The supports were pulled out, the seam collapsed. Everyone understood that this meant if and when someone came looking for the boy, there had been a terrible "accident."

Mags had not been one of the mine kiddies then, so he had been able to scuttle back to the kitchen, where he shivered through his work. Even the kitchen drudges, usually starving, had little appetite for their scraps that day.

Which, of course, was exactly what the Master intended. The lesson was clear. Take up a weapon and die.

So it was small wonder Mags had difficulty even contemplating setting a hand to a hilt.

Fortunately, no one seemed to think he needed to.

Slowly, he began poking his nose into other places around the Guard Post. He found the office of the fellow who did all the reckoning for this post, and watched in fascination as he made marks that looked like letters, but weren't. The man seemed amused and, after a while, motioned him over.

"I take it no one ever taught ye your numbers as well as your letters, boy?" he said. He was the oldest person that Mags had ever seen; his hair was snow white, and his face as full of wrinkles as the bark of a tree. His eyes could scarcely be seen, but there was a bright look to them, like a bird's eye. And Mags did not "hear" anything at all amiss in the thoughts that ticked away in his head like the regular dripping of water on stone. Numbers — this man thought mostly in numbers. He loved them, loved the patterns they made, loved the pure logic that governed them, loved that three and three always made six, never four, never seven.

Mags shook his head.

"Well then, 'tis time to learn, and as I've time meself, I'll teach ye. Pull up yon stool." He nodded at a tall stool in the corner. Mags obeyed.

The man pulled open a drawer in his desk and extracted a piece of slate and a square-cut stick of white stuff. "Ye'll be usin' this; 'tis slate an chalk. 'Tis easy rubbed out, y' see?" He made a mark and buffed it away with a sleeve. "Now, ye kin count right enough, aye?"

"To a hunner' sir," Mags almost whispered.

"Right enough. Well, there's marks for them numbers, just as there be marks that make letters that make words. On'y these be a bit more straightforward, belike. This be 'one'. . . ."

Mags caught on quickly. And although he had not realized it until the man — who he learned was Guard-Clerk Sergeant Taver — showed him, he *did* know some primitive reckoning. After all, he had to keep track of the sparklies he found. He took to the figuring quickly, learning how to add and subtract double-digit numbers by the end of the afternoon, much to Sergeant Taver's delight. It was Taver who took him in to supper that night, in fact, and much enjoyed letting the "dunderheads" know that already the "wee boy" could outreckon no few of them.

He shook his finger at one particular young man who had pulled his head so far down into his collar that he looked like a turtle. "An' the next time, Brion, ye come t' me an' tell me thet th' two dozen socks ye been issued adds up t' twenty, I'll have *him* come an' count 'em aright for ye!"

Mags was fearful then that the Guard would take it hard, and be angry with him.

Yet as the others laughed, he grew crimson but laughed with them, and Mags sensed nothing more in his thoughts than chagrin and a determination to count more carefully next time.

Sheer astonishment left him dumb through the rest of the meal — but since silence on his part was a more common occurrence than speech, no one really noticed.

He went to bed feeling something he had never experienced before in his life; the warmth of accomplishment. Sergeant Taver had said he was clever! No one had ever said that before to him! He felt Dallen's glow of approval, and decided on his own that if Sergeant Taver would continue to show him the mysteries of numbers, he would continue to pursue them.

But, as it fell out, the next day brought a rather different task for him.

5

In the morning, Herald Jakyr was waiting for him as soon as he had finished his breakfast. He sensed Jakyr waiting outside the room and was surprised to feel a certain happiness when he also sensed the Herald was waiting for *him*. It was an unfamiliar feeling, taking pleasure from knowing someone wanted to see him. In the past, well, the only time anyone wanted to see him was to question him, usually before punishing him. It came to him with a feeling of shock that he actually had not seen anyone punished as such since he had come to this place. Oh, he had overheard men being berated by trainers, or even assigned to some undesirable duty because of some infraction or other, but he actually had not seen anyone punished as he understood the term.

But his pleasure in seeing Jakyr was short-lived. With him was a stranger, a sober-faced man in a dark tunic and trews, who carried a leather case with him and who regarded him with a measuring eye. Mags shrank from the stranger, instinctively trying to hide from that searching look. Jakyr brought both of them to the library, shut the door, and shot the latch across it. The only time he had ever been in a room with a locked door was when something truly terrible was about to happen, and Mags looked at the Herald with alarm until Dallen soothed him. *:Just do what Jakyr tells you, Chosen,:* came the calm voice in his head. *:This is needful.:* Visions of horrible beatings passed across Mags' mind as Dallen assured him that nothing of the sort was going to happen. *:He is only going to ask you questions. That is all.:*

Questions! Questions could lead to bad things, too! What if he got the answers wrong? What if the answers made the man angry?

It was with difficulty that Dallen finally persuaded Mags that it *would* be all right. Both Jakyr and the stranger must have found out in some way that Mags was afraid, and that Dallen was calming him down, because both of them stayed quiet until Mags was finally ready to talk. And even then he was shaking inside and regretting he'd had any breakfast at all.

"This is going to be difficult for you, Mags, I understand that," Jakyr said carefully, as the other man took pens, a pot of ink, and a sheaf of clean paper from his case and set them up on a table. "Your condition, and that of the other children I saw at Cole Pieters' mine is fairly convincing testimony of neglect, if not outright abuse. But I need more than that if I am to be able to take a company of the Guard there and close the place down. I need testimony from you, and as much as you can tell me about the place."

Mags scarcely heard the last sentence, since the one before it was so astonishing. "Close the mine?" he whispered. "But — what 'bout the rest of th' kiddies? If ye close th' mine, Master Cole belike won' feed 'em!"

"Master Cole won't be in charge of them," Jakyr replied, with a certain grim satisfaction. "And Master Cole will have other things to think about. Now, let's start with something simple. Tell me about your day, just an ordinary day from the time you would wake up. Where did you sleep?"

Slowly, haltingly, still trying to comprehend what it was that Jakyr was about to do concerning Cole Pieters, Mags obeyed, beginning with the description of the sleep-hole and moving on.

And that was where things got . . . odd. It hadn't really occurred to him before that there was anything out of the ordinary about how Pieters treated his workers. That is to say, he understood vaguely that Master Cole was not treating them *well,* especially in contrast to how the Guards were treated, but it had not occurred to him that there was anything that other people would see as *wrong* about it. It was, after all, Cole Pieters' mine, and they were his workers, and there were all those priests in the place, and how could anyone prevent him from doing what he wanted with them? Well, short of killing people. Would that ever be found out? Would anyone believe the word of the kiddies over that of the Pieterses? He didn't think so.

When it came to how the workers were treated, well, there just didn't seem any reason why Master Cole couldn't do exactly as he pleased with the workers in his mine. But from the moment Mags began talking, it was obvious that both Jakyr and this stranger were caught off guard by what he was telling them. Not only that, but they both were angry — though not at him. He caught sight of a vein throbbing in the strange man's temple almost at once, and sensed thoughts full of outrage as Mags carefully detailed what life was like at Cole Pieters' mine. That astonished Mags, astonished him so much that he actually forgot his own apprehension. That this stranger would actually *care* that the kiddies went cold, starved, and bare was the most amazing thing he had ever encountered in his entire life. It came near to making no sense at all. Because all he could think of was — *why?* Why should he care? What difference did it make to him? And wasn't that how things were everywhere for the kiddies nobody wanted? If all those priests hadn't been outraged, then why was this stranger?

When he had finished with telling about a typical day, with Jakyr questioning him minutely about the meals, and how one earned or lost those precious slices of bread, Jakyr took him back over a day again, this time in the dead of winter. He asked how they protected their feet from the snow, and how long they had to work at the icy water in the sluices, then what kind of bedding they had once the winter set in. As he questioned Mags ever more closely, Mags described how many of the kiddies would get chilblains and how they had to be careful not to lose fingers or toes to the cold, and he thought the stranger was going to burst. Except that anger was all on the inside. On the outside, he looked just as calm as calm, and never once faltered in his writing down of things. He could have been writing down what everyone here had for breakfast, for all that he showed. It was strange, listening to the silence in the room broken only by his voice and the steady scratching of a pen. Very strange, as it occurred to him that he probably had not spoken so much in an entire year.

Then Jakyr asked about the injuries to the mine workers. And the dangerous question, "How did people die?"

That was when Mags got frightened all over again. This was dangerous, dangerous stuff. Everyone knew what would happen if you told such things, and Pieters found out about it. You'd end up in a "cave-in" yourself. And Mags had suspected more than once that the Pieters boys had a very special punishment for those who really transgressed. He had the feeling that the ones that woke their worst ire were sealed into those played-out shafts — broken, scarcely able to move, but still alive. Though of course, they didn't stay that way, not for long. The question would be whether they ran out of air first or whether they died of their injuries before then.

He could *see* it in his mind's eye. He could see himself in the absolute dark, gasping out his last breaths. Pieters would find a way. He knew it. His insides went cold and knotted up, his hands began to shake, and he wanted to go and curl up in a corner behind something and hide.

"I cain't —" he whispered, tears starting into his eyes, his voice choked off into nothing by the fear. "I cain't. When Master Cole finds out who 'twas told —"

"Master Cole cannot reach you, Mags." It was the stranger who spoke, voice tight with rage and mind so full of the same anger that his thoughts were lost under a red wash. "Master Cole can never touch you again. Now don't you want to make sure the rest of the children get that same protection?"

:Mags, this is not a premonition you see, it is only your fear. Don't let Pieters keep you a prisoner!: Dallen's voice rang with conviction in Mags' mind. Mags quivered with fear, but deep in his heart, he knew the stranger was right, and so was Dallen.

The stranger's reaction had told him so. He knew now that no one should have been treated as he and the others had been. He knew that Cole Pieters deserved to be punished. He couldn't leave the others there, not now that he knew Master Cole was an evil, bad man. And what he had said so far might not be enough to win them free.

But it was hard, hard, hard. He had to fight past the fear of Master Cole that made his throat close up, fight past the knotting of his gut and the hunching of his shoulders against the blows he knew *must* come for breaching the silence.

And then, in a whisper, he told everything he knew.

To the best of his ability, he drew a map of the mine and showed where the bodies were. As far as he could, he detailed what they had *really* died of. And when it was over, he was shaking, his clothing was soaked with nervous sweat, and he felt as weak and drained as if he had run for days.

When they let him go, he had barely enough energy left to drag himself to the bathing room and pour himself a bath. He stank of fear and sweat and — suddenly he was feeling fastidious, being around all these cleanly people. He didn't want anyone to think he didn't know better. Not now. And besides, he was so wet through, and so drained, that he was shivering with chill as well as reaction. His stomach was still in knots, and he still kept wanting to hide. It took forever to fill the bath, his hands were shaking so that the buckets sloshed.

So he stripped and soaked in the hot bath, trying not to think of anything, until his shivering, internal and external, stopped. He lay back against the rear of the tub, his mind emptying, steam rising in his face.

:You mustn't be afraid, Mags.:

Now, until this moment, Mags had accepted whatever Dallen told him unquestioningly. But this was too much to swallow. He knew very well he should be afraid. What was he? Nothing. Now, he was not very smart, and it was clear to him from everything that Dallen had been pouring into him that the way he and the other kiddies had been treated was *not* the way things were usually done. Yet Master Cole had gone on doing it. Mags was not very smart, and he was not at all wise in the ways that the world worked, but there was one thing he did know, and that was all about power. You either had it, or you didn't, or you had some, but not as much as someone else might. The Pieters boys had some, over the kiddies and the other mine workers, and they did whatever they wanted to the people below them. But Master Cole had power over *them* and did what he wanted to all of them.

Now this was a fact: Master Cole had treated the kiddies very badly indeed. Yet he had been able to do so for years and years and years, stretching far back beyond where Mags' memory started. So it stood to reason that somehow Master Cole had plenty of power that extended far beyond his own mine. Or, if he didn't, there was someone with a lot more power who was protecting him.

Now what Mags was telling Herald Jakyr and the stranger was going to turn Master Cole's mine upside down, maybe even shut it. That was going to make Cole Pieters very angry, certainly angry enough to kill. And if there was someone even *bigger* than Cole Pieters involved, it would surely make that person angry, too.

So what reason was there for Mags to *not* be afraid?

Dallen read all that swiftly from Mags' mind, as quickly as he reasoned it out himself. And for the first time, Dallen was silent.

Finally, he spoke.

:You are right, Chosen. You have reason to be afraid. But you have no reason to keep *being afraid. No matter what happens, you can be sure that Herald Jakyr will not allow anyone to know who gave him this information. To be absolutely honest . . . Herald Jakyr can do some of the same things that you can, and*

many, many more that you cannot. He has the means to get this information by himself, once he gets back to the mine. I will warn him to be sure that Cole Pieters thinks he got it all by magic.: There was a pause. *:There. He and Scribe Myrden are conferring now. The only people that will ever know where it all came from are the people in that room and the King himself.:*

Mags thought about that for a moment. *:I s'pose . . . :* he thought, still dubious.

:If you ever trusted me, you should trust me now.: Mags got the impression of a sigh. *:Mags, there will be many things that you should be afraid of. I am not telling you to never be afraid. But you must not let fear rule you. It should guide you, not govern you. And you should never allow it to stop you from doing what is right.:*

He thought about that for a much longer moment. *:Helpin' the rest . . . that was right.:*

:Yes, it was. Just as sharing your bread with the weaker was right. And giving up your extra blanket to the littlest was right. You did not let hunger stop you, nor cold. Do not allow fear to stop you either. If you do that, you do half of the work of evil men for them.:

He swallowed. This was all very well, but . . .

:We will protect you, too, Mags. We may not

113

be able to protect you from everything, but we can from most things. That is why we are here. You see?:

And at the moment, Dallen . . . did something. It was like opening a door in his mind. Except it was a door onto something enormous. Like stepping through the mouth of a cave and finding himself at the top of a very high place. For that moment, he saw, or sensed, rather, a vast web like the enormous web of a spider, except that all of the points in the web were people, and all of the strands connecting them were their Companions. And what one knew, sooner or later, the others knew. And what happened to one of them happened to all of them.

That was when he *understood.* Understood that, even though he would not always get along with some of the people who wore this white uniform, they would *always* protect him, as he, when he was older and stronger, would always fight to defend them. Understood that this was a bond that went deeper than blood and bone. He even understood now, what it was that had made Dallen pick him.

That door in his mind shut again, for it was rather too much for anyone to bear for long. But the sense of it stayed with him.

That was when, elated and humbled all at the same time, he began to cry quietly. He had always known he was a very small and insignificant thing; he had been called "maggot" so often by the Pieters boys that he had come to think of himself as exactly that — a thing that was not even an insect. But now . . . now he had seen that he wasn't so insignificant, that he was a part of something huge, and that he would always be part of it, no matter that he would never feel quite worthy of it all.

This time Dallen did not soothe him, since this was not something anyone should be soothed out of. The tears were one part happiness, one part awe, and one part release, and he let them fall.

Finally, he found words at the end of his tears and the end of his wordlessness; he ducked his head under the hot water to wash the tears away and considered what still left his guts in a cold knot. There was still a fear in him, a new fear, and not of Cole Pieters nor what the man might do to him. Mags had made so many mistakes in his few years. And he was tracing a path through a wilderness he didn't understand. What if he made the most terrible mistake of all?

:What if I do something that makes you hate

me?: he thought fearfully.

:You won't,: Dallen replied firmly. *:You can't, so long as you never close your mind to mine, so long as we make decisions together. Together we will find solutions. They may not be the best, but they won't be the worst, and if we make mistakes, we will make them together. Is that a bargain?:*

He splashed more lukewarm water on his face to wash away the last of his tears. *:Sounds right to me.:*

:Good. Now, I have an idea. You've not ridden me, not really. Come out to the stable. I think it's time you learned to ride, and ride well. The books can wait for a few candlemarks. Come out into the sun, and let's see what we can make of you.:

He was climbing out of the tub when Dallen hit him with *that* idea, and it left him stuck for a moment, half in and half out. *:But . . . but . . . but . . . :*

:I have my own tack, a Companion almost never goes out to fetch his Chosen without it. It's made to be secure for even a rider that is hurt or dozing. And you should know by now I will never let you fall. Come out. Borrow a warm coat. Come and be in the snow when it is a pleasure for once.:

Swiftly he dried himself off and put on his clothing, then went in search of one of the

Guards who seemed able to get him the few things he had tentatively asked for.

"A coat for you, and harness up your Companion? Shouldna be a problem. I thought we give you a coat already —" The man looked at him quizzically. When Mags shook his head, he shrugged. "Well, that's easy remedied. If there's naught in stores —" He got up from the stool he had been sitting on to polish his boots, set his task aside, and steered Mags toward a part of the building where he'd not yet been. This, it turned out, was "stores," which was where everything not in immediate use was tucked away. Unfortunately, there were no coats or cloaks in storage that were not so big they completely enveloped Mags and pooled on the floor.

Fortunately, there was a tailor.

In a remarkably short time, Mags was headed to the stable in a coat that was still too big for him, but which had had the sleeves and hem shortened by the simple expedient of cutting them off so he didn't fall over them, and which was held in with a belt improvised from a bridle strap. The tailor was doing a "proper job" of shortening another coat while Mags "made do" with this one, which, so the tailor averred, "Wasn't fit for anything but the ragbag."

Mags couldn't see what he was talking about to be honest. There seemed nothing whatsoever wrong with the coat to *him*. But then, it was the first time he'd ever had a coat, and certainly no one else seemed to be wearing one with as many patches on it as this one. He didn't see where they made a difference; certainly he was toasty warm in this thing.

He knew where the stable was already, for he had been to visit Dallen several times there. This time, when he pushed open the door tentatively, and stood blinking in the horse- and straw-scented gloom, he saw one of the Guards was already pulling tight the wide strap that held Dallen's saddle on his back.

He stood back uncertainly. The Guard didn't seem to know he was there. *:Now what do I do?:* he thought.

:You ask Tennit to help you onto my back.: Dallen cast an amused glance at him out of one blue eye, and the Guard turned.

"Heyla," the man said in a friendly enough tone. "Got this lad all tacked up and ready for ye. Are ye gonna be needin' a bit of help, then?"

Relieved that the man understood without Mags having to say anything, the boy nodded.

"Right ye are. So, ye come over here, yah? Then ye get yer left foot inta this thing, yah? 'S called a stirrup. Now ye grab that there — that there is the pommel of the saddle. If ye was alone, ye'd haul yerself up, but since I'm here, ye step inta my hands, ya?"

Awkwardly, Mags did so, gingerly putting his right foot into the man's interlaced hands. And suddenly, he found himself shoved right into the air, practically over Dallen, saddle and all, and it was only by hanging onto the pommel thing for dear life that he avoided going right over Dallen's back to fall in the straw on the other side of the Companion.

With a *thud,* he landed in the saddle and awkwardly fitted his right foot into the other stirrup.

The man fussed about with the stirrups for a moment, shortening the straps holding them to the saddle. Finally he was satisfied, as Mags sat there feeling unbalanced and precarious — and *very* far from the ground. "Right then, off ye go! Have a good ride!" He patted Dallen on the shoulder, and before Mags was ready, the Companion was moving.

Once again he held to the pommel of the saddle for all he was worth, and the feeling that he was never going to get the hang of this riding business, that he was going to fall off at any moment and break his skull, and that Dallen was surely laughing at him.

:And why would I laugh at you?: came the indignant response.

:I dunno, 'cause . . . 'cause . . . :

:I would much rather make a decent rider of you before we have to start on our journey to Haven. So, Chosen, you are sitting there in my saddle like a bag of grain. Let me show you . . . :

And now, Mags felt something he had not experienced until this moment. It was as if he and someone else were sharing the same body. But the second person understood exactly how to ride, and ride well, ride expertly in fact. And that person lent to Mags the *experience* of how a good rider felt in the saddle. It was a very, very strange sensation. A little like sharing his body with a ghost. But as Dallen continued to move at a brisk walk, Mags shifted his weight, his posture, even small things like how his legs gripped Dallen's body, until what he was feeling matched what the ghostly presence had experienced.

In a moment of brilliant epiphany, it all came together. Mags no longer felt as if he was going to tumble off at any moment. As Dallen kicked his way through fluffy, sparkling snow, still moving at a brisk walk, Mags began to feel elation. It was like the first time he chipped out a really big sparkly without damage. Only better.

Now Dallen started moving in and around the trees surrounding the Guard building, curving his body first one way, then the other. Mags felt his balance changing and followed that intangible guide to get it back. Then Dallen changed to a different gait, a bouncy sort of movement.

That was painful at first. Mags and Dallen were no longer moving at the same rate, and the first couple of paces, Mags hit the saddle hard enough to jar.

"Ow!" he exclaimed indignantly. "What're ye doin' that for? Why'd ye change?"

:*You have to learn how to ride at all my paces, Mags. This is the trot. And this is how it* feels.:

His confidence slipped a good deal at that point; he could tell what he was supposed to do, but he couldn't figure out how to get there, and Dallen was not letting up on him and going back to the walk. Mags gritted his teeth, clutched the pommel, and concentrated on making his body move the right way. And then, finally, he and Dallen were moving together again. And muscles he was not aware that he had began faintly protesting.

:If you think this is bad now, wait until we have been on the road for an entire day,: Dallen said mercilessly.

"A day!" Mags exclaimed, aghast. He could not begin to imagine what riding for an entire day would be like.

:It is more than seven days to Haven,: Dallen replied, appalling Mags even further.

From the trot, Dallen moved to the pace, then the canter, all the while keeping up those weaving patterns in and around the trees, coming so close that the fabric of Mags' coat caught on the bark. He was going fast, too, by the time they got to the canter. But Mags wasn't afraid now, he couldn't be. He was so busy thinking about what he should be doing that he had no time for fear.

Finally, as the bell that summoned them all to the noon meal sounded, Dallen slowed down to a walk again, and turned around to head back to the stables. Mags heaved a sigh of relief, even as he winced from the pain in his legs. When they arrived, the same Guard was waiting for them.

He helped Mags down out of the saddle and caught him as he almost fell with an involuntary groan of pain. "Ah, lad, ye'd better be getting' yer horse-legs an' get tough," the Guard called after him, as he limped off toward the building again, thinking of nothing more than yet another hot bath and maybe, only then, some food. "Heralds spend their whole lives a-horse."

:*And if someone had told me that . . . :* He didn't finish that somewhat sour thought. Dallen's sympathetic chuckle managed to soothe his injured spirit, if not his legs.

6

That night, Mags was sore, despite a good hot soak. The next morning he woke in considerable pain. He wasn't about to complain, however; he had actually expected the pain. Every time he'd been set to a new task by the Pieterses, he'd hurt, from simple soreness to being in agony. That was just the way it was; you did something new, you used muscles you hadn't before, and you hurt. And he knew what to do about it, too. He crawled out of bed, with his legs screaming at him, and slowly began to stretch. When his legs were only whimpering, he went to breakfast, then went back to the barracks room and stretched some more. Dallen noted this with quiet approval, and sent him in search of the Healer, who gave him a bitter tasting tea to drink and a bottle of something that smelled rather like pine sap to rub on. And both helped. By afternoon, most of the worst of the pain was gone, which was when Dallen summoned him to riding practice again.

On the one hand, he wanted to rebel. On the other . . . well, there was no doubt at all in his mind that this was not something he could refuse to do. He knew from all of his reading and all of the things he had picked up, listening to gossip around the Guard Post, that Heralds rode, and spent most of their time in the saddle. It wasn't just the long ride to Haven, whatever that was — if he was going to stay with Dallen, he would have to learn to be a Herald. If he was going to be a Herald, he would have to learn how to ride, and ride well.

For something had changed inside him, when Dallen had shown him that intricate web of lives all linked together, lives that now included his. He had made a commitment without even having to think about it. It had begun when he had accepted Dallen, all unthinking, understanding only dimly that he would never be alone again. Now he had extended that acceptance to other Heralds and Companions, and to all that it meant, all he would have to do to become a Herald. Again, it was unthinking, because it was right. Not that this was something he was somehow "meant" to do, but because it was the right and proper thing to do.

So complaining, and rebellion, were irrelevant.

Out he went, in his oversized coat. This time, under Dallen's direction, he got one of the Guardsmen to help him put all of Dallen's stuff on him, and tell him the names of the things as he put them on. Then it was off into the snow again, for a repetition of yesterday's lesson.

This time he was so tired that after a hot soak and more of that pine-scented liquid outside of him and the bitter tea inside of him, he went to lie down. He didn't exactly sleep, but he wasn't entirely awake either, when one of the men came to tell him that Jakyr was looking for him. Hastily, he sat up and tried to get his fuzzy head working, then limped to the library.

Jakyr was standing at the window, looking out. "I thought you would like to know what is going to happen to Cole Pieters and his mine, Mags," Jakyr said, without turning around. "The evidence was presented and relayed to Haven, but the local Court has already decided that there is more than enough there to warrant removing him and his family from the property. Administration will be taken over by Lord Astley, who was genuinely horrified to discover the extent of his abuse. The children are to be taken away at once, and given into the custody of a Temple on Lord Astley's property. From there, good homes will be found for them, which is what *should* have been done in the first place. The adults will be given a choice of continuing to work at fair wages or going elsewhere."

Mags frowned and tried to put all the pieces of that together. It just wouldn't come clear in his mind, as if it wasn't real. Still . . . "They won' leave," Mags felt impelled to tell him. "They don' know nothing else. Some on 'em are crazy."

"I have no doubt of that." Now Jakyr turned to face Mags, and his face wore a look of grim triumph. "The mine will probably be shut temporarily, and only reopened when it has been determined what can be done with the adult miners, and what should be done with Cole Pieters and his family. Pieters *does* own the mine; that is clear enough. We can't dispossess him and his family of it without a legal cause. Even if we punish him, the law in this land is such that we have to determine just how much guilt is on the heads of the rest of the family. If there are guiltless minor children, it is entirely possible that the profits will be kept for them in trust while those who are guilty get turned out to find a more honest way of making a living. It is going to get very complicated, and I wanted you to know that. This could stretch on for a year or more . . . but . . ."

Mags tilted his head to one side, waiting. All this felt as if he was reading about it.

". . . if we find bodies where you say we will, it is very likely that Pieters and at least one of the sons will be charged with murder."

Mags considered that. His brow creased, and he felt that cold jolt of fear again, until Dallen comforted him. "It's only my word 'gainst theirs," he said finally, willing his hands to stop shaking. "Ain't no one else gonna say nothin', ye knows that."

Jakyr lost the look of triumph, and he nodded. "That is not all, because he will have time to get rid of the bodies, and thus, the evidence. That surely occurred to him when I took you out of there. He knows what Heralds are, even if none of you children did. He might well guess that I would have these things out of you, one way or another. That is why right now I am speaking with the Justiciars about whether we should pursue the murder charges. I fear that unless he was very careless and remains so, he will get away with murder, literally."

Mags just shrugged. It was very hard to

muster up any sort of emotion about all this except the dread of what might happen if Cole Pieters found all this out. Mostly, he just felt odd. He supposed he should be angry that Master Cole would probably get away with the worst of what he had done, or feel elation that he had helped find the man out, but he just couldn't. Besides feeling odd, he was still deeply uneasy, as if there was someone standing behind him, ready to strike him down when he least expected it. It was hard to believe that Pieters would be unable to exact some sort of revenge.

Jakyr looked at him curiously. "Is something the matter? I thought you would be pleased about the other youngsters, or angry with Cole."

Mags struggled to understand his own feelings, or lack of them, and put it all into words. "I guess . . . I dunno. Like I don' feel anythin' strong about it. Like this ain't finished yet, an' till it is, no point in thinkin' anythin'." He pondered. "It's good the kiddies is got away, and it's good Master Cole cain't keep on, but anythin' other than that . . ." He shook his head. "It's like somethin' in a book. I know it's real, but it don' feel real. It don't feel finished." He shook his head uneasily. "Y' know, it wasn't smart t' get too friendly with nobody. You tell half them kiddies m' name, they won't know who I am. Mebbe that's it."

Jakyr sighed, and got up to walk to the window. "And the ones that died?"

Mags felt badly then. He knew he should have been angry about it all. When it happened, though, he had to be honest — it scared him, it terrified him, in fact, but he had never been angry. "I reckon I'm a bad lot, sir," he sighed, feeling a sick sinking in his stomach. "I reckon yer gonna tell me so."

"Why?" Jakyr asked.

" 'Cause when people died? All I could think was I was glad it weren't me. I'm still glad it weren't me. Them as is dead, is dead, an' nothin' is gonna make 'em not dead." He hung his head. "Reckon 'm as bad as Master Cole."

Jakyr turned to stare at him. "Good gad, Mags, I certainly don't think that!" When Mags looked up at him, it was his turn to struggle for words. "Look, I think what you are feeling is a great deal like what I felt when I was a young man in the Guard, and I was in battles. I mostly did not know my fellow soldiers, there was no time to get to know them and, Mags, when they died, I felt the same. I was glad it wasn't me."

He swallowed, and searched Jakyr's face for a hint of falsehood. He found none. "For true?"

Jakyr nodded. "For true." The Herald looked away again. "It may have been a battlefield for you your entire life, Mags. How can I think you are a bad person because of how you handled it?"

Mags swallowed. It was comforting, and yet . . .

Oh, well.

"Well, is it important to you to actually see it? See the man get his punishment?" Jakyr seemed to be finding something very interesting outside that window to look at.

Mags shook his head dismissively. "Nossir. It don' matter. Not a bit. I guess . . . I dunno why, it just don' matter. 'S like the Mags you hauled outa there an' me, they're two different kiddies." He shrugged again. "The ol' Mags, he woulda danced on Master Cole's grave. The new one . . . Cole don't matter. I got stuff to do, and Cole don't matter. 'Cept that he's trouble. I cain't 'splain it any better nor that."

"Then I'll take your word for it." Jakyr nodded decisively, just as the bell rang for supper. He seemed satisfied. "Go nurse your aches and get fed. The sooner you can ride well, the sooner we can be gone."

Mags limped off.

He himself was more than a little puzzled about his own lack of emotion. Once, nothing would have pleased him more than to see with his own eyes Master Cole being humiliated at worst, and punished terribly at best. Now . . . now he had other things to think about. His mind was so crowded with all of those things that, no, it just didn't matter.

Well, all but a feeling of warmth when he thought about the other kiddies, especially the youngest, being taken somewhere that they were getting the same sort of care and treatment he was. And he had been the instrument of that. *That* felt good.

And if Cole Pieters got away with the worst of the things he'd done, at least there was this much: he would never be given a free hand in the running of his own mine again. No new kiddies would be slaving in the tunnels. He would have to pay miners an honest wage.

Last of all . . . there was the thought that Cole Pieters was, indeed, trouble. And the farther Mags got from him, the better Mags felt. He didn't want Master Cole to ever think about Mags again. Cole Pieters was a bad, mean man, and Mags hoped that Cole Pieters would forget about him entirely. The sooner that happened, the happier Mags would be.

He thought all that over while waiting for his aching muscles to settle down and let him sleep, and it occurred to him that being at the mine and having to run it the proper way, actually being forced to part with his money to *pay* his workers, was possibly the worst punishment that could be devised for Master Cole.

Mags fell asleep with that thought in his mind and it gave him at least a level of satisfaction.

And even though he ached, he knew it wouldn't be for long. He was used to hard work and sore, tired muscles. In a few days, even if he still wasn't a good rider, he would be fit enough to stay in the saddle all day. Then they could leave, and Master Cole would be left far, far behind.

His dreams were disturbed only once, by something too vague to be called a nightmare, a dim dream of hunting for something, or someone, knowing that there was something else dark and dangerous that was hunting for the same thing. And knowing that if the other hunter found that thing . . . something terrible would happen.

The way to Haven unrolled before them,

there was a good breakfast in Mags' belly, and the air held the scent of snow to come. If Mags was not sitting in the saddle with the easy and careless grace that Herald Jakyr had, at least he was no longer sitting in the saddle like a sack of grain about to fall off. And if Herald Jakyr was worried about him being able to handle the long travel, he didn't show it.

Those were all the positive things. Also positive — since the night he had had that dream of hunting something, all of his fears, while still in the back of his mind, seemed to have been *pushed* to the back of his mind. He had no good reason to feel so — so trusting. Well, other than that Dallen kept telling him that he could and should be. But it didn't seem to matter that he had no reason for feeling this way; it even felt a bit as if he was dreaming while wide awake. As a consequence, he was feeling good; a sort of drowsy contentment, like the aftermath of one of those once-a-year feeds when he was full and warm and allowing himself the incredible luxury of *not* thinking about the next day. And maybe that was stupid, but right now, it didn't matter.

Herald Jakyr, on the other hand, looked as if he was fretting enough for both of them. It seemed he was more worried about the weather than about Mags falling off, and as they got packs strapped to the two Companions, it seemed to Mags that he was rightly concerned. Mags didn't like the way the sky looked, or the air felt. It was a little too damp, the sun a little too bright, and yet there was the sense that there was something lurking just over the horizon. He was not weather-wise, but it felt as if there was a storm coming.

Herald Jakyr had wanted to be off at dawn, and when they finally set off down the road, with as much stuffed into the bulging packs on both Companions as they could easily carry, the sun was still touching the horizon. And the pace that Jakyr set was easily as hard as anyone trying to outrun a storm could want. Very shortly, Mags had his hands full, so to speak, with thinking about his riding. He didn't have attention to devote to anything else.

Dallen did his best to spare his rider, but Jakyr did not stick to the road for very long, and Mags hung on grimly to the pommel of the saddle as the Companions followed tracks only Jakyr could see, up and down the hillsides, leaping frozen streams and bouncing over fallen trees. They cut right across farmers' fields more than once, sometimes startling grazing livestock. But the wind was picking up by midmorning, and it whined in the uppermost branches of the trees with a tone that Mags knew well. There definitely was a storm bearing down on them.

Jakyr stopped at running streams only long enough for both of them to take care of the needful while the Companions got a drink. At noon, with the sun blazing down on the snow, and Mags' stomach growling, they didn't even stop long enough to eat. Jakyr put bags with sweetened grain in them over the heads of both the Companions so that they could eat while they loped toward whatever it was that Jakyr wanted to reach by nightfall, and Jakyr handed Mags a cold meat pie, some cheese, and an apple after they had both mounted up. All four of them ate while moving, with Jakyr glancing back over his shoulder from time to time, though what he could see through the trees, Mags could not venture to guess.

He was used to hard work, but this was harder than anything he had ever done in his life. He had thought he was used to riding, but it was not riding like this. He found entirely new muscles to stretch and strain as the Companions scrambled up and down slopes, or vaulted over fallen trees, and he fought to stay balanced. And every time he went in one direction while Dallen went in another, he got another tooth-jarring jolt.

Finally, in late afternoon, when Mags was wondering if they were ever going to see another human being again, they broke through the trees and onto the surface of a much wider, cleared road. Ahead of them, the eastern horizon glowed blue and clear, with only a few wispy white clouds tracing across the brilliance. A few more paces, and they were at the top of a ridge, and Jakyr finally pulled up to peer back the way they had come. Mags turned to look, too.

Sure enough, the western horizon was a far different prospect than the eastern. Absolutely black clouds boiled across it, like a wall, and they were moving fast.

But they were moving more northward than eastward, and Jakyr sighed with relief. "The worst of it'll miss us, or at the very least, we'll be in good shelter in town, provided we keep moving until sundown," he said, and looked at Mags with some concern. "Can you handle a gallop till then?"

"T' not get caught in that? Aye," Mags said, with a shudder. "That's naught t' chance with." He had seen the sky like that before, when storms had all but buried the buildings around the mine. This was not something he wanted to meet while in the open. He had too-vivid memories of the kiddies desperately tunneling through the snow with their half-frozen hands to try and get to the kitchen, because the food was certainly not going to be brought to them, and it was better to lose fingers and toes than to starve.

They both turned their heads to the east, and without any urging, both Companions moved from a walk to a full gallop in a few paces.

They were not the only folk on the road, nor were they the only ones trying to outrun the storm. Jakyr actually stopped twice to advise people driving slow-moving carts to seek shelter with farmers ahead or behind them. But after a league or two, they drove on grimly without needing to stop, because it seemed that more and more of those they passed were coming to the conclusion on their own that they could not beat the storm and were turning their steps toward the nearest farmhouses. Mags could well imagine the reaction Master Cole would have had to people turning up on his doorstep. They'd have been driven right off; Master Cole would have been sure that they were there to steal the sparklies, and not even a looming storm would have convinced him otherwise.

With travelers clearing off the road of their own volition, the way was open for as far as they could see. The road was as deserted as if it wound through an empty wilderness now, and in the distance, they could hear the howl of the blizzard. The sun cast long shadows on the road before them, right up until the moment that the towering clouds swallowed it. Then the world plunged from sunset to red-lit dusk within moments.

But now every time they crested a hill, they could see their goal in the distance. Lots and lots of buildings, more buildings than Mags had ever imagined, even when reading about cities and towns. Part of him stared at all of those houses in bewilderment, while part of him looked at them with relief. If they were going to get hit by a storm, being in a place like this would be far better than being anywhere else. Even with all the travelers looking for shelter, surely someone would have space for them.

A series of images, rather than words, came to him from Dallen, and then he understood more of those words he had read. "Inns" and "taverns" and "innkeepers." Visions of rooms full of small tables and stools, of food and drink exchanged for money, of beds hired out by the night. He understood that there would be no looking for shelter in a stable, that as a Herald and a new Trainee, they would be treated at one of these inns as well as they had been with the Guard — or that, if Jakyr chose, they would seek shelter with the Guard again.

Darkness closed in, the howl of the storm seemed right at their backs although not a speck of snow had fallen yet, and ahead of them, dim lights began to appear in the gloom. The rise and fall of the land alternately revealed and hid the town from them, and it never seemed to be getting any closer.

Just when Mags despaired of ever reaching their goal, suddenly they were there. They crested a hill to find the town spread out before them.

There was a wall about the place; not a high one, but enough of a wall to keep wild animals out and straying animals in. There was also a bar across the road, and a Guard at it, bundled up in furs and illumined by a torch. The Companions slowed and walked the last few paces to that bar, sides heaving. Mags clung to the pommel, feeling utterly drained. The Guard raised the bar for them, and they passed under it, Jakyr giving him a kind of vague salute.

They turned immediately to the right and

followed the wall until they came to a large building built right up against the wall in the form of a hollow square. They entered the hollow through an arched passage; there were a few men about, and all of them were busy putting up shutters and hurrying around, making other preparations for the storm. Quickly. Jakyr dismounted and motioned to Mags to follow him. They went into what was obviously a stable, led the two Companions to two huge loose-boxes at one end, and prompted by Dallen and watching what Jakyr did, he got all of Dallen's gear off him, wiped him down, bundled him in a blanket, fed him, watered him, wiped the gear down, and only *then* did the two of them make their way into the Guard building proper.

No one paid too much attention to them as Jakyr motioned to Mags to follow him. Evidently he had been here before, since he went straight down a corridor to the stairs, up the stairs, up another set of stairs, finally ending in an unoccupied room with six beds in it and a fire in the fireplace at one end. It was lovely and warm, and Mags hastened to throw his saddlebags on the bed, and following Jakyr's example, hung his coat, stiff with cold, on a peg next to the fire.

"Hungry?" the Herald asked. Mags nodded. In fact, he was ravenous. A couple of meat pies and a handful of dried fruit had not done much to assuage his hunger, especially now that he was used to eating regular meals.

Once again, Jakyr motioned to him to follow; they went down to an enormous kitchen where a sleepy-eyed fellow gave them bowls of thick soup and slices of buttered bread, a couple more cold meat pies, and an apple apiece. They ate it all there, in the kitchen, perched on stools. When Mags looked around for more, the fellow smiled, and went to the pantry, coming out with a wedge of cheese and another apple.

"Bed," Jakyr said shortly, and Mags nodded, following him back up to the room on the third floor, eating his cheese and his apple on the way. He finished the last bites of each as they reached the room itself, tossed the core in the fireplace, divested himself of his outer garments, and crawled into the bed. A moment later he was asleep.

He woke to the sound of bells, which was entirely expected. Jakyr was still asleep and didn't look likely to move, but he was ravenous again. He followed his ears to the washing-up room and an indoor privy, then his nose to the kitchen and the eating hall. This time, when he sat down at a table as he had been used to do at the first Guard House, the Guardsman doing the serving asked him who he was, and what he was doing there. He had a moment of paralyzed fear, sure as he was sure of his own name, that he was about to be uncovered as some sort of imposter —

:Just tell him your name, that you are with Jakyr, and you are Chosen of Dallen.: Dallen gave a kind of mental chuckle, and Mags coughed and complied. His answer seemed to satisfy the man. There were no more questions, and there *was* a great pile of hot-cakes and honey, along with a platter of bacon, in front of him shortly.

He kept his mouth busy with food and his ears open, and soon learned that the worst of the storm had missed the city, but had hit the countryside to the west very hard. The Guards were going out in teams to look for stranded travelers, and to check on isolated farms, before getting to work clearing the road.

It appeared that he and Jakyr were not the only people lodging with the Guard. An old man in bright scarlet asked how the road was to the east.

"Clear and clean; we got snow falling still, but naught like what's to the west. Yon Herald must've brought us luck," laughed one grizzled fellow. "I tell ye, little as I fancy going out to look for strays, I fancy being snowed in here with no one for company but you ugly dogs a lot less."

That earned the man a laugh and some remarks about where he was likely to be spending that night. That interested Mags not at all, so he went back to his food.

After eating his fill, and tucking a couple of apples into his pockets, Mags tiptoed into the room, got his now-warm coat, and went to check on the Companions.

:We will be moving soon,: Dallen told him, after gleefully accepting the apple. *:As soon as Jakyr wakes, nearly. Jakyr wants to get back to Haven as soon as he can. So tell the stable keeper to feed and water us and make up our nosebags with sweet feed. While he is doing that, bring down the big packs, and go to the kitchen, and ask for traveler's pies, as many as they can spare, made up into two packets.:*

Mags blinked at that, for he had seen the trays of waiting meat and apple pies in the kitchen. "We canna eat that many, and surely he don't mean to ride like he did yesterday!" he exclaimed. He was still moving stiffly, though his muscles were loosening.

:Oh, not at all,: Dallen replied with amuse-

ment. *:Most of the pies will go with the rescue parties. Jakyr will just want to be sure that if we have to stay overnight in a Waystation, you don't starve. He is an excellent fellow, but he has one deep flaw. He cannot cook. In fact, he has been known to ruin boiling water.:*

Mags shook his head, but went and did as he was told. And since Jakyr still wasn't awake, he decided to take advantage of the facilities and have a quick hot wash. Not a good soaking bath, though he would have liked one, but a thorough wash-up. No telling when he'd get another chance, and he was discovering that he liked being clean.

Dallen's words proved true. No sooner was Jakyr awake than he was fretting to be on the road. When the Guards asked if he could be of help locating stranded travelers, he regretfully shook his head.

"I've not got the Gift for it, I fear," he told the Guard Captain who asked him. "I'm no better at it than you. And I'm overdue at Haven. I've gotten word I'm needed, and the sooner I get my charge there safely, the better."

The Captain nodded wisely and made no further entreaties. Far sooner than Mags would have thought, they were both on the road again, riding through snow that fell thickly, but not with the fury of the blizzard that had pursued them here.

He set a hard pace, but not the grueling one of the previous day. And they did, indeed, spend that night in what Dallen had called a "Waystation," a one-room structure reserved for Heralds traveling or "on circuit," whatever that meant. Though small, it was stoutly built, and comfortable once they got a fire going on the hearth. Jakyr proved as much of a disaster at cooking as Dallen had foretold, and although Mags did not know a *great* deal about it, after the first two pies were burnt past the point where even *he* would eat them, he firmly evicted the older man from the hearth and took over the warming of the pies and the making of pease-porridge himself. Fortunately, Jakyr had not done too much damage to the pease-porridge before Mags intercepted him.

The remainder of the journey was uneventful and unvarying. They rose about dawn, whether they stayed in a Guard Post, a Waystation, or — rarely — in an inn. Mags cooked at need, Jakyr cut firewood, both tended their Companions, with Mags getting better at it all the time. Jakyr did not speak much; Mags got the sense he had something on his mind that had nothing to do with him. And in a way he felt isolated, but he was also relieved. So much of his time in life had been spent in silence that he was often hard-pressed to make the kind of conversation the Guards they stayed with found so easy.

But finally, after Mags had lost count of the days and nights — which wasn't hard, with all of them being much alike — Jakyr finally gestured to him to come up alongside and spoke.

"We're less than a candlemark from Haven," he said, his eyes on the road ahead except for a single side glance at Mags. "Now, you know what that is, right?"

Mags nodded. Between his own reading and Dallen's memories, he did indeed know what Haven was. The capital of Valdemar, where the King lived, and where the Heralds were headquartered. Dallen's memory also gave him various views of the city, which must be bewildering and confusing; Mags could hardly imagine that many people all crammed together in one place.

"Now, I will get you to the Palace and the new Collegium. I'll make sure someone takes charge of you. Whoever it is, obey him. Or her. What I told the Guard is nothing less than the truth; there is a situation to the east that I am the best person to handle, so handle it I must. I don't like to abandon you in a strange place, but I don't have a choice."

Mags nodded, not really sure of what he was feeling. True, Jakyr was the only person he knew here, but it wasn't as if Jakyr was his bosom friend. "I'll get by," he said, since the Herald seemed to be waiting for him to say *something.*

"Good lad." That satisfied Jakyr, and he turned his attention back to the road. It occurred to Mags after a few moments, and somewhat to his surprise, that Jakyr must have come to the conclusion that Mags was not as stupid as he had first appeared to be.

That made him feel rather good. And that, in turn, was what kept him from panicking at his first sight of Haven.

Because Dallen's memories simply did not convey how overwhelming the place was.

He went into a kind of daze after a while, as Jakyr led him through the city on a winding path that he was sure he would never be able to retrace. And it was not just the sheer number of people either; it was, as they got deeper into the city, the *luxury* of the place. He had thought that the Guard Post was luxurious, and by his standards, it was. But some of the enormous buildings they passed, which Dallen informed him were lived in by single families and their servants, nearly stupefied him. More of Dallen's memories only made it more bewildering. These people had entire rooms as big as the eating hall of the Guard Post, that they only used to *dance* in. People slept by themselves in some of these rooms, sharing the space with no one else. There were rooms just for sitting in, rooms just for playing music in, rooms that went empty most of the time. And all these rooms were filled with things. He had the concept of money now, and had a good idea what the "sparklies" he had been digging out for years were worth, and to be aware that one ring with one jewel in it that one of these women mostly kept in a box was worth more than he could ever have made in three lifetimes . . .

His mind just couldn't quite encompass the idea.

Finally they came to a high wall, which Dallen told him surrounded the Palace and the grounds. This was where the Heralds were organized, for the King was always a Herald, too. It was where it had been decided to build a training center for young Heralds, to match the ones for Bards and Healers, so that all three sorts of folk could share learning.

And despite what he had been told, in the back of Mags' mind, he had somehow pictured something suitable for — at most — two or three dozen people.

But the scene of organized chaos they rode up to was enough to drive the enormity of the Palace itself quite out of his mind for the nonce.

Despite the fact that it was well into winter, there were workmen everywhere, but most were pounding away on two huge, unfinished buildings. There was a third building that looked in use, with people wearing white, green, red, and gray surging in and out of it. It looked very raw and new.

"That will be the *new* Healers' Collegium," Jakyr said, pointing toward one of the unfinished structures, "And that will be the *new* Bardic. I hope to blazes they're done by this time next year. Meanwhile, we have all of you younglings crammed into the one building. Damn and blast Healers and Bards to perdition anyway!" He ran his hand through his hair in the first demonstration of irritability that Mags had seen from him. "Couldn't they just have waited —" He broke off and looked over at Mags with a rueful expression. "Never mind me, lad, I go off on a rant about this —"

"Aye, you do, Jak, and on any excuse whatsoever." They both turned their heads at the sound of the voice, which had been pitched to carry. There was a woman approaching them, sauntering slowly toward them with her arms crossed over her chest. She looked about the same age as Herald Jakyr, but was dressed all in red, with a hooded coat rather than a cloak. "And I'm certain-sure he'll hear it all enough times to be sick of it. Is this the new lad that Dallen called for help in fetching?" She nodded at Mags, and a graying blond curl escaped from her hood at her temple.

Jakyr's expression went very stony. "Aye, Lita, it is. Now, if you don't mind, I've —"

"You've got to take him off to Caelen, and then you have urgent business to be off on," she interrupted him, with just a touch of waspishness. "Which was precisely what you always have. Lots of urgent business taking you elsewhere, and none of it keeping you *here.* Which is why you are in that saddle and your bed is narrow and cold. Nah, be off with you on your urgent business!" she continued, as Jakyr's expression went from stony to stunned. "I'll take the boy to Caelen. You fair can't wait to shake the last of Haven dust from your feet, so be about it. It'd be a sad day when a Bard can't extend a bit of courtesy to a new Trainee."

As Jakyr sat there, looking very much as if he could not make up his mind between going or staying, she added, "You think I'll eat him? You think the leader of the Bardic Circle can't be trusted to take one Trainee from here to Caelen's office?"

That made up Jakyr's mind for him. "Thanks, Lita," he managed, as if he was strangling on the words. "I really do have —"

"Urgent business, aye, I know," the woman sighed. "Go, and wind at your back. I'll not wish you ill, no matter what our differences."

There was no other word to describe Jakyr's abrupt departure but "fled." And when he was out of sight — which happened so quickly that Mags suspected he had deliberately chosen the route that would put buildings and trees between them the soonest, the woman looked at Dallen. "Well met, Dallen," she said, reaching out and giving the Companion a friendly pat on the neck. "So you finally got you a Chosen?"

Dallen nodded. She smiled, and then looked up at Mags. "And what would your name be, then, lad?"

"Mags." He stared down at her, feeling rather dumbfounded. Whatever had just happened here left him entirely in the dark.

"Don't mind Jak. He and I have some history betwixt us." She sighed. "Not always good history, especially toward the *parting* end of it. And now I can't help myself. Whenever I see him, I goad him." She shook her head. "Come along, we'll turn Dallen over to his minders and get you in the hands of yours." She turned and headed up a stone-bordered, well-swept path, without looking back to see if he was going to come along.

Feeling rather as if all control of everything had been snatched out of his hands, Mags dismounted and followed.

7

Mags sat gingerly on the edge of a short wooden bench. Gingerly, on the edge, because the rest of the bench was taken up with a huge pile of books with a pillow balanced inexplicably on top. It was, however, the only available seat in Herald Caelen's office, as the rest of the room was also taken up with books. Herald Caelen's small desk, however, was immaculately clean, and the blocklike fellow gazed at the piles of books with distaste. Mags immediately got the sense that Herald Caelen had not put those books there himself, and the man's words confirmed that. "I don't know why *my* office should be the repository of every book that the librarian thinks is too valuable to keep in the library," he said, aggrieved. "When it was only one or two, or even a dozen, I didn't mind . . . or at least, I didn't mind that much." He shook his head. "My own fault. I'll deal with it. Now — you would be Dallen's new Chosen, according to Merlita — I didn't get your name? No, wait a moment —" He opened a drawer, pulled out a sheaf of paper, and leafed through it quickly. "Ah, yes. Mags. Just Mags. Mixed up in that business with the mine. Well, let's see . . ." He read some more. Mags tried not to squirm; his natural inclination at the moment would have been to make himself as unobtrusive as possible; Dallen had to keep reminding him that he was not in trouble, and that Herald Caelen might have his feelings hurt if Mags tried to hide from him. "Hmm. Hmm." He looked up again, and Mags held himself very still; not quite the paralysis of fear, but not far from it. "You've probably gathered that we are chronically short of room. And, in fact, there *is* no room. I haven't got a bed to put you in. And if you were from some other background, I would never ask you to do this — but would you be willing to sleep in the Companions' stables? Not in a stall or anything of that sort," the Herald added hastily. "There are some perfectly good rooms, with heating that makes them as cozy and warm as anything in this building and as clean and all, that the stableboys use. But it *is* the stable —"

Mags blinked. Here he was, someone who

had, a few weeks ago, been sleeping in a hole under a barn floor — and this man was asking if he *minded* sleeping in a bed, in a warm room, just because it was in a stable. "Be fine, sir," he said, in a voice just above a whisper.

Herald Caelen let out a huge sigh of relief. "Bless you. I pray to the gods that the next Trainee we get in here will be Healer or Bard, because finding space for him will be Lita or Paako's problem, not mine. Unless we can get some of you graduated to field trials and out of here, I am going to be stacking you like so many hens in nestboxes atop one another soon." He went back to his papers, occasionally looking up to ask Mags a question. When he had finished, he took out a fresh sheet and began writing on it, then got up and edged his way around the desk, taking care not to topple over the piles of books. "Follow me, then, and I'll get you taken care of. Uniforms first."

Right. Uniforms. He had some memories from Dallen about that. He nodded, and followed Herald Caelen out of the office and into a building that was clearly half finished on the inside. There were still workmen putting up wall panels and plastering the ceiling.

The borrowed memories sharpened, and

he understood what was about to happen when they were halfway down the corridor. He would be a Heraldic Trainee, and he would wear a gray uniform, identical to Jakyr's and Caelen's except for color. That was how they did things here; Trainees — they might as well be called apprentices, really — wore something in the same color family as the Bards, Heralds, and Healers, but it was more than enough different to let anyone who saw them know that they weren't exactly ready to act like the real thing yet.

They went through a set of double doors at the end of the corridor, and then made an abrupt turn to go down a set of dark little stairs. This brought them to a cramped room piled high with neatly folded clothing in white and gray. Herald Caelen pulled tunics from the top of piles, held them up against Mags, muttering to himself, refolded and stowed them away again until he found something that met his criteria. At that point, Mags found himself burdened with a staggeringly tall pile of things. "Do those boots fit you?" Caelen asked abruptly. Mags peered at him over the top of the clothing.

"Uh —"

"Do they pinch your feet?"

He had to think about that. His feet were

so tough, he probably wouldn't have noticed otherwise. "Nossir."

"Are they falling off you? Did they rub blisters anywhere?"

Well, that he was sure of. "Nossir. Mebbe a bit big . . ."

"Wear extra socks, then." A couple more pairs got tucked under the top of the pile. "Right. Come with me." He grabbed a couple of cloaks, draped the gray one rather haphazardly over Mags' shoulders and the pile of clothing, and slung the other, white one, around his own neck.

Again, Caelen set off briskly. Mags stretched his legs to keep up. They went back up the stairs, then outside via a nearby door, and headed down a path that clearly ended at a stable building. "That's the Companions' stable, and that is where you'll be living," Caelen explained. "We'll arrange for that now."

Mags was slowly getting the lay of the place as they headed for the stables, where he had left Dallen. The Heralds' Collegium was actually attached to this other building, which was roughly four or five times its size. The unfinished buildings, which he vaguely gathered would be Bardic and Healers' Collegiums, stood alone. The Companions' stable was across a big stretch of open area and on the other side of a broad lane, of course . . . the road that had brought him here was *there* —

In the stables, he felt a little more relaxed. Not so many people. Companions all about. Dallen peering over the wall of a loose-box just ahead. He took a deep breath and smiled; they must keep this place as clean as a room in the Guards' barracks, for the only scent in the air was of crisp straw and sweet hay, with an undertone of clean horse. Herald Caelen gave a sharp whistle and waved over someone who proved to be the Stablemaster. He quickly explained what he wanted, and just as quickly got an answer.

"Aye, I'd just as soon that room there at the end got used. Been a bit of a temptation, that, come evenin' — empty room, quiet stable, willin' kitchenmaids?" The Stablemaster waggled his eyebrows, and Caelen cracked a wry smile.

"Then I am happy to be able to solve two problems with one solution. Can we get a couple of the lads here to help make it livable?" the Herald asked.

In answer, it was the Stablemaster's turn to whistle, and within moments, Mags was helping another strong fellow carry a bed in from a storage room, while a second went off for linens and a third carried out the odds and ends that had been stored there, swept the place, and found a couple of chests in the tack room for Mags' use. The Stablemaster himself scoured up a table and chair and a couple of lanterns. The room was already warm, thanks to the brick ovens built into that end of the stables. The whole end wall was brick, actually; the ovens, according to Dallen, served two purposes. A certain amount of cooking and water heating was done there, but mostly, they were there to keep the place warm. They were fired from outside, and heated the stable and the rooms that the stable workers lived in with the heated brick rather than the direct heat from the fires. With all that grain-dust and straw and hay about, the risk of fire was taken very seriously, and minimized.

When the furnishings were in place, the room was left to Mags and Herald Caelen, who had extracted some folded paper and a bit of lead pencil from a pocket, and was writing on it. "All right, Mags, given where you come from, I am going to assume you know practically nothing. Your teachers will find out quickly enough if that is not the case, and will promote you. So, here is the list of your classes."

He handed over the paper to Mags, who

took it, puzzled. "Classes, sir? I'm t' go to classes?"

Caelen looked at him oddly. "What did you think you were here for?"

Mags shrugged. The truth of the matter was he hadn't thought about it much because thinking about it only reminded him of how much he *couldn't* do. "I dunno, I guess, I figgered . . . work? Diggin' snow, scrubbing floors, belike?"

"How did you think you were going to become a Herald?"

Mags blinked. "I . . . uh . . . I guess I figgered . . . that was the kind of Herald I'd be. One that does for the others. Some'un t' do th' work, aye?" He really hadn't spent any time dreaming about it at all. Despite all the things that Dallen had shown him, he had never pictured *himself* doing the things he knew Heralds did. It didn't seem . . . fitting. After all, what did *he* know about law and justice, or fighting, or . . . well whatever. He couldn't do those things. But he *could* see that the ones that knew how didn't have to worry about other stuff. After all, hadn't he taken care of the cooking and cleaning in the Waystations?

Caelen stared at him for a moment then shook his head. "No, Mags, what a Herald does is something no one else *can* do. And you will be doing that, eventually. But, for right now, you need to learn a great deal before you know how to do those things, so you will be taking classes."

Mags looked at him dubiously. But all he said was, "But who does do all the cleanin' and things?" Surely all those people bustling about weren't here just to take classes?

"We have plenty of people for that, don't you worry about it." Herald Caelen chuckled a little.

Mags could only think that it might have been better if they hadn't had quite so many of those people. If Herald Jakyr had ever learned how to cook, maybe he wouldn't be trying to eat half-burned stuff all the time now.

He didn't say that, though, and a moment later, he was glad that he hadn't when he saw the eye-popping list of things he was supposed to be learning about . . . it seemed utterly impossible. How could anyone get through all these things and not have his head explode from trying to pour learning into it?

History, Geography, Mathematics, Riding, Weapons' Training, Languages, Mindspeech, Grammar, Speech . . . The whole day seemed to be filled with classes . . .

"You'll be taking some of those with the

Trainees of Bardic and Healer's," Herald Caelen said, nodding at the list. "And you will be taking more and different things as you master these."

Mags stared at the list in mingled elation and despair. Elation, because he could not think of a grander thing than to be able to do nothing all day but learn things. Despair because — he could barely read and write, he knew nothing about reckoning beyond what he'd learned after Jakyr had rescued him, and he already knew how little of the outside world beyond the fence of Master Cole's mine he had even been aware of. He was going to cover himself with shame over this.

"I know it looks formidable, Mags, but you'll do fine," Herald Caelen began, then paused as Mags looked up at him dumbly. He faltered. "Mags, plenty of younglings arrive here knowing very little."

He must have continued to look stricken, for Herald Caelen bit his lip, and sat down on the as-yet unmade bed. "Mags, the reason we've started the Collegium is because we have a problem. It used to be that every Herald took one or two Trainees under his or her wing and taught them everything personally. It was like the arrangement between a master and an apprentice. But we can't do that anymore. There are too many Trainees, and the Heralds are going farther and farther from Haven on their circuits. It's not possible to send an apprentice out of danger, if danger looms. And, more to the point, there isn't the leisure time to teach you younglings everything you have to know and do the job of a Herald at the same time. We have to train you as a group now, and only send you out at the side of a mentor when you have everything except the hands-on experience."

Mags nodded, though he had no real idea what he was agreeing to. He was only now beginning to grasp how different his new life was going to be. It was a new life, an *entirely* new sort of life, and he felt as if he had awakened from a sound sleep to find himself on the top of a mountain. The view might be amazing, but he had no idea of how he had gotten here, and more importantly, where he was, how he was going to get down, and if he ever managed to do that, what he was supposed to do when he got down there. It was no longer about just going where Jakyr told him and doing what Jakyr said to do. He felt hopelessly adrift.

And also split, as if there were two of him. One, the old Mags, kept thinking, "You can't trust these people. You can't trust anyone. Why should they help you? They're leading you on for some reason of their own." The other, the one that shared Dallen's memories, kept thinking that everything was going to be fine, and although this whole Collegium thing was new to him, to them both, it was a good thing and it would make everything easier. . . .

And the old Mags was thinking "Make *what* easier?"

In the back of his mind, he felt Dallen, very quiet. *:I could . . . cushion you again. I could help you to not think about these things. . . . :*

He understood then that the calm he had felt so far was all artificial. It was something Dallen had imposed on him to help him deal with all of these new experiences. And now Dallen was taking that away.

And that was when old . . . instinct? . . . or was it experience? . . . rescued him. *When you don't know what to do, do nothing, watch, and wait.* He was not calm, but he could pretend to be. He could stay quiet, not draw attention to himself, and wait to see what happened. People always revealed what their intentions were when you did that. Always. When you did nothing, you forced them to act even when they didn't intend to.

He sensed Dallen being startled by this reaction, and made uneasy, as if now it was the Companion who didn't understand and had no idea of how to react.

Meanwhile, Herald Caelen, who had no idea of what was going through Mags' mind, took his silence as assent, or something positive at least, and seemed satisfied.

"You'll see," Herald Caelen said with confidence. "Just give it time. Now, come along, and I'll show you where everything is."

The Herald walked Mags through the buildings; one thing that Mags was very glad to see was a bathing room like the one in the Guard Post. Another was a huge room devoted entirely to eating — it was shared by every person working at this place, so there were people coming and going all the time. He saw Trainees of all three sorts: Bards, Healers, and a smattering of Heralds among the blue livery of what the Herald and his own — or rather Dallen's — memories told him were servants of the Palace. There were everything from very fine looking outfits indeed, finer than anything that Master Cole ever wore, to very rough clothing that must belong to heavy laborers. And mixed with *them* were men also in rough clothing spattered with paint and plaster, dusted with fine white dust or yellow saw-dust. He didn't need any prompting to know that these were the men working on those two buildings out there.

There was some separation into like groups, but they all ate the same food, it seemed, going to get it themselves at a hatch, leaving bowls and plates to be cleaned up by boys in that rough blue Palace livery.

For someone who had to learn to navigate the maze of twisting tunnels of a mine, find-ing his way around the "allowed" area was child's play. Herald Caelen made it very clear that there were places he was not sup-posed to go, and Mags had no interest in trespassing. Instead, as he obediently went about where he was directed, collecting the things he was told he would need and bring-ing them back to a room that was going to be all his, shared with no one, he commit-ted to memory every bit of the buildings and grounds that he was allowed in. And as he did so, another strange thing began to happen.

He knew this place. He knew many of the people he saw. He knew them, because Dallen knew them.

It was disorienting in a sense to share Dallen's memories now, for these were not just the memories of putting name and purpose to things he didn't recognize, these were immediate and personal memories. Dallen had lived here for a very long time, it seemed. It was a shock to recognize people he didn't know, and to sense Dallen's memories just waiting to be brought out. And every time that happened, it eroded his certainty that people could not be trusted, that *these* people were certainly hiding something dire and sooner or later he would find it out.

Not all the memories were "good." He would have distrusted that, now that he was thinking for himself, everything that seemed so perfect only alarmed him the more. Except . . . except . . . these were a lifetime of memories, or at least, enough to equal *his* lifetime. How could you make all of that up?

So as he made up his room — *his* room, with a door he could latch from the inside or the outside! — he thought about all of this. As he slipped in as unobtrusively as possible to eat and clean up, he thought about it. And when he laid himself down in his bed, sleeping alone for the first time in his memory, he thought about it. How . . . why this had happened, he could not begin to imagine — but happen, it had. And he was forced to come to the conclusion, by himself, that nothing in the world was really the way he had always thought it was.

Still, he trod warily. He woke to the first bell, dressed for the first time in one of his new uniforms, and again slipped in quietly to get food, and eat it sitting in the most remote corner he could find, watching everything and everyone as he did so. However, he was not permitted to remain in obscurity.

He noted the approach of an older boy in Trainee Grays immediately, as the fellow did not swerve off to join his presumed friends at any of the tables populated mainly by gray tunics. And when, to his alarm, he sensed that the boy was looking for *him,* it was all he could do to keep from bolting. He told himself firmly there was no reason to run.

Dallen, using an admonishing tone, echoed that thought. *:No one here is your enemy yet, Mags. This boy is just going to show you where things are.:*

:But I know where things are!: he protested, finally mindspeaking comfortably with his companion. He couldn't hear Dallen's snort, but he could sense it easily enough.

Too late for anything more, the rangy, rawboned blond boy stopped at his table and gave him a friendly nod. "Trainee Mags?"

Mags ducked his head by way of answer. That seemed enough for the boy.

"I'm here to show you about." He took a scrap of paper out of a pocket and perused it. "Your first class's at Old Bardic. You done?"

By way of answer, Mags stood up, plate, bowl and cup in hand. Taking that as a "yes," the boy led the way out of the building.

More of Dallen's memories guided him. It seemed that the buildings once occupied by the Bardic and Healers' Collegia were being replaced. Classes were still being held in "Old" Bardic Collegium; it would not be torn down until the replacement was finished. It was set very near the Palace, and was a third the size of the new building being constructed to take its place.

The Bards, from what Mags had learned from Dallen, actually had had a Collegium here first. It had been the first Collegium here, as the Healers had originally been happy enough to train other Healers wherever student and teacher happened to be, and the Heralds had their own system of apprentice and mentor. Then the Healers built their own small Collegium, mostly just to train all the local Healers in Haven, but also to get especially gifted Healers special advanced training. But when far, far too many new Heralds began appearing for the old system of master and protégé to work, and it had been decided that the Heralds needed a Collegium of their own, suddenly the Healers wanted expansion, too, and the Bards insisted on a *much* bigger one than they had. And both Circles got their demand, but since there were only so many skilled workmen in Haven to build such large structures, it was going to take three times longer to build them all.

According to Dallen, this had given rise to some aggrieved feelings among the Heralds, who were annoyed at their perceived overcrowding, though to Mags' mind, they didn't have a great deal to complain about. Still, there were bad feelings on the part of some toward the Bards, who were thought of as being greedy, and who — it was presumed — had also egged the Healers into demanding a Collegium of their own.

Dallen didn't know the truth or falsehood of that last. All he knew was that some among the Heralds were definitely holding a grudge.

As for "Old" Bardic, it was definitely going to be taken down, as was "Old" Healers'. The King wanted the space for pleasure gardens for the courtiers and all of these new Trainees to use.

The place certainly looked old, worn, and tired, Mags thought as he followed his guide inside. A long corridor stretched the length of the building, with doors all along it. Wood floors were black with age, and the floorboards worn, gaping in some places, cracking in others. Walls of white plaster showed spiderweb cracks. The ceiling, also of aged wood, was blacker than the floor from the soot of countless candles and lamps. The building itself must have shifted slightly over the years, since nothing quite sat true. Doors wouldn't close properly, windows wouldn't open, and there were signs of extensive repairs.

Mags — the old Mags — would never have noticed these things. The old Mags would simply have been grateful that he was inside four walls, in a building with heat in it, and not out in the snow. The new Mags did, wondering if the building was actually becoming dangerous, and found himself in sympathy with the Bards.

"Here's the class," Mags' guide said abruptly, stopping in front of a polished, blackened wooden door with the number "three" on it, cast of age-tarnished brass. "All the rest of 'em are on this corridor. Got your list?"

Dumbly, Mags pulled it out.

"Good, the numbers are next to the name, see?" He pointed to the relevant column. "You just go in the room with that number on it when time comes for your next class."

The boy didn't stay for Mags' reply; instead, he turned and headed for another room, as, suddenly, doors at either end of the corridor burst open, and a flood of people in gray, rust, and dark green came pouring in through them. Mags hastily pulled the door open and ducked inside the designated room.

It was arranged with rows of benches and narrow tables, a larger table at the front, and a fire in a fireplace at the front. Front would be the most desirable seats; fairly certain of that, Mags took a seat at the rear, near the windows, figuring to be ignored.

It was a futile hope, of course. He was new, and everyone in that class already knew each other. He got plenty of curious looks as they filed in, and a knowing one from the adult who was presumably the instructor, a wizened little fellow in Herald Whites.

When the rest had all settled on their benches, the instructor cleared his throat and got instant attention. "Our newcomer is Trainee Mags," the man said simply, in an aged voice that was nevertheless firm and strong. "You may all study him at leisure later. Turn your attention now, please, to the fourth chapter of our text."

The others all pulled out books. The instructor asked some question of one of the Bardic boys dressed in rust. The Trainee stood up to make a long answer of it — Mags understood neither the question nor the answer, but while the youngster was talking, the instructor pulled a battered old book out from under his desk, walked back to Mags, and dropped it in front of him. When the Trainee was done, the instructor nodded. "Well put, Brion. Very well put. Mags, we are currently on Chapter Four. By the time we reach Chapter Five, I expect you to be caught up. Now, Tre, what can you tell me about —"

Taking this as a tacit order to begin reading, Mags opened the book and concentrated on the words in front of him. At least this history book did not assume he knew *anything* about the history of Valdemar. Possibly because it began before there actually was a Valdemar.

And it was nothing like as dry as some of the books he had looked at in the library of the Guard Post. He was able to ignore the curious glances, even though he certainly was not reading as fast as they could. At least he *could* read now.

He watched the others as the bell for dismissal rang, and saw that they had picked up their books and were taking them away with them. Assuming he should do the same, he tucked it awkwardly against his chest, and went looking for his next class.

If he had been under the impression that it would be easy to sit and learn things — as opposed to chipping sparklies out of rock — he was swiftly disabused of the notion. By the time the list in his pocket said he was to get something to eat, his head was spinning, and he felt as if he would *rather* be chipping sparklies out of rock. He also had a pile of five books to deal with, and realized he had better get a bag for them like the others seemed to be carrying.

He ate without tasting his lunch, because although the afternoon was going to be devoted to physical rather than mental work, he was a bit dubious about half of it. "Weapons class" . . . he'd never been allowed a weapon before. He was pretty sure he was going to be awful at it, and just as had happened back at the Guard Post, the mere idea of taking up a weapon made him shake inside.

Not that his other classes didn't make him

shake inside for a different reason; to be honest, if he hadn't had a couple young fellows in his classes who were just as mud-ignorant as *he* was, he'd have been mightily discouraged. But they were, so he wasn't.

The other thing that kept him from being discouraged was that so far nobody was making fun of him — or worse — for being so behind. That was a relief, all the more so for being unexpected. Again, he had been blindsided by people being —

:Decent?: Dallen suggested, as he changed into the suggested "outfit for weapons work" that had been given him. *:Humane? Reasonable and kind?:*

:Well, aye,: he admitted reluctantly, pulling on trews with leather patches at the knees, and a tunic made of heavy canvas.

There was a moment of deep quiet, then Dallen added something else. *:You know that all Heralds are linked to their Companions as you and I are, right? And all Companions are linked as well.:*

:Aye.: That had been pretty obvious once he and Dallen began sharing memories.

:So given that, why would any *Herald do anything to cause distress to another Herald?:* Dallen asked forcefully. *:Doing so would cause distress to that Herald's Companion,*

which would spread to the other Companions, and eventually get back to him! It's like that old saying, "cutting off your nose to spite your neighbor." True, your neighbor then has a very ugly thing to have to look at, day in, day out — but you have all the pain of cutting your nose off! Do you see what I mean?:

Mags blinked. He certainly did. And more, that coiled serpent of suspicion in his belly saw it, too. He scratched his head in thought. *:Makes sense,:* he ventured.

:Good. Then keep reminding yourself of that. And go approach Beren and Lyr. The three of you should go to Herald Grevien and ask him for extra tutoring. Don't worry; he will grumble, but he will also tutor you in other things, like maths. But if you don't ask for the help, you won't get it. You'll see them both at weapons class.:

Mags had the feeling that if he *didn't* do as Dallen suggested, he was not going to get any rest on the subject, so the first thing he did was approach both the boys before the class began and suggested it. Thankfully, they were both younger than he was; if they had been older, he would have been terrified to talk to them. But Beren and Lyr, who, it turned out, were old friends from some place in the wild hills where *no one* knew how to read and write, took this suggestion with relief and exuberance, grabbed it with both hands, and Beren immediately volunteered to approach the Herald himself at dinner. Mags felt limp-kneed with relief of his own at that. He promised he would stick around until Beren had an answer and a time and place for these extra studies, and that was when the Weaponsmaster showed up.

These classes were held in another separate building called the "salle," a huge barn-like place with one wall lined with something that Mags had never seen before — and would have walked straight into if Beren hadn't grabbed him in time.

Glass mirrors.

Beren explained them to him hurriedly, but then the Weaponsmaster interrupted them.

"Is this necessary, Beren?" the wiry little man asked, looking them both sharply up and down. Beren was not in the least intimidated, though Mags shrunk back as far as he could.

"Aye, that, sirrah," the boy replied, in a drawl that Mags understood only because he listened so closely. "Less ye be wantin' t' replace 'nother mir-roar."

"Ah, like that is it?" The Weaponsmaster turned to Mags, who wished he could hide from those penetrating black eyes. "I've not been briefed on you yet, Trainee. You're from where?"

"Master Cole Pieters' mine, sir," Mags whispered.

"I meant what part of Valdemar." The look the man gave him made him wish he was invisible. His knees began to shake.

But then — suddenly — the Weaponsmaster blinked and looked off to one side. He stared at the wall for a moment, then nodded and turned back to Mags. "I beg your pardon, Trainee. I have been briefed now. I'd like you to stand over there while I sort the rest of the students out, if you please."

Mags was only too happy to move over into a corner, away from the mirrors, while the teacher paired everyone up, more or less. He had a couple of people left over, so those he assigned to one of the pairs with orders to do — well, something — and the three of them take it in turns. He surveyed the room for a moment until he was satisfied that all was going well, and only then did he return to Mags.

"Now," the Weaponsmaster said, his voice firm, but not quite so hard. "I am most put out that Caelen didn't tell me about you yesterday. Evidently, it didn't occur to him that I needed to know you hadn't set your hand to anything in an offensive capacity in your life. This is not altogether bad; you won't have to unlearn anything. I trust you are not going to be upset because I set you to work with a singlestick instead of a sword?"

Since Mags only knew what a singlestick was because the image of one obligingly appeared in his mind courtesy of Dallen, he shook his head dumbly.

"Good. I expect you'll be working with it for some time to come." The Weaponsmaster drew him farther over to the side of the room, where there was a padded pole, and handed him a thick, straight stick as long as his hand and forearm, picking up another himself. "Now, watch me, and do as I do."

It was not the most exciting thing Mags had ever done, hitting the pole in places where the padding had been marked with red paint, over and over and over in a series of repetitive patterns. In fact, it was not much worse for boredom than chipping sparklies. But all that careful chipping had given him pretty good control over where and how hard he hit things, and the Weaponsmaster seemed pleased enough with him. Most importantly, to Mags' mind, he had *not* been required to do anything that involved raising his hand to another person.

A big pole, he could hit, and not have the sense that he was going to be punished for it. Especially when he took care to not think of the pole as anything other than a pole. He was mostly hitting it in the right places when they all broke up to go off for riding lessons.

The riding lessons, however, *began* with saddling lessons. Mags was altogether shocked to discover that Beren and Lyr were utterly clueless about how to put on *any* of the tack. Couldn't their Companions tell them?

:Ah, actually, no,: Dallen replied, at Mags' mental query. *:Not everyone has Mind-speech. Certainly not as clear as you share with me. No, Beren Fetches and Lyr is a Far-Seer, which does very little for him being able to put on a saddle. And until their Companions turned up, neither of them had ever seen anything larger than a goat.:*

Well . . . that was interesting. Through Dallen, he had a good idea of what a Fetcher and a FarSeer did. It occurred to him that if the kiddies had had such talents among them, they could have lived a great deal better.

But no matter. He waited quietly while the stablehands patiently showed the two what they should be doing, and then mounted up at the signal. He was obviously not the worst in the class, and certainly not the best, so as a consequence he was left alone with Dallen for the Companion to continue his riding instruction.

And so ended his first day as a Trainee. After supper, he waited while Beren arranged for the special tutoring, then retreated to his warm little room with his books to study until he couldn't keep his eyes open anymore. And then, with the latch slid across the door, feeling *safe* for the first time, ever, he slept.

8

He stayed quiet, very quiet, in all his classes; at meals, he took a seat as far from everyone else as he could and pretended to be engrossed in his food, or in a book, once he realized it was not forbidden to bring them to the table. He went straight to his room when his day was finished and chose times when no one else was using the bathing room to get clean. Even in the tutoring sessions he never spoke until he was spoken to. If he spoke more than a handful of words in a day outside of being asked direct questions, it was a rarity. People seemed inclined to leave him alone, which suited him completely; he wanted to watch them and listen. There was a war inside him, a war in which everything he had ever learned about people fought desperately with everything that Dallen was telling him. He wanted Dallen to be right . . . but he feared the consequences if Dallen was wrong.

After several days, he still hadn't seen or heard anything to make him think that Dallen was mistaken. But all of his instincts still kept him wary, and he only really felt relaxed when he shot the bolt home on his room, locking himself in. That lock represented the first time he had ever been able to keep anyone away from him, and he could have kissed it. Its mere presence allowed him to sleep more deeply than he ever had in his life.

Dallen had been moved to the loose-box right outside his door, another measure of protection that allowed him to sleep soundly through the night *without* Dallen's mental intervention.

But, oh, the amount of learning he was having to cram into his head; sometimes it seemed as if his skull was going to burst. It wasn't that he disliked it! Oh, no. This was like meat and drink to him. Every new lesson seemed to open up a little more of his mind, and he actually felt starved for the knowledge. But there was so much of it that if he had not been so physically exhausted by the end of every day, he would have been unable to sleep with his brain a-buzz with new information, new thoughts, and new ideas.

After the first two days, they had taken

the measure of his learning — or perhaps the depth of his ignorance — and had canceled some of the classes he had been supposed to take in favor of extra sessions of tutoring. Somewhat to his surprise he was not the only one getting the extra attention; the hapless Beren and Lyr were also the recipients of special attention, as well as a fourth, a Bardic-trainee named Callin, who had the voice of an angel and could play virtually anything by ear on his harp, who made up melodies as easily as breathing, and who was utterly and completely illiterate, without even the basic reading lessons Mags had gotten at the mine. They were taught, not by a Herald, but by a woman named Lilli, who wore the Palace livery of dark blue and silver. Whatever her function was in the King's service, she was a good teacher, patient with their fumbling and ready with an explanation.

By his fourth day, all morning was spent in classes, half of the afternoon in riding and weaponry training, and the rest of the afternoon and early evening after supper with the tutor. By the end of the week, it felt like routine, although a routine that, in its way, was just as tiring as the work in the mine.

He spent every waking moment when he

was not at work in some way watching all the people around him and waiting to see if there were any indications that all was not as it appeared. Between that and classes and tutoring, he had so many things buzzing around inside his mind when he went to bed that he was sure he would never sleep — but he was so tired from all the thinking *and* the work under the eyes of the Riding Master and Weaponsmaster that he did, as soon as his own eyes closed.

Nor was he allowed full respite from the work even when he slept. Dallen had a thing or two to impart to him in dreams, and that was exactly what his Companion did. Since he was not getting lessons yet in this business of hearing the thoughts of other people, Dallen had taken it upon himself to provide the instruction. Mags might have thought himself rather overworked and ill-used — since not even Master Cole had invaded his dreams of a night — except that the way he kept overhearing what people were thinking was beginning to become uncomfortable. It was one thing to get vague hints of general intentions; that was useful and didn't leave Mags open to knowing things he would rather not. It was quite another to be keeping his eye on someone, only to hear, as clearly as if the fellow had shouted it, just how much the man wanted get the approval of a certain favored tavern wench, and exactly what he wanted to do if he got it. And if anyone was worried about something, really worried that is, Mags got an earful of it even if he *wasn't* concentrating on that person.

Thanks to Dallen's timely lessons, *that* wasn't going to happen again. Dallen had taught him how to do something the Companion called "shielding," and Mags was never going to eavesdrop on anyone's private thoughts unless he wanted to, and he was very, very sure that it would take a lot more motive than curiosity for him to want to. It had made him feel rather happy, though, when Dallen praised him for how quickly he had mastered the mental discipline it took to keep those unwanted thoughts out. It turned out to be not that difficult for someone who was used to concentration — and it certainly took concentration to be able to chip a tiny sparkly from its bed of rock without destroying it. Dallen promised that eventually, this would all become second nature to him, so much so that he would never think about it anymore.

By the time two weeks had passed, he settled into a routine that suited him.

Knowing that he was behind, but also knowing that he was doing his best to catch up, the teachers left him to himself to do so, although they expected him to pay close attention to their lectures in the classroom and what the tutor said as he and the others met in that empty classroom.

And so, on yet another icy morning, he found himself tucked unobtrusively at the back of the History classroom, doing his best to understand what was being discussed — treaties, agreements, alliances. Without the background, he was pretty well lost, and he left the class feeling as if everyone there had been speaking another language entirely.

He slipped into the next classroom behind some of the others — as usual, a mix of Trainees from Heraldic, Bardic, and Healers' — and took his usual seat, still feeling vaguely unsettled. But no sooner had the last of the students dropped into his place, when someone in Healer Greens popped his head through the door. This was unusual enough behavior to stop the buzz of idle conversation cold.

"Your instructor has had the poor taste to contract a rather nasty case of stomach disorder," the Healer said, with a wry smile. "I'll thank the rest of you not to do the same. You will be seeing him in another few days; come back here as usual tomorrow and we'll have found a substitute. Meanwhile, consider yourselves dismissed."

The Healer vanished again, leaving the students a bit dumbfounded. Finally, someone at the front — Mags didn't see who — gathered up his books and bolted for the door. It didn't take long for the rest to follow him.

Mags was the last to leave, and stood in the hallway for a long time, trying to make up his mind what to do next. Dallen was no help; the Companion was otherwise occupied; Mags got the impression that he and a knot of his equine friends were enjoying a good gossip. Finally, for lack of a better goal, he went out the door nearest "old" Healers' Collegium and some of the herb gardens.

The new Heraldic Trainees were a lively sociable bunch, and that left Mags right out. He could scarcely bring himself to talk to any of them, because most of the time he didn't know what to say. He had nothing in common with them; no parents, no siblings. Nothing he left behind with regrets — he certainly had no fond memories of the mine! When they weren't talking about each other or the Heralds who were their teachers, most of them traded reminiscences of home, so what would he have told them? Chances were they wouldn't believe him about his life anyway, and if they did, well, the idea of being pitied felt uncomfortable.

In their leisure, they often got together with other Trainees for impromptu singing and dancing. Many of them seemed to be musicians, and he wondered where they found the time to practice! He never learned to play anything, of course, never learned to dance, never heard any music but the drunken bawling of the Pieters family on the rare occasions when they celebrated anything. The Trainees were not the only ones who gathered for impromptu fun; the Heralds often came down to Companions' Stable to do the same, according to the stablehands. They hadn't yet, but Mags had passed by the Trainees' rooms or even a classroom before he went to bed, on his way back from the library, and heard the other Trainees laughing and talking and singing together. He didn't precisely feel left out — it was more that he felt as if he simply didn't understand them.

The Guards had done much the same thing, actually, when the day was done. He didn't understand them either. He had felt awkward, as if he *should* want to join them,

should want to do what they were doing —
but his head wouldn't quite shape itself to
what they were doing, and all he could do
was gawk and try to figure out what they
were laughing about.

Sometimes he noticed that the Trainees
would play games, or tell stories, even over
meals or when waiting their turn at something. He had seen gambling games, but of
course never had the leisure to play them,
and the only stories he knew were about the
mine . . . not a good choice for telling, even
if he had been inclined to do so.

Until now, the height of his ambition had
been to go to sleep with a full belly. They
were as strange to him as if they were some
sort of exotic bird. He felt as if he moved
among them like a ghost; they scarcely
registered his presence and none of them
seemed to even remember his name without
prompting from a Companion.

So, gifted with this unexpected bit of free
time . . . he found he had nothing with
which to fill it. On the other hand, the one
thing he had *not* done yet was explore
around the Collegia; he had been so busy
that he hadn't seen much outside of his
classrooms, the salle, the riding grounds,
the eating hall, and the stables. Curiosity
was not encouraged at the mine, but now

he slowly felt it stirring. There would be no harm in looking about a bit.

There was nothing to see in the Healers' herb gardens; everything was under a cover of mulch and snow, and in the gray light that filtered through the heavy clouds, there was nothing to distinguish it from an ordinary, snow-covered, hummocked field.

But the gardens around Old Bardic Collegium, in back of the building itself, were a little more enticing. Bards, it seemed, needed inspiration from nature, and even in winter the gardens were interesting, a kind of tamed wilderness, dotted with secluded places to sit, lit even at this hour with a variety of outdoor lanterns. It was the very opposite of everything Mags was familiar with. These gardens were not utilitarian, the way the herb and vegetable gardens were; they were not laid out in formal patterns as the ones nearer the Palace were. But they were also utterly unlike Companion's Field, which was just that, a field allowed to grow wild, with groves of trees and spreading bushes. Mags had never actually wandered about in there before; he had always been too busy during the day, and at night sleep had seemed preferable to stumbling around on half-lit snowy paths. Especially when he had overheard no few of the Trainees making plans to meet there after dark with someone. It seemed unlikely that he would run into a couple slobbering over each other by daylight, though, so he decided to explore further.

He hadn't penetrated very far past the boundaries when he heard something. For a moment, he stood quite still, trying to identify it. After a moment, he realized what it was.

Muffled sobs. Someone — a girl by the high voice — was crying.

More strongly than ever before, he was torn between his old self and the new one — the person he used to be might have turned his back on whoever was weeping and pretended he knew nothing about it. After all, this was some stranger. Right? It was no one he had any obligation to. He would not get in trouble if he ignored her. Why should he care if some strange girl was crying? How could it possibly matter if he walked away?

But the "new" Mags — that boy could not walk away. Not with those heartbroken sobs in his ears.

On the other hand, if this girl, whoever she was, was not alone, then him barging in there would not be good. She might be with a girl friend. Worse, she might be with a boy friend. The boy might be the one who was making her cry. Or he might be trying to comfort her.

So he carefully let his protections thin a little. Then a little more. Finally, when he could dimly sense her thoughts, although it was like hearing a voice so far in the distance that he could not make out the words, only the anguished tone, he allowed his senses to check the area around her.

Nothing. Not even the "alive-but-blank" feeling he got from someone who was shielding his thoughts too.

:What are you doing, Mags?: Dallen must have sensed enough to pull his attention away from the rest of his friends.

:I'm going to find out if I can help,: he replied, feeling even more awkward, if possible.

There was silence in his head for a moment. *:It isn't a Heraldic Trainee,:* Dallen said cautiously. *:I would be very careful if I were you. It could be the daughter of someone highborn in the Court. She'd not appreciate your help. Especially not if she is lovelorn or something of the sort. She won't appreciate you coming in and wanting to know her private affairs.:*

He gave a mental shrug, but Dallen wasn't finished. *:She might even be insulted. Some* *of the highborn are rather . . . touchy about being approached by someone who is not of their rank and class.:* Dallen's tone conveyed a certain resignation. *:Much as I would prefer otherwise, there are those who believe that their blood entitles them to look down on the rest of humanity.:*

:Even a Herald?: he asked.

Another moment of silence. *:In some cases,* especially *a Herald.:*

In a way, that statement came as a relief rather than otherwise. So the Heralds didn't get along with everyone. Or rather, not everyone saw them as an unalloyed blessing from the gods. That, to Mags' mind, was far more realistic than the "everyone adores the Heralds" image he had been getting from Dallen and everyone else in Whites or Grays. Instinctively, he had been certain that could not be the case. In his experience, life was not just an apple with a worm in it, it was an apple that was mostly worm, and one could only hope to pick free bits of apple. So here was the worm, or perhaps, many worms, revealed at last.

:But such people are few!: Dallen all but bleated.

:The more reason to know they're there, and who they are.: He began working his way into the gardens, guided by the sound of

sobbing. *:You don't have to tell me now who they are, just warn me when there's one about.:* He might have added more, except at that moment he rounded a clump of three evergreens to find himself practically face-to-face with a young girl, dark-haired, thin, and smaller even than Mags, with a dead rabbit in her lap.

:Don't!: Dallen shouted in his mind, before he could say anything. And rightly so, because Mags' impulse on being presented with a dead rabbit was to ask when she was going to cook it and did she need help in skinning and gutting it. Not that long ago, a dead rabbit would have been cause for the nearest thing he and the rest of the kiddies knew as a feast. He would have welcomed a dead rabbit with all his heart, but the only ones he had ever seen were going into the Pieters' kitchen.

As for himself, Mags had eaten dead crows, dead sparrows — even a dead cat, once . . . it was almost second nature to think of any beast only as a potential meal.

Which, he knew in the next moment, would have been a terrible, and very hurtful thing to say. You didn't stroke the fur of your dinner the way this girl was petting the dead rabbit. And you certainly didn't weep over it the way she was doing. And now, here, he

196

found himself thinking of one of the other kiddies, a creature of indeterminate gender that had attached itself to one of the barn cats, and the cat to it. The Pieterses did not have "pets" as such — every animal in their lives was either food or a beast of some use. But the child and the cat had been almost inseparable until the child took ill the past winter and died. And the cat had vanished.

He coughed slightly to alert her to his presence. She looked up, huge brown eyes bloodshot, tears pouring down her delicate face, and that was when he noticed that she was wearing the rust-red uniform of a Bardic Trainee, and he felt some of Dallen's anxiety ease. "Hey," he said awkwardly. "I heard ye. Ye maybe should go inside. Yer gonna get cold out here like this —"

She stared at him blankly, then sobbed. "He's dead! I went back to my room to feed him, and he's dead!" Anything more she might have said was lost in the torrent of sobs that followed.

Awkwardly, Mags sat down on a garden seat opposite her. "They don' live very long," he suggested. "Mebbe 'twas his time —" Not the most tactful of things to say, perhaps, but at least it didn't cause her to cry harder.

"He wasn't very old!" she sobbed, stroking the rabbit's brown fur. "He was only four!" Mags grimaced. He really didn't think rabbits lived much longer than that; certainly that seemed to be about the average life for a cat around the Pieterses' mine, and cats were about the same size as rabbits. But the young girl wasn't done. "M–m–my best friend Kaley gave him to me; she found a nest a–a–and gave Bumper to me to k–k–keep me c–c–company."

Mags furrowed his brows. "Keep ye company? Why?"

"Everyone at h–home is always so b–busy," she replied, head down, voice muffled. "Kaley had to go to w–work at the inn, s–so she didn't have t–time anymore." The girl looked up at him for just a moment, then back down again, flushing, and broke into sobs again.

Mags was freezing, but gamely remained. "I don't know anyone here," the girl said forlornly. "And I–I–I am not really good at meeting people."

Mags contemplated the irony of that statement, given that he was so bad at meeting people he could just as well have been invisible.

"S–so when I asked if I c–could bring Bumper, they said yes." She paused for another spate of tears, and pulled a square of white cloth from her sleeve to dry them with.

Outwardly, he probably seemed calm. Inwardly, he was beginning to panic. :*What do I do now?*: he begged Dallen. He felt himself floundering. Now that he had gotten himself involved in this girl's grief, he didn't feel as if he should extricate himself, but he also didn't know how to react to it. Some mostly-smothered instinct said *comfort her,* but how did you do that? He'd never felt that much attachment for another human being as to weep over him, so how was he to sympathize with such an outpouring of grief over what to anyone else would have been a feature at dinner?

"Now I'm all alone," she sobbed into the cloth.

"Ah, nah, yer a Bardic gel, no?" he responded, before Dallen got a chance to prompt him. "Ye gots lots of friends, surely —"

"No, I don't!" she cried. "I don't have *any* friends! How could I have, when Tobias Marchand is my father?"

She said that as if she expected that answered all questions. Mags' brow crinkled, but Dallen answered him before he could voice the obvious question.

:*Tobias is a very famous Bard,*: Dallen told

him, sounding surprised. *:I've heard he can play almost every instrument there is, and do it brilliantly — and his songs are popular in at least three countries besides Valdemar. And, besides that, he's supposed to be a simply amazing and witty man, able to hold a conversation on just about any subject. I had no idea he had a daughter — :*

"Well, yer Da can make sure yer looked out for, no?" he ventured.

She looked up, stricken. "Oh, no!" she whispered. "No. No, I couldn't call on my father. And anyway, I hardly know him. He never spent much time with us, he was *much* too busy. He's too important for someone like me to bother."

Dallen reacted to this with indignation, although it seemed perfectly sensible to Mags. Cole Pieters' boys knew better than to bother him with anything that did not have to do directly with the running of the mine, for instance. . . .

Underneath her words, with his protections down, Mags was getting a running match of her thoughts to her words, and he felt more and more at sympathy with her with every passing moment, for all that they seemed so dissimilar. For the past several weeks since her arrival, she had been too shy to open her mouth except to sing —

and in any event, all of the Bardic Trainees at or near her own age already had established groups of friends. She shrank from the mere thought of trying to penetrate those apparently-closed ranks. And as for her teachers . . . she was intimidated, not by them, but by how much they expected of her. She was laboring under the burden of her father's reputation, and that terrified her.

In fact, the memory of that first interview was always lurking in the back of her mind.

"So you are young Lena Marchand."

"Yes, sir." The face of the Dean of Bardic Collegium looked down gravely at her. She bobbed her head awkwardly. Lita Darvalis had a formidable reputation; she had Skill, Creativity, and the Gift, all three. Even her father looked up to her with respect, which didn't happen often.

"We expect great things of you, Lena." She smiled, but her words practically paralyzed Lena. "You have a formidable legacy behind you."

Oh, yes. And how could she ever, ever begin to measure up to that legacy? She wanted to fall to the ground and moan in despair. Instead, she shook Lita's hand, and went to collect her things and be conducted to a room.

The memories and the desperation behind

them flooded over him. Here was someone who was feeling just as out of place as he was, and just as unworthy. Suddenly, he didn't feel quite so alone.

Poor kiddie. She scarcely knew her father any more than Mags knew his, and they were expecting her to be some kind of younger copy of him. Mags sensed Dallen all but spluttering with indignation; Mags ignored him. "If ye need a frien', Lena . . ." he said, slowly, the unfamiliar word leaving a strange, but pleasant, sensation behind it, "I c'ud be yer frien'. If ye want."

He expected her to look away and politely decline. After all, it wasn't as if he had anything worth offering to someone like her. So her reaction surprised him.

"You would? You could?" Two bright pink spots appeared on her tear-blotched cheeks. "You'd really be my friend?"

"I guess everyone'd be if they knew ye," he half-mumbled, staring down at his hands. "Uh . . . I guess poor ol' Bumper there —"

"I wanted to bury him," she replied, choking down a sob. "But the ground is so hard —"

He almost laughed. "Might not know much," he offered, "But I know diggin'. If yer not too partic'lar about where, I'll get ye a hole." When she nodded, he went off to

202

the gardener's shed and came back with a pickax and a shovel. And of course Mags did know digging; after scraping back the snow in several places and examining the ground closely, he found a spot under a bush that was mostly mulch, and softer than the ground around it. With the pick and shovel, he managed to dig a little hole; the girl carefully wrapped her rabbit in her scarf and laid it in the bottom, then looked at him expectantly.

:*You should say something, Mags*,: Dallen prompted.

He gulped. What should he say? He was not good with words at the best of times. Finally, he bit his lip and tried to think of what she might want to hear.

"He was a good rabbit," Mags began desperately. "An he was a friend when Lena needed one. Reckon that's how ye knows a friend, they be there when ye need 'em." He paused. "An' Lena'll miss him. Lots."

Lena burst into tears again, though it did not seem to be because of anything he said or hadn't said. He shoveled the mulch back on top of the little body while she sobbed, and patted it flat with the shovel.

"Best go back inside," he advised her. "Yer goin' t' get sick, out here in the cold."

She nodded, and with drooping head and

sagging shoulders turned to go back to the building. But then she stopped, and looked back at him, tears still slipping down her cheeks. "Where can I find you later?"

"Uh — I got a room. In Companions' Stable. Uh — I'm Mags."

She nodded gravely. "Thank you, Mags. And thank you for being my friend."

And with that, she disappeared into the building.

Mags put his protections back up.

:Class,: prompted Dallen, just as the bell rang for the change. With a sigh, Mags gathered up his forgotten books, and went back on his schedule.

He really did not expect to see Lena again, despite offering to become her friend. It was one thing for her to have flung herself on the mercy of a strange Trainee when she was so distraught. It was quite another for her to actually seek him out and take him up on that offer.

So he went on to his riding practice and weapons practice without giving much thought to her.

He had found over the last couple of days, somewhat to his own amazement, that he liked both. More than that, he was getting *good* at both.

Riding, well, that was all because, for the

first time in his life, he felt in control of something. And powerful. Up there on Dallen's back, he wasn't puny little Mags anymore. And there was the whole sense of freedom he got when Dallen really cut loose and ran or jumped. Their mental link was so strong that he was able to anticipate Dallen's every move and move with the Companion to the point where it sometimes felt to him as if they were one creature. He could scarcely remember now how frightened he'd been, perched uneasily on Dallen's back a few sennights ago. Now, well, he might as well have been sewn to Dallen's saddle, and Dallen had taken to more than just simple running and jumping the past couple of sessions. The Companion called these acrobatic exercises "battlefield moves," and Mags could see where they would come in handy if a lot of people with sharp things in their hands came at you to do you wrong.

Today was like that. Half a dozen of the Guards had been borrowed from the barracks (and Mags suspected, bribed with the promise of drink) and were standing in for enemy fighters. Each of them in turn was set upon by fellows with blunt wooden swords, with ropes, with spear-poles with heavy wads of rag and wool tied to the end, and one man with a very long pole with a padded hook on the end. The object was for Companion and Chosen to hold them off for one turn of a very small glass. This was not as easy as it sounded.

These men knew Companions and warhorses both, and knew what they could do. The first three Trainees that were set upon lost their seats and were dragged down out of the saddle before half the sand had run out. Then it had been Mags' turn.

By then, he and Dallen had had more than enough time to settle into that peculiar merging of minds that left them so aware of each other that the rope around Dallen's hock might as well have been around Mags' ankle. When the six Guardsmen popped up out of "ambush" to take them, the two of them were ready to show what real riding was all about.

Dallen leaped almost straight up into the air, lashing out with his hind hooves as he did so. The men behind them threw themselves to the ground to avoid those hooves, even though Dallen was in no danger of hurting them.

Landing on all four hooves, Dallen spun in a circle, pivoting on his hind feet, snapping at the Guards as Mags flailed the air above their heads with his own wooden sword.

As they scrambled out of the way, Dallen caught sight of the man with the hook. Rearing up on his hind legs, he "hopped" forward, lashing out with his forehooves viciously, aiming for that man alone of the dozen. Unnerved, he dropped the hook and dropped to the ground. Since that was exactly what Mags and Dallen had been waiting for, the two of them soared over his body in a huge jump, whirled again, then bolted for the open spaces of Companion's Field. They didn't return until they were well and truly sure the sands had run out.

As they ambled back, finally, they could see the Guardsmen making short work of another Trainee. The Herald who was in charge of the instruction gave them a brief glance, and an approving nod, then waited for the unseated Trainee to pick himself up out of the snowbank he'd been tossed into.

"People," the Herald said, with just a hint of impatience in his voice, "Show some sense. This is not an exercise in fighting back, it's an exercise in escaping. Stop trying to prove you can out-fight any six attackers, and do what those two did." His eyebrow rose. "So far they're the only ones of the lot of you that beat the turn of the glass."

Mags felt a flush of accomplishment, and Dallen tossed his head and arched his neck a little. Then the Herald sent them to do the jumping course before they could bask in the envy of the others, and at that point they became much too busy to think about anything else.

Mags gave Dallen a good rubdown and turned him loose when the time for weapons training came around. Dallen trotted off with his tail flagged proudly, presumably to take in the congratulations of the others, while Mags shouldered the burden of his practice arms and armor and trudged off to the salle.

His growing expertise with weapons was more of a shock than his aptitude for riding. The revelation that he had a knack for such things literally came out of the blue. When he had been beating on that padded pole for a few days, the instructor had looked him over, then, without any warning at all, had picked up a stick of his own and come after him. Startled, Mags had held onto his stick and scrambled out of the way. And somehow, blocked the teacher's blows. He had been graced with a grim smile and a nod of approval, and suddenly the stick was taken from him, a hilt shoved at him, and before he knew it, he had found himself with a practice sword in hand.

He had frozen then, every memory of every person who had ever been punished at the mine for daring to even raise a hand in self-defense flooding to the fore.

But the instructor had no intention of letting him stay that way.

"Here! Euston!" the Herald had called. "This lad has the patterns down, so come show him how the patterns become fighting!"

A young man with bright red hair, dressed in the Bardic Trainee rust, disengaged from his current practice partner and came straight over to Mags. Without saying a single word, he simply saluted Mags with the "blade," and launched straight into an attack.

Mags reacted without thinking, getting his guard up in time and deflecting the blows. Before he knew it, he was bouting with the Bardic Trainee, a boy who gave no quarter, nor asked for any, and he was too busy defending himself to think about how it was all wrong to be holding, and using, a weapon.

Maybe the fact that he himself had never been punished for using anything weapon-like was the reason why this fear broke down so quickly. After all, he had never even given the Pieters boys so much as a threatening look. But as he got used to the feel of the thing in his hand, those fears and inhibitions melted away. Having a weapon made him feel as powerful as being on Dallen's back. Being able to use it made him feel more confident that no one would be able to treat him as Master Cole had, ever again.

And his aptitude for weapons work was no more of an illusion than his aptitude for riding. His body seemed to have a better memory for things than his mind; he only had to be shown something once to be able to do it himself. It felt like a kind of magic, but the Weaponsmaster said that it was just a natural thing that some people had. It certainly explained why he had been so skilled at harvesting sparklies.

Today the Weaponsmaster took him aside and actually put *him* to drilling some of the others at his old friend, the padded pole, which he now knew was called a "pells." And the two he was asked to help were — Beren and Lyr. The poor fellows were as clumsy with their wooden batons as a pair of puppies. Mags felt horribly sorry for them, for they were clearly feeling terribly humiliated, and he did his earnest best to get them sorted out.

They actually made a little progress by the time the Weaponsmaster dismissed them all — they were at least not smacking each other anymore — and as usual, Mags did his best to fade into insignificance in the rush to get to the bathing rooms and then to the eating hall. He generally slipped off to his own room to get a change of clothing and set the place to rights before getting his bath. Such precautions meant he had the bathing room to himself and after the drubbing he had gotten at the unskilled hands of Beren and Lyr he needed the soak in hot water to ease his bruises.

And after all, there was no need to hurry to get to dinner. He never ate with anyone in particular, mostly choosing his isolated seat where he could keep a wary eye on all the company. So it was with a start of surprise that he felt his elbow seized as soon as he came in the door.

"I've been waiting for you forever, Mags," said Lena, looking up at him with eyes still red-rimmed from weeping. "Come on. I've saved you a place."

9

The thing about having a room in the stable, Mags was discovering, was that people, Heralds included, tended to forget that there was someone here besides Companions. And because he would sequester himself in his room long before most of the other Trainees were in theirs, he was the unintended witness to a lot of conversations he was pretty sure shouldn't have been overheard. Or at the very least, conversations that no one wanted overheard.

Most of those conversations were merely embarrassing; most were stablehands in eager pursuit of women — and women eager to be pursued. Since the Companions' Stable was heated when the others were not — the stable proper was not as warm as the couple of rooms that were here, but with the exception of Mags', those rooms were shared. So when privacy was wanted, maybe a stall was the best choice these fellows had.

He and Dallen often shared a sardonic word or three about some of what they overheard.

Mags got to hear an awful lot of lies, to put things bluntly. *"Of course I love you,"* was the one he heard most often, along with *"You're the only woman in my life,"* coming a close second. Though to be fair, the women lied almost as often. *"You're all I think about,"* and *"Never change."* It was interesting. He'd heard that Heralds could do something that let them know when someone was lying, but it was getting so that he could tell without that — whatever it was. "Truth Spell." Dallen seemed to think this was remarkable, but very useful.

Mostly, when he heard voices on the other side of his door, he just tried to ignore them. He had a great deal of practice at ignoring things, once he was able to decide that what was being talked about didn't matter to him. Back at the mine, there were times when your life, or at least your health, depended on "not hearing" things. He'd "not heard" the boys messing about with the kitchen- and housemaids, for instance, plenty of times. He'd "not heard" the boys saying ugly things about their father. And here and now, he was careful about all those careless, feckless lovers, and careful about Trainees blurting out things they probably shouldn't have. It harmed no one to forget all about those little secrets. But there were some conversations he couldn't just put aside and forget. And one of them started one evening with two mature voices coming into audible range as he was doing sums.

". . . Holden, I'm telling you, this Collegium idea is criminally stupid."

The man had been speaking too quietly for Mags to make out what he was saying for some time now, though it had been obvious from his tone that he was arguing. But this was a rather startling statement for a Herald to make. He assumed it was Heralds, and Dallen confirmed it.

"That's a bit of a leap," came the reply. Evidently the fellow he was arguing with agreed with Mags.

"No? Have you *seen* how these younglings are being taught? In classrooms! Out of books!" Incredulity warred with indignation in the man's voice. Mags wondered what was wrong with learning things out of books. Surely when you did things that way, you didn't stand nearly as much risk of making the same mistakes as someone else. "A Herald doesn't need books to show him what to do, he needs another Herald! You don't learn that sort of thing out of *books!* You learn this sort of thing by seeing it, doing it — hands on, Holden! We've always been hands on!"

"What they're learning out of books are things I wish I had known," the other replied mildly. "I scanted my History, and not to mention that I knew nothing about anyone's religion but my own. Besides that, it's a plain fact that we're getting younglings who are functionally, if not actually, illiterate. Younglings that can barely read simple words and write their own names. You can't teach someone something that basic without tying up an enormous amount of your own time. Our Chosen aren't all coming from the educated folk anymore. I know, I know!" he added, when the other seemed to be about to protest. "I know it's the law that all younglings are to get a basic education! But we've nearly doubled the size of the Kingdom in last few years, what with petty princelings deciding they'd rather have Valdemar's protection than a foreign army on their door, and plenty of those petty princelings thought that pig-ignorance was the proper lot of the peasant."

"Gods, I hate it when you're right," the first man grumbled. "I just got off riding one of those circuits."

"Well, we are getting Chosen *from* those very places. Which is a good and proper thing, since a Herald from the borderlands is going to be able to tell us how to keep from offending."

"Holderkin!" the first man groaned. "Oh, blessed gods, may I never have to ride that circuit again. Even with that briefing — they are as touchy as a hive of hornets, and you would think that *I* was the enemy, not the Karsites!"

"You see my point. We have young Chosen coming in now that need elementary education, and we need to make sure they have the tools to do their jobs before we turn them out on an unsuspecting public."

"Bosh! We did well enough before!" the first man said savagely. "We had Chosen who were as ignorant as butterflies! They got education over at Bardic, but they were under the eyes of their mentors every waking moment. Now what? Now what have we got? No mentors until they go into Whites! Using the Bardic model! They're going to be all shoved together in their Collegium without a single adult present most of the time!"

"It works for the Bards," the second man said mildly.

"Works? Works? Good gods, those Bardic students get into more mischief than a basket of ferrets! And now you want us to do the same with *our* Trainees? Who's going to serve as the check on their antics? Who's going to serve as an example? We've *always* run things this way — a couple of Trainees and a mentor, proper chaperoning, and instruction every waking hour. But this! The gods only know how these youngsters are going to turn out!"

"They have their Companions," the second man pointed out. "It's not as if they're unsupervised."

The first man snorted. "They might just as well be. What's a Companion going to do if his Chosen gets into mischief? Mindspeak him and nag him? And what if the Companion doesn't think it's mischief?" He groaned. "They might as well admit to what is going to go on and install a midwife in the Collegium, because they are going to *need* one before the first year is out!"

But that second man only laughed at him. "Kyle, the Trainees have been up to *that* sort of mischief from the time of King Valdemar, and no looming mentor ever held them back from it. And I cannot believe you are not aware of that fact —"

"Well, other mischief, then," the first man said stubbornly. "If the Bardic Trainees are worse than a basket of ferrets, ours will be worse than a basket of ferrets with hands and wings. Oh, I have no doubt their intentions will be relatively innocent, but the result will be calamity. This whole Collegium idea is going to be the ruin of the Heralds! Let the Bards and Healers have their schools, but we should stick to what has always worked in the past!"

"Good gods, Kyle, where are all these mentors that you want going to come from?" the second man finally retorted. "And where in Haven are we going to put them? We've been assigning the Trainees three and four to a Herald, and there just are not enough of us! The latest influx — that would put us at a Trainee to every Herald, and I mean *every* one of us, even on the most dangerous of assignments. For the ones with ordinary routes, it could be up to six, and how the hell is someone supposed to go riding circuit with a pack of younglings at his heels? You want mischief? What about those four that went out with Herald Elyn? Good gods, that was worse than mischief, if they hadn't had the luck of the blessed, they could have been murdered by that old man! And that was only with *four* Trainees! It can't be done, Kyle. It just cannot be done."

"— but —"

The second man had clearly warmed to

his subject by this time. "And how about those who should *never* be entrusted with an impressionable young mind? What about Baren? The man never intends harm, and he's brilliant at cutting straight through a difficult situation, but his sarcasm has put adults into a killing rage or tears, so what do you think prolonged exposure to him would do to a Trainee?"

"Ah — toughen them?"

"Or break them! Or Bella! There is *no one* I would rather have in charge of victims, but dear gods, a pack of Trainees would run right over the top of her, and they would have *her* in tears! Would you want to be responsible for that?"

"— ah — no — but —"

The two men moved out of earshot, leaving Mags thinking very hard. Finally, he ventured a quiet question to Dallen.

:I thought — I mean, Jakyr was angry only because the building was being delayed so that the Bards and Healers could get bigger Collegia. I thought . . . : He considered that statement, and amended it. *:I* didn't *think this was something anyone was against.:* And why should he have? All he ever heard was eager talk about what would be done once the building was complete, and all the

comforts that were going to be installed there.

There was the sense of a reluctant sigh. *:No, I am afraid that not every Herald is happy with the changes,:* the Companion replied. *:In fact, some of them are . . . very unhappy indeed. There are arguments about it every meeting of the Circle still, even though the King himself has sent down the ruling that this is how it will be. As you heard . . . there are those that believe that Trainees should be very strictly attended to. And . . . and they have good reasons for that. Some tragic things have happened when even mentors were not as attentive as they should have been. Now, with this new system in place, there is less supervision. Many think this is a bad thing.:*

Mags chewed on the end of his pen. *:So what d'you think?:*

:I think that I trust my fellow Companions and I trust those they Choose. I think there will be neither more nor less mischief. I think mischief is not such a bad thing, though there are surely people who would be very angry at me for saying that.: Dallen sounded amused. Mags could almost see him smiling.

:Well . . . I guess.: He wasn't entirely sure just what qualified as mischief to Dallen. Back at the mine . . . well, that word was

generally applied when one of the Pieters boys did something that he was risking a reprimand for at best, and a horsewhipping at worst. It usually had to do with chambermaids, but sometimes it had to do with meddling in things Cole Pieters felt were his own particular prerogatives.

:This is the first year of the new system. And it has been a full year and nothing disastrous has happened.:

:So how did the old system work?: He worked out another couple of problems while he waited for Dallen to collect his thoughts.

:In the past, Herald Jakyr would have served as your mentor, since he was the one that found you and brought you in. If for some reason you just didn't suit, or he couldn't take you, someone else would have taken you on. Then one of two things would have happened. Either your mentor would be assigned to the Court or Haven and you would have spent all your time here as you will now, or you would have gone out on circuit with your mentor. In that case, you'd have spent as much time with him, away from this place, as you did here, attending classes. And it would have been his job to keep you at your lessons.:

Mags thought that over as well. *:I'd'a gotten right lost, doin' things that way.:*

:Well, there wouldn't have been a choice. The Heralds who actually stay in Haven are very few. They *were already mentoring up to eight Trainees. And that was getting to be a strain, not much "better" than having you all in the Collegium. So you would have had to go out with someone who ran messages, served as an envoy and negotiator, or was on circuit. That's what Jakyr does, by the way,:* Dallen added by way of an afterthought. *:He's a negotiator.:*

Mags picked up on what Dallen did not say. *:And I'd'a been in the way.:*

:I'm afraid so. But so would most Trainees. There just is no choice, Mags. As much as some of the Heralds want to keep the "old ways," it just is not possible. Just think how much *you are going to have to learn before you are fit even to think of going with a mentor! And Beren and Lyr are even more uneducated than you. I have no doubt that at some point soon we will get a Trainee who is not even aware that the arts of reading and writing exist. How could a Herald-mentor hope to teach people like that and still continue to do his or her work?:*

It was a good question, and one for which Mags had no answer. Nor did anyone else, he suspected.

It did open his eyes, however. Here was

one issue on which the Heralds themselves were at odds. And in a way that heartened him. He had never quite believed in the attractive mental picture Dallen was painting for him. This cracked that façade. If they were at odds over this, chances were there were other quarrels of which he was not aware.

So even the Heralds were not perfectly in accord with one another. That made him, not uneasy, but conversely more secure. He trusted in his own senses to tell him when someone menaced *him,* and the fact that Heralds were not perfect, could disagree with each other, and still stay a somewhat coherent whole was a cause for relaxing, rather than raising, his guard. It meant that there was nothing worse lying behind the face they showed the world.

Dallen seemed baffled by the reason for his attitude, but accepted the change with guarded relief.

Only later did he realize that if the Heralds could be at odds with one another, anyone who wanted to, and knew how the various Heralds stood on important issues, could drive some serious wedges in the not-so-seamless front of the Heraldic Circle.

This didn't change how he interacted with the other Trainees, of course. The habits of a lifetime were too hard to break. He still said little, listened much, and observed always. But that made him the perfect comrade for Lena. They met every day now, at meals, and often between classes. He would listen, and she would talk. Sometimes very little, and sometimes a lot; most of that was about home, her friends, her mother, the things she used to do. Gradually, he understood that she was bitterly homesick, and that at least having someone to talk about home with was comforting to her, even if all he did was murmur some innocuous word at intervals.

He didn't mind, not in the least, because he found that he enjoyed having a friend. That was repayment enough for him.

But evidently it was not enough for Lena.

"I want to help you," Lena said earnestly over dinner. "With your studies, at night, after dinner."

Mags studied her carefully. Her soft brown eyes were full of determination, and he sensed that she was not going to accept "no." "I gots a teacher," he said, instead of an outright refusal. "I don' think they'd let me have a different one —"

"I know who your teacher is, and I am just as good." Defiantly, she raised her

224

pointed little chin. "I can do this. There's no reason why not."

He sucked on his lower lip. "Ye gots to ask her," he said, finally. "I cain't just not turn up, see?"

For answer, she stood up, grabbed his hand and tugged at it. "Then let's go."

A little amused, and a little alarmed, he let himself be led away; he realized that she must have *some* information about what he was doing at night, because she went straight to the empty classroom he and Beren and Lyr were using for the extra lessons. They were early, and the tutor looked up at the sound of footsteps crossing the threshold. Her eyes narrowed, then widened, when she saw he wasn't alone.

"This isn't the time or place, Mags," she began. But with a toss of her long, brown hair, Lena interrupted, albeit politely.

"Chronicler Lilli," she said, with a little bow. "I'm Bardic Trainee Lena Marchand. I know you've been asked to tutor three of the Heraldic Trainees. I would like to tutor Trainee Mags in your place."

Lilli regarded Lena thoughtfully. "And why would you want to do that?" she asked carefully.

Lena smiled. "Because he's my friend. And that makes me more motivated to help

225

him pass his classes than you are; I want him to get caught up so he can have free time like everyone else. And because you have to teach three, while I will only have to think about one."

The Chronicler scratched the back of her head. "If it was anyone but you — but they talk well of your scholarship, Trainee Lena. And I am confident of Mags' ability to concentrate on his studies . . ." She pondered this for a moment. Then, "Very well. You must take care that there are no distractions. You may use the room next door to this one, and I will drill him afterward."

Now the thoroughly bemused Mags was led by the hand to the designated room, where, with a determined look on her face, Lena set up two chairs, facing each other, with the table between them.

Somehow, and he could not quite reckon how, Lena made a lot more sense than the Chronicler did. He reflected as she drilled him relentlessly that he wished all his classes were maths and math-related. Those things had simple logic. Two into four would always be two, never five, never three. But the things people had done in the past! There seemed no reason for them.

Except that somehow Lena was able to explain the reasons. They might not be logical, but then, neither was Mags all the time. They *were* understandable. Perhaps that was what Chronicler Lilli had missed. Without *reasons* for what had happened, Mags simply could not grasp the events themselves; they became nothing but a series of things to be memorized, and his mind didn't work well on strict memorization.

Having made more progress in an evening than he had in three, after Chronicler Lilli came in, drilled him on what he was supposed to have learned, and pronounced herself satisfied, Mags grabbed Lena's hand and wrung it in wordless gratitude. She smiled shyly at him.

"I dunno why ye wanted t' help a straw-head like me, but — ye're a wonder, Lena," he managed after a moment.

She ducked her head. "I don't mind. And . . . I hate being in my room and seeing where Bumper's box used to be, and —" Her eyes grew bright, and Mags hastily searched for something, anything to distract her. Then he hit on it.

"Ye've never met Dallen," he said quickly. "Come meet Dallen afore ye go back t' Bardic, eh?"

She wiped her eyes with the back of her hand. "All right —" she began, but this time it was Mags' turn to seize a hand and drag his friend off before she could think of any reason to protest.

The stable was very quiet at this time of night, with most of the Companions drowsing in their stalls, warmly covered against any hint of chill with their thick blue blankets. The carefully shielded lanterns glowed golden, so it wasn't at all hard to see, and the air smelled of nothing worse than hay and horse. The atmosphere was strangely cozy for so large a building, and very peaceful. But Dallen was wide awake and alert, having been warned by Mags that they were coming, and looking for them. They could see his head from the doorway, the glow of a lamp gilding it as he peered through the shadows at them.

Lena stopped dead in her tracks at the first sight of him. Her mouth opened in a soundless "o" and her eyes grew very big. Mags found himself smiling; always something that surprised him when it happened. He thought that he had probably smiled more in the few weeks he had been here than in his entire life before Dallen.

:I do believe she has never seen a Companion up close, Mags,: Dallen said thoughtfully. *:Interesting!:*

"Well, go on, he don't bite," Mags urged.

"He says hullo."

"Can I — can I touch him?" she asked, her eyes shining, and her fingers twitching with the unspoken urge to stroke that silver coat.

"Of course ye can touch him!" Mags patted her shoulder encouragingly. "I wouldn' have brought ye here t' meet him if ye couldn'."

:Tell her I quite like being touched.: Dallen's eyes sparkled with amusement, and he lowered his nose to Lena's tentative hand.

"He's a one for bein' made much of," Mags paraphrased, with a waggle of his eyebrow. "Don't reckon he ever turned down bein' scratched."

Lena giggled, and stroked Dallen's nose, then gently scratched his eye ridges. Dallen sighed and closed his eyes in bliss. *:Tell her she can stop in a year or so — but she can take more time if she needs to.:*

Mags chuckled — it sounded odd in his own ears, and it had rather well been surprised out of him. But he liked the sound, and he liked the way it made him feel even more. He told Lena what Dallen had said, and this time she laughed aloud. But she made no move to stop.

"I've never been near to a Companion before," she said quietly, confirming

Dallen's guess. "Heralds never came near our house, I mean, there wasn't any reason for them to, you know. Our home is rather off the road, and we never had any reason for one to come, I suppose. And until I came here, I never really left our land . . ." Her voice trailed off a moment, and she put her cheek against Dallen's. "He's so beautiful."

:Tell her that tomorrow she can ride me.:

Mags blinked. If there was a truism about Companions, it was that they *never* let anyone ride them except their Chosen, unless it was a dire emergency. But, dutifully, he repeated what Dallen had said.

Lena gasped, and the stable practically lit up with her smile. "I can?" she squeaked.

"He says so," Mags shrugged. "I 'spect you had better find somethin' good to ride in by then."

He was not altogether certain that her feet touched the ground when she finally left to go back to her own room.

10

Mags woke a few days later to the sound of irritated voices in the stable; he was taking a nap because he had been studying late with Lena the night before, and was taking advantage of another class canceled because of a sick instructor to get some much needed sleep. After a moment, he had to smile, because of what the Trainees were complaining about.

". . . and I ask you, is it so very hard to find gray thread instead of blue? I've got blue darns on my elbows and knees!"

"Well I've got a big blue seam running up my bum where I tore the trews on a nail," someone else complained.

You could mend 'em yerself, Mags thought quietly. That was what he had done from the moment he got the uniforms. He'd thought everyone was supposed to. Goodness knew he'd had plenty of practice piecing rags together into something like a garment; the difficulty had always been finding anything to take the place of needle and thread. Grass wasn't strong enough; generally he'd used hair pulled from the tails of the long-suffering horses. When he'd first gotten here, he'd asked for needle and thread from one of the servants; he'd gotten a puzzled look, but several hanks of gray thread and a packet of pins and needles had been found for him. And thanks to Dallen, he understood that his dirty uniforms were to go straight to the laundry, and he had dutifully delivered them down the chute in the Guards' quarters, but only after he had fixed whatever was amiss with them.

It seemed, however, that he was the only one doing so. And the servants who took care of such things, now severely overworked with the heavy influx of new trainees, were encountering some difficulties. Like finding enough gray thread to fix all the abuses Trainees wrought on their uniforms. Trainees did not stop sending clothing down to be washed and mended just because there was a shortage of materials, so clearly the servants had done what they could with what was on hand.

"Look at this!" said a new, equally indignant voice. "Just look at it! Do these look like Grays to you?"

"More like Pale Blues," someone snickered. "Looks like a Guard tunic got into the wash."

"How am I going to pass inspection like this?" the speaker demanded, in despair. "It's not *my* fault I look like a Guardsman that's been lying out in the sun too long!"

"I don't know why you are worrying about your uniform when your room looks like a magpie's nest," came the laconic reply. "You haven't cleaned it in a week. You're going to fail that inspection, so a blue uniform isn't going to matter."

Mags could only shake his head, then pull a pillow over it and try and drift back to sleep. It was impossible for him to take these "difficulties" seriously. Really, it was hard for him to believe that he, Mags, was actually here and not dreaming. It seemed utterly impossible, and not for the first time he wondered if he was actually dead and this was that heavenly afterlife that the priests had said that good people would get.

For the first time ever, he could eat as much as he wanted, of food that nearly made him delirious with how good it tasted. In fact, based on how thin he still was, he often got more food urged on him than he could actually eat. He'd overheard some of the other Trainees complaining about the meals — that things were plain, boring, coarse food — and he could only shake his head in wonder. They complained because the cook was formerly with the Guard, and made the same rations the Guard ate. Clearly, they had never gone hungry a day in their lives.

For the first time ever, he knew what it was to be clean. He knew now why he'd been practically scrubbed raw at the Guard Post; not only had he been filthy and probably stank, he'd also been flea-ridden. The soap that the Guards had used on him was meant to kill vermin on horses and dogs, and it did a good job on the "passengers" he'd had along. He had been scratching and itching for so long that when the irritation healed, it was like having a vague headache suddenly stop. He had never realized how miserable that had made him feel because it had been swallowed up in all the other miseries. When your belly aches from hunger, you don't notice you've scratched your arms half raw . . . some of the other Trainees complained because they had to carry the hot water for their baths from the big coppers where it was heated. Mags reckoned they would sing a different tune if they'd had fleas infesting every straw of their beds and every stitch of their clothing.

For the first time ever, he had clean clothing that covered every bit of him and kept him warm in the worst cold. He could march out fearlessly into the snow knowing that he was *not* going to get chilblains all over his feet, that he was *not* going to be aching in every limb, and that he was *not* going to have to hope he could get into shelter while he could still feel his fingers. There were plenty of complaints about the uniforms. Mags could scarcely imagine why. Maybe they didn't fit like the sleek clothing he had glimpsed on some of the highborn of the Court, but for his part, he could see nothing wrong with them.

For the first time ever, he slept in a real bed. A warm bed, in a warm room that was all his own. He slept long and soundly, didn't wake shivering, didn't have to decide what part of him he was going to leave out to be chilled. And if he had to clean his own room, so what? At least he had a room to clean, and if it was a mess, he had only himself to blame.

And what did he have to do to earn all this? Merely learn. So if this *wasn't* a heavenly afterlife, he didn't much care what befell him after he was dead, because the here and now was just fine. And that brought him to *what* he was to learn, which was not just the school lessons, but the other things. He could hardly believe he had been asked to help some of the other Trainees who were struggling with riding — or that the Weaponsmaster wanted him to help those who were still trying to get beyond hitting the pells with sticks.

From the sounds of things, the complainers were saddling up to go out on riding practice themselves. Which is what Mags should be doing soon . . . could have been doing now, except on the whole he preferred to practice alone, and the instructor was inclined to let him now. The instructor was really there for those who had never been on a horse in their lives. Once you got past being afraid to fall off with every step, unless your *Companion* needed instruction in war maneuvers, if you wanted, you were left alone to practice at your own pace. That suited Mags. He sensed that some of the others wondered why he was so slow to make friends, but there was no way he could explain it to them, and he didn't want to try. They would never understand.

Truly, he still didn't know quite why he and Lena got on so well. It made no sense at all, really. There could not possibly be two people in this world as different as he and the little Bardic Trainee, and yet here they were, inexplicably friends.

Friends . . . that was another thing he had never, in his whole life, had before. Not a real friend.

The sounds of hoofbeats leaving the stable let him know that the others were leaving. And he might as well give up trying to sleep anymore. Besides, he needed to get Dallen saddled; Lena was coming for a ride.

He wondered what it was that thrilled her so much about riding Dallen. Without the kind of mindlink that he and Dallen had, it was really not much different from riding a superbly trained horse, and he *knew* she must have had plenty of opportunity to do that. From everything she had told him about her family, they were at least as well-off as the Pieters were. So what was it? Was it just the mystique of the Companions? Or despite not having Mindspeech, could she still sense something about him that was out of the ordinary?

:Of course she can. I am a magnificent creature. Just ask me.:

Mags had to chuckle at that. *:I don't have to ask you,:* he replied. *:You'll be sure and tell me every chance you get.:*

He was wide awake at this point, and there was no use in trying to drowse anymore. He got up, expecting to find the stable empty of anything but Companions, and nearly ran right into a Herald.

The man scowled at him. He had the tightest shields Mags had ever seen; to Mags' extra senses he wasn't even there. Mags stammered an apology, feeling the blood draining from his face.

"What are you doing here, Trainee?" the man barked.

"I . . . I live here, sir," Mags faltered.

"Here? In the *stable?*" The man stared at him as if he suspected Mags of lying.

"Aye, sir." Mags waved in the direction of the open door. "There, sir."

The Herald glanced briefly inside. "Who told you that you could live out here alone?" he replied, not at all mollified by Mags' answer.

"Herald Caelen, sir." He tried to will himself smaller. Maybe if he looked insignificant enough, the man would leave him alone.

"And he sent you out here to live alone." The man was getting red in the face. When Master Cole got red in the face, someone ended up beaten. "Why?"

"There wasn't enough room in the Collegium, sir." Dallen stirred restlessly in his loose-box and snorted.

"Without adult supervision." Now the

tone of voice was a growl.

"I gots me Companion, sir," Mags whispered. " 'S Dallen, sir. He's growed."

The man sneered. "Oh, surely. Who is your mentor?"

"I don't . . . got one. Sir." Mags was having a hard time breathing now. "Herald Jakyr, he brung me, but he's off —"

"Doing something important, no doubt." Still a growl, but one full of contempt. Mags did not look up to try and read the man's face. He stared as hard as he could at his toes. "Leaving you here to frolic about without discipline. No doubt you've got stolen spirits in there, and you are carrying on with serving wenches all night long!"

Dallen's hooves drummed angrily on the dirt of the stall floor.

"No, sir," Mags choked out. "I don't got no drink in there. An' nothin' else neither. I dunno any servin' wenches."

But by now, the Herald had warmed to his subject. He reached out and grabbed both Mags' shoulders and shook them until Mags' teeth rattled. "Tell me the truth, curse you! I'll have it out of you if —"

Before the man could finish the sentence, he was suddenly pushed aside abruptly, shouldered into the wall by Dallen, who shoved in between them.

:*Go back into your room until I say to come out, Chosen,*: Dallen said calmly. :*I will deal with this.*:

Mags was not at all averse to following Dallen's orders. In fact, he fled into the safety of his room, and threw the bolt on the door. Then thinking better of that action, he unlocked it almost immediately, wedged himself into the farthest corner of the room, and sat there staring at the door.

Shortly afterward, he heard more voices, speaking too quietly for him to make out what they were saying. The tone was low and urgent — or in the case of the strange Herald, low and angry. Eventually, he heard footsteps going away.

:*You can come out now, Mags. They've gone.*:

Coming out was the last thing that Mags wanted to do right now, but Dallen seemed to expect it of him, and so with great reluctance he picked himself up off the floor and walked over to the door and opened it again. The stables were empty of everything but Dallen and a couple of Companions in far-off stalls, studiously trying to look disinterested.

:*That is one of the Heralds who does not like the new Collegium organization,*: Dallen said calmly. :*I made it known that he had laid*

*hands on you, and the circumstances, and
some of his peers came to make him understand that he was* quite *out of line with his
accusations.:*

Mags shook his head. He was too shaken
to be able to think clearly. He felt as if he
had been flung right back into his old life,
and it made him sick inside.

*:Mags, you just got caught between a man's
anger at what he thinks is a ruinous idea and
his inability to convince those who have put
that idea in motion. He wasn't thinking.:*

Mags controlled his shaking as he saddled
Dallen and heaved himself up into place. *:It
felt like I was 'bout to get a beatin'. Just like it
used t' be:*

Dallen did *not* say, "Oh, he would never
have beaten you," for which Mags was
grateful. The truth was, he would not have
put it past that Herald to at least hit him,
and Dallen was honest enough to acknowl-
edge that.

Which actually made Mags feel a little
better. At least Dallen wasn't trying to lie to
him. That would have made things worse.

*:I am sure, absolutely sure, that all the man
meant to do was frighten you. He is short-
tempered at the best of times, and I do not
believe it was in his mind to hurt you. He is
not used to someone like you. He is more*

used to the sort of youngling who would take apart a cart and reassemble it in someone's room for fun.:

Mags wondered briefly why that would be "fun" but could not be distracted. "I thought Heralds was supposed t' look out for each other," he said plaintively aloud, realizing after a moment that the sick feeling in his stomach was *betrayal.* Dallen had told him he could trust anyone in Whites.

:Try to understand, Mags. He did not mean to hurt you. He . . . : Dallen paused. *:He would not thank me for saying this, but the truth is that he, and the Heralds that think like him, are afraid.:*

:Afraid!: Mags could scarcely believe that, and his surprise brought Dallen to a complete halt. *:Afraid! I can't hardly b'lieve that! Afraid of what?:*

:Change.: Dallen's flanks under his legs heaved in a huge sigh. *:This is an enormous change in how Trainees are turned into Heralds. They are used to seeing four or five new Trainees come in over the course of a year — suddenly there are more than sixty of you, counting the ones out with mentors. It is an enormous change, and the challenge is that it is not possible for every Herald to personally know every other Herald now. And it never will be again. In his heart, he knows that he*

never will be able to say "I know Herald So-and-so is trustworthy because he is my personal friend." Now he will have to take it on faith because he is another Herald. This changes everything, and the only way he thinks he can be absolutely sure that these new Trainees will be as good as he and his friends are, is to insist that they be under the eyes of himself or one of his friends during their training period.: Dallen started up again at a walk, and Mags scented snow in the air. *:He doesn't have Mindspeech. He can't talk to his Companion. And he doesn't much like people your age.:*

"We're even, then, 'cause I don't much like him," Mags muttered.

:And that is exactly the difficulty for him. There are people he does not much like who are essentially being forced on him by circumstances, and —:

"— and don' think ye can make me feel sorry for 'im," Mags interrupted aloud. " 'Cause I won't."

Again, Dallen's sides heaved with a sigh. *:All right. I won't.:*

He moved from a walk into a canter, and then into a gallop, and began taking jumps. After that, Mags had plenty to think about other than his recent fright.

Following a good workout, they reported

to the stable again where Mags helped Lyr with his seat, and from there, after giving Dallen a good rubdown, Mags went to weapons practice.

The practices were always a mixed lot of Heralds, Bards, Healers, and others. But today there was a knot of young men Mags did not recognize, in clothing that looked rather different from that of the others, and not just in color. The cut was different; the tunics were shorter, and had high collars and an odd side-closing to them. The others were all a-buzz about the newcomers, but no one seemed to know who they were. The Weaponsmaster put an end to the mystery.

"These young gentlemen are the escort for several foreign merchants that have come to negotiate with the King," he said, putting an end to the buzz. "They requested to be allowed to work out and practice among you, and the King has granted that request. They are to be treated no differently than one of you. Now, let's get loosened up."

As the Weaponsmaster ran them through their exercises, Mags was not alone in watching the young men covertly. They moved, he noticed, like the strongest of the feral cats that had prowled the yards and outbuildings at the mine. Very secure in their strength, restless, but with a wary eye on everything around them. And when the Weaponsmaster paired them up with the most skilled, they enjoyed the fighting in a way that Mags had not encountered before. Actually, it was not the fighting they enjoyed — it was *defeating* that brought them great pleasure. They reveled in it, exchanging glances of triumph with each other. And although they said very little, Mags began to note that they were taking pains to bring down their opponents in the most humiliating fashions possible. They disarmed opponents so energetically that weapons skittered halfway across the salle. They delivered blows that left their opponent sprawled out on his face or landing on his backside. One of them even "accidentally" got in a hit on a young Guardsman's groin that left him gasping and unable to speak, tears of pain flowing from his eyes — and *he* had been wearing a hardened codpiece for protection!

He'd seen this before . . . though the Pieters boys were nothing like as graceful as these guards.

Finally after that last incident, the Weaponsmaster paired them off with each other, saying nothing more than, "You are too skilled for my students. I'll have to find you better partners."

Just being around them made Mags feel sick and shaken, especially after the kind of day he had been having. He finally excused himself and, with the Weaponsmaster's permission, headed back toward his stable room.

He got about halfway when he heard footsteps creaking in the snow behind him. With a feeling of dread, he turned and found three of them trailing him. They looked him up and down; he was reminded forcibly of the Pieters boys again.

"C'n I show you where ye need t' go?" he said, mouth dry.

"We were seeing you training the others, and wondered why your teacher did not pair you with one of us," said the nearest. "We would like to test your mettle." He had very cold blue eyes, Mags noticed, and black hair. An odd combination. The other two, more nondescript, shifted restlessly from side to side, the snow creaking under their boots.

"I druther not," he replied, his heart starting to pound.

"But I do not think you have a choice," said the other. "It is not . . . hospitable."

They moved in on him. They did not rush him, but there was no doubt, based on their grins, that they had decided he was a coward, and it would be fun to knock him about a bit.

But Mags had learned long ago the means of fighting back without actually fighting at all, and as they grabbed for him, their hands closed on nothing more than air. He was good at this. He could judge their reach to a hair, and he moved only enough to keep out of their way. He made sure to position himself each time so that they actually hindered and ran into each other. Not that he wasn't afraid, because he very much was. There was a bitter taste in the back of his throat, and it felt as if his heart was going to pound right out of his chest.

Time and time again, the same scene played out. They would try to lay hands on him, or even deliver some kind of blow; he would evade hands and blows alike, without ever seeming to move much. Each time, he left a hand or an arm out temptingly for them, hoping that one or more of them would lunge after it. Finally, the tallest of them grew tired of the game, and *did* make a rush at him. This time he not only evaded being seized, but with what looked like a gentle brush of his hands, landed the for-eigner several arm lengths away, facedown in the snow. What he had actually done was to lure the attacker off-balance, and then, while the young man was still off-balance, continued him in that direction with the slightest of shoves.

He came up, not spluttering as Mags had expected, but angry — and disgusted.

"Bah!" he said, wiping melting snow from his face. "He is cheating, using one of their White Rider magic tricks. There is no point to this."

And with that, just as abruptly as they had begun their attacks, they broke it all off. They turned their backs on him, stalking toward the Palace, leaving Mags to stare after them, numb and shaking.

11

The Herald that had attacked Mags left him alone — and then left altogether, out on circuit.

Why this had come about, Mags did not know. Dallen was silent on the subject. But Mags could not help but notice the occasional careful stare at him that other Heralds did not hide. He was not able to sense any menace, but . . . there was not much doubt in his mind that these Heralds, if they did not actually blame him for their colleague's abrupt departure, were certain that the "encounter" was the cause.

He was not quite sure what to make of that, but he did know what felt most comfortable, and that was to make himself even less noticeable, if that was possible, than before.

The mercenary bodyguards were still in residence, and still showed up at the salle, but the Weaponsmaster made sure to allow them to pair only with each other or with Guardsmen at least as skilled as they were. Mags kept a wary eye on them when they were there, but avoided them whenever it was possible. Dallen came to get him from the salle now, so even if all of them had tried to swarm him at once, it would not have been possible to touch him without causing a serious incident. Laying violent hands on a Companion inside the Palace grounds — No matter what anyone thought of Mags, no one would stand for Dallen being threatened. They must have known that, since there were no further incidents involving *him.*

But aside from his teachers, no one really seemed to know what to make of him. He still kept very much to himself, and although no one was unfriendly, the other Trainees seemed inclined to keep him at as much of a distance as he kept them. Word of his confrontation with the older Herald had spread out to the general population of the Collegia, and Mags suspected there were plenty of wild rumors about what had caused it. The man's abrupt departure did nothing to quell those rumors, since as a rule, one was allowed a minimum of a month between circuits. No one ever told him what those rumors were, but it was obvious from the way people looked at him that they must range from near truth to wildly unlikely. He shrank from those looks.

Lena was his only human friend, although living in the stable and being as strong a Mindspeaker as he was, he had made friends with several as-yet-unpartnered Companions. He would happily have stayed out in the stable all day, but he was required to attend his classes. Outside of those, however, he scarcely left the building except to eat, and he had contemplated asking Lena to bring him food to be heated in the stable ovens when she decided to take matters into her own hands.

He knew he was in for — something — when he heard how she was walking as she came up behind him. There was determination in her step, and as he brushed out Dallen's mane — unnecessarily, since it was already as silky and tangle-free as a pampered girl's hair — she seized his elbow.

"There is someone I want you to meet," she said abruptly. "So come on!"

"But —" he began, but there was no stopping her in this mood. She marched him out into the snowfall. There was another snowstorm just starting, not a violent one, but from the way the fat flakes were drifting down through the air, and the look of the sky, it was going to pile up deeply before it was over. He found himself hoping that it would be *so* deep that classes would be canceled and he could spend the whole day reading alone in his warm, safe room.

Well, Lena was not going to let him do that just yet; this much was clear.

She pulled him along the path that led, not to Heraldic or Bardic Collegium, but to Healers'. Alarmed at what this might mean, he began resisting. "Lena — just 'cause I don' like t' mingle with folk, that don' mean I need a Healer!" he exclaimed. "Serious, now, I'm fine —"

To his intense relief, although she kept tugging, she giggled. "Silly! I'm not taking you to a Healer for *you,* I want you to meet my friend Bear!"

"Bear?" *Bear?* Who would name someone that? And why? The name conjured up a big man, intimidating, fierce and frowning. Dangerous. He must have a temper. Why did Lena want him to meet such a person? It would be worse than —

"Bear!" Lena called, waving her free hand. The figure bent over some dormant rosemary plants, all huddled in a green cloak, straightened and peered at them through the falling flakes.

And every bit of Mags' apprehension

melted like those snowflakes falling on the hot brick of the ovens.

This young man, with a pair of ground-glass lenses perched on his nose, could not be less imposing. He was a little taller than Mags, and looked to be about a year older, and he did indeed look like a bear — but a sleepy, affable bear, with a round face, untidy short brown hair, small but friendly eyes, a pug nose, and a generous mouth that looked as if it smiled often. He stood with a little bit of a stoop, as if he spent a lot of time hunched over. When he smiled at Lena, Mags had to smile back. There could not have been a sweeter smile in all three Collegia.

"I was just making sure the rosemary was going to be all right," he explained to Lena, and looking over at Mags, made him feel welcome with the same smile. "So this is Mags? It must be interesting to be a Mind-speaker. Some of the Healers here are, too."

Bear didn't give Mags a chance to reply to that.

"Come on inside," he said instead. "Lena said she would help me with studying the same things she's helping you with. I arranged to have some supper brought up to my rooms, so we won't have to go out in the cold."

Rooms? At a time when the Heraldic and Bardic Trainees were practically being stacked like cordwood, this young fellow had more than one room to himself? Mags blinked, but he followed the other two inside quietly. They went up four steps to a separate entrance from the rest of the Collegium and the areas for the sick and injured and stepped inside.

And Mags immediately felt like a fool. For the "rooms" were actually a greenhouse with panes of thick, wavy glass, each about the size of his hand and leaded together into a floor-to-ceiling window facing south and a glass roof, with pots and pots of plants everywhere they could catch the light, and two small rooms off it, one of which was clearly used for dealing with the plants. It was very warm and cozy in here, and Mags wondered if it was heated, as his room was, by a big oven built into the wall. . . .

"Fire's below," Bear explained, with a smile and a shrug. "Knew you'd ask, everyone does. Furnace's below, heats the floor, then the hot air and smoke goes up through flues in that wall." He pointed to the back wall shared by both small rooms. "There's some herbs has got to be fresh to use, so we grow 'em here all year."

"Except no one could get them to grow in

winter until Bear came," Lena put in, eyes dancing. "That's what you never tell anyone, Bear!"

Bear just shrugged. "Someone used to, or these rooms wouldn't be here," he pointed out logically. "Stands to reason. Anyway, it isn't a Gift or anything of the sort, I just am careful with 'em, make sure I know what they need, and make sure they get it. Easy. Anybody could do it. Only, I don't have a Gift, you see, so I've got to have the knack for taking care of these little beauties, 'cause that's how I Heal folks."

He gestured at the back of the greenhouse room, where a rough wooden table had been set with three places; a basket of bread and a bubbling pot over a coal brazier waited. "Lena, you said you wanted to try this, so I asked Cook to help me make it up." He grinned. "I think you're gonna like it."

"It," when Mags peered curiously at the pot, was a softly bubbling concoction, much thicker than gravy, of a creamy yellow. Bear sat them all down around the pot, picked up one of the rolls, tore it in half, and dipped the end in. "Careful, it's real hot," Bear cautioned, blowing on the end, as Mags and Lena followed his example. Bear was not exaggerating, it was hot enough as he dipped his bread that he was certain a drop of it would probably raise a blister.

"It" turned out to be melted cheese. But . . . such melted cheese! There was a slight bitterness to it that was not at all unpleasant, and a suggestion of herbs and beer. It was so very good that it made him impatient for the stuff to cool on his bread, and it was pretty clear from the way that dainty little Lena was tucking in that she felt the same. Nor was Bear at all behind. And when they were done and he took the pot off the coal, there was a nice crust of cheese that he lifted out with a knife and divided among the three of them that added a crunchy finale to the feast.

"Oh, that was so good!" Lena sighed.

"Even better when the pot's on the hearth," Bear said complacently, dumping a mug of water on the coal. Now Mags saw he had improvised a stand with a wrought-iron pot stand of the sort that were raising pots above the ones in front of them so all the plants could get sun. "Sometimes we make it with white wine, 'stead of beer —"

It looked as if he was about to wax eloquent on this dish, when there was a knock on the door. Without waiting for an answer, the knocker opened the door. Ignoring Lena and Mags, he addressed Bear.

Mags could not even begin to follow the question, but Bear, who must have been twenty years this man's junior, listened and nodded, then went to the workbench in one of the two smaller rooms and began to take things from various jars. He also came back out for a few leaves from a couple of the live plants. All these things he ground together, then presented the results to the Healer who had interrupted them. The latter took the jar with thanks and hurried back out again.

Bear seemed to take this as a given sort of thing, but Mags was amazed. He grew even more amazed as the evening of studying went on. Bear was just as clueless about history as Mags was . . . but four more times that night, full Healers, many years Bear's senior, interrupted them to ask for some herbal remedy or other. After the third time, Bear turned to them both and shrugged ruefully. "See, now," he said. "This's why I didn't want to study over there at the library, you ken? It's like this about every night."

Mags studied him a moment. "Kin I ask somethin'?"

Bear grinned. "I got no secrets."

Somehow, Mags was sure that was nothing more nor less than the literal truth.

"How come you got all these people comin' t' ye for yarbs, when they kin — y' know — just *Heal.*" That was what was baffling him. There was no reason, so far as he could see, for anyone to be messing about with leaves when all they needed to do was put their hands on someone and will them better.

"Well," Bear said slowly. "There's folks as don't *want* a Healer muckin' about with 'em like that. "I know it don't make sense, but that's how they feel and they feel pretty strong. Then there's stuff that don't respond real good to that kind of Healing. Herbs and medicines actually work better and faster. And sometimes, you just gotta have both. Which is a good thing." He shrugged, with a rueful grin. "See, my whole family is Healers. Every one of them. They all have the Gift but me, and I wanted to be a Healer *bad,* so I started learning this stuff. Big thing I can learn here, besides cures I didn't have the books for at home, is cuttin' and stitchin' and bonesettin'. You *got* to have those even if you got a Gift. And if you don't — you can still do stuff someone with a Gift can't. You know?"

Mags didn't, but he was willing to take Bear's word for it.

Despite the interruptions, they got some

good study in. Bear kept them all going with kettles of herb teas with subtle flavors, and when he finally bid them good night, he gave them a final cup of something that tasted like nothing so much as summer.

"You get into bed soon, now, 'cause that'll put you to sleep right fast," he advised with a smile, as they went out into the still-falling snow.

The falling snow reflected all the light from all the buildings around them, so that the air itself seemed to glow faintly. As they trudged through the new-fallen stuff, Mags scratched his head. "How'd you an' him —" he began.

"He was looking for a tutor, and they recommended me," she said modestly. "But then we realized we have a lot in common."

"Uh . . . you do?" Mags couldn't imagine how.

"Of course." Lena sighed. "People expect really big things from both of us."

"Oh," he replied, feeling stunned that he had not realized this. Of course. He already knew how she felt about those expectations. Sometimes he found her almost sick with anxiety over it.

It was at that moment that he realized how much she must envy him. Not just having a Companion; she would love that, of course.

But because no one expected *anything* of him. For that matter, they appeared surprised when he actually accomplished something.

Poor Lena. He couldn't imagine how it must be to be her, with everyone watching her all the time. And by extension — poor Bear.

"It don't seem fair," he said at last, and got a grateful smile from her. "Not to neither of ye. Well, I guess I can put up with bein' interrupted if you want to be helpin' both of us."

By that point, they had reached Bardic Collegium. "I do, and that would be wonderful, Mags!" She exclaimed. "And I'll see you tomorrow."

She scampered through the snow and disappeared into the building, leaving him to trudge through the stuff to the stables, feeling oddly warm inside.

There was a growing sense of anticipation in the Collegia, though for the life of him, Mags could not imagine why. He overheard whispered questions in class — *"Where are you going for Midwinter"* and *"Did you get your Midwinter present for so-and-so yet?"* But none of these questions made any sense to him. Midwinter was only the shortest day of the year; there was nothing special about it. At least, there had not been, in his world — not unless a blizzard had locked the kiddies in the barn, which was hardly a cause for celebration, since the only way they would get food would be if they dug themselves a way to the kitchen.

He didn't like to ask questions, though. It would only draw attention to himself, attention that he did not want. He thought about asking Lena or Bear, but examinations were scheduled, and all three of them were studying very hard for them. Lena scarcely even came by the stable to see Dallen.

It didn't occur to him to ask Dallen until the Companion finally volunteered the answer himself. Two of the Bardic Trainees in his History class were whispering rather urgently together about presents while the instructor's back was turned, and he almost turned to ask them what they were going on about, when Dallen spoke up in his mind.

:Midwinter holidays are a fortnight long, which is long enough for most of the Trainees to go home for a visit,: Dallen said. *:For most of Valdemar, Midwinter is a big celebration, with a feast on Midwinter's Day and a party on Midwinter's Eve.:* With that, came a series of images that made Mags blink and then

feel a surge of raw envy. No wonder everyone was excited! And then, he immediately felt the heavy hand of melancholy bow his shoulders. The more he was around the regular Trainees, the more he realized just how much he didn't have. Not things; he didn't need things — he never went hungry, never went cold, and all the things he was learning! How could he ever want more than that?

But family and home — he had Dallen, of course, and he would rather die than lose Dallen — but that was all. He had never known before that family could be a good, even a wonderful, thing. Certainly the Pieterses were . . . well, the only thing he imagined Cole Pieters feeling about his children was that they were adequate additions to his workforce. But these pictures that Dallen showed him — things and stories that Bear and Lena had told him —

And he had no one. His throat ached a little.

:Are Bear and Lena going home?: he asked, a further sinking feeling coming over him. They would, of course, how could they not? If this was a time when families made a point of drawing together, then they must go home. Leaving him alone here.

:I'm afraid so. And I am afraid it has not oc-

curred to either of them that you are staying here.: Dallen said apologetically, then added, *:But Jakyr will be here; I expect him in the next few days. So there will be one familiar face at least.:*

It didn't help much, but he decided to put a brave face on it. They were his friends, after all. And Midwinter seemed to mean a season of giving. *:Should I do something about Midwinter presents for them, then?:* he asked, wondering where he was going to get the means to produce such a thing. In the past, the only presents he'd had to give were the grass shoes he wove, or a bit of food. He couldn't give food, and why would anyone want his grass shoes?

But Dallen seemed prepared for the question, and had an answer ready, *:Yes, but leave that to me. I'll manage it, and it will be from both of us. They will like that.:*

Mags blinked, but accepted the assurance at face value. After all, it wasn't as if Dallen hadn't managed seemingly impossible things before. Sometimes he wondered if the Companion was ever surprised by anything.

So he forgot about it until after Weapons class. When he returned to the stable, Dallen called to him, with mind and with a stamp of his forehoof. *:Mags, if you are not* *busy, I need you to come here a moment, would you?:*

Obediently, he went straight to Dallen's stall. The Companion nudged him affectionately with his nose, as he reached out to scratch Dallen's soft ears. *:Come in here, please. I need you to comb out my mane and tail and be very careful. Gather up as many of the hairs as come out as you can, don't stretch or damage them, keep them straight. I'm going to concentrate very hard on shedding some.:*

Baffled by the odd request, Mags did as he was told. Surprisingly enough, when he was done, he had a skein of silvery hairs the size of a thick rope.

:Now take that into your room, and we'll get to work.:

Even more puzzled by now, Mags retreated to the warmth of his room. Dallen instructed him to sit down at his desk, and light the lamp he normally used for studying by. The loose bundle of hair rested beside his right hand; the hairs seemed to shimmer in the light.

:Now . . . I would like you to relax. And let me have your hands. Just — don't think about anything, just concentrate on watching. All right? This is a bit like when I was keeping you calm, except that it is all physical.:

264

Now completely puzzled, all that Mags could do was to sit there and try not to think at all. And when his hands started to move all by themselves, he fought down a brief moment of panic, then suppressed the urge to make them stop, and just . . . watched.

Watched as those hands selected a neat little bunch of Dallen's hairs, watched as they moved deftly and surely, swiftly turning those hairs into a braid, then turning the braid into a bracelet.

Only then did he realize what it was that Dallen was doing. Dallen had the skill to do this, but not the hands — obviously a Companion couldn't finger-weave like this with hooves. He had the hands, but not the skill, although he was deft enough in weaving grasses. This was another skill entirely, and Dallen was a master of it. He watched in fascination as the intricate braid formed under his fingers.

When the bracelet was done, the hands set it aside, then started another braid. This one was much longer. One end terminated in a loop, the other in a fancy knot that was just big enough it couldn't slip through the loop. :*There are a lot of things Bear can use this for, but I think he will decide it should be a bookstrap. He was looking for one the other*

265

day,: Dallen explained, as Mags' hands got to work on something new, this time a round braid, rather than a flat one, which also terminated in a knot and a loop. Then Mags' hands made a second. *:For Jakyr. Jesses for a hawk. He's a falconer; he keeps a peregrine here in the Royal Mews. These are good jesses; if the bird should escape, he can pick them free of the bracelets and not get tangled in a tree.:*

Mags blinked at the images he got from Dallen. Falconers carried birds of prey out into the woods and fields, set them free, and flushed game for them to take down. It was so strange to him that he could hardly encompass it. He had seen hawks in the sky, of course, but cooped up in the mine all day, he had never known what they did or ate, and never knew you could train them to hunt for you. It looked altogether exciting.

"I'd like t' learn how t' do that for myself," he said aloud, as Dallen released control of his hands, and he flexed them.

:I will be happy to teach you.: Dallen's mental voice was both satisfied and relieved. *:But in the meanwhile you should go and get some fancy paper and perhaps some ribbon. Go and talk to the Guard Quartermaster, I am sure he can tell you where to find such things,*

assuming he has not got some himself.:

In fact, the man did have such things, being accustomed to supplying them for his own troops. Such small items as Mags had made could easily be folded into bits of scrap paper left over from the wrapping of larger gifts, and the Quartermaster had no objection to simply giving the scraps away.

By the time the usual study hour came around, Mags had two little packets, neatly tied with bits of blue ribbon. He tucked them into his pocket, picked up his books, and when he arrived, simply presented the gifts to Lena and Bear, ducking his head to hide the sudden blush.

"From me an' Dallen," he said as Lena took hers with thanks and Bear beamed at him. "Jest little things. We made 'em. Hope ye don't mind."

"Oh, *Mags!*" Lena exclaimed with delight. "This isn't a little thing! Do you know how many people would pay anything just to have a Companion-hair bracelet?"

Before Mags could say that no, he had no idea, Bear had already unwrapped his gift, thriftily setting aside the paper and ribbon. "Mags!" he exclaimed with glee. "This is just the thing for a bookstrap! No more dropping books all over for me! How did you know I was looking for one?" He exam-

267

ined the beautifully braided strap carefully. "You did this yourself? You dog, when did you find time?"

Mags decided not to tell him it had only taken the afternoon.

:*I think our little presents are a success,*: Dallen observed with pleasure.

"You tell Dallen I think he's a star for letting you steal his hair," Bear continued, running the strap through his fingers with an expression of bliss. "My brothers are gonna hate me. None of *them* have a Companion-hair bookstrap!"

Now the gifts were nice, and Mags was very proud of the weaving, but he couldn't think why they were both making such a fuss over the presents.

:*It is because we rarely allow our hair to be given to anyone but our Chosen,*: Dallen explained to him as they all settled down to study. :*To have such a thing says that you are the great friend of both a Herald and his Companion.*:

They settled down to their studying, and at the end, when Lena and Mags were packing up their books, Bear asked, "When are you leaving, Lena?"

"Right after my last examination, which is in the morning two days from now," she said. "What about you?"

"The same! Want to travel together as far as my home? You can overnight there, it'll be cozier than some inn full of strangers." He beamed at her, and she smiled happily back. "And this way for at least part of the trip, you won't be stuck with some prune-faced old servant and have no one to talk to."

"Oh, Havens — that would be wonderful! They'll be sending Hamish, the steward, and I think he hates me. Or at least, he doesn't approve of female Bards." She shuddered. "The sour looks he gives me every time I open my mouth would curdle milk."

"We'll do it, then. You'll love my family, they're all mad about Midwinter, they'll probably hold a feast-rehearsal just for you —" Bear continued for a bit longer in this vein, then turned and said to Mags, "So when are you —"

That was when it finally occurred to both of them that Mags didn't have a family, or anywhere else to go. Lena looked stricken, and Bear flushed. Lena spoke first,

"Mags, I am so sorry. We didn't mean anything, we —"

He swallowed, and ducked his head. "Don' matter. I didn' even know what all this was about till Dallen tol' me. So it's not like I hev recollections or anything, eh?"

Lena shook her head. "No Mags, we were really thoughtless, and if we'd taken the least consideration, we would have asked if one of us could have you along."

"Pish. It don' matter. I'd 'a felt as out of place with your kin as a pig in a sheep pen." He managed a smile. It felt stiff and fake, but maybe they wouldn't notice. "Dallen says this's 'sposed to be a family time, so you don' need some stranger shovin' in where he don' fit. Anyway, you'll be back here in no time. An' I'll hev a rest from lessons! I might actually get a chance to look around. There's a mort 'o stuff I never seen before, d'ye ken?"

Lena looked unconvinced, and Bear troubled, but they didn't say anything. Well, really, what could they say? To save them further embarrassment, Mags shoved his books into his bag, making a great show of getting them in there just so. "Anyway, got an exam first thing, so I better get some sleep. See you at breakfast, then?"

He hurried out before either of them could reply.

:That was awkward.: He hadn't gotten three steps down the path before Dallen spoke ruefully in his mind.

:Aye, that,: he replied. He was feeling both sorry for them and a bit miserable himself.

Despite the promise of Jakyr's arrival, he had little confidence that the man would spend much time with him. He was, after all, a grown man and a full Herald, and had very little in common with Mags. There would be no classes and very little to occupy Mags' time during the fortnight or so when everyone would be gone. Once, that prospect would have made him quite happy, but now . . . honestly it didn't. He'd gotten used to having people around, and gotten used to actually having friends.

:Wretched, isn't it?: Dallen said wryly. *:All this time being lonely, and never knowing you were lonely, until you weren't anymore.:*

:Aye, well, I'll only be lonely for a fortnight. Reckon I can last that out.: He pushed open the door of the stable with a sigh. *:Dammit, I am gonna be happy here,:* he told Dallen abruptly. *:I got everythin' I need, an' I got you. If I cain't be happy with that, I don' deserve t' have any of it.:*

The Collegia were quiet for the first time since Mags had arrived here.

Shortly after he had waved good-bye to Lena and Bear, most of the rest of the Trainees had gone their ways as well. There were a handful still at Healers, and a couple at Bardic, but he was the only Heraldic

271

Trainee. Only the workmen remained, taking advantage of the Trainees' absence to do things it was hard to accomplish with people underfoot.

Bear and Lena had given him and Dallen Midwinter presents of their own. Bear's gift to Dallen had been a mane-and-tail comb impregnated with pennyroyal oil, which would keep flies away. His gift to Mags had been a canister full of herbal tea of his own devising; something that would help Mags sleep, but had been made to appeal to his specific taste. How he had known about the nights when Mags would be awakened by nightmares, Mags had no idea. He still dreamed of being pursued, or pursuing something that was going to hurt some unspecified person he cared for, and on those nights when Mags would wake up in a cold sweat and be unable to get back to sleep — well, this would be exactly what he needed.

Lena's gift to Mags was a long scarf of soft, gray wool; her gift to Dallen was a strange little contraption of white net that fitted closely over both ears, and was intended to keep insects out of and off them. Mags nearly choked up; it was clear that they had both put a lot of thought into their gifts.

Now they were gone, the stables were almost silent, and when Mags had awakened this morning, he decided that he was not going to get up and go to breakfast. This was supposed to be a holiday; well, he would treat it as such.

He got up long enough to brew some of that tea, though, and drink it down. It helped, perhaps, that he had been studying so hard and for so long to pass those examinations, and that now that they were over, he felt as if a heavy weight was off him. He did manage to drowse well into mid-morning, then got up, got something that might have been either an early luncheon or late breakfast from the kitchen, and then —

Then wondered what he was to do with himself. The Collegium itself was full of hammering and shouting, and was not a very peaceful place to be.

:*We are going to go into the city, Mags,*: Dallen said firmly. :*You have never seen so much as a village before. So this is what I want you to do . . . :*

By midmorning Mags was dressed in his uniform with Lena's scarf about his neck and a belt-pouch with a few sausage rolls from the kitchen in it. On Dallen's advice, he went to Herald Caelen and asked permission to visit the city; Caelen, deep in some papers that were making him frown, waved at him absentmindedly and told him to be back by sunset. And that was all there was to it.

So he mounted Dallen's saddle and they headed out the "Herald's Gate" in the walls around the Palace-Collegia complex. Mags hardly dared look at the enormous homes of the highborn, now that he knew what they were. Crowded closely together, they occupied every inch of space around the Palace, and most were decorated with banners and garlands of evergreen branches, holly, and other indications that this was a festive season. There was a great deal of coming and going, too, mostly of young children with escorting adults.

:Morning is the time for small children's parties,: Dallen informed him. *:Afternoon for those from about twelve to fifteen. Evening is for the adults and those old enough to be married. Every child and adult will attend at least one party every day during this season, and most will attend two or even three.:*

Mags stared at one of the houses, where so many tots were streaming in the front · door that it looked like a procession of ants, and blinked. *:Is that all them highborn do?:* he asked. *:Go to parties?:*

He'd never been to an actual party, unless

you counted the "feasts" that were held for the mine kiddies in order to make it look as if they were taken care of well. There had been several at the Collegium since he had arrived; he'd heard laughter and conversation from them as he had passed open doors, and took a shy glance out of the corner of his eye, but he'd not been invited. Parties looked like they were fun. Music and talking and food. And games, though he didn't think he would be any good at games. The only games he knew were gambling ones, and that was mostly from watching rather than playing.

:Oh, going to parties is very serious business for the highborn,: Dallen replied shrewdly. :First, you must make sure you are invited to the right parties. Then, you must make sure when you get there that you have brought the right sort of gift, and associate with the right people. You must seem to be having a good time, without seeming to be having too good a time, because then people might wonder what you thought you needed to prove, or if you were hiding something. Once you are with the right people, you must make certain that they are aware that you also are the right sort of person. You mustn't arrive too early, or leave too late. Your arrival should cause a stirring of interest, your departure go *unnoticed. You must talk about the right things when you are with the right sort of people, and of nothing if you happen momentarily to be stuck amongst the wrong sort. You must dance, and again, with the right people. You must not dance anything too* country, *for that is too old-fashioned:*

:What are the right sort of people?: he asked, watching the kiddies in their brightly colored clothing being shooed along like so many rainbow-hued hens by the black-clad nursemaids. Each of them wore more clothing than any six of the mine kiddies put together. Did a child really need boots, leggings, undergown, overgown, shawl and coat, plus mittens and a hat? They were so bundled up they looked like yarn balls.

:In general, people that are higher in rank than you, although there are the occasional exceptions, like an especially honored scholar, Guardsman, exceedingly wealthy merchant, or anyone else who is currently being lionized.: Dallen sounded as if he had been to one of these parties personally.

:Children, too?: Mags asked, wondering how children could possibly be expected to act like anything other than children. Granted, the mine kiddies hadn't acted like children, but the mine kiddies had incentive in the form of beatings and the loss of food

to make them forget about playing and settle down to work.

:Children, too,: Dallen replied, then added *:Usually, it is their nurses that are the ones to make sure that their charges are seen with the right people, but yes. Children, too.:*

A moment before, he had been envying them. Not now. It would be exhausting.

:Oh, and did I mention that if you are of the female persuasion you must wear a different dress to each party? Or, at least, appear to do so.:

That was sheer insanity.

:The ones old enough to marry are expected to use this season to hunt down a suitable partner among the right people,: Dallen continued. *:I have to say that I do not favor Midwinter among the highborn and the wealthy. It becomes a season of partial madness, with everyone scrambling to further themselves or their families, and almost no one getting so much as a crumb of pleasure out of it.:*

Mags blinked. *:Not real fond of them, eh?:*

Dallen snorted and bobbed his head. *:I have my reasons.:*

Whatever those reasons were, Dallen did not elaborate. Instead, he quickened his pace through the area, trotting briskly on the hard-packed snow that covered the road. Mags wondered why they had not cleared it off, then his question was answered when he saw the sled pulled by two matching chestnut mares. It was obvious then. It was better to glide on runners than try to control a wheeled vehicle as it bounced over ruts in the snow.

They passed quickly through the area where the merely wealthy lived, then the well-to-do, all of which were so much grander than the Pieters' house that Mags wished with some amusement Cole Pieters could see them. He'd have gone scarlet with anger and envy.

The farther out from the Palace they got, the more crowded the streets became, until at last, Dallen slowed down to an amble and then moved out of the way of traffic and came to a stop in an open square that was filled with what looked like open-sided tents, each tent holding one or more people with things spread out on tables before them and other people crowded around.

:Midwinter Market,: said Dallen. *:Go walk about and look. Enjoy yourself. No one will trouble you, wearing that uniform.:*

Mags dismounted, and eased himself into the crowd.

Unlike most of the people here, he was too interested in watching what the people were doing to look at what the booths held. Now, while they were engaged in trying to find gifts, they tended not to control their expressions. Some looked bored, or harried; some had the look of a person who knows exactly what he wants and is only hunting for the best possible price. Some looked worried, some uncertain. Some had a kind of serene and happy look to them. Some — rather few — bore a contented, almost lazy look. Those last, Mags thought, had probably already gotten all the gifts they needed, and were just enjoying the market itself.

Booth tenders either huddled with potential customers or cried their wares aloud. Mags ignored this for the most part, until a few words caught his ear.

". . . the finest of yellow topaz . . ."

Topaz . . . that, he had learned, was what his "yellow sparklies" had been called. Feeling a morbid interest in seeing just what became of those bits of glitter so laboriously chipped out of the rock, Mags worked his way in the direction of the voice.

He squeezed between two giggling young women to find himself abruptly at the side of an older man in a sober brown cloak, as both of them stood before what must have been a jeweler's booth. But there was just one problem with the velvet trays of rings, brooches, and necklaces. They were not what the man was claiming them to be.

His "finest yellow topaz" was inferior stuff carefully cut to hide the flaws, but Mags, who had learned to judge to a hair the stones that would get him the most bread, could spot them. And he could not help it. His mouth opened, and the words came out before he could stop them, tinged with scorn.

"Ain't so fine as all that."

The jeweler started, and glared down at him. The man who was examining the ring looked at him with interest.

"Be off with you!" the jeweler barked. "This is none of your business!"

" 'Tis if you be makin' claims that ain't stric'ly true," Mags retorted, quaking a little inside, but determined to stand his ground.

The jeweler glowered. "Go back up the hill, before I call my man —"

"Now, now, I should like to hear what the *Trainee* has to say," the man in brown interrupted, the emphasis on *Trainee* to drive the point home to the jeweler that this was not just some random boy in gray clothing. He turned to Mags. "Now why do you say that this stone is not so fine?"

"Turn her sideway, and tilt her a bit. Ye'll see the flaw. He's cut it t' hide it, but it's there. 'Tis a pretty stone, and 'tis cut well, I reckon, but 'finest,' it ain't." Mags shrugged.

"By the Havens, there it is . . ." The man stopped peering at the stone to look down at Mags. "However did you know?"

"Useter mine them things," Mags replied, and would have slipped away, had the man not detained him with a hand on his shoulder.

"Thank you, my young friend. Please stay here a moment." He turned back to the jeweler. "Now, as it happens, I like the stone and the setting, and I know my niece will as well, regardless of the flaw. "So what would be a fair price for a *flawed* stone?"

Deflated, the merchant named a price, there was a little haggling, and the merchant placed the ring in a small satin bag and handed it over in exchange for several coins.

"Now, Trainee, as you have saved me from being cheated, I would like to treat you to luncheon. Would you permit me?"

Mags gaped at him. "Ah . . . er . . ."

:It's all right, open your shields a bit and you'll see,: Dallen advised. Mags followed his suggestion, and let the man's surface thoughts wash over him for a little.

And Dallen was right; this was nothing more sinister than a kindly man who was grateful for Mags' help. And it did not hurt that Mags was a Trainee. Mags got the distinct impression that the man was getting a bit of a thrill to be around a Heraldic Trainee.

He ducked his head. "Was doin' no more than I should, sir," he said modestly. "But thankee. 'Twould be kind on ye."

The man smiled broadly and held out his hand. "Soren Mender," he said. Mags took the proffered hand and shook it.

"Trainee Mags," he replied. He liked the man's face. Seamed with wrinkles, which all looked as if they had been formed out of good humor rather than bad temper.

"Well, Trainee Mags, there is a nice little tavern just over that way —" the man pointed to Mags' right, "— and if you'll come with me, I suspect you could wrap yourself around the outside of something hot and filling."

Mags laughed. " 'Spect I could, Master Soren," he replied. "Lead on."

12

Mags was no fool. He knew very well that Master Soren could be harboring intentions that were not good toward him.

But they were going to eat in a public place, he *had* done Master Soren a favor, his own brief glimpse at the man's thoughts revealed no guile, and Dallen vouched for the man. All of these things counted for something; Dallen vouching for him counted enough that Mags felt reasonably safe.

And Soren gave him none of the signals he would have thought showed danger. They sat down, one on either side of a small table in the window, where the sun streamed warmly through the hand-sized, thick glass panes. The girl brought them hot cider, poured from the same thick pottery pitcher; Soren gave him no recommendations for food, and ordered the same when Mags asked for meat pies.

"So, you mined gemstones?" Soren asked, when the food arrived. He tilted his head to the side a little. "Aren't you rather young for that?"

Mags surprised even himself with the bitterness of his reply. "Master Cole what owned the mine reckoned th' smaller, th' better. For fittin' inter tunnels."

Soren chewed his lower lip. "I will take it that this was . . . not a good situation."

Mags hesitated. Should he tell his story to this stranger? No one had told him not to. And now that he was here, in Haven and at the Collegium, could even Cole Pieters and his friends touch him? By now they surely had figured out that he was the one who had acted as informant for *everything.* They would have to be thicker than even he thought not to have done so.

Mags nibbled thoughtfully on a bit of crust for a moment, then slowly began to tell Soren just what it was like to work for Cole Pieters. Without the murders; he was relatively certain that the Heralds would *not* want him telling about those.

And Soren had a very interesting reaction to it all. He didn't get angry, as Jakyr had, nor did he act as if it didn't matter because it hadn't happened to *him.* Instead, an expression of grave sorrow slowly moved over his face, and the more he heard, the sadder he became.

Finally, he sighed. "I wish there was a way that all this could be made up to you, and your fellows, Mags. That man stole so much from you — years of your lives that you will never get back." He shook his head mournfully.

Mags could only shrug. " 'Tis what it is," he replied.

"But I never dreamed there could be something like that going on in *Valdemar.* It . . . offends me." He paused, and Mags wondered if he should say something. Then Soren nodded his head as if deciding something. "Now that I know that they do . . . Mags, what would be a good way of keeping youngsters from falling into such places?"

Why is he asking me? Mags wondered, feeling stunned. He opened his mouth to ask that very question, but what came out was not that at all. "Mebbe you c'd do somethin' with the law," he heard himself saying. "Make it bad t' put kiddies to work or som'thin.' "

"It would have to be the 'or something,' " Soren mused aloud. "We don't want to penalize farm folk who rely on their children and extra hands. But, yes, I see your point, and I think that would be a good start." He straightened up again, and nodded decisively. "Well, my young friend, is there anything more I can do to thank you?"

Mags shook his head, blushing. "Ye went well over, feedin' me. All I did was wut I should do, aye? Bein' a Trainee an' all."

"Well, I don't need to ask you why you are still here with Midwinter Festival upon us, so . . . let me do this. If you haven't anything better to do, you are welcome to join our ongoing festivities." Soren smiled at him, but not in any kind of patronizing fashion. "We don't hold parties as such; we keep an open house, and if people are inclined and like-minded, they more-or-less form parties. Here —" He took a small card out of a pouch at his belt, borrowed a pen and ink from the taverner, and wrote out some directions in a careful hand. "Here you are," he said, handing it to Mags. "You can simply arrive, and feel free to bring a friend or friends. The only part of our celebration that is set in stone is the Midwinter Day Feast, and a Midwinter Eve ceremony. All the rest is freeform."

Mags waved the card to be sure that it was dry, and tucked it safely away. "I 'spect I'll have t' get permission," he said, feeling a great interest in seeing this "open house."

Soren nodded. "And I expect that will be no difficulty for you. All right, Trainee Mags," he said, standing up and offering his hand. "It has been a very great pleasure to be in your company, and thank you for the timely intervention —"

"Jes' a moment, Master Soren," he interrupted, suddenly thinking of something. "Kin I see th' ring again?"

With an odd glance, Soren obliged him. Using a ray of sunlight that the windows were inadvertently concentrating, he turned the stone this way and that, peering at the flaw. Finally, he turned the ring upside down and looked at it from the back.

"Ha!" he exclaimed. "Lookit yon. She looks like a bird, flyin'. That there makes it more satisfyin', eh? Still a flaw, but now turns into an asset kind of flaw."

"A bird?" Soren leaned closer, peering at the stone. "By the Havens, it does! You have helped me out twice today, my young friend, and now I am truly in your debt!"

Mags blushed again, a deeper crimson than before, and handed back the ring. "Ye won't say that if I c'n come to yer party, Master Soren," he replied with a laugh. " 'Cause I c'n eat a lot!"

Herald Caelen looked at the small piece of

stiff paper with a look of absolute astonishment on his face. "Mags . . . do you know whose address is on this card?"

Mags shrugged. "Master Soren —"

"Who is the head of the Builder's Guild, which is in charge of everything to do with the construction of buildings, and who is one of His Majesty's advisors about matters of commerce!" Herald Caelen spluttered.

Mags blinked at him. A few fortnights ago, he would have had no idea what that meant. But now? Oh, he knew all right.

"But . . . he was just wanderin' in the Midwinter Market, lookin' fer . . ." He tried to think what a flawed stone would be, to one of the people who lived in those enormous houses near the Palace. ". . . a trinket. He was a-goin' t' get cheated, an' I warned 'im."

Herald Caelen nodded. "He's the sort of man that would appreciate that. As soon as he heard you speak, he must have known that there was no way you would recognize him or his name, so there was no way that you would have done anything out of what is the 'ordinary' for you."

"Aye," Mags agreed. "I'd save anybody from bein' cheated."

"This could not be better for you and your friends from the mine." Caelen didn't rub his hands together in glee, but he came close. "Now Soren will look into your case, since he has heard about it firsthand. He'll discover that not only did you not exaggerate the conditions, you actually didn't tell everything. You said he looked sad?"

Mags nodded.

"He abhors injustice. This will jump your case to the front of the queue. Or rather —" Caelen amended, "— the case of Master Pieters and his abuses. *You* are fairly well out of it right now. I doubt you will even be called as a witness. He might not ever have had an interest in this; it could have gone to one of the ordinary Justiciars. Now, it won't. Cole Pieters and his sons might very well find themselves working as laborers — at a fair wage — in what used to be their own mine."

Mags pictured that in his own mind and found himself smiling.

Caelen paused, his face showing thought. "Let me tell you some things about Master Soren — although, given your Gift and your observational skills, you probably had figured out most of this already. He is unique among the King's advisors in that he does not have a great interest in ostentation, and I have heard rumors that he spends as much or more of his fortune on charitable efforts as he does on himself and his family. Since he doesn't make any sort of public display of his charity, these are still only rumors. I, for one, believe them, however. Because he is indifferent to social climbing and display, he seldom holds any sort of gathering except at Midwinter and Midsummer Festivals — and those, rather than being a series of parties at which it is important to be seen, are, as he told you, a sort of ongoing party, or 'open house,' to which he invites all manner of folk. Artists, writers, musicians and Bards, Healers, the highborn, priests and clerics of all sorts, philosophers and teachers — it really doesn't matter, the one common denominator is that he thinks they are interesting. As a result, despite this not being a social climber's event, there is a certain cachet to being invited. It means that Master Soren thinks you are intelligent and worth knowing. *Not* being invited, in the Palace circles, tends to carry with it the assumption that you are not very bright and uninteresting."

Master Soren thinks I am worth knowing? Mags was so astonished by this thought that he felt a little stunned.

Caelen tapped on the desk to get his attention. "Listen to me, Mags, this does not mean that you need to go to this thing prepared to entertain people with your conversation. Just be yourself, even if that means you are going to be quiet and observe as you usually do. Master Soren saw you being yourself and was impressed. So keep doing just that."

Mags blinked. "So — I should go?" he replied tentatively.

"If you want to. I think you will enjoy yourself. I believe you will be less intimidated than you think." Herald Caelen rubbed his chin a moment. "If I were in your place, I would go, and not just once. There will be all sorts of people there, plenty for you to watch and listen to."

Mags felt encouraged by the fact that Herald Caelen talked about "watching and listening" as opposed to doing any talking himself.

Then he thought of something.

"I . . ." He flushed. "I cain't. I ain't got nothin' good enough t' wear. I'd be . . . I'd make th' Collegium look bad. Like we don' care enough t' dress right."

He looked down at himself. The Trainee uniform was serviceable enough, but it had its share of places where it had been mended, and none of the others in his possession were much better. When he looked back up again, Herald Caelen was chewing his lip.

"Let me see what I can come up with," he replied, and then smiled. "I think I have an idea."

By this time it was well into the dinner hour; Mags went down to the kitchen to get something, not feeling much like eating in the dining hall. Paradoxically, it was very crowded, which might have made no sense until you realized that with the Trainees out of the way, workmen had been pulled in from all over Haven to help on the three Collegia, and part of the benefit of working over Midwinter holiday was being fed from the Palace. The food was no longer the same utilitarian fare of previous months. These workmen and -women were being treated very well to compensate for losing part of their holiday. Breakfast had meats and eggs as well as the usual bread and butter and porridge with various things that could be added to it. Luncheon was meat pies and sausage rolls, or cold sliced meat, cheese, and lots of bread and pickles and onions — the ideal sort of thing for workmen in a hurry. Dinner was generally roasts and hams — something that only happened once a week or so when the Collegia were in session — which then went to serve as the next day's luncheon. The kitchen fixed him up with a heaping plate that they put in a kind of shallow bucket with a lid on it to keep the heat in. This contrivance served very well indeed; his dinner was still piping hot when he got down to the stable.

Instead of taking it to his room, he made himself a little table and chair of a couple of bales of straw in Dallen's stall, and fell to. :Wotcher think?: he asked Dallen.

:I agree with Caelen. I think you should go. I think it is time that you experienced "fun" for yourself.:

Mags stopped with the bite on his fork halfway to his mouth. He put it down. :Wotcher mean?: he asked cautiously.

:I mean . . . you should be with people, and in a place, where you are, for once, doing something only for the pleasure of it. You did a bit of that today, going with me down to the Midwinter Market, but I would like it if you could do more of that.: Dallen nosed his hair affectionately. :You are an awfully solemn fellow. Do you know, I have never heard you laugh?:

Suddenly he felt strangely sad. :Ain't had much reason to,: he responded gruffly.

:Not even here?: Dallen heaved a huge sigh. :No, you need not answer that. You have been so busy in trying to catch up to the rest

293

of the Trainees, you have scarcely had time to breathe, much less learn how to laugh.:

Mags shrugged. :I'm . . . good,: he replied, and bit down on a butter-filled bread roll in sheer bliss. :I got you, I got the best food I ever et, good stuff t' wear, warm bed . . . I got more 'n I ever dreamed I'd get. Dunno as I need t' laugh.:

Dallen sighed again, but he said no more on the subject. Mags could tell, though, that he *wanted* to say more.

Like it's his fault I ain't like Bear an' Lena . . .

Quickly, he changed the subject, to a book he had been loaned by Caelen. Dallen seemed grateful for the change in topic. But as it happened, the book was genuinely engrossing, and Dallen knew a fair bit about the subject. Mags carried his plates back to the kitchen, then had a long, leisurely bath — something he rarely got to do. He reflected, as he soaked, on how far he had come. Bare moons ago, he had no idea that any such thing as hot baths existed. Now?

Huh . . . it's like I'm livin' in what them priests all promised us if we was good.

Mags' intention of being as lazy as possible didn't last any longer than the first day. He was just too restless to sit on his hands. He first embarked on a massive cleaning and

294

organizing of his own room. Then he went out to the salle and practiced alone against the pells. And with bow and arrow. Then again against the pells. Finally, he and Dallen rode a grueling obstacle course which left both of them sore and tired. He gave Dallen a good rubdown, got another hot bath and a change of uniform, then went looking for some food.

It was late by luncheon standards, and it looked as if a plague of rats had overrun the table where the luncheon foods were laid out. There were mostly empty plates and crumbs, although those crumbs would easily have filled up one of the smaller kiddies back at the mine. But he found pieces of cheese here and there, the ends of a couple of loaves, a forgotten piece of ham and a few hard-boiled eggs, and plenty of pickles. He felt well satisfied with his gleanings, and was about to carry it all back to his room. That was when Dallen Mindspoke him.

:Herald Caelen is looking for you. I told Peshta to tell him you would come to his office.:

Well, that was convenient. It was the first time that Dallen had done anything of the sort like that, relaying a message, but Mags could see how useful it was. He borrowed one of the baskets that had held the bread, wrapped his luncheon in the napkin that was still in it, and went on up to Caelen's office. Once again he was struck by how noisy the Collegium was, with the sounds of hammers and other tools echoing down the empty corridors.

"Mags!" the head of the Collegium greeted him, perhaps sensing his presence with some Gift or other, before he even came into view. "I told you I would sort something out about things to wear to Master Soren's Midwinter festivities, and I have. Come along, I have a stack of things for you."

Curious now, Mags hurried to do as he was requested. The office was a good bit cleaner; the number of books was at least halved. Evidently, the workmen had been putting in good progress on the Collegium library.

Herald Caelen indicated a pile of folded gray fabric on one of the chairs. "Some of our Heralds have been highborn or very wealthy, you know," he said with a smile. "And even though they are supposed to wear the same uniforms as the rest of the Trainees, you can't keep their parents from having nonregulation Grays made for them. I just canvassed the Heralds assigned to the City and those that were visiting their families here at Court until I found three sets of personally tailored Grays that I thought would fit you."

Nonregulation Grays? Mags picked up the topmost garment from the pile and the soft fabric caught a little on his rough hand. A few moons ago he wouldn't have known what these things were except soft. Now he had names for them; velvet and damask, doeskin leather, lambswool. No one looking at these Grays would mistake them for the sort worn for classes and more physical lessons; the cut was the same, and the design, but that was where the resemblance ended.

Mags had names for these fabrics, but he had never actually expected to touch any of them, much less wear them himself.

"They told me that you might as well keep these, Mags. They're never going to wear them again, and any youngling in their families that gets Chosen will have his own sets of Grays made to fit him. Or maybe I should say, 'made to fit him exactly.' The highborn never seem to run out of money for new clothing." He shook his head. "Well, everyone I went to said the same thing — they're never going to wear these, obviously, there is no point in them going to waste, so I should take them. Which is not a bad thing at all, since now I'll have some fine uniforms on hand the next time one of you Trainees needs such a thing, and with as much as I had to pick from, I was able to get you more than one change of clothing. There's a couple sets of boots there, too," the Herald added. "Yours are beginning to look a bit grim."

Well, that was true. They'd never actually matched his Grays, since they were the ones he'd gotten from the Guards, and were really "civilian" boots that had been outgrown and returned to their storerooms. And they had only fit with three pairs of stockings. Not that he was complaining. Not when, for the first time in his life, he had warm feet in the winter. Feet like his could take anything a badly fitting pair of boots could deliver, and not even feel it.

At Caelen's urging, he picked up the whole pile and carried it off to his room, not forgetting his lunch, of course. And at Dallen's insistence, once he was done eating, he put on one of the outfits. Instead of canvas tunic and trews, and heavy wool shirt, he found himself in elegant doeskin tunic and trews, and a shirt of lambswool so fine and soft it felt as if it would float. There were hose that matched the shirt, and the deerhide boots that matched the tunic fit his feet as if they had been made for him.

But they hadn't; there were subtle signs of wear on all of these things that made it clear they were second-hand. Not that he cared about a little wear. The outfit, except for the boots, was a little big, but that was easily fixed with the matching belt. When he was clothed, he turned this way and that, trying to see himself.

:*Come out, and I will show you a trick.*: Dallen sounded uncommonly merry, and Mags obliged, stepping back out into the stable and facing his Companion, who was hanging his head over the top of his stall.

:*Now look — do* this *with your mind, and* this, *and . . . there you are. Now you can look at yourself through my eyes.*:

And sure enough, he could. It startled him. He was used to seeing himself in the wall of mirrors at the salle, but now he looked . . . elegant? He looked like the sort of fellow that those mercenaries would not dare touch, for fear of reprisals. His black hair and tanned skin looked a little startling against the gray of his clothing. He straightened, and tucked a thumb in his belt, and smiled at himself.

"I wouldn' know me," he said aloud, and with that, he was looking out of his own eyes again. "Huh. That was diff'rent."

:*You look quite respectable.*:

He smiled. *:Yah, I do.:*

:So let's go to Master Soren's home.:

That startled him. *:What, now? But —:*

:We've nothing in particular to do, and he keeps a Midwinter open house as you have been told. You showed that you are not some social climber by not rushing over there at once. If he did not want you to come, he would not have invited you. So let's go.: Dallen shook his head impatiently and stamped one hoof.

Mags might have tried to argue, but he could think of no good reasons not to go. So, with a sigh, he gave in, saddled Dallen and put on the special bitless bridle that Companions wore, and the two of them trotted out into the afternoon sun.

Somewhat to Mags' relief, Master Soren did not live in one of the first-tier dwellings, the constructions that were little palaces unto themselves. His home was down in the second tier of the "merely" wealthy. It had nothing to distinguish it from the other half-timbered stone-and-plaster homes except that unlike theirs, the gate was standing wide open, there were lights in virtually every window, and the sounds of music and voices carried out to the street. There was a stone wall about the entire property, snow-topped, and within that wall the building faced on an area that was about half snow-covered garden and half paved courtyard.

As soon as Mags entered the courtyard, a servant appeared so quickly he might have materialized out of thin air. "If I may, sir?" he said politely, not to Mags, but to Dallen. "The stables are this way." Now he looked up at Mags. "Master Trainee, just go up to the door and ring; someone will be with you before the sound dies away."

Bemused, Mags dismounted; the servant did not so much as touch Dallen's bridle. He might have been escorting a dignified gentleman. Mags' first thought was that Dallen must have been eating that sort of treatment up.

:Of course I am. Shoo.:

Amused, Mags went on to the door, and rang the bell with a single pull on the strap attached to the clapper. The door flew open and another servant, even more correct than the first one, bowed slightly. "Welcome to the House of Mender, sir," the servant said, and bowed low. "How shall I announce you?"

:As Herald-trainee Mags,: Dallen prompted. *:And nod your head a little to him. And smile.:*

Mags did all these things, and the man waved him through the door, announcing at the same time in a clarion voice, "Herald-trainee Mags." There was a small entryway into which he passed, a tiny box of a room that opened up into another space that was much, much larger.

The enormous room just past the entryway was about half full of guests, but even at only half full, there must have been more than a hundred people in it. It was at least as big as the dining hall at the Collegium. It, too, had a high ceiling, two stories tall at least, and there were many windows along the wall behind Mags. The ceiling was crisscrossed with heavy black beams, from which hung garlands of evergreen branches. The pungent pine scent filled the air, added to by the spice-and-apple scent of mulled cider. The walls were white plaster and black beams just like the outside, hung with gorgeous tapestries, and there was a huge fireplace at the end opposite the door, easily big enough to roast an entire ox. Benches lined the walls with tables between; if they were all like the one nearest Mags, they were laden with things to eat and cauldrons of hot mulled cider. People seemed to sit or stand or walk about as they fancied.

Another servant took Mags' cloak as there was a little stir, and Master Soren came striding up to him, both hands extended in greeting. Today he was dressed as Mags would have expected a man of his rank and wealth to dress; in wine-colored velvet and fine linen, with a silver belt around his tunic and a silver chain around his neck.

"Mags! Welcome!" He took one of Mags' hands in both his and shook it. "Come this way, and I'll introduce you to some of my guests."

Mags followed him with some trepidation; if Master Soren took him to meet some of the King's advisors or other important people — well, he wasn't certain what he would do or say.

But Soren did nothing of the kind; instead, he brought Mags to one side of the huge fireplace where, to Mags' intense relief, there was a group of people about his age.

"Lydia, this is Mags, who found the bird in your ring. Mags, this is my niece Lydia."

Lydia, a sweet-faced girl with a tumble of intensely red curls smiled up at him, her smile warming her eyes which were as green as fine beryls. Mags saw she was wearing the ring her uncle had bought her yesterday. "That is so clever of you! But from what Uncle says, you bought your skill rather dearly. I am glad that horrible man is not going to be able to continue as he has been."

"There's a mort o' folks that're happy

about that, mistress," Mags said, with an awkward half-smile, as Master Soren moved away. So Master Soren had told his niece, at least, quite a bit about Mags. He wasn't sure whether to be pleased or otherwise. He finally decided to be pleased. It probably saved him a lot of awkwardness.

The girl smiled again, warmly. "Just Lydia. And this is Marc, Amily, Tomas, Saski, Jak, Renton, and Dia."

Mags nodded in turn to each of them, fixing their names and faces together in his mind. Fortunately, he was rather good at that, and getting better all the time. Sometimes he wondered if his memory had always been this good, and he finally decided that it had been, there had just been less for him to remember, so he hadn't noticed.

The pale young man called Tomas made a wry face. "Hope you don't think too badly of me, Lydia, nor you, Trainee Mags, but 'tis holiday season, and I had rather *not* think of tales of misery at the moment."

"And from the unease in his eyes, I suspect Mags would rather not talk about them," observed round little Dia, looking at him shrewdly from deep brown eyes.

Mags nodded, though he wasn't sure what he *could* talk about with these sleek, well-dressed young people. It wasn't as if he had a lot in common with them.

"First, have some cider to warm you." Dark Jak, whose skin was nearly as tanned as Mags', pushed a mug into his hands, and motioned him to a seat on one of the cushioned benches. "Then tell us what you know about those mercenaries that lot of merchants brought with them. You have to have seen them, since I know they are doing weapons work at the Palace salle."

He blinked, and sat down gingerly. "Well," he replied, slowly, "Aye . . . but I on'y seen them at that salle . . ."

Tomas, red-haired Marc, and Jak all nodded vigorously. All of them leaned forward eagerly.

"That's what we want to hear about." Somewhat to Mags' surprise, it was Lydia who said that, not one of the young men. "We want to hear what their fighting technique is like."

Well, there, at least, he was on solid conversational ground. Slowly and carefully, he described what he had observed; that they absolutely preferred to gang up on someone in a pack, who in that pack was weakest, who was strongest. With all of them hanging on his words, he detailed the style they used, and where it differed from what the Weaponsmaster taught, and how. They listened hard, nodded, and occasionally made intelligent comments or questions.

Finally — "That's all I c'n think of," he said, spreading his hands apologetically, then looked with surprise at the empty mug in one of them. He didn't remember drinking all of that cider.

"That's enough," Dia replied. "That's more than enough." She looked at the others. "Well?"

Marc nodded. "I think you girls can take them down."

Mags blinked. He had halfway suspected that the boys were thinking of challenging the mercenaries — but the *girls?*

Lydia gurgled a chuckle. "They'll never know what hit them. And they will be utterly humiliated."

Mags blinked again. "There a reason why yer wantin' t' do that?" he asked carefully. It seemed to him to be a very odd sort of thing to want to do. If they *knew* those arrogant young men, if one of them had been bullied by the mercenaries, that would be different. But of course, they didn't, or they wouldn't have been asking him so many questions.

They all exchanged glances. It was Jak that answered.

"These fellows that are supposed to be merchant princes," he replied. "The ones the mercenaries are guarding. They're no more merchants than my pet hound is. Princes — maybe. But why they are here — they're looking us over. Testing us. Call them spies in diplomatic clothing. They've got some of their lot testing the Heralds and the Guards to see what kind of fighters they are. But we want them to discover that if it comes to a fight, it won't be just the Heralds and the Guards that they meet."

"So we're going to challenge them," Dia said, with her little chin in the air. "And we are going to humiliate them. And they will go home knowing that they had better make peace, because they truly do not want war with us, not when the women will fight at the sides of the men, and just as fiercely."

Mags gazed at them all with enormous respect. His initial vague impression of them had just gotten an abrupt shift.

Lydia nodded, her green eyes twinkling. "And before you ask, yes, our parents know about this. And with the proviso that we *could* do this with a minimum of damage to ourselves, they agreed it was a good idea. It is one small part of a larger plan, you see."

"It was my father who saw how they were testing the Heralds and the Guards and sensed something more was going on," Jak said, motioning to a servant to bring them all more spiced cider. He waited while the servant poured, and then until the man was out of earshot, before resuming his conversation. "He came to me to find out if we thought there was anything we could do to help. And so you have it —" He spread his hands wide. "Master Soren and our parents are not at the highest level of rule — but my father says that gives them a broader scope, so to speak. They see things that the ones that sit in Council might not."

"And of course, everything *they* see and do, they consult with the King's Own about." Amily, who had been very quiet until now, spoke up in a matter-of-fact voice. She was nothing like as vibrant as Lydia or as bold as Dia; in fact, she seemed to fade into the background a bit. Even her clothing was in a subdued shade of soft brown. But when she looked up at Mags, he saw a glittering intelligence in those eyes, and he realized that the image she projected was deliberate on her part.

He shook his head. He wanted to say to them all, *I am completely out of my depth here,* but he didn't quite know how to say it.

Lydia patted his hand. "Don't worry,

Mags," she said in a kindly voice. "We've been doing this sort of thing since we were old enough to understand that we could help our parents this way. And our parents have been helping Master Soren for quite a long time. He understood that some of those who sit on the Council are there only because of birth, not brains. He went to the King's Own and offered to put together some people that could help counteract some of the blunders those folk stumbled into, or the troubles they deliberately created. And we are the second generation to follow that path." She tilted her head to the side. "And I'll tell you the truth, and that is we've been testing you, just now, to see how good your memory is, and how well you can report on things you've seen. My uncle asked you here, not because he is kind, which he is, nor because he thinks he owes you a favor, which he does, but because he thinks you are the person we need to tell us things from inside this new Heralds' Collegium."

Now Mags' head was fairly spinning. She thought he would do — what? But — how did he know this wasn't intrigue piled on top of intrigue? Granted, Dallen had said that Master Soren was all right, but how did Dallen know? If he agreed, what was he agreeing *to?*

At just that moment, the door servant's voice rang out over the crowd. *"King's Own Herald Nikolas."*

A figure clad in brilliant white with a silver belt and the crest of Valdemar embroidered on the left breast entered the room. He looked about as if he was searching for something or someone. Mags' mind raced. Could he ask the King's Own Herald about all this? Did he dare? Dallen had said that they were all Heralds, equal, together — but no, there was only the one King's Own, and he —

— and he was coming straight for them!

Amily rose, and Mags saw at that moment, the final bit of irony that the heavy skirts of her gown had concealed. She was lame, and had to use Jak's aid to get to her feet. Her right leg was twisted all wrong —

Herald Nikolas reached the group, and put both arms around Amily, embracing her and steadying her at the same time.

"Hello, my scheming darling," he said, dropping a kiss on top of Amily's head. "Have you finished terrifying the poor lad yet?"

"I've only just started," Amily said cheerfully. "Father, as I am sure you know, this is Mags, the boy from the mine, the one that uncovered that cheating merchant for Master Soren. Mags, this is my father."

The King's Own reached out and shook Mags' hand. "Good to meet you, Trainee," he said. Mags looked up at him.

If you didn't *know* he was the King's Own Herald, you would never have guessed. He had that same ability to fade into the background that his daughter had, only in his case, this was clearly a skill honed to perfection. His face was no particular shape, his hair no particular color, and his eyes were a kind of washed-out neutral. He wore his Whites with no particular air. If you had to pick him out of a crowd, you couldn't.

"I hadn't yet gotten around to telling him what you wanted out of him, Father," Amily said with a smile. "Other than that Soren thinks he can be our eyes inside the new Heralds' Collegium."

Nikolas held his daughter carefully and regarded Mags out of those unreadable eyes. "Amily has put it quite succinctly. Soren thought you might be amenable to acting as a set of eyes for us, if we told you what to look for," he said, in a soft voice that was neither high nor low. "Doing what I presume you just did for Lydia and Jak, since I am sure they quizzed you about those mercenaries. His plan was to not ask you for anything you would feel uncomfortable about. Merely observing and reporting."

The Herald paused, and Mags felt that more was coming. "Aye, go on."

Nikolas inclined his head. "But I have just been speaking with Herald Caelen, and he has a high opinion of you, Trainee. The Companion that Chose you is one of the brightest, and your Gift is strong, mature, and under remarkable control. We think you can do more than that. We think you can be an impartial set of eyes on the Heralds themselves as well as the Trainees. In fact, we think you can report to us about *all* the Trainees, as well as the Bards, and the Healers."

Mags felt as if someone had just doused him with a bucket of ice water. "M–me?" he stammered.

Nikolas nodded. "We are in odd times. Our ranks have inflated. Change is on us, and not everyone likes that change. And we do not know what the sudden increase in our numbers *means*. Historically, when many, many new Trainees are Chosen, they are going to be needed in a few years' time. Which is . . . not necessarily good. Need implies interesting times ahead."

Numbly, Mags nodded.

"Like me, people underestimate you. Because of your background, they are pleasantly surprised when you aren't a village idiot, and then think no more about you unless you impress them further. I would like to train you on ways to *remain* virtually invisible. If you are willing to help us, that is, and serve Valdemar and your King in this most peculiar fashion." Nikolas favored him with a lopsided grin. "And you can say no."

He could say no? Well that was about as wrong as it got. He knew what all this meant . . . he understood why Dallen had been sharing memories with him so much that it sometimes seemed that Dallen's memories were his, and vice versa. Dallen was catching him up on the years of growing up like a normal person did, so that he wouldn't act like an uncivilized feral cat. In fact —

No, he would ask Dallen about that later. Right now, here he was, an unknown quantity in the Collegia. He lived apart from the rest of the Trainees. He had excelled only in weapons work and riding and any sufficiently agile dunce could do that. He had no family ties, he had no ties of friendship. He was a stranger to everyone here, and he was not accustomed to the sorts of things that Valdemarans took for granted.

And the consequence of this was that Mags knew very well what Herald Nikolas was asking him. He was so much an outsider that he was the perfect observer. And yet, he was so much an insider that no one would ever suspect that he was watching everything.

Yes, he understood what was being asked of him.

And he understood why it would be impossible for him, for anyone Chosen, to refuse.

"I'm in," he heard himself saying.

And Lydia dazzled him with her smile.

13

Suddenly the two weeks of Midwinter holiday had gotten a lot more interesting. In the morning, Mags still kept up with his riding and weapon practices, and with reading things that Herald Caelen suggested to him. Then Mags went every afternoon to Master Soren's house, staying until early evening. No one who saw him would have thought he was anything other than what he seemed to be; an awkward youth, severely disadvantaged but very bright, that Soren's niece and her friends had taken under their wing. In a way, that was a part he was playing. And in a way, that was very much the truth. Dallen's shared memories made up for a lot of what he had missed by being raised as a virtual slave, but not everything. Both of them were being very careful that those memories stayed separate. It gave Mags a context for things, but those were still things that he himself had not gone through.

Lydia and her friends spent very little time on intrigue; they *were* very much enjoying the holiday, and they were doing their best to make sure he enjoyed it, too. Now that they had his consent to help them and Lydia's uncle, that seemed to be all they really needed from him for the moment. If he happened to be at the salle at the same time as the mercenaries, he would observe them as closely as he dared. Then he would come to the open house and tell them what he found out — which usually took not very much time. Other than that, since virtually everyone was gone from the three Collegia, he didn't have much to report. Which left him feeling free to enjoy the holiday as well with his new friends. Enjoying a holiday — having a holiday at all! — was a very new thing for Mags, and an unmitigated pleasure compared with all of the other new things. Although he would never want to go back to his old life, that old life was so much simpler than this one.

Well, for these few days, this new life was a bit less complex. And the things he was doing were less mentally taxing. For the first time in his life he found himself playing games.

At first, he just couldn't quite grasp the

concept of games. Doing something just for the sake of doing it? What was the point? There didn't seem to be much sense in blindfolding someone, spinning him around to disorient him, and waiting for him to catch someone and determine who it was. It made no sense, until it was done to him, that is.

And first there was the breathless, fluttering, near-fear moment when he was blinded and spun. Disorientation without actual threat — he knew they weren't going to hurt him, and suddenly the disorientation was . . . well, he didn't have a name for it. It made him feel excited, a thrill of anticipation of something good happening, and the dizziness called up the urge to do very silly things to make them laugh. Then there was standing there, in the dark, waiting to get his equilibrium back, while around him he heard breathing and giggles, and the scuff of feet on the floor. That was exciting, too — something was going to happen, and no matter what it was, the outcome was going to make no difference, so he was free to succeed or not. Free! It was like a sudden drink of strong wine! Suddenly his senses of hearing and smell seemed a thousand times more acute, his heart raced, but in a good way. For some strange reason, this was all terribly exciting in wonderful ways. Every other sense just came alive to the point that he almost didn't need his eyes. And this was *not* his Mindspeaking ability; he was keeping that heavily shielded, as Dallen had taught him, because using it would be cheating. No . . . no, this was like working in the mine, in the near-dark, when you felt your way to your place in the seam, or felt your way out, when you listened as hard as you could to see if you could overhear something useful. And when you had to rely on everything except your eyes. Except this was all good. He could win the game and they would all laugh, or he could lose it and they would all laugh, and what he did simply didn't matter, because no matter what happened, everyone would laugh. This was completely, totally good. He stood very, very still, listening. Waiting.

Then suddenly, he feinted in one direction, and as he heard the circle of youngsters scuttle to evade him, he whirled, and grabbed in the direction he had wanted to reach in the first place.

He caught an arm, and the owner stood stock still. It was female and covered in velvet, which didn't help, since all the girls were wearing velvet. She was about Lydia's height, but so was Saski. Before he had arrived, they had all been outside around a bonfire after having a mock fight with snowballs, so they all smelled faintly of woodsmoke. But he knew her by her breathing, and by the suppressed nervousness of her giggle.

"Saski," he identified at once, and with a crow of laughter, the girl whipped the blindfold off his head.

"You cheated!" she accused playfully, her gray eyes dancing as she tossed her head. "You used some Herald thing! How could you possibly tell between me and Lydia?"

He shook his head and smiled slowly. She did not really mean that he had done something wrong. This was what was called "teasing," and it was completely unbarbed and without venom. "I didn' cheat," he replied without a trace of anger. "I heerd ye giggle. Lydia's more on a chuckle."

"He has you fair and square, Saski," Tomas observed. "No point in arguing."

She made a face at them both, then waited for Tomas to tie the blindfold on her. Mags took his place in the ring and felt something odd happening to his face. Muscles he rarely used stretched, and he realized that he was not just smiling, he was grinning.

Now he had smiled a hundred thousand times more often since he had come to the

Collegium than he ever had until that moment. And that felt good. But then, as he tried to evade Saski's outstretched hands and still remain inside the ring chalked on the stone floor, he realized something else.

His heart thudded with excitement, he was smiling and he felt a strange sensation in his chest, as if something was trying to get out. Then it did get out, an odd gurgle of a noise, rusty with disuse, that he would never have recognized as a laugh in anyone else.

But it was a laugh.

He was enjoying this. He was having *fun*.

He had never had *fun* before. He still hardly understood what it was, he only knew that he was certain he was having it. Dallen's memories told him as much, but his experience made it real.

Nor was that the end of it. When the others tired of the blind-man game, they settled down for something a little quieter. They all moved to Soren Mender's library, a wonderful warm room lined with books interspersed with curios. The floor was completely covered in carpets, and besides three desks and matching chairs, there were padded benches and large cushions for sitting on beside the fire. The ceiling was much lower here, and painted all over with pictures.

That made it eminently suitable for their game. "I Spy," it was called, where one of them chose what it was he was looking at — without looking at it directly — and gave the first letter of what it was. And the rest of them would have to try and guess what it was. Now since the object could be very small indeed (like the tiny bead that had somehow rolled onto the hearth to get lodged between two of the stones) or just as large as anyone pleased (like the pictures in the ceiling!) in a room as full of so many things as the library, it was possible to go for quite some time without a correct guess. And the game kept getting put aside when someone would spot something they didn't recognize and ask Lydia about it. She always knew what it was — she had lived here most of her life — and there was generally a story about it.

And that game was *fun.* He was not the best at it, but he was not the worst by any means, it stretched his observational ability and his deductive reasoning, and it was *fun.* Lydia's stories were *fun,* too.

Master Soren did not serve regular meals at this "open house," preferring instead to have tables spread with food that was constantly renewed over the course of the afternoon and evening, rather like what was being done up at the Collegia right now. Except, of course, that the food on these tables was a cut or more above that which was being put out for the workmen and those few Trainees, Heralds, Bards, and Healers that were still here instead of going home or had not made other arrangements. Mags hardly ate anything at the Collegia now, knowing what was waiting for him when he got to Master Soren's place.

There were roast fowl, for instance, brought there so fresh from the roasting oven that their skins were crackling and still sweating golden droplets of fat — roasts of beef and pork — entire hams. These would have been perfectly delicious had they stood there long enough to grow cold, but there were so many people in and out that they never got a chance to drop below "warm."

There were plenty of breads of many kinds — the usual wheat loaves that Mags was used to, barley bread that was utterly unlike what had been served at the mine, pungent rye bread, golden egg bread, hard-crusted rolls covered in seeds, sweet bread almost as tasty as pastry.

And then there was the cheese. Mags was used to seeing two or three kinds of cheese at a time up at the Collegia (if one could say that someone who had been starved most of his life could ever "get used" to such a thing) — Master Soren served a dozen or more. And, oh, those cheeses! Mild white ones. Sharp yellow ones. Smoked cheese. Pungent cheese with veins of blue running through it. Cheese that crumbled at a touch that was meant to be sprinkled over things. Hard cheese grated and also meant to be sprinkled on things. Soft cheese meant to be spread on bread . . .

Mags loved cheese. This was heaven.

Then there were several kinds of sausage. Sliced thin hard sausage, meant to be eaten cold. Tiny sausages kept warm over candles. Sausage stuffed in pastry. Sausage on skewers with vegetables, and ground sausage stuffed into other good things.

And there were dozens of other tidbits, whole trays that got rotated out as they emptied or grew cold. Vegetables rendered into crunchy little snacks. Tiny meat pies, equally tiny egg pies. Hard boiled eggs and eggs in crust.

Then there were the sweets, an entire table of pastry alone. Cookies, tiny pies and tarts. Tiny cakes, some iced, some stuffed with candied fruits, some so rich they didn't need anything. Candied nuts, fondant balls flavored with spices, little jellies, and syrups poured over clean snow.

The drinks were just as plentiful, although none were terribly strong. Dallen had told him that very strong drink was a hallmark of some of these Midwinter parties, as was the associated intoxication. Mags was just as happy about that; when the Pieters men got drunk, things always turned out . . . ugly. Master Soren's table was meant for tasting, not gulping. There was beer and ale, mulled wine and cider, hot tea of many sorts.

What the guests didn't eat, Mags came to discover after the third day, was gathered up thriftily and delivered at the back to priests of a charitable order who in turn delivered it to the poor. Even the bones and scraps were gathered up and sent off to make soup. Master Soren had strong feelings about waste, and equally strong feelings about the obligations of those who had means to those who did not.

Small wonder he had covertly allied himself with the King's Own.

In any event, Mags was not going hungry by any stretch of the imagination, although he was missing two of the three meals served at the Collegia. In fact, Lydia had discovered a few of his favorite things and made sure that when he left to go back up the hill, he had a little basket made up with them "just in case you get hungry studying tonight." Which was a great kindness, since he *did* study nearly every night, and did get hungry doing so. It seemed as if studying was as much work as the physical practice he was doing.

Even then, when he was done studying, his day still wasn't over. When he was ready to close his books, he would let Dallen know that he was finished for the evening. And not long after that, Herald Nikolas would slip into the stable and take up yet another sort of lesson with him.

These were lessons in how to be unobtrusive, and in how to observe. Interestingly enough, the lessons in "how to be unobtrusive" were not always about being quiet. He was learning how to gauge the mood of people around him, what Nikolas called "reading the room," and when being somewhat boisterous would be more useful, how to counterfeit looking careless, devil-may-care, and utterly oblivious to what was going on around him.

He was hardly the master of any of this, of course. These were like the beginning lessons in weapons work, except this was nothing he had a special aptitude for. So it was going slowly. On the other hand . . . Herald

Nikolas appeared to feel that he was progressing well.

"I hope ye ain't disappointed in me, sir," Mags sighed one night, after repeated attempts to look as if he was more interested in examining a broom (standing in for a young lady) than his "target" had repeatedly failed.

"Not even close," Herald Nikolas replied, with a ghost of a smile. "You are no worse and no better at this than I was when I started. It is very easy to get one noticed; it is a lot harder to remain unnoticed. And you don't have to be perfect at this for a good long time. Right now, most people overlook you because you are a mere Trainee, a callow youth, because your accent and way of speaking give you away as poor and rural, and because you are inoffensive looking." He smiled slightly. "I hope you take no offense at this, but in short, you are no threat at all — in fact, you are beneath the notice of most people."

Mags nodded. He pretty much had counted on all of that to keep him out of trouble since he had gotten here. "Sir, what about m' Gift? You 'spect that I use that, too?"

That . . . troubled him. It seemed like a terrible invasion. And yet, it might be the only way to learn if someone was wearing a mask over his true thoughts.

"Sit down, Mags. I expected you would ask me this sooner or later." Mags sat down on one side of the table he used to study and eat on; the Herald sat down opposite him. Nikolas drummed his fingers on the table a moment, then scratched his upper lip with his index finger. "That is an interesting ethical question. The answer is 'sometimes.' Using Mindspeech in that way is intrusive, and you are essentially forcing other people to allow you to see what they do not want you to see. Or, if you wished to use that Gift for misdirection, you would be forcing them to see what *you* want them to see. From there it is a short step to forcing other things on them. On the other hand . . . if you should happen to be in a room full of potential enemies, and you know that they are dangerous to you — and I mean physically dangerous — you would be foolish not to use your Gift."

"So —" Mags began. Nikolas interrupted him with one of his rare smiles.

"For right now, unless something changes drastically, the answer is 'no, it would be wrong.' " The right side of his mouth quirked up in a rueful smile. "I will make a point of speaking with Herald Caelen about some more lessons I would like you to have — specifically, one which will be less a class and more a series of ethical puzzles."

Mags scratched his head. "Not sure I follow — what's a ethical puzzle?" He knew about puzzles, of course, and riddles. Those were games; he had been introduced to riddle games by his new friends. But why would you take a class in such things?

Nikolas chuckled. "Questions like you just asked me. Ethics — that is the slippery side of 'right and wrong.' Some things are very obvious, but some aren't — like when it is ethical to use your particular Gift. You are by no means the first youngling to be concerned with this sort of thing. Normally, Bards and Healers take these classes — they are confronted with the need to make ethical decisions about how to use their Gifts all the time. The Bardic Gift, for instance, is the ability to use music to influence people, make them understand or feel the song you are playing. And that can be a good thing; it causes your audience to connect with you and with the music. But if you use it to influence someone *outside* of that music — well, your result as well as your intention must be very pure indeed. So we require *all* Bards with the Gift to take this class."

Mags' brow wrinkled. "But wouldn' that

make me stand out? Thought we didn' wanta do that."

Nikolas nodded. "That is correct — but anyone with Mindspeech as strong as yours should attend these exercises, too. There will probably be at least one other Heraldic Trainee there, and maybe more, depending on whose Mindspeech is looking strong enough to need something like this. We can't disguise the strength of your Gift, since nearly everyone that is a Herald is already aware of it. The very best thing we can do, in fact, is to make it very clear that *you* are strongly aware of how it can be used and misused. And after that — we trust the Companions. As long as the Companions are sure you are still trustworthy, then you should be treated as such by every Herald, at least." He sighed. "Even if some of us are convinced that the rest of us are so wrong-headed about the founding of Heralds' Collegium that we should have our ears boxed."

Mags looked at him soberly, very much troubled. "Sir — there be *that* many Heralds bein' at odds with each other? With what's happenin'?"

Nikolas closed his eyes as if in pain and pinched the bridge of his nose between his thumb and forefinger. "That is just the problem, you see. *I don't know.* Some of them have very vocally come up and told me off to my face, but others . . . there are surely others festering in silence. And I would not care about dissent if I knew that it would result in healthy dialogue. I do not in the least mind a good argument, and I think the mere fact that the Companions are in favor of this idea should weigh heavily with those who are in dissent and will eventually sway everyone. But it is possible that some of them may be used by other people whose motives are anything but pure. We Heralds don't know everything, our Companions don't know everything, and very clever people who are good at manipulation can use people's resentment against them, and against the rest of us. I'm not out to expose or expel anyone, Mags. I just want to keep an eye on the people *around* them, so I can, I hope, head off any dangers."

He hates this, Mags realized and, obscurely, that made him feel better.

Then Nikolas looked up and smiled wanly. "And hopefully this will all prove to be the workings of my overstrained imagination and my tendency to worry about everything."

Mags nodded somberly. "Hope so, sir."

"Now, let's try that exercise again. . . ."

14

The days of the holiday flew by. What he had thought were going to be empty and lonely times turned out to be neither. When Herald Jakyr did not appear until Midwinter's Eve, Mags had actually forgotten he was supposed to come at all, and his arrival came as something of a surprise.

For once, the salle was empty. The mercenaries, so the rumor at breakfast said, had gotten into a drinking contest down in a tavern in the city. They had won — barely — but two workmen who had seen them brought back up again in a hired wagon told everyone within earshot that it was unlikely they would be moving swiftly this morning. If at all. From the condition they had been in, and the fact that they were brought up just at dawn, well, the workmen were taking bets on whether they would be seen in public at all that day.

So Mags had the salle all to himself, which

he rather liked. He'd been able to set up an archery target inside, something he rarely had a chance to do, which was a vast improvement over standing in the snow to shoot. When he had shot his required fifty arrows, and had decided that throwing knives at his current skill level was going to be hazardous to the big glass mirrors, he switched to simple exercises to round out the workout. He was working out against the pells alone when he heard someone enter the salle. He didn't look up, however, until he heard a familiar voice say, "Fancy trying your skill against me, youngling?"

And then he whipped his head around and grinned with delight. "Herald Jakyr! I —"

What he was about to say was *I forgot all about you coming,* but fortunately he stopped himself. That would be — very impolite. Jakyr weighed a practiced blade in one hand and said, with a look of embarrassment touched with a bit of apprehension, "I know you were expecting me, but I was detained. And I can't stay —"

"Well, you come at last, so I c'n give ye my little somethin'!" Mags replied happily, resolutely tightening his shields against Jakyr's thoughts. He didn't want to know what the man was thinking . . . but guilt gave them such force that a little of it leaked

through anyway. . . . *not someone else, cling-
ing to me, strangling me . . .*

"Little something? Mags, you didn't get
me a Midwinter gift —" Jakyr betrayed
more apprehension, although if he hadn't
been getting those lessons from the King's
Own, Mags probably wouldn't have seen it.
"That is really unnecessary."

"Come on, 's just a bit of nonsense, but
Dallen said ye might like it." He put up his
practice blade and headed for the door, and
Jakyr had perforce to follow. "I was makin'
stuff for m' friends for Midwinter, 'cause
Dallen said 'twas the thing to do, an' he
reckoned ye'd like these. I got two good
friends who are Trainees — ye'd laugh t'
see us — one's Healer, one's Bard." He
chattered on about Bear and Lena, and
watched Jakyr's tension slowly ease, in the
set of his hunched shoulders that straightened, and in the uncreasing of his brow. So.
Jakyr probably had delayed his arrival
because he had been afraid that Mags was
going to be . . . needy. He had assumed he
would be the only "friend" Mags had.

*Huh. Reckon I'm learnin' more than I thought
I was.* He hadn't been able to read Jakyr
nearly so well before. It had seemed that
nothing could shake Jakyr — but it appeared that beneath his façade, Jakyr was

just as fallible as anyone else. And just as human. This must be Jakyr's big flaw, that he was skittish about being tied down to anyone, afraid of demands on himself. Well, whatever his reason for that was, it wasn't Mags' to sort out.

And he still liked Jakyr, even with having "heard" that unflattering thought. But now he had a lot more sympathy for the Bard that had been his lover. If that was how the man felt about *her* — well, no wonder she was sharp with him. Being thought of as a weight around someone's neck — that was enough to make anyone angry. Especially if they were perfectly competent on their own and had no thought to make demands. It was sadly clear that Jakyr saw such things where nothing of the sort actually existed.

In Mags' case, he had not wanted Jakyr to be a father (as the man seemed to fear he did), nor a brother, nor a mentor, nor even a protector anymore. He had Dallen as a brother, he had friends — and as for a mentor, in a real sense, he had Herald Nikolas, who seemed to have appointed *himself* as mentor. As for a father, well, he had gotten this far without one. He supposed he could continue to function without one.

Protector — well, that had always been up to him, to protect himself.

:*And you have me,*: said Dallen. :*I will always protect you.*:

He smiled a little. That was no small thing. :*Aye, I have you.*:

They headed up the hard-packed snow path, the clear, bright light of a cloudless winter day making both of them squint against the glare. The buildings loomed darkly against the hard, bright sky, and with so little activity about the sound of hammering and sawing rang out in the clear air. Jakyr turned toward the Collegium; Mags had to correct him. "I got a room in th' stable, there ain't 'nuff room up there. I like it. An' it lets me be near Dallen."

Jakyr frowned and looked as if he was about to be angry. "The stable? That hardly seems . . . right. A Trainee doesn't belong in the stable, like some — stablehand."

Mags only smiled. "What ain't right is th' way they got them Trainees packed in rooms up there, like sheeps all penned up t'gether. I got privacy! Ye'll see —" By this time they were inside the stable, and half a dozen Companions beside Dallen whickered a welcome. Mags waved to all of them, then flung the door of his room open and bowed Jakyr inside.

The older Herald looked around and rolled his eyes a little. Mags was glad he had neatened it up that morning; the small window let in a lot of light, even if the panes of glass were thick and bubbly and no bigger than his hand. The thick walls kept out the drafts better than some rooms at the Collegium did at this moment, what with doors being left open, and access to the roof, too. His back wall radiated warmth, since the ovens had been pressed into use by the Palace kitchens to bake bread for the Midwinter Feasts taking place each night. His bed had been neatly made, and over the course of the last few weeks he had managed to get extra blankets, cushions, even a rug. Candles on the table, an oil lamp on the wall; not even the best rooms at the Collegium were better than this. Jakyr nodded a grudging approval. "All right, this is reasonably cozy. If things are as crowded up there as you say — I'd probably prefer this, too."

"Here," Mags said, taking the little package from the shelf where he had left it, and thrusting it at Jakyr. "Happy Midwinter, sir. Jest a liddle thing, kinda t' thank ye fer bein' persistent 'bout gettin' me outa there."

"Nonsense, it wasn't —" He opened the package and blinked. "Jesses! Aylmer jesses! And I take it this is Dallen's hair! But how did you —"

"Dallen said. Ain't much Dallen don't know about," Mags said with pardonable pride. "Him an' me, we worked t'gether on these things. Taught me t' make the braids, he did. Made page markers fer m' other friends, down th' hill. Master Soren Mender's niece an' her lot. Been spendin' most of the holiday with 'em, since Bear and Lena're gone." He did not add that the page markers were his excuse to see them and vice versa, if they needed to get information from him directly. Just undo the braiding a little, and bring it to him to fix. Or send a message asking him to bring another.

Jakyr blinked. "Soren Mender? *Councillor* Soren Mender?" At Mags' nod, he shook his head. "Lad, you are not only like the cat that lands on his feet, you are the cat which has landed on his feet in front of a bowl of cream, and had a trout leap out of the water to land beside him. Next, I'll probably learn that the King's Own has decided to be your mentor."

Mags managed not to choke. Fortunately, Jakyr was looking down at the jesses, which were round horsehair braids with a knot on one end, each about twice as long as Jakyr's hand. Mags hadn't the foggiest clue what they were for, but Jakyr seemed very taken with them.

"In any event, I was hoping you could spend the rest of the morning with me. Have you that time free?" He smiled. "Since you've been so kind as to give me these, I thought you might want to see my bird hunting." Since Jakyr looked as if he meant it, Mags nodded.

Together, they took Jakyr's falcon out for some exercise and enough hunting to satisfy her — she was more than happy to rid the Palace of a couple of pigeons — and Jakyr showed Mags how the little braided jesses worked on the falcon's legs. She had something on each leg that Jakyr called a "bracelet" that was a bit of leather with metal grommets hammered on each end. When Jakyr came to get her, she had something he called "Mews jesses" slipped through the grommets. These had a loop on the ends that was tied off to a leash. When Jakyr popped a kind of eyeless hat that he called a "hood" on her head, and picked her up, he changed these out with the ones that Mags had made.

"You see, if she decides not to come back, these will pull out of the bracelets, and they don't have a slit on them to get caught on a branch," Jakyr explained. "Once the jesses are off, she could rid herself of the bracelets, too."

He seemed unperturbed at the notion that she might not come back as he took the hood off, let her see the pigeons feeding, and sent her aloft. In less time than it took to think about it, she had struck down one of the feeding birds. Jakyr came to take her up, and she mantled her wings over her kill so that he had to move up very slowly and ease his hand under her from behind, taking her up with her kill. She seemed an aloof and bloodthirsty creature to Mags, and he said as much as Jakyr stowed the pigeon in a game bag.

Jakyr laughed at that, as he sent her in pursuit of another pigeon. "Hawks are not pets, Mags. It's a rare hawk that shows you even a morsel of affection. Generally, the best you get from them is tolerance as a hunting partner and provider of food and shelter. I never know when I cast her from my wrist if she is going to come back this time. And do you know, I don't really mind that. I know being with me has made her a better hunter. If she decides never to come back, well, that is how it goes."

She made her second kill, but now the pigeons were all scattered or in hiding.

He sent her aloft again, then looked up at the circling bird, disappointed that all the pigeons were in hiding. He took out an odd contraption of a pair of wings mounted on a stuffed form, all on the end of a long string. He began swinging it around and around his head, whistling as he did so.

The falcon folded her wings and dropped from the sky, opening them at the last minute, hoping to grab the thing. Jakyr jerked it out of the way just in time, and she shot back up into the air.

He let her make another half-dozen passes at this thing — which he called a "lure" — before fastening a bit of her last kill to it. Once more he whistled and swung the lure, once more, she dove for it, and this time he let her catch it.

She hunched over her prize, wings spread, glaring at them both. Carefully, Jakyr came in behind her and worked her and her bit of bloody pigeon back up onto his gloved hand. "So, she didn't leave, and I am her keeper for another day," Jakyr said lightly. "Or rather, the Royal Falconer is. I have an assignment and it's not somewhere I can take her."

Jakyr took his leave of Mags at the stable, just before luncheon, pressing a little bag that jingled into his hand as he did so. "I didn't have time to find you anything, so go and find what *you* want," the Herald said.

"I am not very good at getting people presents."

Mags had the shrewd notion that Jakyr hadn't even tried to get him a present, but that would not have been from lack of generosity on his part. No, it would have been because he had been afraid that a gift would provoke a bond. And a gift of money was impersonal enough — many would say, "too impersonal," which would make it just right so far as Jakyr was concerned.

Jakyr's Companion was already saddled, with everything Jakyr needed for yet another journey stuffed into the saddlebags. Both of them looked ready to be gone. And now Mags had to wonder, just what kind of a personality Jakyr's Companion had, if he fitted well with someone who didn't want any ties on him.

:It is not that Jakyr doesn't want any ties. It is that he doesn't want any more than he already has.: If Dallen had had a voice, it would have been very dry. *:And in his defense, he does do some very dangerous things, and he does not want anyone around him who can't take care of himself.:* There was a lot there that Dallen wasn't saying, and Mags got the feeling, the very distinct feeling, that Jakyr's Companion was a lot like his Chosen.

Still, none of that harmed Mags —

:*True.*:

"Ye didn' need t' give me a thin' — but I ain't likely t' turn it down," Mags said gratefully. He was actually going to have a coin or two of his very own! Not that he needed money, but . . . what if he wanted to get Lena or Bear a present? He couldn't keep making things from Dallen's hair, or soon the poor fellow would be snatched bald. "Thenkee, sir. Reckon I owe ye again —"

"You don't owe me anything, Mags. That is why it is a present." The words were said with more ease than Jakyr had shown earlier this morning, and the Herald even reached out and ruffled Mags' hair. "Looks like you're doing well, settling in and getting on. I am happy for you. I never would have dreamed that under all that mud was a fine young Trainee when I first saw you."

Mags stretched his mouth in a grin. "Me neither, sir. Tha's Dallen's doin'. Seems he managed t' housebreak me."

Jakyr laughed aloud. "You get on down to Master Soren's house and your friends. I have a bit of a ride ahead of me, and the sooner I start, the less ground I will have to cover after dark."

Mags waved to him as he headed off down the road to the Herald's Gate, but didn't linger. Tonight was a highly significant night in a week of special days. It was Midwinter's Eve, the longest night of the year, and the reason for the holiday in the first place. Mags had permission to spend the night at Master Soren's house, by express invitation. Soren Mender was unusually casual in most things, but it seemed he was unusually sober in one; he kept the Midwinter Solstice in the old-fashioned way, or so he said.

Now there had been enough priests prattling about the mine for Mags to have picked up that most religions considered the night significant. And Dallen had explained the whole year-turning religious business to him — how this was, in most of Valdemar's religions, the night that the dark forces tried (and failed) to keep the mother-god from giving birth to the god, or in some, to keep the dead god from rising and being reborn. And none of that really mattered much to Mags —

But it did seem to matter to Master Soren, so he would give this all his due attention.

Since Mags had *no* idea just what was meant by "keeping Midwinter Solstice the old-fashioned way," he had simply nodded gravely, thanked Soren sincerely for the honor of the invitation, and went to get permission to spend the night away. As he had expected, Herald Caelen was only too pleased to give it.

Which was why he was packing up a small bag with overnight things now.

"You told me you'd explain," he reminded Dallen, as he slung his slender pack behind his saddle. "You told me you'd tell me what it is that Master Soren is going to be doing tonight."

:Oh, it's simple enough. Midwinter Eve is the longest night of the year. Most religions here in Valdemar consider that significant; that on this night, the boundaries between the material world and the spirit world are thinner, that spirits can cross over, and that dark and evil things can, too. So on Midwinter Eve, the "old-fashioned" thing to do is spend the night in vigil and do what you can to keep evil at bay. Music usually, and singing, and remembering good things. There is a special ceremony at midnight. Then when the sun rises, everyone has a breakfast feast of foods that are supposed to be lucky, and goes to bed — or to celebrate further, depending on how hardy you are.: Dallen shook his head. *:There will be many sore heads the day after tomorrow. I can promise that there will be no hammering on that day either.:*

Mags considered this. *:So I'm —:*

:To hold as much of the vigil as you are up

to, and to join everyone at the breakfast feast. The hardest time is just before dawn, anyway, and I can promise you that it will be lively enough you aren't likely to fall asleep. In fact, things are likely to get a bit rowdy: Dallen looked back over his shoulder at his Chosen. *:I have every intention of holding vigil. I am rather old-fashioned myself.:*

Well, if Dallen was going to, Mags didn't intend to be outdone.

:They'll take you to your room when you get there, and it would be wise to get a bit of a nap if you can,: Dallen added, stopping for a moment to let a swirl of partygoers cross the road in front of them. *:I certainly will, and so will most of Soren's guests. They'll wake you when it is time for the vigil to start.:*

When he arrived at Soren Mender's house, it was, for the first time since he had begun coming there, completely quiet. The Great Hall was empty, and the only person visible was the man who opened the door to his knock. "Where is everyone?" he asked the servant at the door.

A smile warmed the man's eyes. "Today and early tomorrow are for only a few, select guests, Herald-trainee Mags. In the evening the usual open house will prevail until the end of the season, but this is what the Master calls his 'quiet holiday.' You will find that the opposite prevails among many other households here; there are so many parties tonight that people may attend as many as twelve between now and dawn."

Mags head spun. "Twelve! How c'n anyone do that?"

The servant shrugged. "It is not my place to say. However . . ." He raised an eyebrow. "It is perhaps easy for those whose time is almost entirely taken up in the pursuit of pleasure." He consulted a list by the door. "Ah, you are the last of our expected guests. I can close and lock the gate now, while someone sees you to your room." He rang for another servant. "Now, you are certainly free to do whatever you choose, sir, but as we are keeping vigil, most of our guests are sleeping before dinner, and you might want to do the same. Dinner will also be later than you may be accustomed to." A boy a little younger than Mags appeared, and the servant gestured to him. "Dur, show Herald-trainee Mags to his room, if you please."

Given what Dallen, and now the servant, had told him, Mags was not at all averse to getting some sleep. The room that the boy brought him to was certainly decorated with sleep in mind. The walls were covered by green embroidered hangings showing nothing more exciting than stylized flowers, small birds, and rabbits. There were heavy curtains over the window and a screened fire blazing cheerfully on the small hearth. A fleece covered part of the floor beside the bed, which took up most of the space. *That* construction was almost a room unto itself, curtained and covered with some soft but heavy green fabric, with a reading lamp and a bookcase built into the headboard. All of the mine kiddies could have fitted into it at once — a bit snugly, but they would have fit. The boy showed him what he called (to Mags' vast amusement) "the necessary room" that was shared between his room and the next. There was a mug warming on a little shelf at the hearth that the boy offered to him. As he put down his bag, he noticed that on the same shelf was a plate of the little egg pies he had come to like so much. That was good, if dinner was going to be late.

Ah, Mags, ye've got spoiled! T' think yer worried about one meal bein' late! He almost laughed at himself. But still, it was hard to sleep if you were hungry, and he'd skipped luncheon to go hunting with Jakyr.

"What be in the cup?" Mags asked with interest.

"Milk, honey, spices and brandy wine," the boy replied. "To help you sleep."

347

Now Mags had never in his life had trouble sleeping, not even when he had nightmares, but he was not at all going to object to being served something that sounded so tasty. He thanked the boy, and since the youngling seemed to be waiting for something, wolfed down the pies and drank the potion down. And it was tasty. He found himself wishing there might be a little more, and handed over the cup.

"Thankee, sir," the boy said. "Good rest to you." He left, closing the door behind himself, leaving Mags alone in the room.

After a moment of indecision, Mags elected not to spoil his clothing by sleeping in it. Instead he took it off and folded it neatly over a rack at the foot of the bed and got in wearing only his singlet. To his delight the bed was already warm, although he could not imagine how they had managed that. And it was soft, softer than any bed he had ever slept it; he literally sank into it. The sheets were crisp and smelled of lavender. It felt like being in a warm bath, but without the danger of drowning if you fell asleep and without the water getting cold around you. Between the warm, soft bed and the drink, he found his eyes starting to drift closed before he could investigate the books in the headboard. But he had plenty of books to read already, and he had never felt more comfortable in all his life, so he just let his lids drop closed —

The next thing he knew, there was someone stirring about the room, lighting more candles over the hearth and poking up the fire. He blinked and sat up. How long had he been asleep?

"Here to wake you for dinner, sir," said yet another servant, straightening. "Will you need assistance in dressing?"

Mags coughed, surprised. Assistance in dressing? What kind of booby couldn't dress himself?

"Ah, no, I'll be fine, thenkee," he said carefully.

The servant bowed slightly. "There is hot water laid on in the necessary room. I believe we have anticipated your needs. You will hear a bell when dinner is ready, or if you would care to, some of the others are gathering in the Great Hall beforehand. Is there anything else?"

Mags silently shook his head, and the servant went away — perhaps to "assist" someone else in dressing. Mags hopped out of bed and into the shared room; there was indeed hot water in there, a large pitcher of it, steaming away. There was not enough for a bath, but he'd already gotten one after the hunt with Jakyr. He gave himself a quick wash just to wake himself up, donned his uniform, and headed for the Great Hall, blowing out the candles behind him for safety's sake as well as thrift as he left.

"See, I told you he wouldn't be laggard!" Lydia called gaily as he appeared in the doorway. The Great Hall had a very different appearance tonight than it had the rest of the week. Comfortable chairs and padded benches had been arranged in a semicircle at the hearth, at the center of which, quite oddly, was a large ornamental pot filled with earth, and beside that, a table with a small brass box, a stack of candles and a tinderbox. He could guess that the candles were for the rekindling ceremony at midnight, but he could not imagine what the pot of earth was for.

Mags didn't get a chance to wonder or ask about that, though, because Lydia claimed him for the evening, coaxing him to come and sit beside her. Most of her friends were oddly absent —

"For people like Uncle Soren, this is a family night," she explained, as she seated him in the circle between herself and Amily. "Since there's only me and Uncle Soren here, he invites more people who like the old-fashioned sort of festival, people that he thinks highly of —"

"More sad and solitary little orphans," Amily interrupted, smiling and looking like neither. "People he likes who haven't families to spend this night with, and who are not the sort to chase the hours from party to party."

Mags blinked. "But your father —"

"Spends Midwinter Eve with the King and his private gathering," Amily replied. "Which I *am* invited to, make no mistake about it, but it's either folk who are a lot older or a lot younger than I am. And it's the *King.* They have *far* too many priests there, and it is all terribly solemn and portentous, there is a great deal of prayer and remembering people who died in the last year. Instead of the hearth, they hold vigil in the Royal Chapel, which is *freezing* and, really, I prefer coming here."

Lydia hugged her friend. "And we like having you."

:Mags, tell Amily that we'll bring her back up the hill tomorrow, so her father doesn't have to fetch her and Soren doesn't have to get a servant to take her.:

Mags started; he hadn't realized that Dallen was "listening in," but he willingly relayed the offer.

"You'd do that?" Amily asked and smiled

351

broadly. "That would be perfect. Should I send word —"

:Tell her no need, I have already told Rolan, Nikolas' Companion.: There was a pause. *:Nikolas sends to thank you and me and asks you to tell Amily she's to stay as late tomorrow as she wants.:*

"Herald Nikolas says you're to stay as late as you want. Which's good, 'cause that means I got a reason t' stay as late as *I* want." He smiled at her, and she chuckled and shook her head.

At that, Amily seemed to relax a bit more as some of the rest of the guests began to trickle in. Mags recognized all of them, although he still didn't know most by name. They had all been in attendance at the house throughout the week. They were a wildly assorted lot. Some were clearly important and respected; some were, it seemed, just as ordinary as Mags was.

One was a Bard named Aiken, a man older than Master Soren, though brisk and vigorous. From the look and the cut of his scarlet tunic and trews, he was considered a Master in his own right. There were twin young men, a little older than Lydia, greeted by her as cousins, Blake and Eddin.

"Distant cousins," said one of them, with a grin. "We've been sent up here to learn the business from Uncle. When he reckons that we've learned all he can teach us, we'll be off home again and set up our own business."

Mags nodded, and finally asked the question he still didn't have the answer to. "So . . . what is 't Master Soren *does*?"

"Oh, good gad, we've never said!" Lydia laughed, her hands going to her mouth. "He makes buildings. He plans and designs them, and oversees them being built, and sometimes does very fiddly bits himself."

"Less now than I did before. The bones grow old and object to being made to climb ladders. Welcome, Mags," said the man himself, motioning for Mags to sit as he began to rise. "I am what is referred to as a Master Builder, although I have yet to construct anything *I* would call a Masterpiece."

Mags was saved from having to make any sort of response to that by the arrival of several more of the guests: a priest, Father Gellet, that Mags had enjoyed listening to — very much more than he would have ever imagined — another builder and the man's nephew, who was apprenticed as the twins were to Master Soren. There was a ramrod-straight granite-faced fellow by the name of Okley who was the Royal Falconer and, in fact, tended Jakyr's bird along with the King's and any others that the King saw fit to be permitted to be lodged in the mews. With him came Marc, and only now did Mags learn that Marc was the Royal Falconer's son, but had no aptitude for the birds and instead was in training to be the Master of the Royal Hounds. There were three highborn gentlemen, and five ladies, all of whom had grand homes built by Master Soren and had become fast friends with him in the process. There was another Master Craftsman, this one a fellow who built bridges and roads. This was the group, and they all had but two things in common. They all thought the world of Master Soren and he of them — and for all of them, this would have been an evening spent alone or with one or two others.

By the time they all went in to dinner, Mags was convinced that this was going to be a very interesting evening.

15

Once they were all seated, Master Soren rose, and the company fell silent. "We have a young man among us who is with us for the first time. This is Herald-trainee Mags, and as the host, I bid him welcome to our Vigil Night."

"Welcome," the others murmured, most with smiles.

Mags nodded. "Thenkee," he said, feeling a bit awkward. "Right honored, sir. 'm glad t' be here."

Dinner was served then, and Mags sensed Dallen watching through his eyes. He smiled with some amusement. *:Might as well stop lurkin',:* he thought. *:I don' mind ye bein' there, do y' ken.:*

Dallen sounded amused when he replied. *:I should have thought so. Well, there are several dishes that will be served that are highly symbolic. Would you like to know about this feast?:*

:*Please*,: he replied, thinking wistfully that he wished he had first-hand knowledge of what was going on. The way that Lydia and her uncle shared warm glances made him wonder, with almost a start, what it would be like to have *family.* How would it be to have someone that close to you that you could say things to them without words? To have people you had shared this sort of night with all of your life?

His thoughts were interrupted by Dallen.

:*Well, the first thing they will serve you is — there it is. Those are sprouted beans. The story is that in the first winter of the world, in the dark and the cold, the first people began to sicken. You know what I am talking about, Mags, when the teeth get loose, and the gums bleed?*:

:*Aye*,: he replied. :*An' we grubbed up grass-roots an' cured it, back at the mine. Roots, anythin' green, that cures it.*:

:*As do these. They're quite good, so don't be afraid of them.*:

Since Mags had never once encountered a food he was afraid of, he conveyed a mental snort of derision to his Companion, watched what the others were doing, picked up his fork and tried them. And they were good; crisp and tasty, with some sort of vinegar dressing.

:So the story is that people were sickening and afraid they were dying. They prayed for help, and the Goddess of Spring begged Winter to allow her to come early to save the people. Winter who was her husband and kept her with him three seasons out of the year, permitted it just long enough for the beans to sprout, and only those that were as white as the snow. And the Goddess of Spring told the first people to eat the beans, and they would be healthy again. And they did.:

There were several more dishes scattered throughout the meal that had similar stories attached to them. All of the stories followed the same theme: in the despair, the dark, and the cold of Midwinter, something happened to bring the hope of spring, and to bring life back to the people. Or sometimes to bring it back to the gods themselves.

There were, it seemed, a great many versions of how and why spring returned and a god or goddess was born or reborn, and Master Soren honored them all impartially. Which was noble, but contradictory and a little confusing.

There were a lot of dishes — but no more than a taste of anything was served. Mags instinctively understood the reason for this without Dallen telling him; this was not a feast meant to remind you of plenty, it was to remind you of hardship, of the privation of winter, of seeing the stores you had gathered shrinking, and knowing you must husband what you had left, for who knew when — or if — spring would ever come. A lot of the food was nothing one would expect on a rich man's table: a soup made with the inner bark of trees; tough, coarse bread of the sort he and the kiddies used to eat; cabbage boiled to transparency. Mags caught Lydia or Amily giving him a knowing glance from time to time, or a curious one, as if they were asking silently, *is this what you used to live on?* They were too polite to ask directly, but he nodded a little and saw Lydia's eyes darken in sympathy and Amily's lips tighten with anger. That actually made him feel good, though he flushed just a little. They were both rather different from Lena, who seemed in a knot half the time with worry.

Finally, the strange meal was over. He had, of course, eaten far more than he'd had to subsist on at the mine. But he could see that Lydia was not the only one who'd been struck by the realization that *he,* someone they knew, someone they had spoken to, had actually lived, or rather, starved, on such food. It made it all more real to them. And he thought that there was something else in those looks of theirs. That they would never again take their good fortune for granted.

Huh. That's not a bad thing.

They all returned to the Great Hall, where most of the candles had been put out, and most of the light came from the fire on the hearth. They took their seats, and Mags wondered what was going to come next.

What came next, was that Bard Aiken reached down for his lute, and made sure of the tuning. Once the strings were set to his liking, he began to play, very softly. Mags listened to the wandering notes, thinking about Lena, wondering what her night was holding. Was she feeling happy and warm and safe, surrounded by her friends and family? Or was she feeling anxious, strained, wondering if she could possibly live up to the expectations they had for her? He sometimes thought that her anxiety over doing well would eat her alive.

Aiken spoke over the music, his voice as soft as the notes, but startling Mags nonetheless.

"This is a song I learned from my mentor, who was taught it by his mentor, Bard Stefen, who wrote it," said Aiken, as his fingers moved from aimless half-melody to the first chords of the song itself.

:Bard Stefen?: he thought, startled. *:The famous Bard Stefen?:*

:Yes,: Dallen replied simply, which made Mags' eyes widen. He had read about Herald Vanyel and Bard Stefen, and they had seemed as unreal and impossible as just about everything else he read of. Yet here was someone who had learned this song — written by Stefen — from someone else, who had in his turn learned it from Stefen directly.

Suddenly the tale of Vanyel became real. Just as tales of starvation and poverty had become real to the guests at the dinner table because of his presence.

It was . . . unsettling.

As the song was unsettling, a vivid word picture of another, long-ago Midwinter Eve, when the writer was snowed in, stuck in some remote place, all alone, with only his music and his memories to sustain him through the long, bitter night.

The Bard finished the song, and somewhat to Mags' surprise, handed the lute to the man sitting next to him.

"I can't boast of having a song at my fingertips written by Stefen," said the man, who Mags had not recognized in the dark but who he now saw was the priest, Father Gellet. "But this is what I do have."

Mags expected something religious, and indeed, it could have been described as a hymn — but it was never meant for choirs. This was a song in a melancholy, minor key, and yet, it was about hope. It began in the depths of this, the longest night of the year. "What if morning never comes?" it asked. But there was a reply.

"When rose the pole star bright, the world was filled with light, and in the killing cold, a song breathed through the night."

In the song, one by one, all the birds that had been shivering in the chill raised their voices at the sight of that star, singing the hope, the surety, that the gods were good and morning *would* come again, because it had so been promised.

It put the hair up on the back of Mags' neck in a way nothing before ever had. *Not* in a bad way. It was hard to put a finger on how it made him feel — shivery, very aware of everything around him. It made him want to hold his breath, and his eyes stung a little.

When the priest was done, there was silence. Finally, the Bard coughed and cleared his throat. "When you took holy orders, Gellet, the world lost one of its finest Bards," he said gruffly. "You make the music come alive in ways I can only dream of and envy."

"You say that every year." The priest handed back the lute, and the Bard took it with a rueful smile.

He cradled the lute against himself. "I say that every year, and every year I mean it. Your Gifts are wasted —"

"My Gifts are used in the service of something other than my own vainglory. But that is an argument for another night, Aiken. Mags, have you any song or story to drive winter away?" The priest turned his head toward Mags, and in the flickering firelight Mags could see his face holding only curiosity.

Mags shook his head. "Nothin' cheerin'," he said quietly, thinking of all the Midwinter Eves that he had spent, huddled with the rest of the kiddies, trying to keep warm enough to enjoy the little bit of extra rest on this, the longest night of the year. "Nothin' anyone wants t' hear. Some of ye might know I was one of them mine slaveys, an' . . ." he paused a moment, and decided to err on the side of the least discomfort for everyone. ". . . an' we didn' keep the holidays. Mostly, we didn' even know they was holidays."

"I do, I have a true story from today," Amily said, and told an odd little story about finding a bird that very morning, lying stunned in the cold — how she had taken it up and warmed it in her hand until it recovered, how it had stayed on her hand, flicking its wings and looking at her, and only after what seemed to be a period of deliberation, flying away.

The priest laughed deep in his chest at her clever descriptions. "I often wonder what they think in those tiny heads when we do things like that. Do they mistake us for gods, do you think? After all, we take them up when they are helpless, we heal them and warm them, and let them go again."

"My pet birds have never mistaken me for anything other than a source of seed," Lydia laughed. "But now I have a story I found when I was searching in some old books for something for Uncle Soren."

Lydia's story was more like a fable, of how some long-ago Prince of Valdemar had looked out of a window one terrible Midwinter Night, and had seen a ragged woman struggling home through the snow laden with fallen branches — how he had bundled up his own as-yet untouched dinner and followed after her to find that she was caring for two aged parents and had little food and less wood. And how, even as he built up the fire for her and spread out the feast for them, the storm was worsening, until by the time that he left, he could not see his own hand before him. And how, just as he was starting to be overcome with the cold, a glowing figure appeared before him, neither man nor woman, and guided him back to safety.

It had to have been a very, very long time ago, since the forest was long gone from anywhere near Haven, and branches that fell or needed to be trimmed within the Palace walls were always taken away to be given to the poor. It was a nice story, though, and it made Mags feel very warm inside, even if he rather doubted that it had ever happened. And if it had, well . . . did that Prince give away his dinner every time he saw a poor woman? It was a good gesture, but it was only that, a gesture, and there were a lot of poor people to be fed and warmed. . . .

"I believe I will sing," said Marc, and surprised Mags who had been expecting one of the drinking songs Marc was so fond of, by singing of how on Midwinter Eve, all the animals got speech at the stroke of midnight, and how they used that time to pray to their own God of the Beasts that Man might be kinder to them in the year to come.

"You know," said Marc's father into the silence when Marc was done. "That is why I came to work with the birds. So let that be my tale."

And a strange tale it was. It seemed that when the older man had been a boy, he had heard that very song and was determined to hear the birds speak at midnight. So he had slipped away from the bed he was supposed to be in and got into the Royal Mews. "And whether it was at midnight or no, I swear to you, when the birds quieted after my disturbing them, they *did* start to speak. Before long, I knew every little thing that was troubling them, from the little hobby whose perch was too big for his small claws to the eagle who hated the man who cleaned his stall. At some point I fell asleep in there for true, with my head pillowed on a sack. The birds woke me when morning came and my parents and all found me, and I got a round scolding for being there, but when I rattled off all that the birds had said in the night, the Royal Falconer then started and looked at me like I had grown a tail. 'I was going to change that hobby's perch this morning,' was what he said in answer. 'And I'd suspected that old Char had got on the wrong side of the eagle somehow. And as for the rest of it — well, I don't *know* it to be true, by damme if I'm not going to act on it. And as for you, my lad, I am going to be talking to your da.' And so he did, that very moment."

Marc nodded. "So that was how you ended up 'prenticed to the Royal Falconer."

"Did you ever hear the birds speak again?" Lydia asked, her eyes wide.

He shook his head. "Not in words. And I can't swear I heard them that night, either. I could've dreamed it all. But I have always known how the birds were feeling, what troubles them, what ails them. Marc has none of that for birds, but he has for the dogs."

Marc nodded. "Though I can't say I've ever heard them speak at midnight on Midwinter Eve."

"That's because your old papa always made sure you weren't creeping about in the kennels on Midwinter Eve," the Falconer chuckled.

And so the first part of the evening passed. There were no sad stories, no sad songs. Everything spoke of hope, even if some of the tales were, in Mags' estimation, entirely absurd.

And then, just before midnight, they all stopped talking, and Lydia picked up the candles, distributing them to all the guests.

As if that was a signal, the servants came in, doused the remaining lights and smothered the fire with a blanket. And they all sat there, in the dark, with the room growing colder and colder.

Mags wondered what it was they were waiting for. As the dark and cold closed in around him, he shivered, reminded all too clearly of those winter nights in the sleep-hole. None of the kiddies had ever actually died of cold in their sleep . . . but some of the older miners had. . . .

Then, into the silence, bells began to ring.

Mags thought they began up at the Palace, but soon enough, bells were ringing all over Haven. And that was when the priest struck a light, using an iron, a flint, and a little ball of lint, all from the tinderbox on the table.

One spark jumped into the lint on his first try, and he managed to breathe it into a tiny flame successfully. Quickly he added bits of wood that must have been oil soaked from the way they flared up, and used it to light his candle.

Lydia began to sing.

"Spark of light, in the night, pass the flame burning bright —"

The others evidently knew this song, for they immediately joined in, as the priest touched his candleflame to Aiken's, who touched his to Marc's, and so on around the circle to Mags while they sang.

"Heart to heart, let it dart, pass the hope, let it start —"

When the flame came back to the priest, he exchanged his candle with Master Soren's. Solemnly, Master Soren went to the hearth and rekindled the fire.

"Darkness fly from the sky, pass the flame burning high —"

Servants came then with small shovels, each taking a coal as the fire roared up again. After a moment it occurred to Mags that they must have put out all of the household fires, and now they were going to restart them as Master Soren had, from the first tiny spark of the new year.

The last of the servants remained, relighting all of the candles as the song ended.

Soren looked at the priest with a grin. "A good omen as always, Gellet, getting a flame with the first spark."

The priest mock-saluted him. "Now I know why you invite me every year. For my fire-starting skills."

Soren laughed. "Among other things. Now, my friends, we have one more thing we must do."

He handed his candle to Lydia and opened the little box that had been beside the other things on the table, reaching into it and coming out with something small, black, and shiny. This, he pushed into the earth in the pot, and passed the box to Lydia. She did the same. When it got to Mags, he saw that they were seeds.

When they had all planted seeds, the priest held his hands over the pot and blessed it. "And may we all grow as strong as these seeds, and prosper," he finished.

:You are planting the seeds of the new year. Soren will put this out in the garden to be dormant until spring, then the seedlings will be transplanted. They are probably trumpet vine, which is very hardy.:

Soren nodded, and stood up, looking expectant. "Well, shall we join the rest of the household for the vigil bonfire?"

Mags had no idea what that was, but he was more than willing to go along. They left their candles, still burning, in a special holder with enough sockets to take them all that stood beside the door. Then they all gathered up coats and cloaks and went out to an area of the home that Mags had never seen before — the kitchen yard and garden in the rear.

There was an enormous bonfire there, although from the look of it, it had only just been kindled and had been aided to its roaring state by the liberal application of oil. The servants were all gathered around, laughing and passing mugs of mulled cider and sausages impaled on sticks. The smell of both — the sausages especially, as they were toasted over the fire — made Mags' stomach growl, and he was happy to accept one.

There was a glimmer of white in the darkness beyond the reach of the fire, and Dallen threaded his way through the humans with his head bobbing at every step. He nudged Mags with his nose. *:Finally, now I can join you!:*

He hugged his Companion's head to his chest. *:Well, we wouldn' want hoofprints all over Master Soren's fine floors.:*

:Bah. Bring logic into it.: Dallen whuffed at Mags' hair. *:Well, now we will be having sausages and roasted apples and drinking songs and games until the sun comes up. The ashes from this fire will be very good for the kitchen garden underneath; sometimes people bring objects of things they want to forget and burn them in this bonfire, but Master Soren, I hear, frowns on that sort of thing. It seems harmless enough, but it's possible for such things to be used as digs at someone else that they know will be attending. And in some parts of the countryside, newly betrothed*

couples jump the fire together — once it burns much lower than this one is! Most people find this the really enjoyable part of the festivities, but I rather like the part up to midnight better.:

Mags thought about that. "I think I'm on yer side," he agreed aloud.

"What side would that be?" Amily asked, hobbling up to both of them. She was able to get about reasonably well for short distances using a crutch, Mags had learned. He had also learned to ignore the crutch since that seemed to be what she wanted. "You two sound just like Father and Rolan, with your one-sided conversations."

"Dallen likes what we did better nor what we're doin' now, before midnight," he explained. Dallen nodded vigorously, and Mags regarded the young woman for a moment. She looked awkward and uncomfortable and she was too short to really see anything, which was hardly fair. But it also didn't seem fair for her to spend the rest of the vigil back inside, where no one else was. "Ye know what, there's no reason why ye have t'stand there."

:Oh, good thought, Mags,: Dallen agreed, picking up what Mags was considering. *:Go ahead.:*

"I don't know what you — *eep!*" Amily squeaked, as Mags put both hands around

371

her waist and hoisted her up onto Dallen's back.

"There. Now ye kin see, an' yer safe as houses," Mags said with satisfaction. Amily stared down at him with round eyes.

"I've never ridden bareback —" she said faintly.

"Then shame on yer Pa's Companion fer not teachin' ye," Mags retorted, handing a toasted sausage on a stick to her, and holding out a roasted apple on another for Dallen to nibble. " 'Sides, 'tis a Companion. Ye know ye won't fall. He won't let ye, an' that's a fact." He found a wooden bucket and overturned it to stand on.

From their vantage point, they could see everything. The musicians, who looked and sounded professional, struck up a very fast and lively dancing tune. Some folk began a ring dance around the fire, which then broke and turned into a spiral dance with people being added to the end of it when the rearmost reached out and grabbed them. They watched Lydia and Marc get added to it, and laughed to see them romping like children. The dance kept snaking out longer and longer as more people were added to the end. Finally, it reached the point where those at the end couldn't keep up, but rather than falling apart, it broke into two with Lydia at the front of one. It looked like fun, but Mags was not going to desert Amily and Dallen. The dancers wound around and around the fire, as sparks flew all about them, with the two chains snaking in and out and around those who weren't dancing. At last, the musicians themselves ran out of breath and brought it to a halt by the simple expedient of stopping the tune.

That was when someone — Mags didn't recognize who — spotted Amily sitting regally atop Dallen, and set up a cry.

"The Midwinter Queen! The Midwinter Queen! She looks like a Queen on her throne! Make Amily the Queen!"

Literally everyone seemed to think this was a fine plan. Soon everyone was shouting the same thing; some people ran off and came back with evergreens in their hands. Blushing furiously, trying to protest, Amily laughed as the whole crowd converged on them. Dallen soon found his neck hung with garlands of soft cedar and apples, and Amily was adorned with a crown of holly on her head. Then the two of them were paraded ceremoniously three times clockwise around the fire while the musicians played a march, Amily was handed a branch twined with ivy for a scepter, and the entire gathering knelt in homage to her.

"Tell us your decree, O Queen of Misrule!" Lydia laughed. "Rule us! Rule us!"

Everyone else took up the chant. "Rule us! Rule us! Rule us!" until Amily waved her branch for them to be silent.

Amily's eyes sparkled, although her cheeks were crimson. "I say that since we ladies get fair weary of waiting to be asked to dance, now every woman who wishes to tread a measure must choose a man to her liking and dance! And no man may deny her! Musicians! Let the dance be 'Sir Tyral Devale'!"

Cheers greeted this pronouncement, and Dallen ambled genially to one side as there was a mad scramble for desirable partners which Mags escaped by virtue of the fact that there were more men than women. The musicians started up again, and the dancers cavorted in the space around the fire in pairs. Mags made his way to Amily and Dallen's side again. She glowed, as much from happiness and pleasure as from the firelight. Dallen stood like a statue, his neck curved proudly.

"Ye make a good Queen," he said, looking up at her. She flushed.

"It's usually Lydia," she replied, almost apologetically. "I don't know what they were thinking . . ."

"That ye'd make a good Queen," he said, and felt gratified when she ducked her head with modest confusion. "Just as simple as that. What're ye supposed t' do, bein' Queen an' all?"

"Think of things they should do." She laughed. "It needs to be things that will keep them awake! Lydia always had them dancing most of the time."

"Well, ye're a clever one. I reckon ye c'n think of somethin'." He nodded

The rest of the night was taken up with games and other nonsense that Amily devised, as silly as possible. She was a very good Queen, since that was what the Midwinter Queen was supposed to do. After the first dance was over, she called out, "Duck, Duck, Goose! And Marc is Goose!" That was utterly incomprehensible to Mags, but shouts of laughter erupted, and soon the entire company was arranged in a circle around the fire, watching covertly as Marc walked behind them all. He tapped each person he passed on the shoulder, solemnly pronouncing the word "duck" each time. That is, until he came to one of the twins. "GOOSE!" he shouted, and ran. The twin chased after him but was unable to catch him, and Marc dashed into his place. Then the twin repeated the formula.

It must have been a children's game, but that seemed to be what people wanted. When Amily judged that people were wearying of it, she decreed another dance, this time with the oldest dancing with the youngest. And then, another game. She seemed to be enjoying herself, too, and Mags wondered if part of her quietude most of the time was because she worked just a little too hard at being overlooked. He didn't know a *lot* about girls, but one thing he was sure of — no matter how hard they might work at being in the background, deep in their hearts they really wanted to be seen and made much of once in a while.

As for himself, he got a great deal of enjoyment out of *her* pleasure, and when at last the sun crested the horizon and was greeted with cheers and toasts, he felt as if he had done a very good thing, putting her up on Dallen's back to be noticed like that.

Nor was she allowed to hobble back into the building on her own as they toasted the sun and the new year with the last of the cider, shared in the breakfast feast that was brought out from the kitchen, and then went off to their beds. The twins hoisted her up onto their own shoulders and carried her in triumph at the head of another parade back to her room. Smiling, Mags divested Dallen of his garlands, led him back to the stable, and made sure he had hay and water and was warmly covered in his blanket.

:*That was well done,*: Dallen said as Mags refilled the manger. :*I've not seen her have that much fun in a very long time.*:

:*How long's she been like that?*: Mags asked. :*Crippled, I mean.*:

:*Since the accident that killed her mother when she was very small. There were no expert Healers where they were, and by the time they got her into good hands, it was deemed too painful to rebreak the bones and reset them.*: Dallen sighed. :*There are many who are surprised she wasn't Chosen.*:

Mags pondered that. :*There's a good reason, aye?*:

:*Her father. She is the light of his life, and being a Herald is dangerous. He has more than enough to worry about, being King's Own. If Amily was Chosen, and he had to worry about all the dangers she faced along with all the cares of the King, he might kill himself with the strain.*: Dallen shook his head. :*Amily knows why, and she agrees this is for the best. We had to tell her, of course. It didn't seem fair, when she was pining over the Field every day.:*

Now, Dallen had never lied to Mags . . . but he got the feeling that there was more to it then just that. *:Anythin' more ye'd like t' tell me?:*

:Oh, just that it is frustrating for her, I think, being unable to dare *as much as she would like to. And for those of us who know her . . . well, seeing her as only her father's helper is sometimes like seeing a fine dagger being used as a paperweight. It serves the purpose very well, but that is not what it is* for.:

Mags had to agree. But what could he do, that the Companions couldn't?

Still this night had made her happy. That had to count for something.

He was one of the last to come in, and the halls of the house were quiet once again. He found his room, buried himself in that lovely cloudlike bed, and dreamed of nothing at all.

16

The holiday had not been kind to Bear or
Lena, as it transpired.

They arrived together, but Mags was not
there to see it. He was carrying out his assignment to keep an eye on the foreign
mercenaries, and there was something
exceedingly peculiar going on with them.
They seemed nervous, wary — and yet they
were, so far as he could tell, oblivious to the
people around them. Instead, they were
looking constantly over their shoulders for
something. What? There was no clue in their
behavior or, at least, nothing that Mags
could interpret. If they had been worried
about an attack on their overlords, they
would have been sticking more closely to
them. They were not; They were, in fact, going about their usual business.

All he could do was make careful note of
how they were acting, and what set off their
odd reaction. Not that he could go into the

Palace to watch them — on the other hand, when they were on duty, they probably were a lot more careful to keep up their façades.

He had first gotten wind of their peculiar behavior that morning, when he overheard two of the Healers talking about it. He had been slowly eating his breakfast, enjoying one of the last leisurely meals he would have before classes started again. Already most of the extra workmen were gone — but the fruits of their labors were visible in newly opened sections of all three Collegia. More rooms for Trainees in all three, all the work on the Heraldic Library was complete and now the books just needed to be moved in, the dining hall was finished but the kitchen still needed work, and there were rumors that there was some sort of addition for the bathing room that would make all that tedious heating of buckets of water a thing of the past. It wasn't a reality yet, however.

So he had just had a morning bath and was savoring eggs and sausages and biscuits when two Healers sat down on the bench across from him and picked up what sounded like an interrupted conversation.

"It's bad enough that they are rude and arrogant, and that half of my work consists of patching up injuries they've inflicted during 'practice,' " one of them said as he got a bowl of porridge. "But this . . . how can I tell if something is wrong with someone if he won't tell me the symptoms?"

"Perhaps they don't speak our language well?" the other suggested diffidently. The first snorted.

"They speak it just fine. They just won't tell me. 'Something is wrong with us, Healer. Fix it.' Just like that, in so many words." The first one stirred currants into his porridge with irritation. "I finally got just as rude as they were. 'Well, perhaps all your problems stem from the amount of strong drink you're putting away every night down in the city,' I said. 'I can't fix you if you keep making things worse by getting blind drunk every night.' "

"Good for you!" the second applauded. "Then what happened?"

"They threatened to kill me, of course. Fortunately, with the Guard there, they didn't dare do anything other than threaten." The Healer snorted. "I've told everyone that those threats were the last straw, and I am sticking to it. I would not put it past them to ambush me and beat me senseless for not groveling and making them all better. It will have to be a royal command before I have anything to do with any of that lot again."

They finished their breakfast, with Mags lingering over his, but said nothing more about the mercenaries. He left just after they did; Dallen had not heard anything either. But Dallen took care to point out that Lydia's friends would want to know anything at all about this — and probably, so would Herald Nikolas.

So with that tantalizing knowledge in hand, Mags decided he would intercept them on their way to the salle, fall in behind them and watch.

That was just what he did, making himself look as unobtrusive as possible, lurking about the herb garden and waiting for them to come out of their usual door at the Palace at their accustomed time. He sauntered along the path right behind them, close enough to take note of everything they did, and far enough he thought they wouldn't notice he was there, or if they did, they would just shrug because this was his usual time at the salle, too. And that was when he realized that there was *something* spooking them. But whatever it was, it wasn't human. They didn't even seem to notice *him* — or if they did notice him, they considered him not worth bothering about, and surely they couldn't tell which Trainee he was at this distance. But something had them looking over their shoulders with every twig that cracked in the cold, every wren that darted out of a bush. What was wrong with them?

He took a chance, speeded up a little, and walked right past them. Nikolas' lessons had taught him how to look sharply at people without seeming to look at them at all. If they had been friends of his, he would have been alarmed at their condition. Their eyes were dark-circled and their expressions harried. Their eyeballs were bloodshot. They looked as if they had not slept well last night or the night before.

They relaxed and acted normally when they finally reached the salle, although their reflexes were a bit off. But if they hadn't slept, that was probably why. As he worked out with another Trainee, he kept a watch on them out of the corner of his eye. They didn't challenge anyone today; in fact, they declined partners offered to them, and sparred only among themselves. They tired quickly, they managed to disarm each other without trying very hard. And in the end, they left before he did, not after, looking as if the short session had completely exhausted them. He decided this was enough out of the ordinary that he ought to go tell one of Lydia's group. And, fortunately, he had a contact right here in the Palace.

So instead of going and having a leisurely luncheon, he grabbed enough sausage rolls for two and a pair of apples and headed for the Royal Kennels.

He had never been there before, so he was at a bit of a loss for where to look first when he got there. The outbuilding was easy enough to find, and he knew that it held dogs, but other than that . . . well if it was anything like the stable, if he couldn't find Marc right away, probably someone would be able to tell him where the apprentice was.

The sounds of dogs barking would have led him there once he rounded the corner of the Palace and entered the grounds where the stable for the regular horses, the kennels, and the mews were located. Even if he had not known where it was, he could have followed his ears. The structure was very like a stable, but one with fenced runs for the dogs to use, as well as quite a few animals roaming free. Much to his relief, he saw Marc right away, feeding a pen of small, brown-and-white, short-haired, floppy-eared dogs with long, furiously wagging tails.

"Marc! Brung ye some luncheon!" he called out, holding out the napkin that contained the sausage rolls.

"Bless you, Mags, I'm behind on the work

and fair perishing." Marc wiped his hands on a towel at his waist and accepted the napkin gladly. "Two of our men are out, as you might expect from trying to drink a barrel of beer dry, and I'm having to do the work of three."

Mags shook his head sorrowfully, which gave him a chance to look around to see if there was anyone near that could overhear them. In an undertone, while Marc wolfed down the sausages — proving that his hunger was no ruse — Mags told him what he had heard and seen.

"Huh. Now that is a peculiar tale. Well, the Healer could be right. Seeing things is one of the signs of someone that's a habitual drunk, and from what I've heard, these fellows have been setting records in the taverns since the holiday began." He grinned. "Seems they can't get drink strong enough at the Palace. For some reason, no one will serve it to them, or even admit that it exists in the cellars."

Mags nodded, but something still didn't seem right to him. "But wouldn't they be seein' creepy-crawlies all the time if it had to do with drink?" he objected. "They stopped actin' peculiar when they got t' the salle."

"Hmm. You have a point." Marc finished

the last of the rolls and wiped his hands. "I'll pass it on to the others. You see what else you can learn. I'm thinking we might want to put off our plan for a bit."

"Won' be much," Mags warned. "Mostly rumor, I guess. Not like I c'n get inter the Palace."

"Rumors often have a bit of truth at the core." Marc's head came up at the sound of a bell from the Collegium. "And that would be your reminder to get back to classes, I expect."

"No classes yet. But aye, should be getting back, I got things as I need t' tend m'self."

He hurried back up the path to the Collegium, intent on his own thoughts, and trying to decide what, if anything, he should be doing about listening in at Bardic Collegium. At the moment, he had no real excuse to linger there and eavesdrop on the teachers and resident Bards. The best he could do was to position himself during meals where he could overhear as much as possible through the hum of conversation. He was already on his way to Healers' with an eye to asking about things to prevent the miserable sneezing and coughing that some of the early arrivals had brought back with them. Not that he thought he was likely to get sick — but it gave him a good excuse to eavesdrop as Herald Nikolas wanted.

And that was when he ran right into Bear, or nearly. Bear was ploughing along the path with his head down, paying no attention to where he was going, and since Mags was doing the same, they bumped shoulders and started, becoming aware of what they were doing only at that moment.

Mags recognized Bear first. He stared at his friend as if at a ghost for a moment. Then he grinned, and grabbed both of Bear's shoulders. "Bear! Yer back!"

Bear grinned, but it looked strained. Mags let go of his shoulders, his glee changing to concern. "Ye look worrit," he stated flatly. "An' it ain't like ye t' go bumblin' along, payin' no heed to anythin' but yer feet. Summat wrong?"

Bear shrugged. His normally cheerful face took on a masklike blankness. "Nothing really. My holiday wasn't much of one. But then, neither was Lena's."

"She's back, too?" Mags asked, suddenly feeling very uncertain. This wasn't like Bear at all. Bear never temporized. There was no doubt in Mags' mind that Bear was hiding something, probably the cause of his unhappiness.

Bear nodded. "We came back together;

we got in last night, but you weren't about anywhere obvious, and you weren't in your room, and we didn't know where to find you." Bear shrugged. "And anyway, we had unpacking to do and we were both pretty tired, so we went back to our rooms. I don't know what Lena did, but I just got something to eat and then went straight to bed."

"I was down th' road with some people —" He hesitated; how much did he dare say? He had been down at Master Soren's house, of course, all of Lydia's group had gotten together to enjoy the last night of the holiday, the last night all of them would be free to get together as a group until the next holiday of the Spring Equinox. They had not yet made up their minds about when the girls were going to humiliate those mercenaries . . . and in fact, Mags was getting the impression that they had begun to have second thoughts about that idea, and Marc's words a few moments ago had confirmed that. But he couldn't tell Bear about any of that. And he couldn't quite figure out how he could readily explain how someone like *him* was friends with the circle around Master Soren's niece.

" 'S no matter anyway," he continued. " 'Cause if I'd 'a knowed you were comin' last night, I'd 'a been here, not there!"

Bear shook his head. "We weren't in any mood to be around, Mags. Things didn't go well at home for either of us. And we would rather not talk about it, if you don't mind."

He was rather taken aback by his friend's words, in fact, he was rather hurt. Wasn't he their friend? They had obviously confided in each other, so why not in him?

He wanted to blurt out all of this, but his mouth had other ideas, and said nothing more than, "Well, we gonna study t'gether tonight? Or at least hev supper t'gether?"

"No studying, that was mostly all I did at home," Bear replied. "But supper, absolutely. And you can probably find Lena up at Bardic if you want to go look for her."

He ducked his head, and hurried on his way, leaving Mags staring at his retreating back in puzzlement.

Although Bear had not seemed particularly encouraging, Mags went up to Bardic, looking for Lena. He realized as he was halfway there that he had never been to her room, and he suddenly felt very diffident about trying to find it. There were implications to looking for a girl's room that he wasn't sure he wanted to deal with. His steps slowed, and finally, when he reached the door of Bardic Collegium, stopped altogether.

He stood uncertainly, looking up at the wooden façade of the building, noting that it was getting pretty shabby. What to do?

Finally, another girl, a little older than Lena but also in Trainee rust-red, came up from behind him and moved to go around him. "Hey —" he said awkwardly, and she stopped. "I don' s'pose ye know Trainee Lena? Little bit of a thing, dark hair."

The girl looked at him as if he was mad. "*Everyone* knows Trainee Lena," she replied, with a lot of undertones to the words that he couldn't quite read. Still this was his chance.

"Could ye tell 'er that Mags an' Bear wants t' meet her fer supper?" he asked. The girl rolled her eyes, as if to say *Why don't you tell her yourself?* but refrained from making any such statement.

He had to reflect that just keeping your mouth shut on things you wanted to ask or say was a much more difficult thing than he had thought.

The girl hesitated a moment, probably weighing her options, inconvenience or a stern lecture from one of the instructors about proper manners.

Evidently the thought of a lecture decided her. Instead of brushing him off, she replied politely, "If she's in her room, I'll tell her, and if not, I'll leave her a note." She smiled at Mags, and Mags found himself feeling very warm of a sudden.

He stuck out a hand; she shook it. "Thenkee!" Mags said, with gratitude, and turned to go back to the stables.

It felt a little odd not to be heading to Master Soren's house at this time of day, but the holiday was officially over and, besides, he had a puzzle to unravel. He thought best when he was away from other people and he wanted to get Dallen's ideas on it, too.

Dallen was, of course, entirely aware of how oddly the mercenaries had acted this morning, and he was just as eager to talk about it. So after Mags settled onto a bale of straw in his loose box, they both went over how the men had acted in their minds.

"Ye know," Mags said, looking up into Dallen's bright blue eyes. "If I didn' know better, I'd 'a thought they'd seen a ghost, and was still lookin' for it. You ever heard tell of somethin' like a haunt around here?"

Dallen bobbed his head. *:The Collegia are not haunted, let me promise you. Believe me, we Companions would know if they were. Neither is the Palace, even though by all rights it should be, if emotional turmoil is what creates a ghost. But you're right. They did act as* *if they were expecting something supernatural to manifest at any moment.:* He bobbed his head thoughtfully. *:People can be haunted as well as places, you know.:*

:Ye think mebbe they brung a haunt with 'em?: Mags hazarded, but then shook his head. *:Or one followed 'em here? Nah, if they had a haunt followin' 'em, they'd be used to it, don' ye think? An' it'd have to be hauntin' all of 'em for all of 'em to be so jumpy. How likely is that?:*

Dallen rubbed his nose against his knee. *:I don't know. I am rather out of my experience when it comes to ghosts. All I know is the ghost stories other people tell. I've never actually seen one myself, nor has anyone I know.:*

Mags pondered. *:Well, ye reckon I ought t' follow 'em?:*

:No. You are too obvious in your Trainee Grays, and you would be even more obvious in civilian garb, since the Palace servants all wear livery. No, you let Marc deal with that end of it. You and I will ask some careful questions, not too many, and not all of the same person. I have some ideas where you might go within the Palace that you might hear things without exciting any suspicion. And above all, you will listen.:

Mags grinned. *:Now that, I c'n do.:*

So he spent the afternoon doing just that. Dallen had excellent ideas, and more than just ideas, he had sound advice that not even Herald Nikolas could better.

He started in the kitchen, since in his experience, that was where most gossip took place, and Dallen agreed. Even in Cole Pieters' household, as tightly controlled as it was, the servants in the kitchen and the ones that came into the kitchen shared gossip.

Now any Trainee could come and go freely from the Collegia kitchen as the cooks dispensed food to any Trainee or teacher out of mealtime hours with no questions asked. That was where he went first, professing hunger, which was no lie since Marc had eaten all of his sausage rolls and Mags' share as well. Once fed, he loitered, knowing that as long as he stayed out of the way, no one would chase him out.

The kitchen that served the three Collegia was rather devoid of anything other than talk about who had done what during the holiday. He moved to the kitchen that served the Guards, but it was empty of everyone but the head cook, who was putting loaves to rise. He left without alerting the cook to his presence, not really disappointed since he honestly had not expected to hear anything about the foreigners there.

That left the Palace kitchen. And truth to tell, that was where he expected to get the most information.

Now, the best way to be unnoticed, Herald Nikolas had said, was to look as if you belonged someplace. And while it was true that *most* of the Palace servants wore livery, not all of them did. Not the ones that did very menial work; they wore ordinary clothing. That included those who served in the kitchen, for certain. Dallen had absolutely agreed with him on this score, and had some good ideas on how to get into the kitchen without arousing any suspicion. It wasn't as if he could go loiter there without knowing anyone who worked there, and a Trainee of any sort was going to excite comment showing up to beg a snack.

So he went back to his room and changed out of his Trainee Grays and into civilian clothing, his oldest and most worn outfit. *:All right,:* he thought at Dallen. *:Where's the Palace kitchen?:*

Wordlessly, Dallen showed him exactly how to find it while avoiding most people. And having been in two large kitchens within the Palace walls already, Mags had a pretty good notion of how the third was likely to be laid out. So he made his way circuitously to the kitchen — making his way from the stable to the wall, from the wall back to the kitchen gardens, and from the kitchen gardens to the kitchen door. He waited patiently and once there, slipped inside on the heels of someone who was bringing in supplies. For once it was an advantage to be small.

The heat and the smells of cooking hit him with a kind of shock, though a pleasant one. This kitchen was easily twice the size of the one that served the Collegia, and had three times as many people in it. Which was ideal since it meant he could probably remain completely unnoticed in all the bustle. It had an entry, a kind of alcove in immensely thick walls, which were thick for a good reason. The baking ovens were built into one side so that the chimney could go straight up the wall, taking the excess heat with it. Rooms above this would be very cozy in winter, and although in summer that could be a bit problematic, one solution might be to use them for storage of things that needed to be kept dry — linens for instance. At any rate that meant there had to be an alcove about as long as a bed, which made for a good place for him to stand in the shadows and examine everything.

From his vantage point in the entryway,

he could see a line of aprons on pegs across the room. Walking quickly, but without any urgency, he threaded his way directly through the bustling cooks and helpers, got himself one of them, pulled it on over his head, and rolled up his sleeves. He walked as if he belonged here, as if he knew exactly what he was doing and what his job was. He was dressed no differently than the lowest of the servants here, and he was small and unthreatening. No one paid any attention to him.

Then he headed straight for the pile of dirty pots and the huge double sink they stood beside, also right on the outside wall, but on the opposite side of the entryway. You needed light when you were scrubbing pots and dishes — at least, you did if you wanted to be sure you were getting them clean. Beneath the high windows, covered in oiled parchment that let in light but nothing else, was an arrangement of two huge side-by-side sinks and two hand pumps, where a tow-haired scullion scrubbed manfully away at the dirty pots with a stiff bristle brush and plenty of soap. Just as Mags got there, he let out the dirty water through a drain at the bottom of each sink and began refilling the sinks from a hand pump. Mags took over the one he wasn't pumping and copied him. When both sinks were mostly full, the scullion added hot water to both from steaming buckets at his feet.

Now, Mags was no stranger to pot scrubbing. He'd done plenty of it before he was big enough to work in the mine. So he grabbed a second brush and set to, and the scullion didn't even look up.

There was a science and a rhythm to doing this sort of work. Nasty, crusted pots with things burned in them, you filled full of water and put to boil, unless they were very bad indeed, in which case you filled them with coals until everything was ash. Pots that had only been used to simmer something gently, you gave a quick scrub and rinse. The rest, you soaked in hot water before you tried scrubbing them — something that the other scullion evidently had not learned. So Mags took the hard ones away from him — filled them full of hot water, of which there was, miraculously enough, a plentiful supply — took the very worst ones and put them to boil, leaving them on the hearth where there was an entire calf and an entire pig roasting, with a clanking mechanism to turn the spit instead of a boy as there had been in Cole Pieters' kitchen.

It had to be said that the worst of the pots

were nothing like the worst ones in Master Cole's kitchen. There was not a one he would have consigned to the coals here.

That might have been due to the huge metal vessel of hot water with a fire under it that stood in one corner of the kitchen — this made cleaning ever so much easier. No burned pot ever got quite clean unless it was filled with coals back at the mine, but when you did that, you ruined the finish on the inside and made it more likely that things would stick. But it was most probable that it was due to the cooks. There could always be accidents — something left a little too long — but there were not that many of those with a good cook about. None of Cole Pieters' cooks had ever been more than "adequate," or so Mags realized now. It was very strange; he had gradually come to understand that it was not only that the ingredients of the food here were so much better, it was not only that he was getting good, wholesome food instead of scraps. It was that the cooks themselves were good. They didn't let things burn — and the kitchen at the mine was always full of the smells of something burning.

:I can't ever 'member a loaf of bread without th' bottom crust burned. . . . . :

:Ugh. That is . . . well, awful.:

:So were the cooks.:

Now the scullion watched him from under a thick fringe of straw-colored hair that almost obscured his eyes and looked as if it had been hacked off with a knife. He still said nothing, but as Mags' remedies loosened the crusts so that most of the nastiness could be *washed* off rather than *scrubbed* off, he began to copy what Mags was doing. It was very clear that this boy was no fool. Mags began to wonder if maybe he ought to cultivate him. With another set of ears in the kitchen, he himself would not need to be there.

Meanwhile, Mags was listening.

Most of the gossip was ordinary kitchen chatter. A maid sent to fetch food and drink had got a glimpse of someone being in a gentleman's chamber who shouldn't have been there, since she had a husband of her own. The kitchen knew who was quarreling with whom in the Court, and how the alliances were shifting. They knew who was going to have a child, often before the lady herself did. They knew what young men the daughters were seeing, often when the parents were unaware.

And within the kitchen there was plenty of gossip, too. There was always someone romancing someone else in the kitchen staff, and plenty of jibes about that.

Most of it was harmless. Wasn't so-and-so the handsomest young lord you ever had seen? And Lady thus-and-such was angling to marry off her daughter to the highest bidder, so to speak, and the poor thing only had eyes for that nice young fellow up from the country with whom she would never be allowed to keep company.

Mags let all the gossip flow around him, although he very quickly realized that this was going to be very useful stuff to the King's Own. That made him feel rather cheerful.

Finally a serving maid came rushing in, all a-flutter, and not in the sort of way that anyone would connect with "being interfered with," which was kitchen code for a maid who'd been taken advantage of. "Oh!" she exclaimed, as her entrance caused a stir. "If you had just seen what I've seen!"

One of the cooks looked at her indulgently. "Na, missy, if ye'd seen as many things as *we* hev, ye'd think twice afore ye said that."

But when Mags angled himself so that he could get a good look at the girl he saw that she was white as paper — and so, at that moment, did the cook. "Mercy!" the woman exclaimed. "Girl, ye look fear-struck!"

"And I should be!" The cook pushed a

stool toward her and she sat right down on it, groping after a mug of water that was shoved into her hands. " 'Tis them terrible furriners, the bodyguards! They're haunted!"

Mags started, almost dropping the pot he was scrubbing.

"Haunted! Never!" By this time the head cook, an enormous man, had taken notice, and reacted to the statement with scorn. "There's never been a spirit in this Palace, and there never will be! The Companions and Heralds keep us safe from such unholy things, and even if they didn't, the Bards could sing it away!"

"I tell you, I seen it! With me own two eyes!" Normally a girl like this maid would have been overawed by the big man, but whatever she had seen had frightened her too much for her to be in awe of anyone. She stared at him with passionate, if terrified, defiance. "I did! And they seen it, too! They're as scared as I was! I swear it! That's why they been looking so seedy!"

"Start from the beginning, girl," the undercook urged.

Hands shaking, clutching the mug, the girl ducked her head. "It begun like this. You know. They never eat with staff — get us to bring them their dinner special, so they eat before their masters, an' then go and stand guard behind the chairs during Court dinner."

"Aye, we know that," the first cook agreed, as the head cook sniffed his contempt.

"Think they're too good for the likes of us," growled the pastry cook. "Think they're highborn themselves."

:Actually they are probably testing their food for poison before they eat it, and they would *need to eat before their masters do.:* Dallen sounded as if his excuse for their behavior made him embarrassed. Mags didn't have the heart to be as rude about it as he would have liked. Dallen always did see both sides of a situation. And, more and more, so did Mags.

"So I brought 'em their dinner on the cart, like I always do," the girl continued. "But yesterday and the day before they've been — different — when I came. Nervous, I would have said, except I've never seen them nervous. And today they were even jumpier. Every time there was a squeak or a rattle, they jumped and looked for what might have caused it. I pushed the cart into the room, just like always. And that was when it happened!"

Her hands were shaking so much that the water sloshed out of her mug and all down the front of her gown.

"What happened?" the cook asked, dabbing at her uniform gown with a napkin. The girl was so shaken she didn't even notice.

"The ax! There was an ax in the room, on the wall in the room! And all of a sudden it just *leaped* off the wall, and flipped over three times, and *split* that dress-helm the tallest one likes to wear because he's going bald!" She shuddered. "It didn't just fall! It just about flew! Like someone was throwing it!"

Some of the kitchen staff looked apprehensive, and there was some murmuring back and forth. The maid spoke right over the top of them.

"I saw it and *they* saw it and they just went white! And the sly one pushed me out of the room and shut the door, which was a good thing, because I couldn't possibly have moved otherwise! And I ran here." She wasn't as close to hysteria as she had been, but Mags had no doubt that she was very near some sort of breakdown.

So did the head cook, who snorted again. *He,* at least, was not at all impressed. Then again, he must have been serving here for —

:Almost thirty years that I know of.:

"I've seen things move around here many a time, girl. A Herald with the Fetching Gift can move things just by thinking about it." The head cook shook his head. "You've got no call to go bringing ghosts into it, when there's a perfectly reasonable explanation. Like as not, it's one of the Trainees, pulling pranks. They aren't supposed to do that sort of thing, but boys will be boys, and those mercenaries are a hateful lot. I couldn't fault the boys for making 'em sweat."

"But a Herald has to see what he's moving, right?" the maid demanded. "He can't just decide to move things without knowing what they are and where they are, right?"

"Ah . . ." She had caught him off guard, it seemed. He would like to pretend he was an expert in such matters.

"I *believe* that is true," he said finally. "I believe that in order to move something, the Herald has to be able to see it."

"And there were no Heralds anywhere about!" she exclaimed. "They couldn't have seen in the window. Those awful men keep that closed up as tight as tight, and I have never seen anyone in their rooms but *them.*"

"And why split a helm?" mused the cook. "I can't imagine what that was supposed to mean. Truly, this is baffling."

"Unless you were a vengeful spirit and

were sending a message," replied another, silent until now. "Well, I wouldn't care to be in their shoes, I can tell you that. I would not be at all surprised to find out they had some dark secrets, that lot. And a lot to hide. And maybe someone they wronged badly enough to come looking for revenge from the grave."

There was more, much more, of the same. Mags didn't hear all of it, since he finished the pots with a speed that the scullion must have found gratifying, and slipped back out of the kitchen again.

:Well . . . that was interesting.:

Mags didn't pause on his way to the stables — he didn't have time. He'd have to hurry to change back into his Grays and be at the dining hall in time to meet Bear and Lena. But he definitely caught something in Dallen's mind-voice.

:You're thinking on something.:

:It does sound like someone with Fetching. And the cook is wrong, you don't have to see what you want to Fetch — if you did, the Gift would not be very useful. You just have to know where it is and what it looks like.:

:Aye, so?:

:The thing is what the ax did, not that it moved. It flipped end over end and landed hard enough to split the helm. You would virtu-

ally have *to be there to see in order to do it. Unless . . . :*

:Oh, get on with it!:

By now he had reached the stables. Dallen whickered a greeting as he passed. He dived into his room and began frantically wiggling out of his clothing and into his Grays.

:If someone with the Fetching Gift worked with someone who was a FarSeer, then he wouldn't have to be in the same room:

Mags stopped, one boot on, the other in his hand. *:But who?:*

:A good question.:

17

Bear seemed to have had no real improvement in his attitude since that afternoon, and he might have thought he was covering it well, but so far as Mags was concerned, he wasn't. Mags would have given just about anything to have a topic of conversation that would distract his friend from whatever was bothering him, but most of the interesting things he had done over the holiday would only have opened up more questions than he was able to answer.

"Ever been down into th' city?" he finally asked, as Bear toyed with his food and they both waited for Lena.

Bear shook his head.

"Herald Caelen said t' go." He shook his head. "Never seen that many people in m' life. Never seen that much stuff neither." After the Midwinter Eve vigil and Midwinter Day celebration, he and Marc and Dia had gone back to the Midwinter Market —

and since he now had some money to spend, he'd gotten something for Lena and Bear. He'd brought the presents with him to — he hoped — cheer them up. "Since Jakyr give me coin, got ye somethin'."

He pulled the cloth bag that held the present out from under the cloak folded on the bench beside him. Bear finally seemed to wake up a bit.

"Mags, you shouldn't — you shouldn't spend money someone gave you on presents for others —"

"Why not? 's mine now, right? S'pose to get things as make me happy? Well, gettin' you an' Lena somethin' makes me happy."

With a nonplussed look on his face, Bear opened the bag, revealing the sheepskin mittens that Mags had gotten him.

"I hardly know what to say — this is exactly what I needed!" Once again, Mags got the feeling there was more behind that statement than he could properly comprehend. But some of it slipped out. "I think you know me better than my own family, and we haven't been friends for more than a couple of moons." The last was tinged with bitterness.

:Oh, dear . . . :

:Mebbe families ain't all shiny an' flowers.:

:Sometimes not even with the best of intentions.:

Fortunately, what could have been a very uncomfortable moment indeed was salvaged by Lena's arrival. She did not look happy, but she didn't look as miserable as Bear was.

She helped herself to the food, but Mags could not help noticing that she took less than half of what she usually did. If only he had something he could talk to them about, something to distract them!

Oh, wait — he did!

"Ye know them nasty bodyguards? Them furriners?" he began. "Well, hang if they ain't actin' strange."

He went on to tell them what he had overheard, then what he himself had seen. Bear and Lena both perked up — with a certain amount of very unsympathetic comments — as he gave some pretty elaborate descriptions of their behavior, helped out by Dallen.

He didn't have to figure out how to tell the story of the "haunted" ax, though. Lena suddenly looked as if something had occurred to her.

"Oh, Havens!" she exclaimed. "I wonder if —"

"What?" Bear asked before Mags could.

"Well, there is a rumor going around that

the Palace is haunted. Some wild story about weapons flying off of walls and cutting things in half. I wonder if this has anything to do with why those bodyguards are so nervous?" Her eyes sparkled. "I wonder if it is the ghost of some Royal Guardsman who is offended by them?"

"Where d' ye hear these things?" Mags asked, both amused and puzzled. Amused because at least he wouldn't have to figure out some way of telling the story without revealing how he had learned it.

"Bards hear everything, because anything could lead to a new song," she replied, now actually eating instead of shoving her food about on the plate.

"And Bards gossip worse than a pack of old women," Bear added, but with a smile. "Do you really think it's a ghost?"

"Well, I 'spect *they* do," Mags put in. "They sure act like it."

"I can't think of why something like that would happen otherwise." Lena's eyes were shining now. "There aren't any classes for another two days, I am going to poke around and see what else I can find out. A mystery! I love mysteries!"

Now that she had cheered up, Mags felt it was a good time to give her the present he had gotten her. He reached into his tunic and brought out the pretty little wooden box that Lydia had helped him pick out to hold it. "Went t' the Midwinter Market. Jakyr come in late an' only stayed a day, I reckon 'e felt guilty, so 'e give me some money an' I reckoned I'd get ye both summut. So . . . 'ere." He handed her the box, which had a harp carved on the top of it. She exclaimed over the pretty thing, then opened it. Mags was very pleased with that find, which had been a stroke of pure luck. Just as there were merchants who tried to pass off inferior articles as more valuable than they were, there were also those who didn't know what they had. He had found, in a secondhand dealer's booth, this very pretty string of deep red beads. The merchant thought they were glass, but his expert eye had seen that they were, in fact, garnets.

"Oh, Mags!" She pulled the beads out of the box and ran them through her fingers. "Please tell me they didn't cost you a fortune!"

"Bah, this's me!" he scoffed. "I got help bargainin'." In fact, it had been Lydia who helped him bargain for that, and for the pretty carved wooden charms he had attached to all the page-markers. "I still got coin fer me."

Thus reassured, she flung her arms around his neck and hugged him quickly. "It's so pretty! And Bardic Scarlet, too! Thank you!"

"Show 'er yer mitts, Bear," Mags urged, and Bear displayed his mittens. "Can't have his precious fingers froze, now c'n we?" he teased, and she laughed.

"He needed mittens like those on our trip," she said. "He had to borrow a pair of mine, and they weren't nearly as nice and warm as these. His poor fingers kept getting cold and stiff." Then she snapped her fingers. "And that reminds me of something else. On the way home, Bear and I were talking, and — Mags, do you want to find out what really happened with that raid on the bandits where you were found?"

That came as such a complete surprise to him that all he could do was gape at her and say, "Wha—" He stared stupidly at her for a moment, then gathered his thoughts. "Uh, I — guess —"

"Well, we can do that. The records of all the Guard reports are kept here, and Bards get access to everything but the sealed stuff. All we need to do is find the report of that raid and see what it says." She looked at him in triumph. "What's the worst that can happen? We find out you are just what that horrible man claimed you are, a bandit child, which is scarcely your fault. But *I* think he lied. I think we should look into it."

Mags felt a little thrill of mingled apprehension and excitement. Could he —

:I think you should, too, Mags.:

Well, that settled it.

"We'll do it," he said decisively.

With both boys in tow the next morning, Lena went in search of where and how to get at the Guard Archives, and that was when they ran into their first snag. Although Bards had access to the Guard reports, Bardic Trainees needed special permission.

"You'll have to get one of your teachers to give you a letter stating that you need to use the Archives for research, Trainee," said the stolid old man in Guard Blue sitting behind the desk at the entrance to the Archives. "We can't have every young Trainee in here poking around just to satisfy her curiosity or to win a bet. Those are the regulations."

Lena sighed, but she didn't push the subject. "I'll be back with that letter," she said firmly.

"And when you are, I'll let you in. Not before." The man crossed his arms and gave her a stern look. "There is sometimes sensitive and personal information in those reports. Things other people would rather not have bandied about. As a courtesy to them, we don't let just anyone come in here and start reading through things."

It was witheringly clear that he was not going to budge an inch on this. Mags tapped Lena on the shoulder. " 'S all right, we c'n come back later," he said. Reluctantly, she nodded.

All three of them left the Guard barracks, which was some distance away from the rest of the complex of buildings, and trudged back through the snow to Healers. "D' ye think you c'n get that letter?" Mags asked anxiously. Now that he had committed to finding out the truth, he wanted to get on with it.

Lena snorted delicately. "He's making a big fuss about nothing. Hardly any of the Trainees want to come here; it takes a lot of work to read something in a Guard report and come up with a song. Everything has to match — you can't change the story just because you don't like the way it came out or the person that should be a hero is a really unpleasant person. That is why people *trust* Bardic news and Bardic history songs. It's a lot easier to just make something up for a tale song. I can get that letter. I just need to figure out which of my teachers is most likely to give it to me."

They pushed through the door into Bear's quarters. And there was someone waiting for them. One of the Palace servants in the special blue-and-white livery rose from his seat, a look of relief on his face. "You're the herb Healer?" he blurted.

"Trainee," Bear corrected. The man waved that off.

"Everyone says that you are the one that knows everything there is to know about herbs. I need something to make people sleep. Those wretched bodyguards are demanding it for one of their masters." The poor fellow looked exceedingly harried.

"Such things are dangerous —" Bear warned. "Too little and they don't work, too much and they can kill. And you can become addicted to them."

"Frankly, Healer, if that man doesn't stop moaning about being watched all the time, *I* may kill him. He hasn't slept in three nights. Please, give us at least one night of peace!" The man gestured entreatingly. "I'm begging you!"

Mags, Bear, and Lena all exchanged looks. "I'll get my bag. My friends are coming with me."

"I think that is a good idea, Healer. I don't

trust those men. I wouldn't be alone with them for my own weight in gold." He waited patiently while Bear gathered up his necessaries and loaded Mags down with them. Then he gestured to them to follow.

They followed him up to the Palace, with Mags struggling to contain his excitement at being asked, invited in, to see the very men he was supposed to be keeping a remote eye on. Lena did not even try to pretend to calm. Her eyes sparkled, and she almost skipped.

They went in through a door he would never have dared use if he had been here alone. It was, however, clearly a servants' entrance, since it was plain and let out into a utilitarian hallway, not at all dissimilar to the ones in the Collegia. And, to be fair, Mags would not have known it was "utilitarian" if he had not had Dallen's point of view to give him a comparison.

Shortly, however, he had a comparison of his own as they entered into a hall that clearly housed something other than servants.

Whitewashed plaster and black beams gave way to rich wood paneling. The wooden floors were polished to a soft gleam, and shiny metal polished lanterns were mounted at intervals along the walls.

Though they were not lit at the moment, it was clear that this hall would be as brightly illuminated at night as anyone could wish.

This, of course, would allow the visitor to admire the beautiful little tables holding statuary that stood beneath each lamp, and the paintings between them. None of them got a chance to do anything of the sort, as the servant hurried them along as fast as he could manage.

He tapped once at a door in the middle of the hallway, and quickly ushered them all in. When Mags entered, he saw two of the bodyguards standing at strict attention, one on either side of the window, and a man huddled with his head in his hands, sitting on a padded chair beside a small table. This was so opulent a room that it made his head spin a little. It was completely carpeted, with stunning hangings softening the effect of the wooden paneling. He had thought that Master Soren's house was the height of luxury. Now he had a new benchmark. This was the height of luxury.

There was a fourth man standing in the shadows. He emerged when the three of them entered with the servant. Now, Mags had *heard* of something called cloth-of-gold, but he had never actually seen anyone wearing it.

This man was.

He wore a tunic of peculiar cut, half black velvet and half a shining fabric that could only be cloth-of-gold. It was very short, and very tight, and with it he wore trews that were also half gold and half black, but on the opposite sides. He had the sort of face that, even had Mags not been getting the feeling of *danger* from him, would have made him cautious. It was an angry face, and the face of a man who is not used to being told "no."

"Who are these children?" he barked at the servant, who quailed.

"The young man is the best herbalist at Healers' Collegium," the servant said, turning his wince into a bow. "The other two are his assistants."

"And where are the Healers, the *adults?*" The man seemed outraged.

"Your man will not tell them anything, my Lord," the servant replied. "And they tell me there is nothing wrong with him that their powers can heal. They suggested medicines. This young man can compound those."

The man with his head in his hands moaned, and said something in a foreign tongue.

"What's he saying?" Bear hissed.

"He's saying something about eyes," the servant whispered back, as the man in gold and black glared at Bear, looking him up and down with contempt. "*The eyes, the eyes, always watching!* That's about all he's said for the last three days."

"The eyes," Lena murmured. "Something about that sounds familiar."

"Well, you think about it while I look at this fellow." Paying no attention to how the apparent leader glared at him, Bear walked up to the man on the couch and forced him to sit up and take his hands away from his face. He peered in both eyes, together and separately, checked him for a fever, and then got out some instruments from his case and began doing other things with the help of the servant, who translated.

"Mags, would you get out the mortar and pestle, and start grinding up those herbs I brought with me? Lena, you keep them all separate in those dishes that are with the mortar and pestle." Bear was tapping the man with a little hammer, though what purpose that could serve, Mags had not a clue.

Now grinding things was no new task for Mags. He'd been put to that sort of work about the time he first remembered being in Cole Pieters' custody. So he fished out the implements and the little packets of herbs and started grinding. He left one sprig of each intact and put it on the pile of powder he spilled out into the dish Lena held out for him.

Meanwhile the man kept glaring, while Bear asked questions in a coaxing tone of voice and the man occasionally answered with something besides "the eyes." And Lena had her brows creased and her lips pursed in that way that Mags knew meant she was thinking very hard indeed.

Bear left off his examining and questioning when Mags finished the last of the herbs. Motioning both Mags and Lena out of the way, he began measuring things into the mortar, added a bit of liquid from a little flask he took out of the bag, then began mashing it all together with the pestle until he had a paste. Then he took bits of the paste that he carefully scooped out with the tiniest spoon Mags had ever seen, dusted his hands with what looked like flour, and began rolling the paste, scoop by scoop, into pellets. And when he had finished everything in the mortar, he began his measuring and mixing again.

Eventually it was done; he threw the remaining ground-up herbs on the fire, where they went up the chimney with a smell like bitter burning leaves. And now, at last, he turned to the man in gold and black, who was fuming furiously.

"First of all, your servant here hasn't slept in so long he's not even able to think anymore," Bear said matter-of-factly. "Now maybe you know better than me why he hasn't. But these pills I've made him are going to make his thoughts stop running around so he *can* sleep. But he says that this started when he crossed into Valdemar, and he claims it won't stop until he leaves, so if you want to keep him *alive,* I suggest you send him home. He's doing you no good here, and my pills won't shut everything out for him. I tell you true, if he doesn't get real sleep, he'll die, and that's a fact."

The man's face turned a deep crimson, and Bear added, "And if you don't do something about your temper, you'll burst a vein in your head like your father did and die."

At that, the man went deathly white. "How did you know about my father?" he gasped.

Bear shrugged. "The way you are? Some things I can see about you? That runs in families. Cut down on red meat, stay away from strong drink, watch your temper if you want to see your son grow to be a man. Otherwise . . ." He let his voice trail off. "At any rate, my lord, I've done what I can. Whether or not there actually is anything here in Valdemar to bother this servant of yours, *he* thinks there is, so get him out of here if you want him to live. Give him three of those —" He nodded at the pills. "Four times a day, at regular intervals. Even when he finally sleeps, wake him up to give them to him."

He picked up his bag, and motioned to Mags and Lena, who followed him out. The servant closed the door behind them all.

"I think you may be the first man other than the King to get Lord Krahailak's respect," the servant said, looking impressed. "And you just a boy!"

Bear shrugged. "I just acted like *my* father. Hang if I can figure out what has that fellow so spooked, though. You sure you translated him right?"

The servant nodded as he led them back through the hallways. "He has been raving about the eyes for the last two days. But before then, in fact, ever since he arrived here, he has been acting . . . nervously. As if he felt that something was watching him, but couldn't see it. It is very strange. The Lord sent for him, and now, whatever it was he was supposed to do, he clearly can't. That is why the Lord is in such a rage."

"Well, he can be in a rage." Bear shrugged. "Isn't gonna change anything. That man is not going to do anything, and if he doesn't go home, he may be that way forever."

Suddenly Lena looked as if she had finally remembered what she had been trying to think of, and Mags could see she was fairly bursting with impatience to tell them. But she wasn't going to do it in front of the servant. Only when the man left them at the exterior door, and they were safely out of earshot, did she burst out with it.

"I remember the eyes!" she exclaimed. "They're *vrondi.*"

"They're which-what?" Mags asked. He had read about a lot of things, but this was nothing that had shown up in any of the books he'd been going through so far. It sounded like a foreign thing.

"*Vrondi.* They're in a song about Vanyel, how he made a spell to keep Valdemar safe." She waved her hands around while she talked, excited now. "In the song, they are incredibly important to protecting Valdemar from supernatural threats. They're sort of little spirit-tattletales. They find people that aren't Heralds or Bards or Healers that are doing — things — and they run and tell the

Heralds about it."

"All right," Mags said, puzzled. "So how come I ain't never been told about 'em?"

"I don't know . . ." She shook her head. "I can look for more things about them, but I don't know. But here is the other thing; they also watch the people that are doing those things until a Herald comes. And watch. And watch. You know how you can tell when someone is watching you? Well, imagine if there are dozens of invisible somethings watching you, all the time, and you can never get away. That's the *vrondi*."

"That's crazy," Mags said flatly as Bear stared at her. And it did sound incredibly silly, here in broadest daylight, with a perfectly solid building next to them, hard-packed snow under their feet, and enough of a chill wind to tease down the back of the neck as a reminder that winter was not over — oh no, not yet — and the coldest moons were yet to come.

She glared. "Don't blame me, it's what the *song* says. I found it in our archives when I was researching music that was written about being a Herald by other Heralds. When I asked my teacher, he laughed and said it was just one of those songs to scare children into being good, but what if it isn't? I mean, it was written by another Herald after all, and one who knew Vanyel if the dates are right." She crossed her arms over her chest, looking annoyed, a gesture a little marred by the heavy coat she wore that prevented her from actually *crossing* them.

"Yes, but —" Bear objected. "Dozens of invisible creatures who only exist to catch someone doing — what? I mean, it can't be something common, or there'd be dozens of people like that man back there. It doesn't make any sense."

"I don't know," Lena replied stubbornly. "The page had gotten spoiled, and I couldn't read what it was that the *vrondi* were supposed to watch for. I don't know what it was. All I can guess is that there aren't any Heralds that can see them anymore, and maybe that's the problem. Since no Herald can see them, they can't get one to pay attention, so they have to keep watching. And you're right, that foreigner has to be uncommon and whatever he was doing, it has to be bad for Valdemar. But you just think about that man back there, and you think about what he was saying. Bear, you're the Healer, I'm not. You would know if he had some sort of sickness. Can you come up with anything that *does* match his symptoms?"

Bear paused right there in the middle of

the path, his brows furrowing in thought as they both watched him. "Well," he admitted reluctantly. "No."

"Hmph." Lena nodded, satisfied.

Bear clearly wasn't. "That doesn't prove anything, Lena. You can't prove a cat's a cat by disproving it's a dog. But on the other hand . . . Well, I thought maybe he might have some Gift that was coming on him late. You know, something like Mindspeech." He shrugged. "So I gave him some stuff that blocks Gifts, and something to quiet his nerves, and willow because by now he's got a powerful headache. I figure if that works, he'll fall asleep on his own. If it doesn't —" He shook his head. "I'm not allowed to handle the strong things, things that can really knock you out. One of the full Healers will have to do that. Whatever it is, it's a mystery and —" Now he looked sharply at Lena, "— if your song is right — what was it he was *doing* that called those things down on him?"

A shadow seemed to fall over them all. She nodded soberly. "That's the real question, isn't it?"

"— and that's the real question, isn't it," Herald Nikolas said slowly, when Mags finished telling him about the day's surprise.

"I know that song, and I always assumed it was one of those children's tales, too."

Mags was bone-weary. It had been a very long day. And if he hadn't thought the problem was *that* important, he'd have begrudged every moment Herald Nikolas sat in that chair at his table. Mags himself was slumped over some cushions on his bed, and the moment Nikolas left, he planned to be *in* that bed.

"But what if it isn't?" Mags asked. "What if them things is real, an' if they are, why was they watchin' that man hard enough to drive him near crazy? An' if they're invisible and most folks cain't see 'em, why could he? Or at least, know they were there, ye ken?"

Nikolas got that *looking inward* expression that Mags had come to associate with a Herald talking to his Companion. The lamp next to him sputtered a little and cast flickering shadows over his face. Slowly, his brows creased, and he began to look pained, physically pained, as if he was either having to concentrate very, very hard, or something was hurting him. Mags had never seen that particular expression on the face of a Herald talking with his Companion. He felt a cold chill, and wondered if it was a draft, or fear. Why would just thinking cause the King's

Own pain?

Then his expression cleared, and he looked up at Mags. "We think you have uncovered something, and a good thing that you did, Mags. If you hadn't, we would never have known of this danger. Now, as it happens, the situation was well under control, but you saw the effect of it."

Now Mags truly felt a thrill of fear. This was far, far more than he had thought he would get into when he agreed to assist Nikolas. "Ye mean, that fellah was doin' something against Valdemar or th' King?"

Nikolas shrugged. "The answer to that has to be *we don't know.* Rolan agrees that the man was, indeed, being watched by the *vrondi* and that it was driving him mad. There are any number of reasons why his Lord would bring him here. But whether he was actually doing anything, we can't say." Nikolas curved his hand around the back of his neck and massaged it as he continued to speak. "He could have been a perfectly ordinary spy, which is something we expect and guard against, Mags. He could also have been here for reasons of comfort for His Lordship — men with his Gifts often act as Healers, and as Bear pointed out, His Lordship is in very real danger of harming himself with his temper." Nikolas got up from the seat at Mags' table and began to pace slowly, looking at nothing. "The *vrondi* do not react to intent, they react to the presence of a particular kind of Gift, so Rolan tells me. He has that kind of Gift, and he probably tried to use it in some minor way. So there simply is no way of telling how that unfortunate man was going to use that Gift further. We can assume, probably correctly given His Lordship's behavior thus far, that it would not have been good for Valdemar. But we can't know."

Mags let out his breath in a sigh. "So Bear's medicine worked?"

Nikolas nodded. "So Rolan tells me." Now he looked up at Mags. "The King's Own Companion is . . . rather special."

"Tha's in the stuff they first tol' me, when I got here," Mags offered diffidently.

Nikolas smiled slightly. "Well, to be honest, no one but the King's Own, usually, is quite aware *how* special the Companion is. Rolan has spoken to Kitri, whose Herald is keeping an eye on our guests for me. He just talked to the servants for me. When last heard, the man dropped off to sleep as soon as the medicine took effect and has remained that way except when being awakened to take his dose. His Lordship has requested a wagon and escort back to the border." His mouth quirked up in another half smile. "I think your lad Bear impressed him, mostly by not being intimidated. According to the servants, His Lordship is having those instructions followed to the letter. That sort of respect could be useful to us. If he calls on Bear for other remedies, can you try to arrange to go along?"

"Yessir." Mags ducked his head. He was not at all averse to this plan; His Lordship made him profoundly uneasy, and he really, truly did not want Bear alone with the man. Not that he thought he would be able to fend off those highly trained bodyguards! But if anything happened, it would be impossible to silence a Trainee *and his Companion.* Dallen could raise an alarm before either of them came to serious harm.

He hoped.

:If anyone harmed a hair on your head . . . .: The rest of the thought, though Mags was not at all good at sensing feelings, was awash in red rage that shook him a little . . . and gave him a strangely warm and happy feeling at the same time. *:They would have to tell me where a door was wanted, because that is where I would kick my way through to get to you.:*

"Sir, what about them mercs? They ain't feelin' them *vrondi,* surely? An' *vrondi* ain't throwin' axes around neither —" Mags scratched his head and looked up at his mentor, who paused in his pacing. "We got th' answer, mebbe, to the sick fellah, but what 'bout the haunt?"

"A very excellent question, and one I do not have the answer to." Nikolas pursed his lips. "It's just barely possible that all of them *do* have this Gift, but suppressed and undeveloped, and since it was hidden that way, the *vrondi* didn't react to it and swarm them. But once someone with a working version of that Gift appeared, and the *vrondi* began to congregate, the men *could* see, or at least feel, their presence."

"But the ax!"

"Does not sound like *vrondi,* no." Nikolas shook his head. "I'm baffled. And to be honest, unless they were all from the same family, or at least the same bloodline, it is wildly unlikely that they would all have the same suppressed Gift." He grimaced. "It does sound like a haunting, but the Palace has never been known to be haunted, and none of the Heralds have detected any such thing. I have to say, I do not like this very much. It seems to be another complication, and complications are something we can well do without. But now that we know about it, thanks to you, we will keep our senses alert."

He smiled then, and it was a full smile, an approving one, and one meant for Mags to see. "Mags, I was not mistaken in my trust of you. You are proving to be a clever and resourceful apprentice. So, is there anything that *I* can do for *you?* Within reason, of course."

It was not a question Mags had expected, but something immediately flashed into his mind.

"Get me, Lena, an' Bear inta the Guard Archives," he said instantly. "On'y ye prolly ought t' make it look like it come from one of her teachers. She's gone an' talked to 'em about it, but they ain't given her permission yet."

"The Archives?" Both of Nikolas' eyebrows shot toward his hairline. "But —"

Again, he suddenly got that gazing-off-into-the-distance look.

"Ah . . . your parents." He nodded. "Yes, I can arrange that. In fact, I think it is a very good idea. The worst that you may find is what you have been told all along."

Mags grimaced. "Aye." He hesitated. "Do *you* b'lieve in Bad Blood, sir?"

"No, I do not," Nikolas said, immediately and firmly. "I do believe that sometimes there are people who are born . . . defective in the understanding of morality, and empty of empathy. But I don't believe that has anything to do with who or what your parents were, and . . ."

Now he hesitated and sat down again, looking at Mags very earnestly over his clasped hands. "It's very complicated, Mags. But I have encountered people like that, and they are truly evil. What is more, they know they are being evil, they make a conscious choice. They simply do not care about anything other than themselves. You will know them if ever you meet them, I suspect. They can be very charming when they choose, but it is all surface charm, and you will always look beneath the surface."

Now he smiled warmly at Mags again, another approving smile that made him flush, then stood up to come stand next to him. "Mags, if anything, you are the opposite of that. So no, no matter what you came from, I not only believe, I *know* your heart is good." He reached out unexpectedly and ruffled Mags' hair. "Your head, now, that remains to be seen," he finished with a chuckle.

That night, Mags went to bed for the first time feeling good — completely, totally, and without reservations.

Unfortunately, it didn't last. Because he spent the night in his dreams, hunting

through the dark for something lost, precious, and in peril. . . .

18

Mags was deeply mired in the middle of a complicated sum, so buried in concentration that his tongue was sticking out of the corner of his mouth a little, when Dallen jarred his focus.

:Mags —: the mind-voice came, breaking into his thought and making him lose track of what he was doing. *:Mags, a moment.:*

Carry the one. Or was it carry the three?

:Mags —: came the voice again, insistently.

:I'm a little busy here —:

:I know but . . . : Dallen sounded embarrassed. *:I found out who threw the ax. At least I believe I found out who threw the ax.:*

For a moment, Mags could not imagine what Dallen was on about.

Then he got it.

:Hell!: Mags almost burst out of his seat. *:Where? When? What —:*

:I will answer all those questions if you will come out to my stall. But quietly. I don't want

them to know we are watching them.:

Mags slammed the book closed and eased his door open. He slipped out, ducking low to be below the level of the stall walls, and into Dallen's stall. The Companion had his head down and his eyes half closed, for all intents and purposes looking as if he was drowsing.

:Well?: Mags demanded.

:At the back of the stable there are five youngsters. Two are Heraldic Trainees, one is a Bardic Trainee, one a Healer Trainee and one a young man who is getting an education at the Collegia but will be apprenticed to a Master Artificer or Builder once that is complete. They are in the stall of a Companion called Colby. I believe that they are responsible for the ghostly activity in the bodyguards' rooms.: Beneath his half-closed lids, Dallen's eyes glittered.

:And how come you think that?: Mags ventured a peek over the top of the stall. There were indeed several people in the loose-box of a Companion far in the rear of the stable. And there was some smothered laughing going on.

:Because I know Colby and his Chosen Barrett are pranksters. Last summer they and their friends were the ones responsible for the circles and glyphs laid down in corn fields by

night. Most of the countryside was convinced they were signs from the gods. The pranksters were never caught, and we, the Companions, never told on them, but . . . we knew who it was. If the doors to the stable are wide open and every horse running loose in the fields, it is a sure bet Colby was responsible.: Dallen heaved a sigh. *:He is . . . very young, is Colby. He is well matched to Barrett. Colby ghosts up behind people, steals hats, or startles them with a loud whinny. No apple is safe from him, no picnic or quiet tete-a-tete in Companion's Field goes unobserved or uninterrupted. Neither of them really consider the further implications of what they are doing.:*

:But ye still haven' told me why ye think it's them.:

:Barrett has the Fetching Gift. And the other Heraldic Trainee with him is a FarSeer. Both have Mindspeech of the sort that allows someone to see images of what another is seeing or remembering.:

Mags felt his eyes widening. Yes indeed, there was the answer. A FarSeer could easily "peer" into the rooms. And with that, someone with the Fetching Gift could move things.

Should he do something about it? What were his options? He could report them to Herald Caelen, he supposed —

:Not advisable, although you certainly should tell Nikolas once you are certain it is them. Barrett is highborn, and his father has the same sense of humor. If he's caught — which I don't think at all likely — his father will pretend to be harsh in public, but in private will demand details and howl with laughter. That is what has happened before, and probably will continue.:

:So. Well . . . : He thought about what had been going on. Thought about how the mercenaries had gone out of their way to humiliate and hurt. *:Well, let's find out for sure if that's what they're doin'.:*

Mags slipped through the stalls until he was right outside the one belonging to Colby, and paused to listen.

"Right, now use your Fetching to pull the string on the bull-roarer, but slow," said a voice. "Do it slow and it sounds like someone groaning."

"I can't believe you were lucky enough to get that thing into their rooms," someone gloated. "They never leave their rooms without at least one of them in it!"

A third voice answered with a chuckle. "That was Gordo's doing. After I threw the ax at them, they didn't want any more sharp things up on the walls, and what they had up there, they wanted riveted in place. So

438

Gordo snuck in and put the bull-roarer inside the breastplate before it got hammered onto the wall. Nobody knows it's in there but us, and it was put up in plain sight of all of them."

Well, if that wasn't an admission of guilt, Mags had never heard one. He straightened, and hooked his arms over the wall of the stall. "That don' seem real friendly to me," he said, startling all six of the occupants of the stall.

Barrett was the first to recover. "I don't mind being friendly to people who are friendly back!" he said, with a cocky smile. "But I doubt you are going to find anyone willing to put in a good word for those bodyguards."

"Nor their master," the one in Bardic colors said sourly. "But none of you have had to deal with him."

"Not d'rectly," Mags admitted. "But I seen him. An' — does seem a nasty piece a work. You doin' this for any reason but 'cause you can?"

Barrett looked incensed at that, and so did the rest. "Of course!" he snapped. "I got tired of seeing them swagger around and bully people! I wanted to give them something to think about besides harassing folk! And I wanted them to feel what it felt like to be harassed and bullied!"

"An' c'n ye give me a good reason why I shouldn' tell Herald Caelen 'bout this?" Mags persisted.

He flushed and looked down. "Uh —" he replied. "No . . ."

Mags regarded all of them carefully. Just how much did he want to reveal to them? "Reckon y'oughta tell some'un," he said slowly. "Ye're scarin' the servants, an' that ain't right."

Barrett started at that, as if the possibility hadn't occurred to him. "We — are?" he faltered.

Mags nodded solemnly. "Happens they talk t' me, 'cause I ain't highborn an' I got no money an' no fambly," he said matter-of-factly. "Y' skeered one wee mite near outa her skin w' that ax. That fair?"

Barrett flushed a deep, shamed crimson. So did the others.

:Dallen —: he thought with a sudden burst of inspiration. *:Talk to Rolan. Get Nikolas here fast.:*

:Oh, I see where you are going with this! Yes!: Dallen's burst of enthusiasm heartened Mags, and even more so when Dallen continued. *:We told him what's going on. He's coming now.:*

"They keep tellin' me," Mags went on,

deliberately stalling for time, "thet now I'm a Herald, I gotta think 'bout what I do afore I do it. Aye?"

Barrett nodded, and wouldn't look at him. "And —"

Foosteps behind him, deliberate, but brisk, told him that Nikolas had entered the stables. He waited for the King's Own to make a show of "seeing" them.

"Well, is this some sort of impromptu gathering?" Nikolas' voice sounded relaxed and genial. "Can't quite give up Midwinter holidays, lads? Not that I blame you —"

He came up beside Mags, and looked with feigned astonishment at the furiously blushing Barrett, at his shame-faced coconspirators. "Why, what is all this?" he asked, quite as if he had no idea. "This doesn't look like a celebration."

Barrett cleared his throat. "It's — not — sir," he said, and then launched into a rapid, but painful, explanation of what they had been up to.

"Hmm." Nikolas raised an eyebrow. "I . . . see. And how is this not misuse of your Gifts?"

"I . . . uh . . ." Barrett looked even more shamefaced if that was possible. "Uh . . ."

"It is one thing to pull pranks on people, Barrett. I find some of your antics rather amusing. The circles in the corn fields now, that was inspiring. Very clever, to use boards to press the crops down, and a little sight on your hat to keep the lines straight."

Barrett gaped at him. "You . . . knew . . ."

"And using the string to make your circles perfect was a very good use of your geometry class," Nikolas continued, oblivious to the stunned looks on the pranksters' faces. "But when it comes to misusing your Gifts . . . no. We have to draw the line."

Barrett stared down at his hands.

Nikolas cleared his throat, causing Barrett to look up. The King's Own crooked his finger.

"All of you, come with me now," he said, with a deadpan expression. "We are going to have a conference with some interested parties about this."

Without a backward look, Nikolas led them all out of the stable, leaving Mags behind.

:Rolan says to tell you that Nikolas says good work.: There was definitely a feeling of pride about that statement behind Dallen's words. *:Now, I think it would be time to get back to your sums. Yes?:*

Mags sighed. *:Aye,:* he replied, and trudged back to his room.

■ ■ ■ ■

The King's Own Herald was definitely amused.

He sat at Mags' table, sipping hot tea, and for once there was a smile on his face. It transformed him from forgettable to rather remarkable; there was a liveliness about him that suggested that, back in his past, he might well have been as much of a prankster as Barrett.

"Mags, I must congratulate you and Dallen. You succeeded in solving the 'haunting,' you caught the perpetrators red-handed, and you did it in a way that neither revealed your interest in our foreign visitors, nor compromised your connection to me." Nikolas drank the last of the tea, and set the cup down on the table with a chuckle. "And as a consequence you have managed to allow me to recruit them to my own purposes."

Mags blinked in sleepy satisfaction. "Gonna let 'em keep hauntin'?" he asked.

"I believe so. A bit more to the purpose, however, and with a great deal more art. We don't want any more servants terrified. That is not fair to them." Nikolas turned the cup around and around on the table. "With their

Gifted fellow incapacitated, they are, we think, inclined to believe that there are spirits here leagued against them. We'd like to encourage that thinking, but more specifically than Barrett and his gang were originally managing to produce."

Mags scratched his head. " 'Scuse me, sir, but . . . I thought they was here t' make an alliance? How come now ye wanta scare 'em?"

"Because I do not believe they came here to make an alliance," Nikolas replied firmly. "This was urged on the King by members of the Court whose lands border on Doste-land and Karse, and who would much prefer to see an alliance with these folk against Karse. I was . . . less than enthusiastic about this plan."

Mags nodded. Now this was getting into realms he truly did not understand, and didn't think he ever would.

"At some point, I will explain all of this," Nikolas promised. "But the long and the short of it is that I've modified my stand on this. I think we can make a very useful, temporary alliance with them, if *they* think we command some very powerful abilities. So long as they are afraid of us, they will be honest with us. The King is inclined to give this approach a trial. So —" he spread his hands wide. "There you have it. Your friends and fellow Trainees are hereby given leave to prank them all you like."

Mags laughed. "On'y prank I did on 'em was t' use that slip-away stuff when they tried t' get me alone t' beat on."

"Well, should they try again, use it again. Only this time, see if you can't — make it more — showy?" Nikolas suggested. "Make it seem as if some spirit is assisting you."

Mags' brow creased. "Well . . . all right. Doubt they'll mess with me again, though."

"Ah, probably not, but it was a thought. Certainly you've done more than enough on that head already." Nikolas snapped his fingers. "Ah! That reminds me. I've arranged for all three of you to get access to the Guard records, with no subterfuge needed. There is no reason why you *shouldn't* try to find out about your parents, Mags. No reason to hide behind some other excuse. Your little Bard friend will probably find something in there that is useful to her, and Bardic Trainees have traditionally gotten access there anyway, and as for Bear the Healer, being one of the first truly outstanding herb Healers we've had here, he should be given a chance to go through those records to see if there is anything there he can translate into medicines. Caelen was exceptionally impressed with how you handled things tonight, Lena and Bear are certainly more than responsible enough to have gotten passes long ago, so there will be permanent passes for all three of you in the morning. Just turn up at the archives, your names will all be on the allowed list from now on."

Mags stared at Nikolas, absolutely speechless. Nikolas seemed to understand that he was speechless with gratitude, and smiled.

"There is something else that you accomplished tonight, quite inadvertently, Mags," he continued. "You and Barrett. There has been some . . . strain in the relationships among the members of the three Collegia over all this building. Everyone has his own ideas about priorities, and everyone is watching jealously to see how much effort is spent on what." He paused. "I think you got some sense of that with what went on around Herald Jakyr — although a good part of the strain between Jakyr and certain Bards has more to do with personal issues than the building. Thanks to Barrett's gang, we had members of all three Collegia working together, as it should be — and tonight the heads of all three Collegia had a completely cordial meeting, deciding what to do about the young rogues.

Frankly, this was only aided by the fact that you made Barrett feel so ashamed of himself that he took the whole of the blame on his own shoulders. Very fruitful. I think we went a long way in mending things." He stood up and stretched. "And that is enough work for one night, I believe. I'll let myself out."

Mags was so astonished by the results of the evening that he stared at the closed door long after Nikolas was gone.

The next morning, as promised, when Mags met Bear and Lena for breakfast, the other two told him with great excitement that they had been told if they appeared at the Guard Archives their names would be on the list of those allowed in. Mags couldn't help but enjoy their enthusiasm, and filled his plate with flatcakes, buttering them and adding honey. "Well, there we go, then," he said with a decided nod. "You'll both get t' root around in there whenever ye want now. You two reckon it'll take long fer me t' find out what I want?"

Lena shook her head. "It shouldn't. We know the time period we are looking for, and we know the location, right? It should be fairly straightforward. I can go with you and show you how to do archival research right after breakfast if you have the time."

Bear looked disappointed. "I have a class,"

he said reluctantly. "Hang it! I wanted to help!" Then he made a face. "And aye, I wanted to go looking for herb lore, too . . . nobody ever thinks to tell anyone about local herb lore. But the Guard does a lot of their own rough-medicine, and I know they use whatever they can get locally."

Lena patted his hand sympathetically. "It's all right, Bear, we understand. Once we find what Mags wants to know, we can plan on afternoons or evening when we *just* hunt out references to medicines and we all three go together."

Bear had to be satisfied with that. Mags was both on fire with impatience and a little sick with apprehension. No matter what Nikolas or anyone else had said to him, it was still there, that horrible feeling. To find out for certain that Cole Pieters was right, right about him, right about his parents . . .

He and Lena hurried over to the Guard Archives as soon as they finished eating. This time the stern individual on guard at the desk looked over his list when they gave him their names. He nodded, and waved them into a short hallway behind him without a word. They opened a door at the end of that hallway, and stepped into what was for Mags a very strange room indeed.

He had expected something like the library. This was nothing like the library.

First of all, they had to go up three stairs to get into it. This was a huge barn of a building, not just a room, with floor-to-ceiling shelves packed very closely together. There were ladders at intervals along the shelves — it was pretty obvious you would need those ladders to reach the upper shelves. On these shelves were identical wooden boxes. Shelf upon shelf, row upon row . . . with only a single table with several chairs around it at the door end of the room. He would have thought such a huge room would be freezing cold, but they had some way to heat it that he couldn't see. Then it occurred to him — the place must be heated the same way that Bear's indoor herbarium was heated, from beneath the floor. The place had a stuffy feel to it, as if the air wasn't moving at all. It was also very dry, and the air was scented with the smell of old paper, but oddly, not of dust. In fact, he couldn't see any dust at all. The lighting was fairly good, too — there were narrow windows up near the roof all the way around, with glass in them.

"Oh, my," Lena said faintly as she went up to the nearest shelf. "It's a lot . . . bigger . . . than I thought it would be. The Bardic Archives aren't much bigger than the library. Well," she said, her voice sounding muffled as she moved behind the shelves, "At least they dust regularly."

Mags followed her. She peered at the end of the box, then at the box next to it, and the one down from it, and perked up. "All right, this isn't as bad as it looks. These are all nicely organized. I was afraid they were just stuck in here, any which way."

"I should hope they are well-organized, Trainee. The Guard prides itself on organization."

Mags could almost hear the unspoken addition. *Unlike some other groups I could mention. . . .*

From the back of the room, another old, but erect, man in a blue Guard uniform came walking toward them. He was balding, expressionless, and as impersonal as a lump of stone. "I am the Archivist. I assume since you are here, you have permission, so how can I help you find what you are looking for?"

This time, despite shields, Mags *did* hear the unspoken addition. *I can't have you running about pulling things down and never putting them back in order, or where they belong. Or worse, putting them back wherever you find room.*

Now Mags, who had, up until this moment, loathed his geography and mapmaking class with a sincere and undying passion, suddenly was just as passionately grateful to them. Because now that he had been in those classes, he knew where Cole Pieters' mine was, so he knew what the nearest town was. And he knew that he had come from somewhere in the vicinity of that town, because he didn't remember a long journey. He *did* remember the shouting and screaming, he remembered cowering in a corner, then he remembered being put in a cart and given sweets to suck. It could not have been a very long journey. It had ended in a bare stone room, from which, after several boring days, Cole Pieters fetched him.

"We're lookin' for th' reports from around about a town called Blueflower Hill an' a place called Cole Pieters' mine, from about . . . twelve, fourteen years ago, sir." He tried to make his tone and his expression as respectful as possible. This man would respond to respect.

The Archivist nodded. "Very good. That narrows the search down considerably. There are three Guard Posts in that area. Come with me."

He led them between two of the rows of shelves, and stopped when they were so deeply in that Mags could not really see either end of the room. The man took ribbons out of his pocket, and sorted out a handful of white ones with little blue beads threaded on the ends. Each of the boxes had a ring attached to it; he tied these ribbons off on the rings of several of them.

"I've marked each of the boxes you will want to look through with these," the man said. "You will probably see other boxes marked in this way; if you look through those, be careful not to disturb or remove any markers in the reports. As you finish a box, please remove the ribbon and either leave it at my desk at the rear, or attach it to a new box you wish to look through." He tapped the end of the box. "The name of the Guard Post and the year are here. The boxes are organized geographically. Put everything back as you found it. You are — ?"

"Heraldic-Trainee Mags and Bardic Trainee Lena," Lena answered for both of them. "We're looking for information for Mags, sir."

Mags waited for the Archivist to ask what that was, but he seemed utterly incurious.

"Very good. These will be your colors until you are finished with this particular research. When you have returned all the ribbons, if you wish to pursue another line of research, let me know what it is you are looking for, and I will assign you another set of ribbons." He smiled thinly. "If it is nothing like as specific as this one, I shall ask you to confine your searches to one small area at a time."

Lena looked as if she might say something. Mags prevented her from doing so by answering immediately, "Yessir, Archivist sir."

"If you need me, I will be at my desk in the rear." With that, he turned smartly about and walked back to the back of the room, heels clicking on the stone floor with military precision.

Mags and Lena looked at each other. Mags shrugged, and reached up, pulling down the first box.

"Well," he said. "Let's get to it."

The box was not as heavy as he feared; he hauled it over to the table, and they unloaded the papers inside. It was all organized with fanatic precision. Each report was folded inside a stiffer, thicker piece of paper, and a moon's worth was tied up with a ribbon or string. There were twelve bundles in each box: a full year's worth. A year began and ended at Midwinter Night, precisely.

They looked at the bundles, and then at

each other. Mags shrugged, and gestured at the box. Lena took out the first moon — Midwinter Moon — and Mags got the second — Ice Moon. They sat down with their bundles and began to skim through them.

The reports were clear and concise, and written in a very legible hand. They also concerned every bit of minutiae on the life of the Guards and the Guard Post.

If I ever can't sleep, gonna see if I can borrow a moon's worth of reports.

Mags went through his quickly, neatened all the reports so that all the edges were square, tied up the stack again, and went back for Thawing Moon. Lena was still deep in hers. Mags wondered what she was finding that was so fascinating.

Whatever it was, 'twasn't in my stack.

She finished hers about the same time as he finished Thawing Moon. She got Budding Moon and he got Flowering Moon. And so it went right through the year to Dying Moon, which was the moon that ended on Midwinter Eve.

"Nothing?" he asked, as they put the stacks back in order again.

She shook her head. "And it's time for class."

He nodded, and hoisted the box up. "I'll

see you at lunch."

He held onto the ribbon, just in case, and put the box back on its shelf. He looked the area up and down, noted the number that had white ribbons tied to them, and repressed his dismay. There were a lot of boxes. . . .

Ah, well. No one told him that this was going to be an easy job. He probably would not have believed them if they had.

If he didn't run now, he would be late for class. He would worry about all of this later.

All three of them met up for lunch, and Bear listened while he and Lena compared notes with every sign of open envy. "Damn these classes," he growled finally. "It's not fair."

"It's not exactly fun, Bear," Lena pointed out, as gently as she could. "These are just military reports, and not even from moons when much happens. It's all about the running of the Guard Post, and it's not very interesting. How much of what was eaten, lost to vermin, and ordered and delivered. What training was going on. How many leagues of roads cleared of snow in the winter, the condition of the roads in the summer. Whatever troubles the nearby people had that the Guard had to get involved with. Disciplinary actions, who was promoted, who was demoted, who retired, who the replacements were. Evaluation reports on each of the men. There were only two reports from the Herald on circuit there the entire year; that was the only times he called there. At least in the year we looked at, absolutely nothing of any importance happened. Much more of this, and I am going to be caught falling asleep over these things."

Bear did not look convinced.

"I'm makin' notes of medicines," Mags offered, handing over a scant paragraph, which was all he'd gotten out of that entire year, written closely on a salvaged piece of paper. Not from the box — oh, no! He was terrified to discover what the penalty would be for such a sacrilege. The Archivist would probably demand fingers. "I don' know enough to know what's stuff you already know 'bout and what ain't, so I just take notes on it all."

As Bear took the scrap of notes from Mags, he looked a little less sullen. "So you were thinking about me anyway — thanks!" He looked them over. "Nothing I can use, but you're a good note taker, Mags, and I appreciate it."

Mags waved it away. "Wouldn't do less for ye, Bear."

19

But they never got the chance to talk any further about doing Bear's research. The elements had other things in mind.

Just as they were finishing their luncheon, there was something of a stir outside; through the windows of the dining hall they could see sudden activity in the form of workmen abandoning their tasks and being mustered in groups, with a Guardsman addressing each group.

"Huh. I wonder what that's about," Bear said, looking puzzled.

Lena shook her head. "Nothing I know of, unless the weather is going to be bad, and they want the workmen to make sure things aren't going to get ruined by it." They all stood up together, and were putting the plates in the tubs to be collected, when a most unusual person entered the dining hall from the door right at Mags' elbow. Now, this would not have been any special occurrence, except that the man was dressed in priestly fashion — and priests seldom came here. Why should they? Not that they would have been unwelcome, but when a priest was invited to the Collegia for any reason, it was generally as an honored guest, and they were treated to something rather better than dining hall food.

Mags nudged Bear with his elbow, and just as Bear turned to see what Mags wanted, the priest did something no one had ever done in all the time Mags had been there. He went up to the big brass bell that was hung on the wall at the head of the room, and gave it three sharp pulls so that it rang out above the murmuring of voices.

All conversation ceased immediately, and all heads turned toward the front of the room.

"Thank you," the man said, in a firm, carrying voice. "I have been asked to inform the Collegia of an impending emergency. Messages from the field have given us warning of the approach of a killing storm. The Herald FarSeer attached to the King's Council has also seen this storm strike Haven, and some of the Gifted among my Temple have confirmed it. We had been informed of this impending storm from Heralds posted west of us; we had hoped it would blow out before it reached the city, but it has only strengthened. It has already paralyzed the countryside to the west of Haven, and it will be on us at about sunset."

Already there was a murmuring; he held up his hand and got silence once more. "This is not a storm to be trifled with. We expect several feet of snow, with such a powerful wind that there could be drifts as high as the rooftops. During the storm itself, movement even between buildings will be very hazardous, if not deadly. All classes are canceled. Trainees are being asked to help carry firewood and stack it at the doors of all buildings. Those who are not Trainees are asked to report to your immediate superiors for assignment to other work parties. We must ready each building here to be self-sufficient for a minimum of three days." The murmuring began again, and the priest raised his voice. "Quickly! There is no time to waste!"

With that, people began to head out of the building, some of them on the run. Mags stared at his two friends, who looked incredulously back at him.

:This is no prank, Mags,: Dallen said. *:Come get me. We'll haul logs.:*

Lena and Bear looked at him still as if they could not believe what they had just heard;

he nodded as the babbling that had broken out all over the room turned into a roar of voices. Heralds and Trainees were explaining to their friends what he was about to tell his. "It's no joke. We gotta get goin'. Dallen says him 'n me are gonna haul logs. We best get at it." He gave them what he hoped was a stare that conveyed the gravity of the situation. *He* had been through blizzards like this. They might not have.

Lena took a deep breath, looking as if she didn't quite believe it could be that bad, but didn't dare disbelieve him either. "Well, in that case —"

"We get to it," Bear said firmly. "We daren't lose my plants. Lena, let's get wood stacked against the wall by my furnace in case no one thinks of it. Mags? In case no one thinks of my furnace?"

He nodded, making an instant decision. Dallen, he was sure, could make it right. But better to take care of it now than to wait for permission, which might come too late or not at all. "Dallen an' me'll bring ye logs, but getting 'em split'll be up t' you." Mags went to the line of pegs where all the coats and cloaks were hung; he wiggled his way in among all the others going after their gear, grabbed his coat, and hurried down to the stable where all the Companions, partnered or not, were being put into abbreviated harnesses with chains on the sides. Mags recognized these from his lessons as the "pulling harnesses" all Heralds took with them into the field. Dallen seemed to know where he was going, so Mags just hauled himself up onto his Companion's bare back and joined a procession of similarly mounted Trainees, Companions alone, and even stablehands with common horses down a little road he hadn't paid much attention to before this. It ran along the inside of the wall around the Palace and Companion's Field, and it ended in the biggest pile of logs he had ever seen in his life.

Until this moment it had never occurred to him to question where all the firewood came from for all the buildings within that wall. Now he knew. It looked as if an entire forest had been brought here and stacked up. There were three men in heavy clothing with iron bars on the top of each stack of logs, carefully levering logs away so that they tumbled down the side of the stack to land on the snow. Once a log was down, a Companion and Trainee, or a Companion alone, or a regular horse led by a stablehand, went up to the log. Chains were hitched around it, the chains from the harness fastened to it, and off they went, heading for the Palace.

When it was Dallen's turn, Mags, who had watched the procedure carefully, jumped off and did his own chaining-up, much to the approval of the log tenders. He didn't bother getting back on; Dallen couldn't go fast with that heavy log behind him, and he didn't want to burden his Companion any more than he had to.

Already there was a sense of urgency in the air that Mags entirely approved of. No one who hadn't tended a fire himself had any idea of how much wood was going to be consumed over the next three days. In a way, he hoped that there *were* snowdrifts up to the rooftops. Those drifts would seal off the wind and insulate against some of the worst of the cold.

:I have approval to take our logs to Bear, Chosen.: Dallen's muscles rippled as he pulled the dead weight forward. Mags wished he could take some of that burden himself. *:Bear was right. Some of those medicinal plants are absolutely without price, and we cannot risk them freezing. That was good forethought on his part.:*

:I'll tell him ye said so.: Mags raced ahead to pull a fallen branch out of the way, then returned to Dallen's side. He watched the log as it plowed a furrow through the snow to make sure it didn't get hung up on

463

anything, and ran ahead to get obstacles out of Dallen's way.

After that, they both saved their breath for work. Despite the unspoken feeling of urgency, there was no outward sign of a reason for that urgency. Overhead, the sky was blue and mostly cloudless. But Mags remembered very well that first blizzard of the year, the one that he and Jakyr had barely beaten. It, too, had begun with cloudless skies, and had churned up over the horizon like some terrible monster.

They left their log with Bear, who had managed to round up three woodcutters, all in the green of Healers, and returned to the log pile at a trot. Soon the steady procession of logs had worn the road smooth, which made pulling easier for horses and Companions. Each time Mags got to the buildings, he could see them swarming with people bringing in supplies of all sorts, workmen nailing shutters on the windward side of the building closed, and a steady procession coming toward the stable of carts hauling hay from what must have been a storage barn. He wondered where they were going to put it all, then ceased to worry. Let them figure it out; his business was not in the stable. Right now, he and Dallen had logs to haul.

After six runs, something had changed up at the Palace, heralded first by a *crack* that sounded as if lightning had struck the place and made everyone jump. It turned out that there were some mechanical aids for reducing all that wood to manageable size. For the life of him, Mags could not see how the things worked, but there were two devices that were splitting entire logs lengthwise into quarters, which were then taken to two-man saw teams to be reduced to fireplace and furnace size. The sound of the logs splitting was startling even when you knew it was coming, and the horses shied every time it rang out. They were all working as hard and as fast as they could; horses and Companions alike steamed with sweat, their breath coming in great moist clouds as they pulled on their burdens.

Finally, as dusk fell, the sound of horns rang out over the entire complex, joined by all the bells of the Collegia.

:That's the signal,: Dallen said, heaving at the log. *:No more. The storm is almost on us, and these will be the last loads.:*

And, indeed, those Companions and horses that were not already carrying logs were turning back, heading to their stables.

Mags had long since delivered plenty of wood to Bear; the last couple of can-

465

dlemarks he had been taking their loads to one of the Palace entrances. Now he and Dallen delivered their final burden, Mags tucked the chains up into the harness, and they plodded wearily back to the stable.

And there they found one solution for the hay storage problem. The Companions were no longer in commodious loose-boxes. The stable was full of rectangular bales of hay, from floor to ceiling. One by one, the Companions were being rubbed down to take off the sweat before they chilled, covered with not only their own blankets, but extras. Then they were backing into narrow slots in those enormous stacks of hay bales. They looked for all the world like toy horses being put away on a shelf. The bales were stacked so closely together that they touched the Companions on either flank.

They won't be keeping the stable warm with the fire, Mags, so you had better get what things you need and find someone at the Collegia to stay with,: Dallen told him. *:All this hay will keep us cozy, but there is no point in keeping the fires going in the ovens right now, when the wood could go elsewhere and we can tend ourselves.:*

:What'll ye do for water?: Mags asked in dismay.

:I think there will be plenty of snow,: Dallen

pointed out drily. *:And we know how to open and shut doors. Now hurry. Go to the eating hall. You can probably find someone with room there. Bundle up in as much as you can, wear both pairs of mittens. Wrap up your face. Take your bedding and whatever else you think you will need.:*

He dove into his room, and took a quick look around. Well, what he would need would be clothing . . . the bedding, as Dallen had pointed out. If he was going to be up at one of the Collegia, the last thing he would need would be books. There didn't seem to be much else. He pulled on extra knitted shirts, then another tunic over that, and a second pair of trews. He packed Dallen's saddlebags with more of his clothing, made all of his bedding into a fat roll that he strapped across his shoulders over his coat, grabbed both packs and reached for the door of his room —

Just as the blizzard hit the stable like a battering ram.

The walls boomed. The wind *howled* around the walls, which shook with the storm's fury. Atavistic panic clutched at his guts for a moment before he managed to fight it down. But some fear still remained, and despite all the layers of clothing, he suddenly felt cold. Mags went out into the stable to see the lamps going out one by one, blown out by the cold drafts forced in through every tiny crevice.

He froze in place, suddenly picturing what it must look like out there. Not only was it dark — not only was there going to be snow so thick he'd have had trouble seeing in daylight, but that wind was going to make it hard to walk, and all the lamps on the buildings must have blown out instantly. How was he going to *get* to the Collegia?

:They've already strung rope while you were putting on more clothing and packing up. There are ropes between every building. Go out the door we usually use and feel to the right, on the frame, about waist-high.:

As he reached the door, the last of the lamps was blown out, leaving him to fumble it open in pitch-darkness. The door was in the lee of the building, so it wasn't torn right out of his hands when he opened it. But he couldn't see a thing; it was dark both behind and in front of him, as dark as being in the mine without a lamp.

All right. He was used to the dark. He took a deep breath to calm himself, and reminded himself of that. He closed the door behind himself and felt to the right until he encountered the rope — a good thick one that hummed and vibrated with the force of the wind on it. He grasped it in both mittened hands — and as Dallen had advised him, he was wearing not one, but two sets of mittens, felt ones inside sheepskin — and stepped away from the shelter of the building.

He was immediately glad that he had both hands on the rope. The wind nearly blew him over when it hit him, and within moments every inch of him was snow-caked. What little skin he had left exposed stung and burned with the snow being driven against it. The scarf around his mouth was damp and ice-rimed; his breath froze as soon as it hit the fabric.

:Go, Mags. The longer you take, the worse it gets.:

From that moment on, he thought of nothing more than the next step. Hunching his shoulders against the wind, head down and eyes closed — it didn't matter if his eyes were open or shut, since he couldn't see anything — he hauled himself along the rope, hand over hand. He had never been outside in a storm like this before. At the mine, he had either been in the mine or in the sleeping hole, and had no reason to go anywhere. He would have been terrified if he'd had the strength to spare for terror. He was already tired from the hauling; shortly, he was exhausted, and every step was agony.

In the back of his mind, he could hear Dallen encouraging him, cheering him on. That was the only thing that kept him going, as his feet got heavier and harder to lift, as his arms felt like lead, as his hands numbed and his body ached with the cold.

:Keep going, Mags!:

The harsh air burned in his lungs, his throat felt raw, and every intake of breath brought a stab of pain at the end of it. His toes and fingers burned.

:Don't stop! They know you are coming!:

All he really wanted to do was to sit down and rest, and he knew that was the last thing he could do right now. If he stopped, even for a moment, the cold would get him. The simple journey to the Collegium stretched on into a hellish eternity —

And then, suddenly, *at last,* it was over. He had expected to have to get the door open himself, but as Dallen had said, there must have been a crew of rescuers waiting right there for him. He felt people grabbing his arms and pulling him along, felt a blast of air on his face so hot in comparison to his chilled flesh that it felt like a furnace. His eyes were caked with snow and frozen shut; he just let people hustle him along, passing him toward another set of helpers who pulled off his pack and saddlebags. More of them unwrapped the scarves from around his head and face, and helped him take off a coat that was so ice-caked it was as hard as armor. As soon as the coat was off, someone else came to wrap him in fire-warmed blankets. That same someone pushed him into a seat and he just fell back into it; he found a hot mug in his hands, and as the snow finally melted from his eyelids, he was able to open his eyes.

At first all he could see was a fire, and feeling still numb inside and out, he stared at the flames, thinking that he could never, ever get enough of them. He was not the only person here; there were two more blanket-wrapped figures trying to thaw themselves on the hearth, both Guardsmen.

He sipped at the hot liquid in the mug; it was spiced cider, but there was a good amount of something else in it. Something much stronger than wine!

He was right next to the fire in someone's room and he wasn't the only one crammed in there, bundled in blankets. Besides the two Guards right at the hearth, there were two of the stablehands and another Trainee, all with identical mugs in their hands and identical glazed looks in their eyes.

"Is that everyone?" He recognized Herald

471

Caelen's voice.

"I'm not sure —" someone else replied uncertainly. "There's no way to know if there is anyone fallen or lost out there unless it's a Herald or a Trainee —"

By this time, Mags' mind had woken up enough for him to realize that the second speaker was right — almost.

He gulped down another big swallow of his drink, coughed, and spoke up. "Herald Caelen — they tell me I got a *strong* Mind-speakin' Gift. Reckon I c'n see if I c'n find anyone out there, if that's — uh — not mis-usin' —"

He didn't even get a chance to finish that statement. Caelen shoved his way through the people nearest the fire and grabbed Mags' shoulders. "That is most certainly *not* misuse of your Gift!" he exclaimed. "Please, Mags —"

"Right. Here." He shoved the mug at Caelen, huddled up in his blanket, rested his head against his knees, wrapped his arms around his legs, and closed his eyes. *:Gonna need yer help with this, Dallen.:*

:Absolutely. First, drop all those shields I showed you how to set in place.:

He had not done that in all the time he had been here. Dallen had warned him that he shouldn't — had cautioned him that because he had been Chosen, his Gifts would be opening up at a tremendous rate.

Now he realized just how much that Gift had burgeoned. The moment he dropped those shields, it felt as if he was in the center of the Midwinter Market, only a thousand times more crowded, and everyone was talking at once. Worse, it was mostly fear, as people all over the complex, all over Haven, reacted to the storm. It *felt* like being in the storm all over again; all those minds, all those internal voices, none of them putting a watch on what they were saying — it all overwhelmed him, threatened to wash him away in the flood, and he felt as if he was drowning in it —

Then he sensed Dallen, strained to hear him, and got the sense of what Dallen wanted him to do. He began raising the shields again, but one at a time this time. First, all those people farthest away, down in Haven. He didn't need to listen to them. He couldn't help them now if he wanted to, anyway. And they, almost certainly, would not want *him* to know what they were thinking.

That cut the clamor down to a fraction of what it had been, and he let out a sigh of relief. The next shield was easier: to screen out those who were closest to him, in the same building. They wouldn't want him to hear their thoughts either.

And that improved things a very great deal indeed.

Now he was able to actually pick out individual "voices." One by one, he sorted through them, not really listening to what they were babbling, because most people just had a running internal babble going on, but looking for the nuances that told him they were safe and indoors. Their fears, while real, were not immediate. And their minds were . . . well, they weren't *numb,* the way his mind had been when the cold was getting to him.

He found five that were not.

"Gardener —" he heard himself mutter. "Just at Palace kitchen door — ah — in. Guard — Guard needs help. In th' rose garden, lost the rope. 'Bout — 'bout a horse-length from it. Fell an' slipped an' lost it. Got sense to stay where he is —"

He heard Caelen shouting directions but paid no attention. There were still three more. "One 'f them pesty furrin mercs. Headin' for town t' drink. Near th' gate, I think. Damn fool." He had never quite realized how brutal and how crude these men were until he got a glimpse of their thoughts. His lip curled with distaste as he heard more from that mind than he wanted to. There was a Herald in the gatehouse, with the Guardsmen on duty there. "I got that one."

He had never done this before . . . he hesitated a moment, then realized that if he waited for Dallen to do the contacting, he might lose some details. He did a kind of mental cough, and — well it felt as if he was tapping on the outside of the other's mind, as if on a door.

The reply was instant, if wordless. Shields dropped; he got the feeling that the Herald's Mindspeaking ability was minimal. But it was enough. He "showed" the other where the mercenary bodyguard was, and got a sense of thanks before the shields came back up again.

"All right. Herald at gatehouse an' three Guards'll fetch 'im in." He tried not to chuckle with a certain nasty satisfaction. Because the idiot refused to heed the warnings, now instead of spending the storm in luxury with the rest of his fellows, he would be spending it sleeping on a stone floor and eating the trail rations that the Guards had stocked in the gatehouse.

He moved on to number four. "Cook's helper, gettin' wood, slipped an' fell an' the wood fell on 'im. Collegium kitchen, so many people in there he ain't been missed yet."

He heard Caelen relaying the orders, and he checked briefly back with the Guard and the gardener. He found the gardener already back inside, and three people picking the Guardsman up out of the snow.

He moved on to the last one. "Bardic Trainee, wants t' get snowed in w' his girl; she's a Heraldic Trainee. He's halfway between Bardic and Heralds' an' he just ran out 'f strength. He's set down in th' snow an' he don' know if he don' get up now, he never will. That's all."

He was about to put up all of his shields again, when — something — brushed against his mind.

His throat closed on the scream he wanted to utter, choked silent with fear. This — *this* was the thing in his dreams, the thing that pursued him, or pursued something he needed to protect! It was cold, it was evil — and it was not sane.

Dallen sensed it in the same moment, but Dallen's reaction was not fear, but fury. He felt Dallen gathering all his mental power, like a thunderbolt, and aim it ready to strike this vicious thing down where it stood —

Too late. Whatever it was . . . was gone.

:What — was that?: he managed to get out.

476

:I don't know, Chosen,: his Companion replied grimly. *:But whatever it is . . . there is something it wants here. Something . . . or someone.:*

Mags poked listlessly at the remains of his stew, and listened to three of the most senior Heralds in the Circle debate what he had felt over his head. They had cleared everyone else out of this tiny room as soon as he had recovered enough to get what he had sensed out in coherent sentences, and Herald Caelen had sent for Nikolas and a third man, who evidently had been in the Palace, doing some searching of his own. From all Mags gathered, he was as strong a Mindspeaker as Mags, and a great deal more practiced and disciplined. *He* had "gone looking" for what Mags had sensed, and had come up with nothing. He looked enough like Nikolas to have been his father, although there was nothing in their manner to indicate that was the case.

Now here Mags was, sitting on a cushion on the hearth, head aching, body feeling as if he had been beaten black and blue, utterly exhausted. In that sense of unreality that comes with exhaustion, he was feeling less and less with every passing moment that he had ever sensed anything at all that

477

wasn't some dream-fragment out of his own mind. After all, if it couldn't be verified . . .

"Stop that," came a calm voice to his right. He turned and stared at the Herald, the Mindspeaker.

"Sir?" he managed, meeting those calm gray eyes. He wished *he* felt like that, so calm, so sure of himself.

"Stop second-guessing yourself. You sensed *something*. Your Companion, who was snug in his stable and *not* half frozen and having hallucinations, also sensed it. All we are trying to do is figure out what it was that you sensed." The Herald smiled at him. "Storms like this can do some peculiar things. I have heard, although I have never seen it myself, that they can carry with them the echo of thoughts from incredibly far away."

"Ye thin' that's what I got?" Mags asked hopefully. He really did not want to think that there was something with a mind like *that* snowed in or near the Collegia. Truly, he did not. He would never be able to close his eyes again.

"It certainly corresponds to what I felt near a colddrake, long ago," the older man said cautiously. "And according to the theory, since they are very powerful, mentally, it is certainly possible for a colddrake's thoughts to have been carried on a storm like this one. Especially if the drake was anywhere about where it started."

Mags nodded and finished his stew, conscious that there must be no wasted food for as long as they were all snowed in.

"I'm not convinced —" Nikolas said warily. "That's just entirely not reasonable to me. How could the thoughts of a beast from beyond our borders get here? And *why* would Mags sense it wanted something here? That is the part that makes the least sense of all! What could it want here, of all places? No one here is — cursed, or haunted, or —"

It was Caelen who snapped his fingers then. "Of course!" he exclaimed.

Nikolas raised an eyebrow. "Of course what?"

"That's the answer. Those bodyguards — why in the name of all that is holy would they have been so convinced, *immediately,* that they were being haunted?" Caelen smiled broadly. "Anyone else, any other hardened fighters I have ever seen, have always been extremely *skeptical* of hauntings, rather than credulous. Unless — ?"

"Unless they have had visitations before," Nikolas said slowly. "That . . . Caelen, that makes altogether too much sense."

Mags stirred uneasily. Something about this theory didn't feel right.

"And if one is being troubled by a vengeful spirit, perhaps in dreams, how does one deal with the nightmares?" Caelen persisted.

The third Herald answered, a little grimly. "Steady drinking, usually. And if the visitations were ugly enough, the nightmares bad enough, it might just drive a man to ignore warnings of an impending blizzard to try and get to a source of really strong drink."

He turned to Mags. "Trainee, did you get any sense at all of whether this — thing's — target was Valdemaran?"

Mags had to shake his head, even though he had some grave misgivings that the solution was this simple. After all, this was not the first time he had had a brush with this thing. And when he had, it had been pursuing something *he* cared about, and he didn't give a crumb about those bullying mercs.

But the answer certainly seemed to satisfy the others. "I think it might be wise to make sure these men have access to either distilled spirits or that herb Healer's sensitivity-deadening potions for as long as they are snowed into the palace," Nikolas was saying. "Things are going to be tense enough as it is before we dig ourselves and the city out. The last thing we need is for one of those men to go mad."

"Agreed," said the third Herald. "And just to be on the safe side, I will keep watch for the revenant myself. If I sense it, I will see if I can find a priest about to cast it out."

"Well, historically, they never stay cast out for long," Nikolas observed, as Mags shuddered at the thought of having *that* in his head again.

"True, but by then, they should be gone." Caelen looked down at Mags. "And so should you, young Trainee. You look as if you would not make it as far as the second floor before you passed out."

" 'm all right," Mags said, struggling to his feet. "Just a bit —"

He blinked as he found himself sitting again. "Huhn —"

Caelen brought over a roll of bedding, which even if it was not his, looked enough like it not to matter. He unrolled it and pointed at it. "You. Here. Sleep."

Even if they hadn't been the three most senior Heralds in the Circle, Mags would not have had the strength to argue with them. He was just so tired —

And yet he knew that there was no way he would be able to sleep. Not with that — thing — out there. He'd never be able to close his eyes, knowing it was there somewhere. And he still didn't believe it was after the foreigners, whatever it was. Someone had to stay alert, and that someone might just as well be him.

He rolled over and faced the fire so that the three Heralds, still discussing what they were sure was a revenant, would not be able to see that his eyes were still open. He would just rest here for a little while. Just rest.

Just —

— sleep.

20

The storm had blown itself out, after three days, although only the first day and a half featured the terrible winds that shook the buildings. Mags had slept through most of that, despite being sure he would do nothing of the sort.

Now there was a different problem entirely. The temperature had dropped, making the upper floor of Heralds' Collegium too cold to sleep in, forcing those who had been up there down to further crowd the rooms below. The same was true at Bardic, only more so, since the ancient building was nothing like as weather tight as the newer structures of Healers' and Heralds'. That caused a migration through the narrow slots between the buildings, cut through snow that was waist-high at the least, and further crowding conditions at the other two Collegia.

This was all incidental to the crisis down

in Haven. The cold had caused the snow to harden, making it even more difficult to shovel, and once you did shovel out a path, where did you put the snow you had removed? In some places the snow had drifted so deep that you couldn't cut a path, you had to make a tunnel, but that, of course, meant there was always the risk of cave-in and injury. The problems of getting food and help to people, of keeping people warm, that the Palace complex was experiencing were only magnified down in Haven. And then there were the cold-and-snow-related injuries — slips, falls and broken bones, frostbite or even entire frozen limbs, other illnesses made worse by the conditions — Healers were being called for at all hours of the night or day. It took them candlemarks to get down to their patients and back again. The Guard was doing its best to get the snow cleared so life in Haven could get back to normal, Heralds were acting as rescuers and couriers, Bards were doing whatever they were asked to do — and most of the time, no one knew where anyone else was, unless they were Heralds.

So perhaps it was not so surprising that until Mags asked, no one realized that Bear had been missing since the snow stopped falling.

■ ■ ■ ■

"Ah, Trainee, we seem to be thrown together by circumstance. Would you pass the salt, please?"

Mags looked up to see that he had squeezed in next to the Guard Archivist. Mutely he passed the saltcellar.

"I must compliment you on your research ability," the old man continued, salting his pea soup. "Your friend the Healer thanked me, and so did his superior later. You seem to have uncovered some intriguing information on herbal remedies that neither of them recognized. And that was incidental to your intended search. Very well done."

Mags frowned, then quickly put on a more pleasant expression. "Well, I'd do about anything for Bear," he said.

"So I see." The Archivist ate complacently. "I should like to reward that diligence if I may. Perhaps if you can give me an idea of what you are looking for in those records, I can do some delving for you when my other duties are complete."

Mags was not as surprised as he might have been, because he was rather occupied with the question of why Bear had lied when he'd handed over the notes he had taken.

"Sir, that'd be . . . real good of ye," he said, hoping he sounded grateful and sincere. "Ain't no secret." He described how he had been found, the raid of the Guard on the bandit stronghold, and what little he could remember. The old man nodded. "So, nothing more than due diligence to find this. I will assist you as I can." He finished his soup and Mags got up to let him get out. "Of course, that will have to wait for some time, until things return to normal. We've left the Archive building snowed in; there seemed no good reason to heat it in this emergency, and it didn't seem likely that anyone would want to get in there." He chuckled then, just before moving away. "Well, perhaps your eager Healer friend. He was terribly anxious to discover whether your research privileges would expire when *you* found what you were looking for, and whether his were independent of yours. I was able to reassure him on that score."

With that, the old man worked his way into the press of people trying to get fed, and was gone, leaving Mags feeling distinctly uneasy.

Bear had been acting oddly since coming back from Midwinter holidays. He had tried to act normally, but sometimes he had been sullen, almost angry, and now that Mags came to think about it, when the idea of checking the Guard reports had come up, though Bear had been relatively quiet about it, there had been an oddly keen quality in his interest. And when Mags had gotten them all permission, there had been a light in Bear's eyes that was all out of proportion to the somewhat dull prospect of reading old reports.

And now this.

Why would Bear lie?

He bent his mind toward the stables, where Dallen, like the other Companions who were not immediately needed, was drowsing in a kind of semihibernation. Even the Heralds working down in Haven were mostly not bringing their Companions. There was just no room for them in the narrow snow passages, and there was not that much for the Companions to do except pass an occasional message.

:Dallen?:

It took the Companion a few moments to respond. Mags explained to him what had just happened, when he was sure Dallen was awake enough to take it all in. *:Why would Bear lie?:* he asked.

:I'm not sure.: Dallen pondered that a moment. *:If I were to guess . . . if he is looking for something, and he doesn't want you or*

Lena to know about it . . . he either thinks the information could hurt you, alter your opinion of him, or make him feel ashamed. And before you say that whatever it is wouldn't matter, it clearly matters enough to him *to lie about it. So it matters.:*

Mags moved out of the noisy dining hall to the end of the hallway where there was relative peace. *:I don' like it.:*

:Nor do I. Keeping secrets of that sort almost always leads to trouble.:

:Should I ask him 'bout it?:

Dallen pondered that for a bit. *:I think you had better. I will query Nikolas if you could have permission to reveal your role for him to Bear — trade a secret for a secret, as it were. You see if you can find him. Get Lena; she can be of great help.:*

And that was when Mags discovered that Bear was missing.

". . . no, sir, he's not there." Lena made a better impression on Healer Praston than Mags had. The head of Healers' Collegium, from a very highly placed family, had listened to Mags' uncultured speech, looked at Mags' short stature, and concluded immediately that Mags was a hysterical and unlettered boy, probably overstressed by the entire situation they were all in. Lena, on the other hand, had pulled on every bit of dignity she could manage, as well as the most cultured accent she could feign, and had the Healer listening and paying attention to her with the first few words she spoke. "He had no reason to leave his rooms for this long, and the three Bardic Trainees who were squeezed in there have been tending the warming furnace for him since yesterday." She grimaced. "He wouldn't tell them where he was going, so they assumed it was to see a girl."

Praston grimaced. "All right, chances are he is fine; perhaps he was called down into Haven and neglected to tell anyone. But we should be sure —"

"Sir," Lena said patiently, "We are sure. His medicines are all there, his bag is there. He's very meticulous about organizing his medicines, too; I can tell you that nothing at all is out of place or missing."

Now Praston began to look a little alarmed. "There is always the chance he was called into Haven for something other than a medical emergency —" He pursed his lips. "Nevertheless, let me raise the alarm. Better we do this and discover to our chagrin that he was only paying a visit to some old patient of his. Young man, ask your Companion to find us a Mindspeaking

Herald that can search that way for us."

"Don' have to," Mags replied immediately. "I am one, an' I already tried." When he first realized that there was something wrong, he had done his best to "hunt" for Bear. But his first tentative sweep of the Collegia and grounds had netted nothing; his second, aided by Dallen, had also come up with nothing, and had extended somewhat down into Haven until the press of so many minds had become too much for him to sort through. He was beginning to feel sick with worry. Why would Bear be down in Haven? And if he wasn't in Haven, where was he? There was no way, short of a god plucking him bodily away, that he could have gotten *out* of Haven.

Praston no longer looked a little alarmed, he looked startled and frightened. "You two stay here," he commanded. "Don't move. This is clearly serious."

As Mags and Lena exchanged a frantic glance, he summoned half a dozen of his Trainees by the simple expedient of sticking his head into the hallway and shouting at them. Within moments, they were scattering, to get the Guard, then someone from the Palace Guard, someone in charge of the Palace servants, Herald Caelen, and two others Mags didn't recognize. It took a while for them to arrive, and until they did, Praston quizzed Lena and Mags closely about Bear, especially his state of mind since Midwinter Holidays.

He clearly did not like what they had to tell him.

"Did he seem despondent?" Praston persisted, as the first of those he had summoned arrived. "Did he talk about feeling worthless, or say that no one would miss him if he was gone?"

Mags shook his head, and Lena answered that. "No, sir," she replied. "Nothing like that. He wasn't *happy,* it was because of something that . . . something that happened at home over the holidays. But he wasn't despondent."

"You're absolutely *sure* about that?" Praston asked. "He didn't talk about death, wasn't interested in listening to ballads about death, didn't write about death?"

"No!" Lena replied with force. "Nothing like that. And what — what happened wouldn't — he was angry and unhappy but —"

"Perhaps you had better tell us so we can judge for ourselves," said Praston, as the last person edged into the crowded office.

"I can't." Lena lifted her chin stubbornly. "He told me in confidence."

Praston looked as if he was ready to grab her by the shoulders and shake her until her teeth rattled. It was the head of her own Collegium who interrupted bluntly. "Lena, you are not experienced enough to tell if something would or would not drive a boy to thinking of suicide. Tell us. *Now.*"

Mags had read about *command voice,* but this was the first time he had heard anyone using it. He found himself ready to tell the Bard anything she wanted to hear, and probably plenty of things she didn't, and he wasn't the one who had been directly addressed.

Lena looked stubborn for a just a little bit more — after all, she was a Bard herself, and raised in a Bard's household — but a moment later her shoulders sagged and her face dropped. "His parents wanted him to get married the next time he came home. They'd already betrothed him to a girl. He knew her, her family was from nearby, and he really didn't care about her, but they weren't in the least interested in hearing his objections. There was a big row about it. He slept at a neighbor's house for most of the holiday."

Whatever the adults had been expecting to hear, this wasn't it. Praston opened his mouth, shut it, opened it again, shut it again. Finally, he managed to say something on the third try. "You can't be wedded without your consent, you know," he said weakly.

Lena shrugged. "Have *you* ever tried to go against what your parents want?" she asked bitterly. "Even when it's something you hate?"

Praston shook his head, and looked at the others in the room. Caelen shrugged. "I can see where the boy would be embarrassed about it, and I can see that it would upset him, but no, I cannot see him courting death over it. Not unless he had a previous romantic attachment — ?"

He looked at Lena, who shook her head, and Mags, who grimaced. "Never seemed t' care much fer girls," Mags offered. "Never said nothin' t' me."

"All right, then, that's one thing we don't need to worry about. So unless he's down in Haven, which *you,* Salenys, will send your men to check on, we have to assume he's still here, on the grounds, and for some reason he cannot or will not respond to us." Mags blinked; Caelen had just taken over the search, and Praston was figuratively stepping back and letting him. "Lita, what can your people do?"

"Question witnesses," she said immediately. "And the Trainees can go put on their cloaks and search. I'll send out some of the teachers to do the questioning, starting with the three that are in his rooms. The rest, I delegate to you."

Caelen nodded. "Master Howarth, I leave the Palace to your people. The rest of us can make a *real* search of the buildings and grounds. I'll get that organized. Right now it is sounding as if Bear was injured or became suddenly ill and is lying in an out-of-the-way place, unconscious. The sooner we find him, the better."

Then he turned to Lena and Mags. "And you two," he said, his expression grim, "You had better come with me."

Lena was crying, though it was not from anything that Herald Caelen had said to her. It was because she, like Mags, had suddenly realized that the reason Mags had not been able to "find" Bear was — because Bear was dead.

But Mags was not ready to believe that. He had always known when Death touched anyone in or around the mine, even people he knew almost nothing about, like the house-servants. There was an *absence* when someone died that hit him when it happened, and left a lingering feeling of *void* for at least several days. The last time anyone had seen Bear was yesterday morning, and Mags was sure he would have known if Bear was dead.

Caelen sat them both down in a corner of his office and gave Lena a big handkerchief to sob into. Mags listened with half an ear as he gave orders for the search, occasionally turning to Mags to ask a question about whether Bear had ever gone to this or that place, and if he had, what had taken him there. Mags answered as best he could, but meanwhile, his mind was racing.

Then he heard it. "— no, don't bother with the Guard Archives. The Archivist left it locked up the first night of the storm."

"No!" he shouted, leaping to his feet, startling everyone. "No, don' you see, tha's it! Th' Archives! Bear wanted somethin' in there, somethin' he didn' want the rest of us t' know about! Now they're locked up tight, an' who'd go there now anyway? 'S perfect time t' go lookin'!"

Caelen stared at him. "And — if he had an accident in there, if a box fell on him and knocked him out —"

"Even if it didn', ye cain't hear in there nor be heard outside, all them papers just muffle everythin'." Mags' heart was in his mouth now. "An' it ain't heated. Ye lay

495

there, hurt . . . the cold . . ."

"Lena!" Caelen barked, startling her so that she dropped the handkerchief. "Round up whoever you can, but make sure you get me a Healer among them. Mags, let's go! In this cold —"

He didn't have to finish the sentence.

He snatched up his cloak; Mags shrugged his coat back on. Both of them made for the stairs and the outside door at a run.

And this was where things got . . . interesting. Because there was no direct route to the Archives. Instead, they had to run to and through Bardic, then Old Bardic, then Healers', then the Guard barracks, because that was how the paths had been cut. On the plus side, they managed to scoop up four Guardsmen on their way through the barracks. On the minus side . . . there was no path cut to the Archives.

But there *was* the clear trail of someone forcing his way through the snow to get there.

"Wait —" One of the Guardsmen suddenly held up a cautionary hand. "Sir, I am a tracker. More than one person came through here."

Mags froze. Suddenly, he *felt* that fear from his dreams, from that brush against something horrible the night the blizzard began.

Herald Caelen paled a little. "Are you armed?" he asked quietly. Two of them nodded; the other two went back into the barracks and came out again with four swords, one of which they gave Mags without hesitation. He clutched the hilt in his mittened hand, then tore the mitten away and cast it aside. Better to have a freezing hand than no grip.

"Carefully now," Caelen said, grimly, and the burliest of the Guards began forcing a way for the rest of them.

:Dallen!:

:We have raised the alarm. Help is right behind you.: Dallen paused. *:Keep me tight linked.:*

At the door to the Archives, the second Guard in the line carefully tried the door, as the rest of them flattened themselves against the wall on either side of it. The door was unlocked, and he eased it open, a little at a time. In his mind, Mags showered gratitude on the Archivist for being so meticulous. The door was well oiled, and opened without so much as a creak.

"Outer chamber's empty," whispered the Guardsman, and one by one, they all slipped inside.

:*Open your mind to Caelen,*: Dallen ordered. Mags blinked, then obeyed.

He sensed Caelen then, thinking hard. *Mags, when you "hear" this, tell me.*

:*Got ye, sir,*: he thought back, hoping that he had properly understood those lessons from Dallen about how to think into the head of someone without Mindspeech so that they could hear him.

Good. I want you to relay my orders to the Guards. You have my permission; theirs is implicit.

Whatever that meant. If Caelen said it was allowed, it must be.

He opened his own mind a little further, to the four in his vicinity, and told them what Caelen told him. :*Crouch low, crawl if you must. Stay below eye level. Do nothing until Caelen signals, no matter what you see or hear. Nod if you understand.*:

All four Guardsmen nodded, although one looked a little startled. Caelen signaled for all of them to move forward. *You, too, Mags. You are going to be my eyes and ears. I am too old to crawl; all I will do is give the game away.*

Well, Mags was used to crawling on his belly through narrow tunnels at need; this was nothing to him. He sheathed the sword, turned his belt around so that the scabbard

498

was at his back, and flattened himself on the floor, skittering along noiselessly, like a lizard.

The door into the Archive room was open a crack. The large Guard eased it open as well. They all moved inside.

It was brighter here than in the outer room, but still dim. The worktable was overturned, and one of the chairs smashed, a box lying on its side with the contents strewn on the floor. Mags reported it all to Caelen.

Tell the redheaded Guardsman to work his way around the wall, with the rest of you following. I want you directly behind the redhead.

Once again, Mags relayed the instructions. This time he was the one to give the signal, and the designated Guard, who was almost as good at belly slinking as Mags, eased forward.

:Keep your mind open to me, too, Mags,: Dallen urged.

They all inched their way across the frigid floor, their breaths puffing out and hanging in the still air in tiny white clouds. Halfway down the length of the room, the silence was broken by a low moan.

"Hushabye baby," said a strange, high voice. "They haven't come for you yet. Here. Drink your drinkie, there's a good baby." The voice giggled. "Oh, and when they come for you, there will be *such* a surprise! They'll be so pleased!"

Oh, dear gods . . . that sounds like a trap. Mags was pretty sure he wasn't supposed to have heard that thought. But he had — and so had Dallen.

:*Tell Caelen that Nikolas is getting something ready. Mags, we are going to need you; you are the key to this. I want you to ease close until you can see what is going on, get a good look, and then ease back.*:

I've been told, Mags, came Caelen's thought, hard on the heels of that. *Do what they tell you.*

:*I need to scout,*: Mags thought at the Guardsmen. :*Ain't getting closer than I have to.*:

All four nodded, and he slithered past them, trying to breathe as slowly and silently as he could.

When he got to the end of the shelves, he moved over across the aisle so that he was sheltered by their bulk, then peered around the corner.

The Archivist's desk was here, and a strange, thin, dark man was seated at it. Behind him, tied to another chair, bound hand and foot and with a gash on his forehead, was Bear, unconscious, but still alive. The man was dressed in odd clothing of a very dark gray; his head and hands were wrapped in what appeared to be bandages, and despite the fact that it was freezing in this room, his arms were bare. Laid out on the surface of the desk was a glittering array of knives.

The man seemed to sense Mags looking at him. He glanced sharply at the shelves, but he was looking high, not low, and Mags pulled back out of sight. He waited, listening for footsteps, but none came.

He slithered back to the others.

:Mags, Nikolas says that is a very dangerous man, some sort of highly trained killer. He can easily fight all five of you at once, and if he thinks you are going to win, he'll kill Bear.:

:But — !:

:Don't worry, we have a plan. All we need you five to do is to fight him, distract him, get him as far away from Bear as you can. And stay alive! He'll concentrate on the one he thinks is weakest, that will be you. So your job is to be the lure, drawing him away from Bear. The Guards are to keep coming at him, but never let him close with them. Have you got that?:

Mags motioned to the others to put their heads together with him. Carefully, Mags thought those instructions into the heads of the Guardsmen as hard as he could, staring into their eyes. All four of them nodded slowly. The redhead pointed at Mags, and mouthed the word "bait." Relieved, Mags nodded.

:Tell them the weapons might be poisoned.:

Gulping, Mags did so. The big man looked angry, the redhead narrowed his eyes, the third shrugged, and the fourth smiled grimly.

Mags looked at the fourth curiously. The man stared back at him, hard. Slowly, Mags sensed a thin mental voice. *It won't be the first time we've handled cowards of that sort, boy. You just see to it that you don't get scratched.*

Mags nodded.

:All right. We are getting something in place. Stand up carefully and wait for my signal.:

They got to their feet, one at a time, so slowly and carefully that even their clothing didn't whisper. And they waited in the semidarkness, Mags feeling ready to scream with the tension, as a tuneless humming threaded its way toward them from the back of the room.

Finally —

:Now. But don't charge him. Walk out until he can just see five of you, but not who you are. And let him hear your footsteps.:

Mags relayed that. And at his signal, they moved forward, soft footfalls muffled by the shelves and boxes all around them. They rounded the last shelf to find the strange man on his feet, waiting for them, a knife balanced on the tip of one finger.

:Now you step into the light, Mags.:

Mags did so, his hand clutched to his sword hilt.

The man stared at him.

"Not YOU!" he screamed. *"YOU are not supposed to be here!"*

He threw the knife, but Mags was already anticipating the action, and ducked back behind the shelf. The knife thudded into the wall and stuck there, quivering, as the man grabbed a handful more, and sent them flashing after the first. Mags showed himself just long enough for the man to see he was untouched, then jumped back into shelter again.

This time the man was tempted enough to rush them. And he was faster, a *lot* faster, than anyone Mags had fought before.

For a moment his mind raced in panic. But then, a curious calm came over him.

Don't attack. Just evade. He didn't have to fight back — the other four would do that for him. All he had to do was to keep from getting hit. And with his mind open to the others, he could sense what *they* were going to do, where *they* were going. All he needed to do was to move with that.

And then, as he ducked and sidestepped, used his sword to deflect an oncoming blow and slid under it, he saw what Dallen had been talking about.

A door in the rear of the building slid stealthily open, and through it came —

Barrett.

Barrett and his gang of pranksters, one of whom without a doubt must have been good enough to pick that lock.

Mags did not allow himself to get distracted, but as he danced his way out of the man's reach, he got glimpses of the gang slowly hauling Bear, chair and all, toward the door.

Meanwhile it was all he could do to avoid the whirling maelstrom of blades that the man had become. He knew, instinctively, that he *had* to keep the killer's attention; that if the man got sight of Bear being taken out, it would be all over. So he danced and capered as he never had in all of his life, allowing his terror to show on his face. He sensed that terror was a better lure than defiance or bravado. Which was just as well, because he was *so* frightened now that he couldn't have squeaked out a single challenge or boast.

And then — at last — the gang reached the door.

A forest of arms reached forward, grabbed them all, and yanked them out of sight.

The door slammed.

The killer whirled.

"It's over, mate," the redhead said. "You might as well —"

Give yourself up, was what the Guard was probably going to say. But he never got the chance to finish the sentence.

With a scream of outrage, the killer threw away all his weapons, turned, and ran himself onto the redheaded Guard's sword.

EPILOGUE

"I c'n think 'o better ways t' get a holiday," Mags said weakly.

Bear nodded as a servant girl handed him a dose of his medicine. "Wouldn't have been my choice either," he replied.

They were not in the Collegium; they had been set up in a luxurious suite of rooms in the Palace. The very rooms, in fact, that had been occupied by the arrogant foreigners.

"Still . . . this's better than my room or the stables," Bear continued. "And nobody's going to come all the way over here to ask me some stupid question about herbs that they can look up the answer to."

He sounded more than a bit cross, and Mags didn't blame him. Exactly that sort of thing was why he and Bear had been moved over here in the first place.

Bear was still not supposed to leave his bed or couch unless he had to, but Mags was under no such restrictions, and spent much of their first day here searching the room for anything the foreigners might have hidden there.

He knew of course, that far more competent people than he had already gone over the place; if they had actually found anything useful, he and Bear would be the last people to be told. But he couldn't help hoping he'd find something overlooked. After all, they had left in a terrible hurry, so much so that it was hard to tell if they had taken anything with them.

"No luck with the beds, I suppose?"

Mags shook his head. He had gone over the bedsteads in meticulous detail, examining every seam, every place where the finish seemed to be a bit rougher than it should be, every place where even the tiniest of objects could have been hidden. He had found nothing, of course, and it was no use to look in the mattresses and pillows as he was certain those had been replaced and taken apart before he and Bear were brought here. In fact, it seemed that only a few innocuous things had been left behind by the first group of searchers.

"Do you ever wonder if those men were even from the country they claimed to be from?" Bear asked.

"I s'pose they could be." He shook his

head. "Not sure it matters."

"And why did they wait a whole day after that madman killed himself to leave?" Bear continued. Clearly, he had forgotten that he had asked that question already, not once but several times. It was the effect of the medicine, Mags had been assured — just as he had been told that he was here with Bear as much to keep an eye on his friend and provide him with company as to recuperate himself. He didn't mind. In fact, he was rather pleased that they trusted him so much.

"I reckon — I reckon they had somethin' they needed t' get or someone they needed t' talk to." Truth was, he didn't know, and really couldn't hazard a guess, but Bear seemed to find the answer satisfactory.

"And how could they get out and not be seen?" Bear continued — as he always did.

"Oh, they went over th' wall. Guards found the place even afore anyone knowed it was them that went." *That* had been all over the Palace and from there to the Collegia in very short order.

"They must have been better in snow than they made out." Bear sighed. "I wish I had paid more attention when I was treating them."

"I wisht I had paid more attention to 'em

508

in general." Every tiny bit Mags had observed had been gone over by so many people that they all blurred together in his memory. "Mebbe somethin' would have tol' us how t' catch 'em."

But according to rumor and the very, very little that the King's Own would tell him, the foreigners had managed to very quickly muddle their trail in a manner that astounded even the best of the trackers. And now? Well, they'd had more than enough opportunities to arrange for escape routes, for people to conceal them, for ways to disguise themselves. The snow would probably hinder them, but not as much as it would hinder pursuit. There were people in the city who would not scruple to help them for enough money. There were probably even people in those huge manors near the Palace who would do the same.

Mags poked at an odd book written in their tongue and illustrated with incredibly beautiful colored drawings of plants. It seemed strange that so violent a set of men could create such art — and poetry, for that was what was in the book. Love poems. It made no sense.

Nor did what the killer had screamed when he first saw Mags. *Not you?* Mags couldn't shake the impression that the man had recognized him. And that was just as disturbing as everything else.

And they still didn't know why it had been Bear that had been used as bait in that trap. Had it just been opportunity? Had they *really* wanted him for his Healing skills? Had it been something else entirely?

"I shouldn't have gone to the Archives alone," Bear sighed. "I should have told you. But . . . I didn't want you to know I was looking for —" He flushed. "I thought I remembered some pretty nasty rumors about that girl's family. I thought if I could confirm them with Guard reports, my parents would give over the idea of marrying us." His face turned a deeper red. "That's a pretty underhanded way of trying to get out of it."

Mags shrugged. "Whatever works," he replied. "You don' got to answer to us."

"Yes, I do," Bear said softly. "You're my friends."

Mags shrugged again, but he felt warm inside. Friends. That wasn't at all bad. Maybe he didn't need to know about his family. Not when he had friends like this.

And right now, all those other questions could wait, too. He was hardly the one best qualified to puzzle out the answers, after all. He was only one Heraldic Trainee in his first year.

:Only?: Dallen seemed amused.

:Quiet, you.:

"Well, then ye answer t' me in a couple a days," he replied, and chuckled. " 'Cause right now . . . I be on holiday. And so be you!"

ABOUT THE AUTHOR

Mercedes Lackey is a full-time writer and has published numerous novels and works of short fiction, including the bestselling Heralds of Valdemar series. She is also a professional lyricist and a licensed wild bird rehabilitator. She lives in Oklahoma with her husband and collaborator, artist Larry Dixon, and their flock of parrots.

The employees of Thorndike Press hope you have enjoyed this Large Print book. All our Thorndike, Wheeler, and Kennebec Large Print titles are designed for easy reading, and all our books are made to last. Other Thorndike Press Large Print books are available at your library, through selected bookstores, or directly from us.

For information about titles, please call:
   (800) 223-1244

or visit our Web site at:
   http://gale.cengage.com/thorndike

To share your comments, please write:
   Publisher
   Thorndike Press
   295 Kennedy Memorial Drive
   Waterville, ME 04901